The Dressmaker's Secret

CHAPTER ONE

1876

'I'm just walking over to the church, Mrs Fudge,' Reverend Michael Redfern called to his housekeeper. 'I shan't be long.' He opened the door and stepped out into the cool May evening. The low sun had set the western sky aflame with its dying embers and a fat, creamy moon was rising in the east. Shrouded in shadow, an owl hooted in the boughs of a nearby horse chestnut tree. Michael breathed in deeply, filling his lungs with the pungent scent of wild garlic.

He had arrived in the Anglo-Saxon market town of Blandford Forum as a humble curate twenty-five years before and had been the incumbent of the Church of St Mark the Evangelist ever since. Having never married, his parishioners were his family. He advised them, comforted them and rejoiced with them. He married them, baptized their children and, when their time came, he buried them. He was a man perfectly content with his lot in life. Whistling cheerfully, he threaded his way through the kissing gate, the gravel crunching beneath his feet as he followed the path to the centuries-old church.

It was a short walk from the rectory to the church, yet by the time he reached the wooden porch, he was breathing heavily. He was a thickset man with a shock of greying blond hair and a paunch which had, thanks to May Fudge's excellent home cooking, expanded considerably in recent years. Pausing to catch his breath, he made a mental note to ask his housekeeper, once again, to please reduce the amount of cakes and puddings she plied him with.

Thinking about the supper he'd recently consumed, he pushed open the heavy oak door but stopped in surprise when his eyes fell on the girl seated in the front pew, dark auburn hair shining in the pale candlelight like burnished copper. Her shoulders were hunched and it was clear to Michael from the way they shook that she was crying bitterly.

Momentarily unnerved by her unexpected presence, Michael shut the door quietly behind him and started up the aisle towards her, the soles of his shoes squeaking softly on the stone floor. He coughed as he approached, hoping to alert the girl to his presence, but if she heard him, she gave no sign. The church was otherwise deserted, evensong having finished well over an hour earlier. Michael slid silently into the pew beside the sobbing girl. That was when he noticed the baby on her lap.

It was swaddled in a frayed shawl, fast asleep, pale lashes resting on porcelain cheeks, wisps of strawberry-blond hair curling from beneath a knitted cap.

Suddenly aware of his presence, the girl turned her tear-stained face towards him. Michael recognized her immediately.

'Bea? Little Beatrice Cullen, my star Sunday school pupil?'

'Yes, sir.' Bea bowed her head, a crimson stain spreading up her pale neck and flooding her cheeks. Her green eyes were red and swollen from crying and carried such a look of abject misery and despair that Michael found himself momentarily lost for words. He handed Bea his handkerchief. Shadows danced on the walls as the candles flickered and sputtered in their sconces.

'And who is this little mite?' he asked, once Bea had wiped her face and blown her nose. She bundled the handkerchief in her fist and sighed.

'This is my Lily,' she replied in a small voice. 'Lilian Mary, after my ma and my nan.'

'Both very fine women.' Michael nodded. Lilian Cullen and her daughter-in-law, Mary, both resided in St Mark's churchyard, carried off by a particularly vicious strain of influenza that had swept through the town a decade before. Unable to cope with his six-year-old daughter, Bea's father had sent her to the Union Workhouse up at Shaftesbury. Soon afterwards he had left the county and, as far as Michael was aware, no one had heard from him since.

'As I recall, you were working at Bay Willow House.'

'Yes, sir. I was a scullery maid, sir.'

'You've come from there tonight?'

Bea shook her head. 'No, sir, from Shaftesbury.'

'You walked here from Shaftesbury?' Michael exclaimed, aghast. 'That's nigh on twelve miles of hard road, and with an infant besides.'

Bea shrugged. 'A passing drayman let me ride along with him most of the way. I only walked the last three miles or so.' She yawned and Michael was reminded of just how young she was.

Now Michael noticed the drab Union Workhouse dress and the worn shoes, and the severity of Bea's plight began to dawn on him.

'Lilian was born out of wedlock,' he said matter-of-factly.

Bea nodded, her eyes filling with fresh tears. 'Yes, sir. As soon as my condition became noticeable, I was sacked without references. I tried to find work but no one would hire me because of my situation.'

'And what of the baby's father?' Michael asked, his brow knitting together over his nose. 'He must be called to account and made to marry you.'

'That is not possible, sir,' Bea replied with a sorrowful shake of her auburn mane. 'He is engaged to be married.'

'Then the engagement must be broken off,' Michael fumed, his mind's eyes picturing a cocky farm labourer who had played fast and loose with Bea's heart while planning to wed another.

Bea fixed her gaze on the plain wooden cross suspended on the grey stone behind the altar. 'He is engaged to Miss Cynthia Lovett,' she said dully. 'You may have seen the announcement in *The Times*.'

Michael's shoulders sagged in resignation. 'Ah,' was all he could say.

'I'm not a trollop like Mrs White said, sir. Freddie told me he loved me and I believed him.'

'I take it we're talking about Master Freddie Copperfield, eldest son of Sir Frederick and Lady Copperfield?'

Bea's expression was one of abject misery and Michael's heart went out to her.

'So, after trying unsuccessfully to find employment, you ended up back at the workhouse?'

'I had no choice, sir. I had nowhere else to go.' She met Michael's gaze. 'That's why I came to find you. You were always kind to me when I was a child, and I know you will do right by Lily.'

'There is always the Foundling Hospital,' Michael said. He rubbed the bridge of his nose with his forefinger as Bea shook her head vehemently.

'I do not want Lily's future left to chance. I know you will find her a good family, people who will love her like their own.'

Michael sighed deeply. He steepled his fingers and bowed his head as if in prayer. Silence stretched between them. Lily stirred in Bea's arms but didn't wake. Bea cuddled her close, aware that her time with Lily was drawing to a close.

'You are certain?' Michael asked finally, breaking the lengthy silence.

'You know I have no choice, sir,' Bea said sadly.

'Then I believe I know of the perfect family right here in Blandford. Jim and Martha Hayter. They buried their infant daughter just three days ago. I shall call on them in the morning, but for now you and Lily will spend the night at the rectory. Mrs Fudge will no doubt enjoy having the little one to dote on, and you're in need of a good supper and a decent night's sleep.' He got to his feet and helped Bea up. She managed a small smile.

'Thank you, Reverend, sir,' she said softly. 'I knew you wouldn't let us down.'

The moon was bright, lighting their path. An owl hooted nearby, followed by the high-pitched screech of its unfortunate prey. It was a mild night with just the faintest breeze rustling the sycamore trees that surrounded the old rectory. Smoke curled from one of the chimney pots and light spilled from a downstairs window. A dog barked and the front door opened, lamplight spilling onto the path as an overweight, grey-muzzled retriever came bounding out, tail wagging in welcome.

'You were a long time, Reverend.' The ample figure of May Fudge, in hat and coat, filled the doorway. She was in her late fifties, with wiry grey hair worn in a bun, and facial features that gave the appearance of sternness, belying her warm, compassionate nature. Her brows arched in surprise at the sight of the young girl hovering at Michael's side, a tiny infant cradled to her chest.

'And who do we have here?' she queried as Michael bent down to pat the dog, which was sniffing around Bea's skirts.

'It's me, Mrs Fudge,' Bea said shyly. 'Bea Cullen.'

'Mary Cullen's lass? Well, I'm blessed. I haven't laid eyes on you since you were knee high to a frog. Come on inside, girl. There's a pot of cocoa warming on the stove and plenty of stew left over from the reverend's supper.' Shooing away the inquisitive retriever, May ushered Bea down the hall and into the front parlour where a fire crackled cheerfully in the grate.

'I told Bea she could spend the night,' Michael said, meeting May's gaze over Bea's bowed head. The old housekeeper nodded, her expression one of compassion. She had noticed the lack of a wedding band on the girl's left hand. Bea Cullen wasn't the first girl in the town to get herself into trouble and May doubted she'd be the last.

'I'll fetch the cocoa,' she said once she'd settled Bea on the sofa, Lily sleeping contentedly beside her amidst a nest of cushions.

Some time later, Michael lay tossing and turning in his bed listening to the familiar sounds of the old house creaking and settling. His usual contentment had completely deserted him as his mind explored every possibility.

For propriety's sake, May had insisted on spending the night. 'You don't want to set tongues wagging,' she had told Michael firmly when he'd protested. 'You know what busy-bodies some of your parishioners can be.' And Michael had had to concur. The last thing he wanted was to sully Bea's reputation any further. So, while Bea ate her stew and fed Lily, May had made up the double bed in the front bedroom where the women both now slept, Lily tucked snuggly in the crook of Bea's arm.

Bea had cried herself to sleep, sobbing quietly into the pillow as May gently stroked her hair and whispered meaningless words of comfort.

Sleep still eluding him, Michael threw off the covers and padded to the window. The moon cast a silvery light over the back garden, neighbouring rooftops and the hills beyond. From his vantage point he could just make out the sloping roof of the police station, and the Hayters' cottage adjacent to it. Little Annie Hayter, second child of Constable Jim Hayter and his wife Martha, had lived only a few weeks. He blinked, unable to erase the memory of Jim and Martha sitting in the front pew, stoic and white-faced in their dark mourning clothes; little Charlie, their bewildered five-year-old son, wedged between them. Please God, he prayed now, the Hayters would be willing to take on Bea's child and, he sent an urgent petition Heavenward, please let Martha still be able to nurse, otherwise it would be the Foundling Hospital or the workhouse for the little mite and God alone knew what would become of her then.

CHAPTER TWO

'Will you have another slice of toast, Jim?' Martha Hayter brushed a strand of blond hair out of her blue eyes in a gesture of weary irritation. She knew she looked a mess but she was too tired and too sad to care. Ever since the funeral three days ago, she'd wanted nothing more than to climb into bed and sink into blissful oblivion.

'You're all right, Martha, love,' Jim replied from where he sat beside the fireplace polishing his shoes. 'I don't have much of an appetite.' He glanced over to where Charlie sat at the scrubbed pine table, his natural childish exuberance stifled in the face of his parents' grief.

'What about you, Charlie, lad?' Jim said, attempting to inject some lightness into his tone. 'Think you could manage a slice of toast?'

Charlie looked up from his porridge. A good-looking boy, he had inherited his father's olive skin, dark brown eyes and unruly black curls. His dark eyes flicked towards his mother who was standing at the sink, staring out the window. He shook his head.

'No, thank you, Father.'

He cast another anxious glance in his mother's direction before venturing hopefully, 'Am I going back to school today, Father?' Much as Charlie had loved and missed his baby sister, Jim could see that the thought of another day of oppressive silence, punctuated by his mother's weeping while waiting for the chimes of the mantelpiece clock counting down one long, dreadful hour after another, hung heavily on his young shoulders.

'If your mother has no objections, I reckon it will do you good to get back to school. What do you say, Martha, love?' He looked at his wife sadly, awaiting her reply.

He'd fallen for Martha the moment he'd laid eyes on her dancing round the maypole at the annual Mayday Fair in the marketplace. It was an event that drew crowds from near and far and Martha had travelled across the river from Blandford St Mary with her older sister Doris. Jim had been a fresh-faced lad of seventeen, Martha just fifteen.

Her blue ribbon had worked its way loose and her long blond hair tumbled around her shoulders; her white lawn dress swirled, every so often affording Jim a tantalizing glimpse of her bare feet and ankles. Jim could picture her head thrown back as she laughed, the garland of wildflowers encircling her head jauntily askew. Her carefree beauty had taken Jim's breath away and he hadn't been the only one captivated by Martha. Sam Elkins, a local scoundrel with an eye for the ladies, had elbowed Jim aside, determined to claim the prettiest girl at the fair for himself.

But to Jim's immense gratitude, and surprise, Martha had been quick to make her preference known. She and Jim were married three years later. Nine months after the wedding, little Charlie had come along, followed by Annie five years later.

Jim forced down the tide of grief that threatened to overwhelm him at the thought of his precious daughter and reached for his wife's hand. It cut him to the quick that he couldn't make things better for his beloved Martha. Never before had he felt so useless, so helpless.

Martha pulled her hand away and shrugged her shoulders. 'Whatever you think best,' she replied listlessly.

It was market day and, even though the kitchen was situated at the rear of the airy five-room police cottage, Martha could hear the carts and wagons lumbering down the street out the front. The smell of animal dung, the bellow of oxen and the shouts of drovers and market traders drifted in on the breeze for, although they were officially in mourning, Jim had insisted the curtains and windows remain open. Charlie needed fresh air and light. It wasn't healthy for the boy to be cooped up in a dark, airless house. Too stricken with grief, Martha hadn't been able to summon the energy to argue.

She stared out at the backyard. Someone had left the privy door unlatched but she couldn't even bring herself to be irritated by the resulting intermittent banging. She spent her days in a fog of grief and despair. Having fallen pregnant so quickly with Charlie, Martha had imagined a houseful of babies, but as the months and years went by, she and Jim had begun to despair of ever having any more children. Then Annie had come along and their joy had known no bounds. For six blissful weeks Martha had thought her life complete.

Then came that terrible day. Not a minute went by that Martha did not berate herself. Surely there had been some warning sign she had missed? Some indication that something was wrong? But try as hard as she might, she could call nothing to mind.

Annie's skin had been a little warm, perhaps, and she had been a tad more fractious than usual, but Martha had put it down to the unseasonably warm weather. Everything had been as it should that Monday afternoon when she put Annie down for her nap. She had just settled down to her mending when Annie let out a strange, high-pitched cry. Martha had gone to her immediately, scooping her from the cradle. In her mother's arms, Annie stretched out her tiny body and went limp. By the time the doctor arrived, it had been too late. Little Annie was gone.

The knock on the door startled them all. Jim and Martha exchanged glances. As a rule, friends and neighbours would come around the back. Who could be knocking on the front door at this hour?

'I'll go,' Jim muttered. Lacing up his shoes, he got to his feet and, ruffling Charlie's tousled curls as he passed, went out into the hallway.

'Reverend Redfern.' Jim's voice rumbled in the hallway.

'Morning, Jim. I'm sorry to call so early. Is there somewhere we can talk? Privately?'

'Of course.' Jim's reply was followed by the sound of the parlour door being firmly shut. Martha could hear muffled voices coming through the wall.

She looked over at Charlie who was watching her, his wide eyes wary, and she felt a pang. Poor boy; she had neglected him of late. With supreme effort, she forced her lips into a semblance of a smile.

'If you're going to school you'd better wash your face and comb your hair.' She glanced at the clock on the wall. 'If you get a move on, you'll catch your friends as they're passing.'

The look of pure delight on her son's face choked her so much she had to turn away, her eyes swimming with tears as she filled the washing bowl with warm soapy water so Charlie could wash his hands and face.

She was just helping him to button up his jacket when she heard the parlour door open and turned to see Jim in the doorway, a peculiar expression on his face.

'Martha.' His voice faltered. 'Martha, the reverend would like to speak to you about something.'

Martha straightened up and smoothed down the skirt of her brown wool dress. Kissing Charlie goodbye, she saw him out of the back door, waving until he ducked through the archway and disappeared from view, before following Jim into the parlour where Michael Redfern stood by the window, staring out into the bustling street where a herd of black-faced sheep were being driven along the road, bleating and kicking up dust. He turned at the sound of Martha entering the room, greeting her with genuine warmth.

'My dear Mrs Hayter. How are you managing?'

'I'm coping one day at a time, Reverend,' Martha replied, perching on the edge of the sofa and folding her work-worn hands primly in her lap.

'Time will heal, Mrs Hayter, of that I am a great believer.' Not wanting to contradict the reverend, Martha simply nodded. She looked up at him expectantly, wondering what it was he wanted.

'Now, Martha,' Jim said nervously, coming to sit beside her and taking her hand in his. 'The reverend has something he wishes to speak to you about. The decision is entirely yours but promise me you'll hear him out.'

Puzzled, Martha nodded. 'Yes, all right.' She focused her attention on the vicar. 'What is it, Reverend?'

The reverend coughed into his fist and took the chair closest to the empty fireplace. There was a chill in the room and Martha wished she'd thought to light the fire but, of course, she hadn't been expecting company. The endless stream of friends calling to offer their condolences had dried up after the funeral.

The vicar steepled his fingers and leaned forward, regarding Martha with earnest.

'My dear, I am aware how difficult the last few days have been for you. It is a terrible thing to lose a child and I don't wish to cause you any further distress, but yesterday a young girl came to see me.'

He coughed to clear his throat before continuing to relate the events of the previous evening.

When he had finished, a heavy silence descended over the room, broken only by the tick of the carriage clock on the mantelpiece and the lowing and bleating of animals in the marketplace. Martha frowned.

'You want me to take this child in place of my Annie and raise her as our own?'

At her words, the reverend squirmed uncomfortably. 'She won't take the place of Annie in your heart, of course not, but perhaps you could, in time, grow to love her alongside Annie, as you do Charlie?'

Martha rubbed her temples. Could she take on another woman's child? As she wrestled with the thoughts swirling around her head, it was as if her body had decided to take the decision for her. Her breasts, which, on the midwife's advice, were tightly bound in an effort to suppress her milk flow, began to tingle and soon she was aware of a warm dampness seeping through the bodice of her wool dress.

Her cheeks flaming with embarrassment, she tugged on a shawl left conveniently folded over the back of the sofa and draped it around her shoulders, aware that both her husband and the vicar were watching her expectantly. She closed her eyes. Every maternal instinct in her body was screaming for her to say yes.

'What do you think, Jim?' she asked, her voice thick with emotion.

Jim shrugged. 'We've always wanted a houseful of children,

Martha, but for some reason God's decided not to give them to us. Perhaps this child is his roundabout way of answering our prayer. He took our Annie, for whatever reason.' He shrugged wearily. 'Who are we to question his will? But perhaps he's given us this little girl instead.'

Slowly, Martha nodded her head and, without a hint of hesitation, said firmly, 'Very well, Reverend. For better or worse, we will take on this child.'

The vicar let out a long sigh of relief, clearly glad not to have had to find some other fate for the poor child. 'Her name is Lilian Mary. I shall bring her round within the hour. Her mother is anxious to be on her way.'

Having lost her own child, Martha was at loss to understand how any woman could abandon her baby. As if reading her thoughts, the reverend laid a hand on her arm as Martha and Jim walked him to the door.

'Don't think badly of Lilian's mother, Martha,' he said gently. 'Her circumstances are untenable. She is heartbroken but you surely understand that her situation leaves her no choice. She must give up her child.'

Martha bowed her head, suitably chastened.

Jim shook the vicar by the hand. 'We'll see you soon, then, Reverend.'

'I'll be back within the hour,' he promised, striding purposefully away.

Blinking back tears, Bea hugged Lilian against her breast. As if sensing something was wrong, Lily had been fractious all morning, refusing to feed properly and screaming, her tiny fists beating the air in red-faced indignation.

Bea had woken early, her heart heavy with dread at the day to come. Once Lily was gone, she would make her way to Dorchester. Perhaps there she would be able to find work. She studied Lily's face, trying to commit her features to memory. She wondered sadly how long it would take until Lily's face faded to an indistinct blur.

She could hear Mrs Fudge bustling about in the kitchen. Today the housekeeper remained stoically silent. There was none of her cheerful humming as she tackled the morning's chores. Lily had quieted for the moment, lulled into contentment by the rhythmic rocking of the chair in which Bea sat. From her vantage point, she could see the road from the village so was watching when the vicar came into view. From the determined set of his jaw and his purposeful gait, she knew immediately that his mission had been a success.

Swallowing her own grief, she got swiftly to her feet and left the morning room, meeting him in the wood-panelled hallway. The reverend stopped on the threshold, clearly surprised to find her waiting for him.

'They agreed?' she asked in a matter-of-fact tone.

'They did. I will take Lily to them as soon as you are ready.'

'Do it now.' Bea bit her lip in an effort not to give in to the torrent of tears threatening to overwhelm her. Lily was gazing up at her with eyes on the cusp of changing from violet to emerald-green. 'Here.' She thrust Lily at him. He took her awkwardly in his arms, his expression one of bewilderment.

'Are you sure? You don't have to leave immediately.'

Bea shook her head vehemently. 'No,' she said sharply, turning her back on her child. 'Please, sir,' she said, her voice shaking as her resolve began to weaken. 'Just go.'

Surreptitiously wiping her eyes with the hem of her apron, Mrs Fudge emerged from the kitchen. Meeting Michael's gaze over Bea's head, she gave him an imperceptible nod, before draping a comforting arm around Bea's set shoulders, and ushering her into the warm kitchen where Bea collapsed onto a chair and dissolved into a flood of tears.

CHAPTER THREE

'Lily's very sweet, isn't she, Mama?'

'She is indeed, Charlie, love.' Martha gave her son an indulgent smile. They were in the front parlour of her sister Doris's house and Charlie was crouched on the threadbare rug encouraging the five-month-old Lily to roll over. She had been close a number of times but had yet to execute the momentous feat.

'I haven't any sugar, I'm afraid!' Doris came into the room bearing the tea tray. 'And the milk's off.'

'Black will be fine. I'm trying to cut down on the sugar anyway,' Martha replied, wrapping her hands around the chipped mug Doris handed her. The glowing embers in the grate did little to expel the room's chill and she was glad she had thought to put the children in an extra layer of clothing. She sipped her tea. It was stewed and bitter to the taste. Placing her mug on the low table beside the faded chintz armchair in which she sat, she glanced around the dingy room. She knew her sister's marriage wasn't a happy one.

Doris and Sam Elkin had begun courting shortly after Martha and Jim, and they had married in haste. On whether Doris had actually been expecting and had, as she claimed, suffered a miscarriage shortly after the wedding, Martha was inclined to give her the benefit of the doubt. Sam, on the other hand, had treated Doris like dirt ever since, convinced that she had deliberately set out to trap him.

He earned a liveable wage as a brewer yet, according to Jim, he squandered most of it down the dog track and on cheap liquor, while his wife and son lived in poverty.

'Where is Jez today?' Martha asked, suddenly realizing why the cottage was so peaceful. Five months younger than Charlie, Jeremy was a stocky child already half an inch taller than his cousin. With his dark hair and large, almond-shaped eyes, he was destined to be a heartbreaker one day, like his dad. Yet Martha had never warmed to the boy. Ever since he was old enough to walk and talk, he had displayed a mean streak that had, at first, startled her and now made her feel downright uncomfortable. He had started at the junior school in September, a year behind her Charlie, and barely a day went by that he wasn't hauled into the headmaster's office for fighting or some other display of spiteful behaviour. And while Charlie wasn't exactly afraid of his cousin, he was certainly wary of him, and avoided him whenever possible. He was becoming more and more reluctant to accompany Martha on her visits to see her sister with every passing week.

'Sam took him down the track,' Doris replied, with a weary shrug of her shoulders. She was Martha's senior by two years, yet she looked a decade older. Her miserable existence had etched itself onto her face, her dirty blond hair was lank and streaked prematurely grey and her washed-out blue-print dress hung limply on her thin frame.

'Is that wise?' Martha asked, appalled. 'Surely the dog track is no place for a child.'

'I can't stop Sam doing what he wants,' Doris snapped crossly. 'You know that. Sam's dad used to take him, so he takes Jez.' She shrugged her bony shoulders. 'I don't expect he'll come to any harm, not if he's with his dad.'

Martha wisely didn't contradict her sister but she couldn't help thinking that, once Sam had had a skinful, there was no telling what Jez would get up to. Sam certainly wouldn't be keeping an eye on him, that was for sure. He'd be too focused on whichever dog he'd wagered this week's pay packet on.

She kept an eye on the mantelpiece clock, wanting to be long gone by the time Sam rolled in worse the wear for drink. She shot her sister a pitying glance. Unless Sam had, by some miracle, managed to shrug off his losing streak, poor Doris would be in for a hard time tonight.

It saddened Martha to see her beloved sister so miserable. She mourned the happy, carefree girl Doris had been before marriage to Sam had stripped her of her dignity, her pride and self-worth. Now her once-pretty face was etched with bitterness and discontent, her once-bright blue eyes dull and devoid of hope.

'Why don't you come over to us next Saturday?' Martha suggested. 'It'll do you good to get out.'

Doris stirred in her chair. 'Sam won't like it.'

'Well, he can just lump it, can't he?' Trying to keep the note of exasperation from her voice, Martha gave her sister a hard stare. 'Sam is a brute and a bully. You've got to stand up to him, love. If only for your Jeremy's sake. He's turning out to be exactly like his dad, and the lad's barely five years old.'

'You leave my Jez out of it,' Doris snapped. She tugged her sleeves over her thin wrists but Martha's sharp-eyed gaze had already noticed the livid fingerprint-shaped bruise. Doris narrowed her eyes. 'You think you're so smug, Martha Hayter, with your boring husband and comfortable lifestyle, and your nice clothes.' She gave Martha's simple wool dress a disparaging glance. 'Everyone thinks you're so wonderful, taking on that slattern's by-blow when your own kid was barely cold in the grave . . .'

'Doris!'

Charlie looked up in shock. His mother seldom raised her voice but when she did she could stop a grown man in his tracks. Lily began to cry.

'Don't you dare,' Martha hissed, getting to her feet and gathering Lily to her breast, rocking her gently as she faced her sister, anger colouring her cheeks. 'I loved my Annie, and not a day goes by that I don't think of her, but I will not have you making derogatory remarks about Lily's birth mother. She'll have a hard enough time of it as it is, when she's older, without you adding to her distress.' Martha gave her sister a pitying look. 'What happened to you, Doris? You used to be such a kind, loving girl.'

Doris pouted. 'I just think charity should start at home,' she said sullenly, her eyes flashing as her thin lips twisted into a sneer. 'Instead of lavishing your love and attention on that kid, you should be helping your own flesh and blood.'

Flabbergasted, Martha could only stare at her sister. 'Doris, Jim is always bailing you out. Who got the rent man off your back just the other week? And I never come here empty-handed. If you got off your backside and took care of your garden, things might actually start to grow. You don't help yourself, Doris, that's your problem. You're bone idle.'

'You don't know what life is like for me, Martha,' Doris whined, getting to her feet. Tears sparkled in her eyes and her nose was beginning to run. She swiped at it with the back of her hand. 'I could have had my pick of husbands,' she said, wrapping her self-pity around her like a heavy cloak. 'Why did I have to pick Sam Elkin?'

At the sight of her sister's anguish, Martha's anger dissipated. Holding Lily in one arm, she pulled Doris to her with the other. 'Like our dear departed mother would say, you've made your bed, now you've got to lie in it.'

'It's a damn uncomfortable bed,' Doris muttered into Martha's neck, her hot, bitter tears soaking into Martha's collar.

'I'll get Jim to have a word,' Martha promised, disentangling herself from Doris's arms to lay Lily down on the rug. Her happy equilibrium restored, Lily lay kicking her legs and gurgling up at her brother. 'I'll make us another cup of tea, and then we really must be getting off. I don't like the look of those clouds. I think a storm's coming.'

Sure enough, Martha had barely stepped in through her own back door when the heavens opened. She set Lily on the kitchen rug and took off her coat and hat, hanging them on the back of the door. She lit the lamp and stoked up the fire. The rain was coming down in stair rods and a cold wind rattled the window frames and shrieked under the eaves as she set about preparing the evening meal.

Her argument with Doris had left a queer taste in her mouth. She hated losing her temper with her sister, she mused as she rattled the pans on the hob. Doris wasn't the first girl to be taken in by a charmer only to find herself lumbered with a feckless gambler. And, for all Sam's faults, and there were many, he had stuck by her when Doris thought she was expecting. There were many who wouldn't. Like poor Lily's dad, whoever he might be. Martha sighed, biting her bottom lip as she turned to watch her daughter gurgling happily on the floor, her wide green eyes fixed firmly on Charlie who was setting his toy soldiers in neat rows under the kitchen table.

From the moment Reverend Redfern had laid Lily in Martha's arms, she had been smitten. The first time she had nursed her, Lily had latched on to Martha's engorged breasts without protest and it was as if a dam had burst inside her. All her pent-up grief and anguish had coming spewing forth along with her milk, and for the first time since Annie had died, she felt as though she had a future, a life to live instead of an empty existence.

She loved Lily as if she were her own flesh and blood and, while she had expected to feel that she was somehow betraying Annie, she found it was the opposite. Like she told Jim, she felt as though she was in some way honouring Annie's memory by loving Lily. They made a point of visiting Annie's grave every Sunday after church and, one day, when she was old enough to understand, Martha would explain everything to Lily.

But that was a bridge she wouldn't have to cross for a few years yet, she thought idly as she slathered butter on thick slices of bread.

She caught a glimpse of a dark shadow crossing the yard and a moment later the latch lifted and Jim blew through the door in a gust of wind and swirling rain. He stood grinning in his oilskins, water dripping onto the stone floor.

'Jim, you're soaked.' Martha hastened to help him out of his wet clothes. He kissed her cheek, shed his wet coat and sank down into his favourite chair close to the fire where he unlaced his shoes and massaged his cold feet.

'Here, get this cup of tea down you.' Martha handed him the steaming mug, which he took gratefully. Charlie came to lean on his knee and Jim ruffled his hair affectionately. The fire was crackling in the grate, casting a warm glow over the kitchen. Steam swirled over the stove top, forming beads of condensation on the windowpane.

'How was Doris?' Jim asked, as his fingers thawed around the mug.

'The same,' Martha replied, lifting the lid on a pan and letting the aroma of mutton stew waft into the air. 'Sam was down the dogs again, with Jez.'

'And Mama and Aunty Doris had an argument,' Charlie added, sliding down his father's leg to duck back under the table where his toy soldiers were waiting. Jim raised a questioning eyebrow.

'Really?'

'Oh, you know how Doris is,' Martha said with a weary sigh. 'She came over all sorry for herself. Implied that we should be doing more to help her.' She turned to face Jim, her hands on her hips. 'She had a dig at our Lily as well.'

'Lily?' Jim frowned, his gaze moving to Lily, who was up on her side, her little fists beating the air with a determined air, her cheeks bright red. He held his breath but the effort proved too much and Lily rolled back onto her back, chubby legs kicking in frustration.

'She's so close to rolling over,' he remarked, his gaze returning to his wife. 'Doris needs to watch herself,' he said sternly. 'I won't have her making disparaging remarks about my family. You do far too much for her as it is. Has Sam paid the rent arrears?'

'I don't know.'

'Old Trowbridge won't wait for ever. I managed to get them a few days' grace but if they don't pay what's owed pretty soon, they'll be out on their ear.'

'I know, I know.' Martha sighed. Her sister's predicament was a constant source of worry to her. Every night in her prayers she was conscious to thank God for Jim. She'd married a good man there, and no mistake. She fetched the bowls from the dresser and was about to ladle the first steaming spoonful when Charlie gave a yell.

'She did it! Mama, Father, look. Lily rolled over. She did it.'

Beaming with pride, they watched Lily flopping about on her stomach like a fish out of water, arms and feet beating the rug, her face one of gummy-mouthed triumph.

'You clever girl,' Martha breathed, stooping to gather Lily into her arms and covering her little face with kisses. Lily giggled and wriggled in her mother's embrace. Watching his wife and daughter, little Charlie at Martha's side, standing on tiptoe so he could stroke Lily's hand, Jim was overcome by a deep, abiding love for his family. Could a man ever be more blessed?

CHAPTER FOUR

1885

'Charlie!' Nine-year-old Lily skipped across the schoolyard, overjoyed to find her brother waiting for her at the school gates. Wisps of auburn hair had worked themselves loose from her plaits, curling around her head like a fiery halo. The warm June sun had turned her pale, freckled skin the colour of golden honey and Charlie had a few seconds to reflect, once again, on how pretty his little sister was before she launched herself at him. 'Have you got the day off? How long can you stay? Are you able to stay for tea? Oh, Mother will be so pleased to see you.'

Charlie returned Lily's embrace, his chin resting on the top of her head. The sky above the dark school roof was a vibrant blue with fluffy clouds scudding across it. Two sulky-looking crows squabbled noisily on the clock tower. The air was filled with children's voices as they streamed up the street, pigtails and satchels flying out behind them.

Lily skipped happily alongside Charlie as they made their way up East Street towards Market Place. Since Charlie had moved up to Shaftesbury to take up an apprenticeship to a cabinetmaker two years ago, Lily only got to see him once a month and she chatted away happily, filling him in on all her news. It wasn't until they turned into Laundry Lane that it dawned on Lily that they were heading in the wrong direction.

'Charlie?' Lily halted and dragged on Charlie's hand. 'Where are we going? This isn't the right way.'

He looked down at her. The grim set of his jaw frightened her and her bottom lip started to tremble.

'What's the matter, Charlie? Why are we going to Aunty Doris's?'

'Because you can't go home, Lily.' Charlie hunkered down in front of her. Two years previous, around his twelfth birthday, Charlie's voice had broken and he'd experienced a sudden growth spurt. He was now a gangly five foot nine. It wouldn't be long before he was shaving. He put his hands on Lily's shoulders and looked into her eyes, his expression sombre.

'Why not?' Lily asked in a small voice. Her stomach hurt and her throat was aching with the effort of holding back tears.

'Mother and Father are sick, Lily,' Charlie replied with a deep sigh. 'Very sick. You know they both had sore throats over the weekend? Well, they got worse this morning. It's something called diphtheria. It's spreading around the town. You have to stay away, Lily, in case you catch it.'

'I don't want to go to Aunty Doris's. Can't I stay with you?'

Charlie shook his head. 'Lily, I live in a boarding house with nine other lads,' he told her, straightening up. He took hold of her hand.

Lily dragged her feet. 'I don't want to go there,' she wailed. 'Please don't make me. Aunty Doris doesn't like me. She called me a bad name and she told Mother that my real mother was nothing but a dirty trollop. I heard her.'

Charlie gave a snort. 'Take no notice of anything our aunt says. Remember what Mother said: your mother gave you to us so you would have a better life. She loves you very much and so do Mother and Father.'

Lily nodded, fat tears rolling down her cheeks. She must have been about four or five when Martha and Jim had sat her down and told her about Beatrice. She'd been too young to understand, knowing only that somewhere in the world she had another mother. She had cried and clung on to Martha, terrified they would send her back to her other mother. It had taken all Martha and Jim's love and patience to persuade Lily that she was their little girl, and forever would be. The implications of being born out of wedlock had only become clear as she grew older and the stigma of illegitimacy had become a weapon for the inevitable few to use against her, Doris most of all.

They walked along the row of old washerwomen's cottages that made up Laundry Lane. The road underfoot was dusty and years of passing wagons and carts had gouged deep ruts into the road. A small child in a grubby pinafore, her nose streaming, scratched in the dirt outside one of the cottages. She watched Lily and Charlie go by with mild curiosity.

Doris's cottage was at the end of the long row, a ramshackle building with peeling paintwork and weeds sprouting up around the doorstep. Despite the day's warmth, the door and windows were firmly shut. A plume of smoke curled from the chimney.

Shooting Lily an apologetic glance, Charlie took a deep breath and rapped his knuckles on the bare wood. 'If there was any other way, Lily,' he said, looking down at her sorrowfully. 'It shouldn't be for too long. Mother and Father are strong; they'll be fit and well again in no time.'

Lily refused to be mollified. She stared down at the tips of her black shoes. She could feel glances prickling her skin, aware that curious eyes would be watching them from the surrounding windows. Laundry Lane was one of the poorest streets in town and any visitors attracted attention.

When their knocking drew no response, Charlie let go of Lily's hand and peered through the grime-smeared window into the dim room beyond, chewing his bottom lip in consternation. If Doris wasn't able to take Lily, he was at loss as to what to do. He was in no position to rent a room for the two of them on his meagre wages. And he was determined to keep Lily out of the workhouse. He was scratching his head, unsure of what to do next, when a shout echoed from down the street. He turned, relief overriding his usual aversion to his cousin Jez's appearance.

Jez, a good couple of inches taller than Charlie, came strolling down the street looking as cocksure and arrogant as ever.

What he did for a living, Charlie had never really been sure. Whatever it was, he doubted it was on the right side of legal.

'Charlie, old chap.' Jez grinned. 'What brings you two round here?' His gaze slid to Lily who tried to slink behind her brother, eyes downcast. She didn't like Jez and he left her in no doubt that the feeling was mutual.

'We're looking for our aunt,' Charlie said. Jez's smile faded as he aimed a hefty kick at the door. It flew back on its hinges to reveal a squalid parlour. The air smelled fetid. Cobwebs, disturbed by the sudden rush of air, swayed in the dim corners of the ceiling.

'Ma, are you here?' Jez yelled.

Doris had never been what one would call house-proud, but since Sam's death in a drunken brawl up at the dog tracks ten months previously, she appeared to have given up all pretence at keeping house, preferring to wallow in self-pity and console herself with gin.

Out of a sense of loyalty, Martha continued to visit her sister, though nowhere near as frequently as she had once done. It was the one source of discord in her otherwise harmonious marriage. Jim couldn't stand Doris, or her son, and he made no bones about the fact.

Jez elbowed his way past Charlie and Lily into the dank, cluttered room. Lily peered after him into the gloom. Every surface was covered in a thick layer of dust. The few trinkets Doris hadn't yet got around to pawning were shrouded in cobwebs.

'Ma, where are you, woman?' Jez's footsteps resounded on the bare floorboards, sending dust motes swirling into the air as he strode across the room and pushed open the adjoining door to the kitchen. He swore loudly and Lily heard what sounded like someone kicking the legs of a chair, hard enough to cause the legs to squeak across the flagstones. Her aunt's voice reverberated through the open doorway, thin and querulous. Lily and Charlie exchanged uncertain glances. Lily's stomach ache was growing steadily worse and now she was starting to feel nauseated too. She started to cry again.

'What do you want?' Doris stood swaying in the doorway, silhouetted against the hazy sunlight streaming in through the back door Jez had opened to disperse the smell of gin that hung like a toxic cloud over the kitchen. Her face was slack and crumpled, as though she had just woken up, her dirty grey-streaked blond hair a tangled mess. With the back of her hand she wiped a thin string of drool from her chin and leered at her nephew and niece through her drunken haze.

'She's drunk,' Jez said sullenly, shoving past his mother. Throwing what looked like a pile of old rags from the moth-eaten sofa, he flopped onto the couch and lit a cigarette, glowering at Charlie and Lily through a cloud of tobacco smoke. Not yet fourteen, he had the worldly air of a much older man.

'I am not drunk,' Doris slurred crossly. She took a step forward and would have stumbled had she not grabbed hold of the doorframe. 'What d'you want, Charlie? Did Martha send you? Too high and mighty to come round herself, is she?'

'Mother and Father are ill,' Charlie replied, trying to keep the disgust from showing in his tone. 'Diphtheria. Doctor Billingham said I'm to keep Lily away so I've brought her here. You're our only kin.'

Doris's snort of laughter held no mirth. 'So, I'm kin when it suits you, am I? I barely see my dear sister these days.'

It was on the tip of Charlie's tongue to retort that it was Doris's increasingly erratic behaviour, fuelled by a fondness for the gin, that had tried Martha's patience. He bit his lip, unwilling to get into a fight with his aunt.

'We need your help, Aunt,' he said, making a supreme effort to keep his tone measured and even. 'I can't have Lily with me and it'll be the workhouse otherwise.'

'Why should we take her in? She's not even family,' Jez drawled, squinting at Charlie as he expelled a lungful of smoke.

Charlie shot Jez a filthy look. 'It's no matter that Lily isn't blood, Jez. She's my sister, your cousin, so mind your manners.' Jez grinned sardonically. He might be younger than his cousin but he knew without a doubt that, should it come to it, he had the brawn to wipe the floor with Charlie.

Charlie took a crumpled note from his trouser pocket. 'Here,' he said, handing it over. 'This ought to cover Lily's keep for a few days, at least.' He saw the light flare in Doris's eyes and felt slightly sick.

'All right.' Doris shrugged. 'She can stay.' Jez got languidly to his feet and snatched the money from his mother's grasp, shoving it deep into his pocket.

Charlie led Lily outside. It was a perfect early-summer afternoon. Skylarks swooped above the chimney pots. Children played around the pair, barely affording Charlie and Lily a cursory glance as they chased each other down the dusty street. Someone was whistling. Several buxom women in mob caps and aprons were loading baskets of fresh laundry onto waiting carts. The smell of woodfires and potatoes boiling on the hearth wafted from a myriad of open doors and windows, mingling with the smell of the midden at the end of the street.

Charlie crouched down until his gaze was level with Lily's tear-stained face. Her bottom lip trembled.

'I don't want to stay,' she whispered, her green eyes filling with fresh tears. 'Please don't make me.'

'It'll only be for a few days, Lily, I promise. Mother and Father will get well.' He tweaked her nose and grinned at her. 'Have you ever known either of them to be ill before?'

Lily shook her head. Tears spilled over the lashes and down her cheeks.

'There you are then. They'll be back on their feet in no time, you'll see.'

Lily clung to him, sobbing bitterly into his shoulder until Doris came shuffling out to scold her for showing them up in front of the whole street with her caterwauling.

'I've got to go, Lily,' Charlie said, reluctantly extricating himself from his sister's grip. 'I've got to be back by dark or I'll be in trouble.' He ruffled Lily's hair. 'Be brave. It won't be for long.'

'Stop your snivelling and get indoors,' Doris snapped, grabbing Lily roughly by the arm and dragging her into the house, all but slamming the door in Charlie's face. 'Now, see here,' she snarled, the gin fumes making Lily's eyes water. 'I'm not a charity. While you're here, you can flipping well earn your keep.'

'But . . .' Lily opened her mouth to remind her aunt about the money Charlie had handed over but one look at Doris's face caused her to think better of it.

'You can start by peeling the potatoes.' Doris shoved Lily into the hot kitchen. Sunlight streamed in through the open door. Faded floral-patterned curtains hung limply at a grime-smeared window overlooking a dirt yard, baked hard by the sun, and the privy, which was shared with the rest of the row. A row of raspberry canes stood along the back fence, beyond which were the allotments. Doris's patch was unkempt and overgrown with weeds and nettles. A few scrawny brown chickens scratched in the dirt around the back steps.

With a lump in her throat so huge she could barely swallow, Lily sat slumped at the kitchen table. Doris dumped a handful of potatoes in front of her and handed her a knife.

'After you've done that you can tidy this place up,' she said, giving the filthy kitchen a withering look. 'It's a pigsty.'

Blinking back tears and missing her mother and father so much it was a physical ache in the pit of her stomach, Lily did as she was told. The potatoes were wrinkled and sprouting. She peeled them, trying to keep the knife as close to the surface as possible so as not to waste any of the flesh, and put them on to boil. Doris and Jez were arguing in the other room. It sounded like Jez was going out and Doris was begging him not to. The argument ended with the slam of the front door. A moment later, Doris came into the kitchen, her face puce. Quailing beneath her aunt's hostile glare, Lily carried on with her scrubbing and cleaning. The pot bubbled rapidly on the stove. The room was hot and steamy, and sweat trickled down Lily's spine. After a moment, and without speaking a word of comfort or kindness to her bereft niece, Doris left the room.

An hour later, the two of them sat in uncomfortable silence at the freshly scrubbed table. Lily could only pick at her meal of boiled potatoes and stale bread with no butter. Her head ached and her throat throbbed with the effort of holding back her tears. She missed her mother and father, and Charlie, so much it hurt.

Jez had not yet returned and his meal sat on the side, covered by an upturned plate to keep off the circling bluebottles.

'If you're not going to eat that, you can pass it here,' Doris said, breaking the heavy silence. Without a word, Lily slid her barely touched plate across the table. 'You may as well get off to bed,' Doris went on, stabbing a potato with a fork. She glowered at Lily through gin-reddened eyes. 'You'll have chores to do before school so make sure you're up early or you'll be late for your lessons.'

Apart from an old iron bedstead pushed against one wall, the attic was empty and as hot as Hades. The mattress was stained and musty. Ignoring the foul-smelling moth-eaten blanket folded across the end of the bed, Lily laid down, still wearing her clothes, and curled up on the bare mattress, which sagged slightly beneath her. Listening to the sounds emanating from outside, Lily prayed as hard as she could for her parents to get better. More than anything, she wanted to go home. Silent tears trickled down her face, soaking into the thin pillow as she cried herself to sleep.

CHAPTER FIVE

In the pale light of dawn, Lily threw off her blanket and swung her skinny legs out of bed, shivering as her bare feet touched the cold floorboards. Though there was no clock in the room, next door's cockerel was as regular as clockwork and after that first morning when Aunt Doris had boxed her ears for waking up well after sunrise, and then having had to suffer the indignity of being made to stand in the corner of the classroom for twenty minutes as punishment for being late for school, Lily slept with her ear tuned to the rooster's throaty early-morning alarm call.

Hastily pulling her pinafore over her head, she crept down the short flight of stairs to the upstairs landing where Doris and Jez were performing their nocturnal duet, loud snores reverberating from their respective bedrooms. She tiptoed along the landing, careful to avoid any loose floorboards and made her way downstairs. In the kitchen she lit the stove and set the porridge on. The day before, Jez had given her some money and sent her off to scrounge what she could off the market traders and shopkeepers.

'I want change,' he'd shouted, leering evilly after her.

Lily was well known to the market traders. Martha bought her Dorset buttons from Hannah Titteridge, and her lace trimmings from Amelia Hodder. She bought Jim's pipe tobacco from Robert Short. Constable Jim was known to be a fair-minded man and was well liked and respected by traders and townsfolk alike. Along with sending Martha and Jim their best wishes for a speedy recovery, the stall holders had plied Lily with free vegetables, assuring her with their friendly smiles that they'd go for pigswill otherwise. The market traders' generosity had meant Lily could afford to buy something from the butcher and had surprised her aunt and cousin with a hearty meal of sausages and mashed potatoes with onion gravy and a medley of vegetables.

'Best meal I've had in a long while,' Jez had said, patting his stomach. 'You're not a bad cook for a kid.' He'd flashed Lily a rare grin of appreciation.

'It wasn't half bad,' Doris had concurred, leaning back in her chair with a contented sigh while Lily cleared the table around them. Their appreciation hadn't lasted long. Doris had slapped Lily across the face not five minutes later for breaking a mug, and Jez had sworn at her for tripping over his feet as he sprawled on the sofa.

Now, as she slipped outside, breathing in the cool morning air to gather a handful of raspberries to sprinkle on her aunt's porridge, she was feeling positive. She had been at her aunt's for five days; surely Mother and Father would be well enough to have her home very soon. Humming softly to herself, she plucked the fruit from the canes, barely wincing when a nettle brushed the back of her hand. She rubbed a dock leaf on the offending spot, and carried the bowl of raspberries back to the house and set them on the table. She ate her own breakfast sitting on the back step, watching the shadows dwindle as the sun crested the rooftops.

At a quarter after eight, she carefully carried Doris's breakfast up the narrow staircase and rapped gently on the door. By then she had swept the floor, cleaned the kitchen and tidied the parlour. After school she would be expected to dust and polish, as well as prepare the evening meal. Behind the door Doris's snoring came to an abrupt halt. There came the squeak of bedsprings and then her aunt's voice, thick with sleep:

'Come in.'

Propped up against her pillows, she ordered Lily about as if she were some grand lady directing her staff. Lily wordlessly did as she was told, opening the curtains just enough to let the light in but not enough that Doris was dazzled by the glare. She filled the wash bowl from the chipped jug on the washstand, and fetched her aunt's shawl, which she helped to drape around her rounded shoulders, trying not to wince as Doris's fetid breath tickled her cheek.

Leaving Doris to her breakfast, Lily fled down the stairs, anxious not to be late for school. She left Jez's porridge warming on the stove – he seldom rose before ten – and dashed out of the door.

She had got into the habit of walking with the other children in the street. They were a ragtag bunch, with their clean but patched clothes and worn shoes, but they were friendly and quite happy to allow Lily to walk along with them. In a short time, she had learned that the mothers of Laundry Lane regarded Doris as a lazy drunk and Jez as a troublemaker. Just yesterday, little Patty Miller's older brother, Pip, had earned himself a clip around the earhole from his dad for getting too friendly with Jez. The families in Laundry Lane regarded Doris and Jez as people best avoided.

Still, Lily consoled herself, laughing at something one of the other girls had said, she wouldn't be here much longer.

As they approached the corner of the street, Lily spotted Reverend Redfern and Charlie making their way purposefully down the street towards her and her heart skipped a beat.

'Charlie!' She broke into a run and flung herself on her brother. He held her tight, crushing her fiercely against him, her face squashed against the fabric of his jacket, his lips brushing the top of her head. Charlie's whole body was shaking and it was only when he released her that Lily realized he wasn't laughing, as she had supposed, but crying.

'Charlie?' In her peripheral vision she saw the vicar shooing the other children on their way, but she kept her gaze fixed on Charlie's anguished face. 'Charlie, what is it?' Lily's lips quivered as she searched his face beseechingly.

'Lily.' The vicar said her name so softly it was barely a sigh. She turned to him, wide-eyed with fear as he crouched down beside her, his hands resting gently on her shoulders. Charlie turned away, unable to watch his sister have her heart broken.

'Sweetheart, I'm sorry. Your mother and father have gone to Heaven.'

Lily shook her head. Mother and Father couldn't be dead. She wouldn't believe it. It couldn't be true. She looked at Charlie, her grief-stricken gaze begging him for reassurance. But the look of abject misery on his face finally registered and Lily burst into noisy tears.

Martha had passed away in the early hours of that morning, the vicar told her once her torrent of grief had subsided. Jim had followed some twenty minutes later.

Lily was inconsolable in her grief. The only thing that had kept her going the past few days was the certain knowledge that she would soon be at home in the bosom of her loving family. Now her beloved mama and dad had been so cruelly snatched from her, and her little heart had shattered.

Charlie had been granted five days' compassionate leave, so he took Lily back home to the police house in Market Place. Charlotte Burridge from next door had been in and aired the place. Bunches of herbs and spices hung from the rafters to dispel any lingering germs. The soiled bedding had been taken away and burned.

The moment Lily stepped over the threshold, her parents' absence hit her like a ton of bricks. The house felt cold and impersonal, an empty shell of the loving home it had once been. She shivered. Charlotte was waiting for her. In her mid-sixties, with iron-grey hair swept back in a neat bun, she swept Lily into her arms and rocked her gently while she cried bitter tears. Then, while Charlie went off with the vicar to deal with the formalities and plan the funeral, Charlotte, ever practically minded, kept Lily busy in the kitchen making endless cups of tea and sandwiches for the stream of visitors who called by to offer their condolences all afternoon.

That night, tucked up in her old bed under the eaves in the back bedroom, Lily wept copiously for her parents and for herself. She had heard the words 'workhouse' and 'orphanage' bandied about by insensitive mourners and she was terrified that she would be sent away to some horrible institution far away from Charlie and everything she held dear. She could hear Charlie and the reverend talking quietly downstairs. Unable to bear it any longer, she crept out of bed and crouched on the landing. Dust motes pirouetted in a shaft of late-evening sunlight that spilled from the kitchen into the hall.

'Your father had a small savings account,' the vicar told Charlie. 'There's not much in it, enough to pay any bills that may be due. His wages will be paid up until yesterday, but other than that . . .' Michael shook his head sorrowfully. 'There isn't much, I'm afraid.'

Charlie nodded. He rubbed the bridge of his nose with his thumb and forefinger. He felt very grown-up suddenly. 'How long can we stay here?' He glanced around the tidy kitchen. Charlotte and Mrs Fudge had washed up and put away the crockery. It looked just as his mother had left it that fateful night seven days ago when she'd gone to bed with the beginnings of a sore throat.

'The cottage is tied to the job,' the vicar reminded him softly. 'I doubt they'll give you beyond the end of the month.'

Charlie nodded grimly. 'That's less than a fortnight away.'

'You're due back at Padfield's soon, aren't you?' the older man asked, his brow puckered in concern for Charlie and Lily.

'Monday.' Charlie's anguished gaze met Michael's. 'What will become of Lily?' Charlie's voice shook when he said his sister's name. Huddled at the top of the stairs, Lily held her breath.

'Will your aunt not keep her?'

'She hates it there,' replied Charlie miserably. 'And I don't blame her. My aunt is not a compassionate woman,' he added bitterly.

The vicar's long sigh reverberated up the staircase. Lily scrunched her face up and crossed her fingers but the little flame of hope flickering in the pit of her belly was doused by his reply.

'If your aunt won't have her, it'll be the Union Workhouse, I'm afraid, or the orphanage in Dorchester.'

Lily pressed her fingernails into her palms in an effort not to cry out in terror. She had passed the workhouse off

Salisbury Street many times. The imposing, ivy-clad building with its turret and clock tower was separated from the road by a wide expanse of grass set against a backdrop of tall pine trees. She had caught the occasional glimpse of the inmates in the grounds. Even from a distance, she had sensed the feelings of hopelessness and despair which seemed to hang over the place like a pall.

'I don't know which is worse,' Charlie muttered. His heart sank like a stone. Michael leaned across and patted the boy's knee. 'I could leave Padfield's and find a job that comes with a tied cottage. Then I could keep Lily with me.'

'Don't throw away your future, Charlie,' Reverend Redfern advised him. 'You'll have a good trade once you've worked your apprenticeship. In a few years Lily can leave school and get a job. Then the two of you can get a place together.'

'But she's my responsibility, Reverend. It's my duty to take care of her now.'

The vicar sighed wearily. 'You're a good lad, Charlie, but your parents named Doris as Lily's legal guardian. She has legal rights over her until she's of age.'

Charlie's mouth fell open and he stared in disbelief. 'What? Why would they do that? Mother and Father were both in no doubt as to the sort of woman Doris is. Why would they trust her with Lily?'

'They wrote their last will and testaments a long time ago, not long after Lily came to live with you. I suppose they never got around to changing it. I'm sorry, Charlie. I'll call in and speak to Doris tomorrow.' He yawned and stretched. 'But now I think it's time we were to our beds.' He got up, the sound of his chair scraping on the flagstones sending Lily scuttling back to bed, tears streaming down her cheeks. They were going to send her back to Doris. The thought curdled her stomach, sending a wave of nausea over her as she slipped miserably beneath the covers.

The two voices moved into the hallway and she heard the front door open and close, followed by the sound of the bolts being shot home. Moments later, Charlie's footsteps sounded on the stairs. Candlelight flickered on the walls and he came to stand in the doorway of Lily's room.

'Are you asleep?' he whispered.

In response, Lily sat up. Charlie set the candle on the side table and Lily shuffled sideways so he could sit on the edge of the narrow bed. Lily buried her face against his chest.

'I don't want to go back to Aunty Doris,' she whispered, her tears soaking into Charlie's shirt. 'I hate it there.'

'I know you do,' Charlie sighed. 'I promise it won't be for long. I'm going to save up and get us a place of our own.'

'Why can't I come with you now?'

'I can't afford it at the moment, Lily. Just be patient and we'll be together soon, I promise you.'

He pulled back and smiled down at her. In the candlelight she looked very young and very scared. 'You just have to be brave for a little while. Can you do that for me?'

Lily nodded slowly, her beautiful green eyes welling with tears. Charlie held her while she cried herself to sleep. He doused the candle and stretched out beside her, watching the moon track its course across the room and finally falling into a fitful sleep an hour before dawn.

The funeral was well attended. Lily clutched Charlie's hand throughout the lengthy service. Doris, her face hidden by a black veil, and Jez, sullen-faced and scowling, joined Charlie and Lily in the front pew. Behind them sat the police constables who had acted as pallbearers. The rest of the pews were filled with friends and neighbours. Martha and Jim had been much-loved members of the community.

The sight of the two plain coffins gave Lily a horrible pinched feeling in her stomach and she kept her gaze fixed firmly on her shoes. Charlotte had lent Lily a black dress that had belonged to her granddaughter. It was a little tight under the arms and perhaps a fraction too short but, as Doris had made no attempt to find Lily anything suitable to wear, she was grateful for her neighbour's kindness.

She could barely swallow for the lump in her throat. She stared at her feet, letting the reverend's words wash over her like waves on the sea. Sunlight streamed in through the stained-glass windows, forming rainbows of colour on the cold stone floor. The air smelled of wood polish and damp. She hardly registered the service and it was only when Charlie squeezed her hand and nudged her that she realized it was over and everyone was waiting for her and Charlie to lead them out.

Heads bowed, Lily and Charlie, followed by Doris and Jez, led the sea of black mourners into the warm summer sunshine.

Butterflies flittered between the gravestones and the trees were filled with birdsong. Martha and Jim were to be buried with Annie and in solemn silence the mourners gathered around the gaping hole. The graveside sermon was mercifully brief and Charlie and Lily led the way back to the Red Lion for the wake.

Jez skulked in a corner smoking, while Doris, revelling in her role as sister and sister-in-law of the deceased, worked the room, accepting words of condolence and sympathy with little thought for her bereaved nephew and niece.

'She's no better than she should be,' Lily heard Mrs Fudge mutter to the vicar as she caught sight of Doris dabbing her eyes with a none-too-clean handkerchief. 'Her grief might be genuine, Martha was her sister after all, but what she said to you yesterday, well, I've certainly no patience with that woman. Not after that.'

'Now, now, Mrs Fudge,' Reverend Redfern chided her, arching his brows though, as he recalled his conversation of the previous day with Doris, he had to agree with her.

'I'm the kid's guardian?' Doris had stared at him, one eyebrow raised in mocking surprise. 'What did Martha go and do that for? Why would I want to take on responsibility for the kid? It's not like we're even related.'

'Mrs Elkin, please,' the vicar had beseeched her. 'Lily might not be Martha and Jim's flesh and blood, but they loved that girl like their own. Surely you can show some Christian charity and take her into your home?'

'I don't suppose I've got much choice, have I?' Doris sniffed.

'You wouldn't see your sister's child in the workhouse, surely?' he had pressed, sadly. He wondered what had happened to this poor woman to turn her into the cold, unfeeling person she had become.

Doris had sighed. Much as she resented being lumbered with her sister's foundling brat, the thought of being the subject of her neighbour's gossip when it became common knowledge that Doris Elkin had refused to do her duty by her dead sister's child outweighed her reluctance. And when the vicar mentioned Jim's little nest egg as well as relaying the message that Charlie was willing to send her a portion of his wages to help pay for Lily's keep, that had clinched it.

Now May Fudge snorted in disgust. The vicar had recounted the entire conversation to her the day before and she was appalled at the coldness of the woman. Catching sight of Lily lurking nearby, she rearranged her features into a smile.

'You all right, pet?'

Lily nodded miserably. 'Mrs Fudge,' she said, her voice so low May had to crouch down to hear her over the hubbub of conversation. 'I don't want to live with Aunty Doris and Jez. Do you think the reverend could ask my real mummy if I can live with her?' She clasped her hands under her chin and looked at May imploringly.

May's face crumpled. She gathered Lily in her motherly embrace.

'Oh, Lily, my love. No one knows where Beatrice is.' She smoothed Lily's hair. It was held back from her face by a black velvet ribbon. 'She does love you, though, and I'm sure she thinks about you every day.'

Lily nodded and bit her lip, wiping away a stray tear. Her throat ached from all the crying she'd already done and her eyes felt sandy and rough. She felt totally alone as she searched the sea of black for Charlie. He was in the corner talking to some of Jim's colleagues. Hot and miserable, Lily slunk over to a bench and sat down. It smelled of stale beer and the velvet cushions were stiff and pockmarked with cigarette burns.

'Ooh, it's warm in here, isn't it?' Doris, tired of being rebuffed in her efforts at playing the bereaved sister, plonked herself down beside Lily, fanning her flushed face with her hand. 'Thank God people are starting to leave,' she muttered under her breath, casting Lily a furtive glance. 'We'll be leaving in a minute, too. Say goodbye to your brother. He can arrange for your things to be sent over in the morning.'

'What?' The colour drained from Lily's face. 'But I'm staying with Charlie until the end of the week. He promised.'

'I'm your guardian now, Lily. You'll do as I say.'

'But Charlie ...' Lily whimpered, her gaze searching out her brother among the thinning crowd of well-wishers.

'Say goodbye to him and be quick,' Doris said crossly, her voice low, a tight smile on her thin face. 'Any nonsense and you'll feel the back of my hand.'

At Lily's look of fright, Doris smiled to herself. If she was to be saddled permanently with the brat, she may as well start as she meant to go on. She'd let her Jez get away with murder when he was young and look at the way he'd turned out. Though she wouldn't admit it to a soul, Doris was frightened of her own son. She wouldn't be so lenient with Lily.

CHAPTER SIX

'Hey, Lazy Lily, watch where you're going.'

'Sorry,' Lily mumbled, keeping her gaze averted from Jez's sneering face. He lay sprawled on the sofa, his long legs stretched halfway across the threadbare rug. The November sky was sombre, heavy with the promise of more rain. The room smelled dank and black mushrooms of mould sprouted on the walls beneath the rotting window frame.

If life with her aunt had been hard before, in the five months since Doris had become her legal guardian, Lily's life had become one of endless misery and drudgery. Doris had wasted no time in increasing Lily's workload. She was up before dawn to light the fires and prepare the breakfast, and Doris expected the place cleaned and tidied before Lily left for school. After school she had to prepare the supper and there was always a pile of laundry, ironing and mending to be done. To Doris's delight, Lily was proving to be a good little seamstress.

'Our Martha taught you well, I'll give her that,' Doris said, tossing Lily yet another dress in need of alteration. Though her fingers were bruised purple from the many times she had pricked herself with the needle, Lily enjoyed sewing. She had spent many a happy evening sitting with her mother making clothes for her rag doll, Bessie. But Lily no longer had time for such simple pleasures. It was usually late in the evening by the time she made her way wearily up the stairs to her attic bedroom. For the first week she had cried herself to sleep every night, but soon her grief had been overtaken by sheer exhaustion. She did her homework by candlelight, often falling asleep over her school books only to wake what seemed like barely minutes later to start the day all over again.

Hunched in the corner of the room, Lily rubbed her tired eyes. She winced as her tired fingers slipped and drove the needle deep into the ball of her thumb. A drop of blood dripped onto her pinafore.

'I'll need you to come out with me tonight,' Jez said, glowering at her through a haze of cigarette smoke. He had just turned fourteen. There was no denying he was a good-looking lad and he had more than his fair share of female admirers. He grinned at Lily, enjoying the way she looked at him, like a frightened rabbit caught in a farmer's trap.

Her heart sank. Whatever it was that Jez got up to in the evenings, her instinct told her it wasn't good. She'd tried asking once, after she'd been woken up by Jez returning home in the dead of night, but all she got in reply to her innocent curiosity was the back of Doris's hand.

She bit her lip, absently sucking her throbbing thumb, her gaze on the crimson drop of blood on her pinafore, which seemed to swell before her eyes. Jez's voice jolted her back to the present.

'Hey, Lazy Lily, are you ignoring me?'

Lily shook her head. Tears stung her eyes and her throat ached with the effort not to cry. She wished Charlie were here. He'd sort Jez out. But Charlie's next day off was almost three weeks away.

'I'm meeting some chaps over near the old malthouse and I need you to keep watch. We'll be leaving as soon as it's dark. Be ready.'

They set off just after five o'clock. Despite her woollen cloak, Lily shivered in the cold, damp air. A thick mist had settled over the town, muffling the sound of their footsteps. The street lamps glowed sickly yellow in the gloom. The curtains of the cottages were tightly drawn, with only the smallest chinks of light shining through the cracks. The cold air smelled of wet leaves and coal fires.

They walked in silence, Lily's heart pounding in fear, as she hurried to keep up with Jez. The mist settled wetly on her face and clothes, swirling like an ethereal being around her. She could barely see the end of the street and, though she wouldn't even be here if it weren't for Jez, she was glad of his presence by her side. They were heading for the less than salubrious part of town.

The derelict malthouse, once the home of a thriving brewing business, had been destroyed by fire decades earlier and the family had neither the inclination nor the funds to rebuild. It had remained a blackened empty shell ever since.

Jez spoke for the first time as Lily took in the twisted metal and flame-scarred brickwork looming out of the fog. 'This is where we hold our boxing matches.' He grabbed her cold hand. 'Come on, we're late already.'

The soles of their shoes crunched on broken glass and dried animal faeces. Lily's heart thumped in her chest. She swallowed hard in an attempt to bring saliva into her parched mouth. The ground floor was mostly undamaged and this, Jez told her, was where the fighting usually took place. He swung the lantern, illuminating the weeds that had pushed their way up through the floor. The place stank; both humans and animals often sought shelter from the elements among the ruins. A haze of light drew Lily's attention and from beyond a crumbling wall came the sound of men's voices.

'The lads are all here,' Jez muttered, sounding slightly relieved. 'In case you hadn't cottoned on,' he said, shoving Lily towards what had once been a doorway but was now a jagged hole in the wall, 'these boxing matches are illegal and we've had the Old Bill sniffing around on the odd occasion. Which is where you come in. You're our lookout for the evening. You see any sign of the Old Bill, you yell as loud as you can, all right?'

Lily nodded, too scared to refuse.

'Good.' Jez nodded in satisfaction. 'Do as you're told and you'll be all right.'

Lily stepped through the gaping doorway, blinking in the sudden brightness. As her eyes adjusted to the light, she noticed the men assembled in the vast room. For the most part, they were young and rough-looking. Thickset and naked from the waist up, their greased skin gleamed in the lantern light. They all greeted Jez like an old friend. Lily kept her head bowed. These men frightened her. There were older men too, she realized, hovering on the outskirts. Men in suits and bowler hats, men with pockets full of money.

Jez came over to Lily, rubbing his hands. 'Come with me.' Half-stumbling, Lily allowed Jez to lead her back out into the cold, foggy darkness. 'This is the drill. You see anyone heading this way, anyone at all, you run and tell me, all right?'

Lily nodded, shivering. The area was unfamiliar to her and, in the fog, it was frightening. Jez squeezed her arm, making her wince. 'Don't let me down, or you'll get what for.'

Left alone in the swirling mist, Lily stamped her feet. The cold had leeched through the thin soles of her shoes, numbing her toes. The street was eerie in the fog, silent and slightly threatening. She glanced around her warily, imagining that at any moment some terrifying creature might emerge from the gloom, but the only sound she could hear was the frantic beating of her own heart. In the thick blanket of fog, even the blood-curdling shouts of the men were muffled.

After half an hour, she was numb with cold, and bored. The mist had thinned a little and the halos of light from the distant street lamps appeared to be calling her. She glanced at the dark, hulking building behind her, pale lamplight spilling from the holes in the brickwork. She could hear the muted roars of the men. The surrounding streets appeared deserted. Surely it would do no harm for her to walk toward town and look in the shop windows. If anyone came by, she would have plenty of time to run back to warn Jez.

Her decision made, she set off up the street, stamping her feet in an effort to get the blood flowing in her toes. Her nose tingled and her breath clouded the air in front of her face.

Market Place was further away than she had thought and she was breathless by the time she reached the broad, deserted street. She pressed her face against the cold glass of the confectioners, before wandering further up the road. Her head filled with images of sugarplums and pear drops, Lily's eye was drawn to a shop on the opposite side of the street. The light from the nearby gas lamp lit up the window of what had, until recently, she recalled, been an ironmongers. She brushed her damp hair from her face and crossed the road. Against a backdrop of dark blue velvet stood a wooden dressmaker's mannequin. She wore a dress of peach cotton, trimmed with fine, peach-coloured lace. To the left, arranged in a rainbow of colours were bolts of cloth; to the right, a walnut-veneered sewing box, its polished lid open to reveal a tantalizing display of silk threads, reams of handmade lace and cotton bobbins. The freshly painted sign above the door read, VIOLET UPSHALL, DRESSMAKER.

Lily pressed her hands against the glass, staring in envious wonder at the tantalizing display. The stirring of an idea began to take root in her mind. So absorbed was she by the wonder of the shop window that she failed to notice the fog growing steadily thicker. By the time she realized, she found she could see no further than a few steps in front of her. It was what her dad would have called a 'peasouper'. It wrapped itself around her like a thick blanket, muffling all sound.

All Lily could hear was the rushing of blood in her ears as she tried to work out which way would lead her back to the malthouse. Fighting her welling panic, she took a few steps in what she thought was the right direction, then stopped, glancing around frantically for some clue to her whereabouts.

The buildings around her were all but obscured and by now she had completely lost her bearings. She had no clue which way was which and was trying desperately not to cry when she spotted the light. It bounced on the fog, making it difficult for Lily to work out the exact direction from which it came, but just the sight of the yellow orb floating up and down was enough to cheer her considerably. Thinking it must be the light from the brewery, she quickened her step. It was only when the swirling fog parted a little that she saw that the light came from a gas lamp. A lamp that was being carried by a police constable.

'Hey, lass.' Taken by surprise at the sight of Lily's white, frightened face pinched with cold, the police constable stopped in his tracks, his lantern raised. 'You shouldn't be out here on your own in this weather.' He lifted the lantern higher, frowning under his hat. 'Lily, isn't it?' His eyebrows shot up. 'Jim's girl?' Lily nodded. Her heart rate was slowing now as her panic began to subside. 'What on earth are you doing out here on a night like this, love?'

Lily hesitated. She didn't want to lie, not when the constable was being so kind, but she could hardly tell him the truth. Jez would have her guts for garters.

'I was just out for a walk,' she muttered. Incredulous, Constable Abel King could only shake his head in disbelief.

'I'm surprised at your aunt for allowing you out on such a night.' He shook his head again, as if despairing at the foolishness of some folk. 'Well, come on, lass,' he said, offering Lily his arm. 'Let's get you home.'

Lily hesitated. She daren't go home. Not without Jez.

Suddenly the thick silence was broken by distant shouting.

'What the ...?' Abel frowned. 'Wait here,' he told Lily sternly. 'Don't move. I'll be back as quick as I can.' He blew his whistle, its shrill sound cutting through the fog like a knife, and began to run towards the noise. Lily followed slowly, amazed to realize the ruined malthouse was actually no more than a few yards ahead of her. Now that the fog had thinned sufficiently to see, she could make out its ruined walls and pools of orange light, which were quickly doused the moment Abel's whistle pierced the air. Suddenly men were streaming past her. She could hear Abel shouting after them to stop and declare themselves. No one did, of course. They shoved past Lily, heads low, faces covered by scarves, some still hastily shrugging on coats, knuckles torn and bleeding. One young man who stumbled past her was clearly in pain. He cradled his right hand, face contorted in agony.

Not knowing what to do, Lily leaned against a ruined column that had once been part of the arched entrance, her tired eyes raking the darkness for any sign of Jez. Within minutes the men had dispersed and the street was empty. Still

Jez didn't come. She felt sick with relief at the sight of Abel trudging towards her, his face set, lantern light playing on the ground in front of his feet.

'Come on, lass, let's get you home,' he said, his voice weary. Subdued, Lily slipped her arm through his. She heard him mutter something under his breath, catching the word 'scoundrels' and then 'illegal fighting', but she bit her lip, not daring to say anything that might get Jez into trouble.

Lamplight spilled from the cottage windows and Doris had the door open before Abel had the chance to knock, as if she'd been waiting for them.

'Oh, Lily,' she cried, dropping to her knees and wrapping her arms around her niece in a way that took Lily by surprise. 'Where have you been? Jez and me have been worried sick. Oh, Constable, I can't thank you enough,' she said, looking up at Abel with an expression she hoped conveyed gratitude.

'Come on, now, missy, off to bed with you,' Doris said to Lily, as she got to her feet, one hand on the door, as if ready to usher Abel out into the night. He frowned, and blocked the door with his foot, his gaze landing on Jez sprawled in his usual position on the sofa. His hair was obviously damp, and there was a suspicious rosy hue to his cheeks.

'You been here all evening, Jez?' Abel queried, keeping his tone deceptively light.

'Yes, sir, all evening. Isn't that right, Ma?'

'Yes, that's right, Constable. Me and Jez, we've been here all evening, waiting for this madam to get home. Quite the little wanderer she is.' Doris shot Lily a glare. 'I said bed, young lady.

You've school in the morning. Go on, up them stairs now. I'll be up to tuck you in in a minute.'

Bewildered and unnerved by her aunt's uncharacteristic behaviour, Lily fled up the stairs. She crouched on the landing, listening as Abel continued to question Jez.

'You swear to me you weren't anywhere near the old brewery tonight?'

'On my mother's life, Constable, I haven't left the house all evening,' Jez replied earnestly.

'I'll say goodnight then.' Lily could tell by the constable's tone that he didn't believe a word Jez had said. 'And take better care of your niece, Mrs Elkin. She shouldn't be wandering about after dark.'

'Of course, Constable,' Doris simpered, ushering Abel out into the night.

No sooner had she shut the door firmly in Abel's face than Jez came flying up the stairs, his face puce with rage. He caught Lily by her hair as she was scrambling up the attic steps, and hit her with such force she went reeling across the landing and crashing into the banister.

Stunned, she stared up at him through dazed, tear-filled eyes, her head throbbing in agony.

'You stupid little cow!' Jez fumed, his fingers biting painfully into her flesh as he grabbed her by the arm and hauled her to her feet, shaking her wildly. 'You stupid, stupid fool. You've ruined everything. They're not going to bloody trust me again, are they? You could have got us all banged up.' He shook her again hard, causing Lily to bite her tongue, tasting blood. He slapped her again. She was crying hard now, tears and mucus streaming down her face as she cowered away from the blows raining down on her, begging and pleading with him to stop.

His rage spent, he gave her one final shove that sent her sprawling. She fell awkwardly onto the attic steps. Feeling as though her whole body was on fire, Lily crawled up the stairs to her cold attic room. Sobbing quietly, her bruised body throbbing, she curled up on her bed. She was too frightened to sleep in case Jez came back and she lay shivering in the darkness, her heart heavy with misery. She longed for Charlie to come and take her away. She closed her eyes and dreamed of Martha and Jim, and her real mother.

CHAPTER SEVEN

Doris kept Lily off school for a fortnight. Her bruises faded from livid black and purple to a dull yellow. The evening following Jez's savage attack, Jez and Doris sat down to meat pie. Lily's plate was empty. She had eaten nothing all day and her stomach was cramping with hunger pains.

'You lost me a lot of money last night, Lazy Lily, so you can flipping well go without any tea tonight. I'm not wasting my hard-earned cash on you.' Jez grinned evilly as his knife cut into the soft, flaky pastry, letting the thick gravy ooze out onto the plate. Lily's mouth watered as the rich meaty aroma filled the air. Her stomach rumbled loudly.

'But Charlie ...'

'Pah,' spat Doris, flecks of pastry flying from her lips to land on the table. 'It costs a lot more to keep you than the trifling amount he pays. Why do you think my Jez has to take the chances he does? You nearly ruined everything, my girl. I told him he was a fool to trust you. You're nothing but a stupid, ungrateful wretch. If my Jez gets done for illegal fighting and is sent away, I won't be able to keep you. It'll be the work-house for you, so think on that, you useless dolt.'

'I'm sorry,' Lily said, her voice barely audible. 'I got lost in the fog.'

'You should have done as you were told,' Jez snarled, fork-ing up a mouthful of meat, his greasy lips smacking in anticipation.

'This is a fine meat pie,' Doris burped contentedly and wiped a dribble of gravy from her chin with the back of her hand.

'It certainly is,' Jez agreed appreciatively, through a mouth-ful of beef and pastry. 'It's not often we have the wherewithal to treat ourselves like this, is it?'

'No, well, that's the last of our Martha's trinkets,' Doris said matter-of-factly, ignoring Lily's sharp intake of breath. 'And you squandered Jim's nest egg a while back.' She shot Jez an accusing look. 'So we'll be pulling our belts in after this unless you can organize another match, and soon.'

'That'll take some doing,' Jez replied dourly, giving Lily a filthy glare that made her shrink in her seat. 'I'm going to have to work hard to get the men to trust me again, and I'll have to find another venue. The coppers will be keeping a sharp eye on that place now, thanks to this stupid mare.'

Lily had been forced to sit at the table until both Doris and Jez had cleared their plates. She kept her gaze focused on her empty place setting, her jaw clenched tight in her determination not to cry. The idea that Jez had frittered away her father's hard-earned savings, and her aunt had pawned her mother's possessions, was almost her undoing but she forced herself to push the thought aside. The time for tears would come later.

'You'd better buck your ideas up, my girl,' Doris said, as Lily began to clear the table. She grabbed her wrist with bony fingers. 'You pull another stunt like you did last night, I won't let you see that so-called brother of yours, you hear me?'

Lily's stomach muscles clenched in terror at the thought of not being able to see Charlie. His monthly visit was the only thing that kept her going.

'I'm sorry,' she mumbled, keeping her eyes downcast. 'I'll be good, I promise.'

Doris snorted. 'See that you are.' She released her grip and, grabbing the plates, Lily made a dash for the scullery where she leaned against the sink, massaging her throbbing wrist and wondering if she would ever escape the hell in which she now lived.

'I believe you imagined my sermon would never come to an end this morning didn't you, Lily?' The vicar grinned as he helped Lily into the trap.

'Yes, sir, I mean, no, sir.' Lily bit her lip, feeling her cheeks growing hot. She hadn't meant to offend Reverend Redfern with her fidgeting but she had been so eager to see Charlie and the sermon had been very long. 'I enjoyed your preaching though, sir.'

'Thank you, Lily.' He laughed. Reaching across, he helped her tuck the travel robe around her legs. It was the last week of November and the weather had turned wintery, the fall in temperature bringing a light snowfall during the night.

'Don't look so worried, child.' He grinned at Lily as he slapped the reins, urging the frisky pony on. 'I may be getting on in years but I haven't forgotten what it's like to be a child and to be looking forward to something so much I feel I'm about to burst with excitement.'

Michael saw the relief in Lily's eyes and he was filled with pity. Life with her aunt was difficult for the girl, of that he had no doubt. In the six months she had been living with Doris and Jez, it was as if the light had faded from Lily. She had become a pale shadow of her former self, and Michael was at a loss to know how to help. According to her teacher, Lily had missed quite a bit of school over the last month, but when Michael had called to enquire after Lily's health, Doris had given him short shrift. She'd fobbed him off with some clearly fabricated tale of Lily's sickly disposition, effectively telling him to mind his own business. And that Jez was bad news too. Michael sighed. The sooner Charlie was in a position to take care of his sister, the better.

Seated beside Michael, Lily tried to ignore the throbbing chilblains on her feet. Inside her woollen gloves, her knuckles were red-raw and cracked from hours spent scrubbing the laundry. Often too tired to do her homework, she was falling behind at school. Twice in the previous week her teacher had made her stand in the corner for failing to complete her homework. For half an hour, ashamed and humiliated, Lily had endured the eyes of her classmates boring into her back while she blinked away stinging tears.

But she was determined not to relay any of this to Charlie. He felt bad enough not being able to look after her himself; the last thing she wanted to do was make him feel worse. The reverend too seemed to want to pry, but Lily was astute enough to know that there was little he, or anyone else, could do to improve her situation and any meddling, however well intentioned, would only result in raising Doris's ire, making Lily's life ten times worse.

So, while she wasn't exactly lying to the vicar, she managed to deflect his probing questions by keeping up a stream of chatter.

'Reverend,' she began, as they wended their way down snowy, tree-lined lanes. The surrounding hills were dusted with snow, the hedgerows stark against the white background.

'What is it, Lily?'

'Do you know where my mother is?'

'Why, child, she's with Jesus, in Heaven. Your mother was a good Christian woman. I've no doubt she has gone to her Heavenly reward.'

'No, sir, I meant my real mother. Beatrice Cullen?'

There was silence but for the creak of the wheels and the steady plod of the pony's hooves on the snowy lane. Lily thought perhaps the reverend hadn't heard her and she was about to repeat her question when he turned to her, his expression kind.

'I'm sorry, Lily. I have no idea where she is.' He pursed his lips, his eyes clouding at the sight of Lily's crestfallen expression. 'I can't promise anything, child, but I shall endeavour to do my best to find out. Will that do?'

'Yes, thank you, Reverend.'

The three-and-a-half-hour journey seemed endless but finally, snow flying from her hooves, wheels slipping and sliding, Michael's sleek pony trotted gamely along Butts Knap into Shaftesbury.

The town was blanketed in soft, powdery snow. Smoke curled from chimney pots and children were running along the street, dragging sledges or carrying tin tea trays, heading for the steep bank of St James Park, their laughter ringing out on the cold, crisp air. Lily watched enviously as they passed.

They turned into Victoria Street, a wide road lined with neat, tidy houses, front walls and railings dusted with snow. Smoke from the ironworks at the end of the street belched into the pewter-grey sky. As Michael brought the trap to a halt outside the boarding house, the door flew open and Charlie emerged grinning, rubbing his hands in the frigid air.

'Charlie!' The heartache and misery of the past weeks instantly forgotten, Lily flung herself down from the trap and into Charlie's arms. She pressed her face into his jacket, breathing in his familiar scent, a mixture of damp tweed and woodsmoke. 'Oh, Charlie. I've missed you so much.'

'I've missed you too, Lily.' Squeezing her tight, Charlie met Michael's gaze over Lily's head. The reverend's expression was grim and Charlie felt his heart sink. 'Hey,' he said with forced cheer. 'Let's have a look at you then.' He held Lily at arm's length. 'Isn't my aunt feeding you?' he asked with a grin, though his eyes remained hard. 'I've seen more meat on a butcher's pencil.'

He kept his tone light, yet he was horrified by the way Lily's cheekbones had grown so pronounced. Even in her winter coat, he could see how the weight had fallen off her bones since he'd last seen her. What the hell was his aunt doing with the money he was sending her every week?

Michael rubbed his gloved his hands together. 'Right, I'm going over to the hotel for a jug of ale.' He glanced up at the sky. Streaks of blue had appeared among the grey, but in the west the sky was dark and heavy, and there was concern in his voice when he next spoke. 'We'll want to set off by half past four,' he said. 'No later.'

'Lily will be ready,' promised Charlie. Turning his collar up against the cold and damp, he grabbed Lily's hand. 'Come on, time's a-wasting.'

Laughing, Lily and Charlie made their way arm in arm along Bell Street to the Grosvenor Hotel where a horse-drawn carriage was waiting outside to ferry passengers down to the railway station at Semley. They ordered hot soup, which they ate in the snug, seated close to the roaring fire, softly falling snowflakes hitting the window and sliding down the glass as they melted.

Later, fortified against the bitter cold, they put on their wraps and ventured onto Park Walk. Lily leaned against the iron railings, her breath billowing in front of her face as she gazed out over the snow-covered Blackmore Vale. The view was breathtaking.

'I'm sorry life is so miserable for you at Aunty's,' Charlie said, as they struggled against the wind sweeping down St John's Hill.

'I haven't complained,' Lily said, surprised.

'I know you haven't,' Charlie said, taking her gloved hand and tucking it into the crook of his elbow. 'And you're very brave, but I'm not a fool. I can see how miserable you are, and it breaks my heart. I wish there was a way I could make things better for you.' His breath billowed in the frosty air. 'You look half starved.' His words carried an angry edge, which made Lily hesitate before answering. She licked her lips, and swallowed.

'It's all right,' she said, her voice low as she avoided Charlie's probing gaze. 'I miss you though.'

'I know.' Charlie laid his arm across Lily's shoulders and pulled her against him. 'I miss you too.' He gazed out across the snow-covered rooftops of Enmore Green spread out below them. 'If there was any way I could leave my apprenticeship, I would. But if I leave, I'm liable to repay the cost of my training, and there's no way I'd be able to afford to do that and look after you as well. I'm sorry.' He looked so crestfallen Lily's heart went out to him.

'It's all right, Charlie. It's not so bad at Aunty's,' Lily said. 'It's only for another couple of years. Then I shall be old enough to get an apprenticeship.'

'Oh yes, and what skills are you after learning?' Charlie grinned down at her.

'Dressmaking,' Lily replied firmly. 'Then I shall open my own dressmaker's shop in town like Violet Upshall.'

'And who is Violet Upshall when she's at home?' He pulled his scarf tighter around his throat.

'She has a shop in Market Place,' Lily explained as they made their way along Bimport Street towards Charlie's lodgings. 'She's got such pretty dresses in the window. I want to make dresses exactly like hers.'

'And I'm sure you will.' Charlie dropped a kiss on the top of her head. 'You've had a flair for needlework since you were tiny.'

They slowed their pace, wanting to delay the moment of their parting but dusk was falling and Michael was already waiting in the trap, his cheeks glowing from the public house's roaring fire, several jugs of fine ale and a late dinner of roast pork and all the trimmings.

'I'm sorry to rush you,' he said, lighting the lamp. 'But it's a long road, and in the dark too.'

Lily clung to Charlie. It would be four weeks before she saw him again. He squeezed her tight.

'Chin up,' he said. 'The weeks will fly by, you'll see. It'll soon be Christmas and then we'll get two whole days together.'

Lily nodded, unable to speak past the lump in her throat. Reluctantly she stepped out of Charlie's embrace and allowed him to help her into the trap. The pony tossed its head, eager to be off and the trap moved forward with a jerk. Twisting around in her seat, Lily waved until they rounded the corner and Charlie disappeared from view.

For a long while, they rode along in silence with only the creak of the wheels and the muffled plod of the pony's hooves.

Pools of orange light from the swaying lantern danced over the snow-covered road. The wind sighed through the dark, skeletal branches that crisscrossed over their heads.

'I know life at your aunt's is unpleasant,' Michael said at length as they passed through the village of Melbury Abbas. He was hunched in his seat, his hat pulled low over his ears. 'You've only got to stick it out another two and a half years and you can go into service.'

'I'm not going into service, sir,' Lily said, finding her voice. She tucked the blanket tighter around her legs as Michael turned to her, his brows raised in surprise.

'You're not?' His breath billowed between them as Lily shook her head. 'So what do you intend to do for employment, missy?' One of the wheels hit a rut and he turned his attention back to the road.

'I'm going to be a dressmaker,' Lily said with a determined thrust of her chin. Michael's brows rose even higher.

'A dressmaker, hmm?' He flicked the reins, urging the pony up the steep hill. Its hooves slipped and slithered on the wet ground. A fox, thin and mangy-looking, eyed them from the frosty verge before slinking out of view. Lily clung to the side of the trap for a moment as the wheels struggled to find purchase on the icy road.

'Yes, sir,' she said, tucking her cold hands beneath the rug. 'I shall open a shop like Violet Upshall and make beautiful dresses for grand ladies.'

'Will you now?' Michael smiled. 'Well, that's a fine ambition for sure. Your aunt speaks highly of your stitching.' Albeit begrudgingly, he added under his breath. He would never understand the woman's aversion to her dead sister's daughter. All right, Lily wasn't a blood relative but Martha had loved her as though she were her own, so why Doris couldn't find it in her heart to do the same, Michael would probably never understand.

The lights of Blandford came into view, an orange haze in the distance, and Lily fell silent, her brief burst of enthusiasm for the future curtailed by her dread of her imminent return to her aunt's house.

While most of the windows in Laundry Lane glowed with lamplight, Doris's cottage was in darkness. Her heart sinking like a stone, Lily climbed down from the trap and walked to the doorway on wooden legs. Every step was an effort, as if she were walking through treacle, such was her reluctance to enter. She had to force herself to lift the latch and walk inside. With her hand resting on the doorknob, she glanced back over her shoulder. Michael sat in the trap, watching her with an expression of deep sympathy. 'Take courage, child,' he said softly. 'And I'll try my best to find out what I can about Beatrice, I promise.' Lily nodded. Taking a deep breath, she went inside. Giving Michael one last wave, she closed the door. She fumbled for the matches and lit the lamp and stood listening to the fading sound of horse's hoofs while her eyes adjusted to the light.

Thanks to Lily's hard work, the cottage was no longer the cluttered hovel it had once been. The surfaces gleamed where she had polished them, the floor was swept, laundry washed and folded away.

'Had a good day, have you?' Her aunt's voice emanating from the kitchen startled her.

'Yes, thank you, Aunt.' Swallowing her fear, Lily hastily took off her coat and hat and hung them up. Smoothing down her skirt, she walked slowly into the kitchen. A fire blazed in the hearth. The window was misty with condensation, the yard a grey-white blur through the wet glass. Doris was sprawled in a kitchen chair, the remains of her midday meal strewn across the table. Her eyes were bloodshot, her cheeks rosy. Sweat glistened on her forehead and beaded on her upper lip. She eyed Lily with her bleary gaze.

'It's all right for some.' She pouted nastily, her hand reaching for her teacup which, Lily had no doubt, contained gin rather than tea. 'Gallivanting all afternoon while I'm stuck here. Selfish, that's what you are, Lily. Our Jez is right. You're a lazy wretch. Lazy and selfish. No wonder he calls you Lazy Lily.'

'I'm not lazy,' Lily said in a tremulous voice. She stood against the doorframe, well out of reach of her aunt's hand. She knew from experience that while Doris was in this state she was safe enough, as long as she stayed out of arm's length.

'Are you answering me back, you cheeky minx?' Doris eyed her over her teacup. 'You'd better watch your mouth, girl.'

'I'm not lazy, Aunt Doris,' Lily repeated, her voice stronger this time. 'I was up at the crack of dawn cooking your meal and cleaning the house before I left for church.' Her fists clenched as all her anger and frustration boiled over. 'How dare you call me lazy? If anyone's lazy around here, it's you.'

Doris's mouth fell open. For a moment all she could do was gape at Lily, her mouth flapping open and closed like a fish out of water as she was struck speechless.

'I can't believe you would have the audacity to speak to me like that. You little cow.' She made to get up, gripping the edge of the table but her legs seemed to have a mind of their own and refused to co-operate. She sank back into her seat, glaring at Lily with impotent rage. 'You've a cheek,' she hissed, the colour rising in her already red cheeks. 'I took you in out of the goodness of my heart.' She sneered. 'Look at you! Your own mother didn't even want you.'

'My mother loves me,' Lily shouted. 'Reverend is going to find her and then she'll come and take me away and I'll never have to see you again.'

'Your mother?' Doris threw back her head and laughed. 'A common trollop? Don't make me laugh.' She snorted, conveniently forgetting that it was her own wanton behaviour that had brought about her marriage to Sam. 'You'd be in the workhouse if it wasn't for me. Any more lip from you and that's where you'll end up, madam.'

'Charlie pays you for my keep,' Lily shouted. 'He told me so. My being here doesn't cost you a penny.' With that, Lily turned on her heel and raced for the stairs, Doris's angry shrieking following her up to her attic room.

'You wait until my Jez gets home, you little minx. Then you'll be for it. He'll give you what-for, you ungrateful brat!'

★   ★   ★

Retribution, when it came, was swift and brutal. Lily's anger had long since dissipated by the time she heard the slam of the front door. In her frigid attic room, she cowered beneath her threadbare blankets, trembling with fear as she heard Jez's footsteps pounding up the stairs. Lily squealed as the door flew open and crashed against the wall. Jez stood in the darkened doorway, eyes blazing like something that had risen from the depths of hell.

'You been cheeking my ma?' he said menacingly, advancing towards her. Lily pressed herself against the wall.

'I'm sorry, Jez,' she whimpered. 'I didn't mean it.'

The room was dark, the only light coming from the candle burning on the small trunk where Lily kept her few belongings, so it wasn't until Jez was practically at her bedside that Lily noticed the coiled belt he held in his clenched fist. Before her mind could make sense of the situation, Jez had uncoiled the belt and was laying into her. He grabbed the blankets from her hand and wielded the belt. Lily screamed as the leather strap bit into her skin, legs, shoulders, buttocks, the blows rained down on her indiscriminately as she tried in vain to scramble out of his reach.

Afterwards, her whole body felt as though it were on fire. She lay face down on her bed, shivering and whimpering in pain. She could hear her aunt and Jez talking and laughing as they made their way to their respective bedrooms, the soft click of the bedroom doors, the creak of bed springs. She hated Jez with a passion she had never thought possible. It was this hatred she would need to cling to if she were to get through the following weeks, months, years even, until she was old enough to leave her aunt's house for ever. And once she was free, she vowed, hot tears soaking into the pillow, she would never, ever come back.

CHAPTER EIGHT

1888

Twelve-year-old Lily tucked the wicker basket over her arm and studied the array of meat on display in the butcher's window. Flies hummed around the row of glassy-eyed rabbits suspended above it. Frank, the butcher, appeared in the window in his customary striped apron, wiping his blood-stained hands on a cloth. He winked at Lily before selecting a plump chicken from those on display and returning to his customer, wrapping it in brown paper.

It was a sultry hot July day with not a cloud in the sky. The street was bustling with market traders touting their wares, their shouts mingling with the bellows and bleating of livestock. The hot air was thick with the smell of dust and animal faeces.

Lily's brow puckered as she tried to decide between mutton or sausages. Sweat trickled down her spine and glistened on her brow. She took her time, glancing up the street, eager to delay her return home.

She had been living at her aunt's for three years now and during that time she had learned to keep her head down and her thoughts to herself. Not that it was enough to protect her from Doris's temper or Jez's fists.

Every night she prayed that her real mother would come and take her away. Disappointingly, Reverend Redfern's enquiries into Beatrice Cullen's current whereabouts had failed to produce any results. But the biggest blow had come when Charlie had been attacked and robbed of all his savings. Lily was convinced Jez had been behind it. The police had been sympathetic but unable to do much due to lack of evidence. Charlie had been laid up for a month, incapable of working and having to rely on the charity of his employer, who, surprisingly, had allowed him stay on the premises rent-free until he was able to work again.

He was back on his feet now, thank God, but it would be a long while before he could afford to support himself and Lily even if Doris allowed her to go. She was Lily's guardian until she was fourteen or in full-time employment, which-ever came first, and would be loath to say goodbye to her hefty cut of Charlie's monthly wage any sooner than she had to.

'Lily, how good to see you.' Mrs Fudge's cheerful voice broke through Lily's melancholy musing. She turned from the butcher's window to smile at the vicar's elderly house-keeper, who was standing in front of the cheese stall. May was into her late sixties now, grey-haired and plump.

'Mrs Fudge, good morning.'

May rounded the stall and came over. 'I was just getting some cheddar for the reverend's lunch.' She held a lace-trimmed handkerchief to her face, wrinkling her nose at the ripe smell wafting over from the animal pens.

'Jez did well on the dogs last night,' Lily explained, indicating the display in the butcher's window. 'So I've been sent out to get meat.'

'How is Charlie?' May asked, her eyes narrowing in sympathy. Lily shrugged.

'Physically, he's well, thank you for asking, but he's gutted about losing his savings. He'd worked so hard.' She tried not to let the bitterness show in her voice, but she'd been counting the days until Charlie would be able to afford his own place.

'I know it's difficult for you, love.' May gave her arm an encouraging pat. 'You take care now.' She moved off, shaking her head at the unfairness of a god who would take kind souls like Jim and Martha Hayter, while leaving the likes of Doris Elkin and her son who brought nothing but misery to all and sundry.

Ten minutes later, Lily exited the butchers and darted across the street, dodging carts and wagons. The window of Violet Upshall's dress shop reflected the hustle and bustle of the market and she caught a glimpse of Jez, mooching around a stall selling hot baked potatoes. She held her breath, praying that he wouldn't notice her loitering, and breathed out a deep sigh of relief when he moved on. He was soon lost in the milling crowd.

She turned her attention to Violet's window display. In her mind's eye, she was already matching the ribbons and silks with the bolts of coloured cloth. Her gaze alighted on a card of six buttons. They were shaped like plump blackberries and she was thinking how nice they would look on the bodice of the old black dress she had found in Doris's wardrobe that Lily was altering to wear for harvest supper in the autumn. She usually bought her buttons and thread from the various haberdashery stalls but, if she were frugal with the house-keeping money, she might just be able to buy these slightly dearer ones. She would have to be very careful. Jez was scrupulous in checking her purchases and if he even suspected Lily of trying to cheat him, he would take his belt to her. She was calculating how much she might need when she was startled by the jangle of the bell over the door.

'Hello, Lily?' Violet Upshall was a pleasant-faced woman with light-brown hair pulled back in a neat chignon and soft, pale grey-blue eyes. She was wearing a white blouse with mutton sleeves, a red velvet ribbon threaded through the collar and a dove-grey skirt, sprigged with tiny red roses. Her stylish elegance only served to increase Lily's feelings of scruffiness.

'Good morning, Miss Upshall,' Lily greeted her politely, painfully aware of her frayed cuffs and the shortness of her skirt. She had let the hem out time and again until there was nothing more to let out.

'I've been hoping to catch you, dear,' Violet said in her usual cheerful way. She glanced towards the church. The hands on the clock stood at a quarter past ten. 'Have you time for a cup of tea?'

Lily blinked in surprise.

'If you're in a hurry ...?' Violet prompted, seeing Lily's hesitation.

'Oh, no.' Lily shook her head. 'It's just I mustn't be too long. I need to get this mutton home.'

'You may put it in the pantry, Lily. It will be cool enough in there,' Violet reassured her.

'Then tea would be lovely. Thank you.' She followed Violet inside, thinking that she would have to wrack her brains to come up with a plausible excuse to explain her lateness.

The shop, cool after the summer heat, was like an Aladdin's Cave and Lily gazed around her in wide-eyed wonder. The shelves on the walls were filled with bolts of cloth of every colour imaginable. Glass cabinets were crammed with an array of silk scarves, ribbons, and threads of all colours. Coloured buttons winked like jewels.

'Go through,' Violet said, sliding the door bolts home and turning the sign from OPEN to CLOSED. Barely able to drag her attention away from the beautifully dressed mannequins, Lily pushed through the velvet curtain and into Violet's workroom.

'Oh, hello.' Gladys Turner, Violet's pretty young assistant, looked up in surprise. 'You're Lily, aren't you? Mrs Elkin's niece? I've a cousin who lives down Laundry Lane,' she added, when Lily nodded. 'I'll be ready to start on Mrs Blackman's alterations as soon as I'm finished here,' she told Violet, who bent her head in acknowledgement, her long, tapered fingers smoothing a wrinkle from a bolt of cloth laid out ready for pinning. Gladys's smooth brow puckered in concentration as she leaned over the long workbench, and returned to pinning pattern pieces onto some ruby-red fabric.

How lucky Gladys was to work in such a place, thought Lily enviously, staring round in wide-eyed fascination, inhaling the smell of cloth. Material was draped over every available surface. Paper patterns and drawings were tacked to the distempered walls and there were three dressmaker's mannequins, each wearing an outfit in various stages of completion. In the corner stood a shiny sewing machine.

'Well,' Violet said with a sweep of her hand, smiling at Lily. 'This is where it all happens.'

'It's lovely,' Lily breathed, awestruck.

'Shall we go up?' Violet moved aside a thick brocade curtain that hid a flight of carpeted stairs.

Nodding effusively, and still puzzled as to why she had been invited in, Lily said goodbye to Gladys and followed Violet up the stairs to a small parlour. The noise of the market drifted up from the street, a gentle breeze stirring the lace curtains. A large gilt-framed mirror hung above an unlit fireplace, the cold hearth crammed with red and pink peonies. The walls were papered with cabbage roses and hung with pretty watercolours. A framed photograph of a stern-looking couple Lily assumed to be Violet's parents took pride of place on the mantelpiece. The furniture was dark wood and green velvet and every surface was covered with knick-knacks.

'Have a seat,' Violet said, indicating one of the two ornately carved green velvet chairs placed at angles to a small round table. 'I'll put your purchases in the pantry and make a pot of tea.'

Lily perched on the edge of the chair, careful not to get dust from her scuffed shoes on the pretty carpet. She could hear Violet pottering around in the kitchen. Why had she invited her up here? A flutter of excitement that Lily couldn't quite explain stirred deep in her stomach. She was wiping her sweaty palms on her skirt when Violet returned with the tea tray, setting it on the table.

'I'll be mother, shall I?' Violet smiled. She handed Lily her tea and took hers over to a long, low-backed sofa upholstered in the same green as the chairs.

'Now, Lily,' she said, lifting the delicate floral print teacup to her lips and regarding Lily quizzically through the swirling steam. 'You must be wondering why I've invited you up here today?'

'Yes, Miss Upshall.' Lily nodded.

'I've seen you loitering outside my window – no, don't be embarrassed,' she said as Lily flushed. 'I was curious about you so I spoke to the lovely reverend after church one day. I invited him over for tea and he spoke very highly of you. He also told me of your ambitions to become a dressmaker's apprentice. Is that correct?'

'Yes, miss,' Lily replied, her heart skipping a beat as the spark in her stomach ignited into something more. She set her teacup on the table, hoping Violet wouldn't notice how badly her hands were shaking. It wouldn't do for a would-be seamstress to have unsteady hands.

'I can see that dress you're wearing has been altered. Is that your work?'

'Yes, miss.'

'Well, you're a neat sewer, I can see that.' Violet smiled. 'Can you finish button holes?'

'Yes, miss.' Lily felt herself growing hot as hope flared deep in her belly. Was it possible Miss Upshall might offer her a position? She kept her gaze fixed on Violet's face, hardly daring to breathe.

'Reverend Redfern also told me that things are a bit … unpleasant at home?'

'Yes, miss,' Lily whispered, shamefaced.

'Well, as it happens, I find myself in need of a new apprentice. Gladys is leaving to get married at the end of this month and I shall be needing someone to take her place. I shall need to see samples of your work, of course, but you look like a girl who isn't afraid of hard work?'

Lily almost laughed out loud. She caught herself just in time.

'You would have to be willing to work late into the night should urgency require it. I would expect your work to be of the highest standard. In return, you will have your board and lodging and a minimal wage.' Violet balanced her cup and saucer on the arm of the sofa and smiled at Lily expectantly. 'Well? What do you say? Would you like to come and work for me?'

Lily clenched her sweaty palms. She didn't even have to consider Violet's proposal.

'Yes, please, Miss Upshall.' She nodded emphatically, scarcely able to believe her good fortune. To live here, away from Jez and Aunt Doris? It would be a dream come true. Only one thing marred her joy.

'My aunt,' Lily said hesitantly. 'I'm not sure she'll agree.' How would Doris react upon learning she was losing her skivvy as well as the money Charlie sent every month?

'You leave your aunt to me,' Violet said, getting up to refill their teacups. She dropped a sugar lump into her cup and stirred it absently, an idea forming in her mind. 'As soon as we've finished our tea, we'll go down to my workroom and you may demonstrate your skills with the needle.'

'Yes, Miss Upshall,' Lily whispered, her throat constricting with nerves. She wiped her clammy palms on her skirt, anxious not to disappoint Violet.

'Good, and as I'm conscious that your aunt will be wondering what has become of you, I shall drive you home in my trap. It will give me the opportunity to speak to Mrs Elkin about my proposition.' She regarded Lily with her soft grey eyes. 'If I'm satisfied with your work, you could start within the month.'

Lily swallowed hard, hardly daring to believe that the chance to escape her aunt was so tantalisingly within reach.

'Thank you,' she said, willing her hands to stop shaking. She couldn't let Violet down. She wouldn't.

*   *   *

Lily's stomach cramped with nerves as Violet guided the pony and trap into Laundry Lane. She swallowed hard in an attempt to quell her mounting anxiety.

An elegantly dressed woman like Violet driving a trap was an unusual sight in the street and children paused in their play to stare.

'Hey look, it's Lily,' a little boy shouted, pointing open-mouthed at Lily seated high on the creaking seat. Stout-armed washerwomen, taking advantage of a couple of hours' reprieve, were gathered on their doorsteps gossiping. A fat, red-faced crone with straw-like yellow hair spotted Lily and grinned toothily. 'Oi, what you doing up there, Lily Hayter?' she crowed, causing Lily to shrink low in her seat.

'Don't mind them,' Violet said in a low voice. 'Good afternoon, ladies,' she called pleasantly.

The commotion had brought Doris to her doorway. She squinted into the brightness, arms folded across her chest, her eyes narrowing with suspicion at the sight of her niece riding beside Violet. She pushed herself off the doorframe, stepping out into the dusty street.

Violet brought the pony and trap to a halt outside Doris's cottage. 'Good afternoon. Mrs Elkin, I presume?' she asked, her tone belying the disgust wrought by the sight of Doris's dishevelled appearance. And was that gin she could smell on the woman's breath?

'Yes,' Doris conceded warily. She scowled at Lily. 'Where the hell have you been? You should have been back hours ago.'

'Pleased to meet you, Mrs Elkin,' Violet lied, feeling Lily quail beside her. Ignoring Doris's question, she gave Lily's arm an encouraging squeeze. 'I'm Violet Upshall. I own the dressmaker's shop in Market Place. May I come in?' Without waiting for a reply, she stepped elegantly down from the trap and motioned to Lily to do likewise. 'I have something I wish to discuss with you.'

'Why, what's she done?' Doris glowered at Lily.

'May I?' Violet raised a questioning eyebrow, motioning towards the open doorway with her riding crop.

'What you lot looking at?' Doris shouted to her assembled neighbours as she led the way indoors.

Lily hung back in shame as Violet removed her gloves and surveyed the cramped, shabby parlour, taking in the threadbare carpet, the frayed and faded sofa. At least, thanks to Lily, the place was clean. Violet fluffed up her hair. Her gaze met Lily's in the mirror. 'You keep a clean home, Mrs Elkin,' she said, her tone thick with irony, as she ran a finger along the edge of the mirror. 'I take it Lily makes herself useful?"

'It's only right the girl earns her keep,' Doris protested sullenly as she plonked herself in a chair facing the window. 'You may as well sit down.' She indicated a chair close to the fireplace. The air was a fetid mix of stale tobacco smoke, sweat and cooking.

'All right,' Doris demanded once Violet was seated. 'This isn't a social call.' Lily cringed under the weight of Doris's sly stare. 'Let's have it. What do you want?'

Lily slipped quietly into the kitchen where she stashed the parcel of meat in the lean-to pantry. She could hear the carefree voices of the children playing outside. Apart from walking to school with the neighbours' children, she had had little to do with them. Doris always kept her so busy that, even during the holidays, there had been no time for playing. Whether while scrubbing bedsheets or weeding the garden, she often listened to the shouts of children playing in the street, her heart heavy with longing. She would have loved a friend, someone to confide in and share secrets with, but it appeared the mothers of Laundry Lane tarred Lily with the same brush as her aunt and cousin.

'Mrs Elkin,' Violet said as Lily returned to the front room. The dressmaker sat straight in her chair, elegant fingers folded around her gloves. She looked so out of place in Doris's parlour that Lily had to force down the nervous laughter bubbling up inside her. The absurdity of it tickled her throat and she had to bite down hard on her lip so as not to erupt in nervous giggles.

'I would like to speak to you regarding Lily's future.'

'Her future?' Doris glared at Lily. 'Why? What's she been saying?'

'I'd like to offer Lily an apprenticeship. She has demonstrated to me her skill with the needle and, while she still has a great deal to learn, I have no doubt that with a lot of hard work, she will eventually become an accomplished dressmaker. She comes highly recommended by Reverend

Redfern, and you yourself, I am sure, can vouch for the quality of her work?'

'An apprenticeship?' Doris said, her interest piqued. 'You'll pay her to learn?'

'She will receive a small wage, yes.'

'How small?' Doris asked, eyes narrowed. When Violet told her, Doris quickly said, 'The answer's no.' Lily's heart sank. 'I can't keep her on a pittance,' Doris snorted. 'And you can be sure that so-called brother of hers will stop his weekly support once he gets wind of this.'

'Mrs Elkin, I'm afraid I haven't made myself clear. Lily's apprenticeship will require her to live on the premises. She will receive her board and lodgings.'

Doris scowled and brushed a strand of lank, greying hair from her florid face. She leaned forward, her gaze fixed on Lily, who was still cowering near the front door as if poised to take flight.

'I need Lily here,' she said, jabbing her finger at Violet. 'She's got chores.'

'Mrs Elkin,' Violet said patiently. 'On occasion, we work late into the night. It makes perfect sense for Lily to board with me. If she were going into service, she would more than likely live away from home, wouldn't she?'

'No,' Doris said, getting to her feet. 'I'm sorry. I refuse permission. She can work for you – she's got to work somewhere, I suppose – but I will need her wages and I need her to help me around the house. I can't manage on my own.'

Violet pursed her lips. Lily held her breath and prayed that Violet wouldn't be fobbed off by her aunt's excuses. This was her chance to escape Doris's clutches for ever. Now she'd tasted the offer of freedom, she couldn't bear to stay a single day more. Her heartbeat drummed in her ears. The silence seemed to last an eternity.

'Mrs Elkin,' Violet said, an edge to her voice, 'I really don't feel that you have any choice. I have spoken to Reverend Redfern and, as I understand it, your guardianship of Lily ends as soon as she finds gainful employment. Legally, you cannot forbid her from accepting my offer.'

Taking courage from Miss Upshall's words, Lily forced herself to meet her aunt's sardonic gaze.

'Aunt Doris.' Her voice quivered slightly and she took a deep breath to steady it. Her hands balled into fists, Lily thrust out her chin in a gesture of grim determination. 'I want to work for Miss Upshall and you can't stop me.'

'You ungrateful little brat.' Doris reeled, taken aback by Lily's sudden show of spirit. 'You're just like your mother, no better than you should be. For three years I've fed and clothed you. I deserve a little gratitude, some loyalty.' Doris was on her feet now, her finger wagging, eyes blazing as an angry red stain crept up her neck, flooding her cheeks.

'Fed and clothed me?' Lily took a step towards her aunt, her expression one of incredulous disbelief. It was as though the prospect of imminent freedom had woken something deep inside her. Her fear seemed to dissipate and all the anger she had kept suppressed for years came spewing to the fore.

'You and Jez wasted my father's savings and I've never seen a penny of the money Charlie gives you. You've been milking him for years. I've slogged and slaved for you day in and day out and you've never so much as given me a kind word. Charlie and I have paid for my keep ten times over.' She took a shaky breath, her heart thumping against her ribcage. She'd be for it now, she thought as Doris eyed her angrily.

'Over my dead body,' Doris hissed, grabbing Lily's arm. Pain shot up her arm, making her wince. 'You're going nowhere.'

'Mrs Elkin, please!' Violet exclaimed, eyes wide in shock.

Doris turned her venomous glare on Violet. 'Thank you for your offer, miss,' she said, with a sour-faced sneer. 'But Lily will be staying under my roof.'

'No!' Lily shouted, tears of dismay pricking her eyelids. 'I'm going with Miss Upshall.' She wrenched her arm free from her aunt's vicious grasp. 'I don't care what you say.'

'Mrs Elkin, surely we can discuss this in a rational manner?' Violet said, appalled at the scene unfolding before her eyes.

'It's nothing to do with you, miss,' Doris shot back. 'Mind your own business. Go on, get back in your fancy trap and get lost. This is family business.'

Lily turned her desperate gaze on Violet. 'Please,' she begged. 'Don't leave me here.'

'Make no mistake, Mrs Elkin,' Violet said, her cold gaze resting on Doris's flushed face. 'I'm not leaving here without Lily. I had expected her to move in with me in the next week or so but I cannot, in all good conscience, leave her here a moment longer.'

'What?' Doris spluttered. 'How dare you?' Violet ignored her, turning instead to Lily.

'Lily, gather your belongings.'

'She's going nowhere!' Doris screeched, her shrill tone reverberating across the street, where it reached the ears of Michael Redfern.

In the front bedroom of the cottage opposite, Michael's forehead was so deeply furrowed that his brows had merged over the bridge of his nose as he heard old Maggie Owen's breath rattle in her influenza-ravaged lungs. Poor woman. He was doubtful she would last the night. Her husband of twenty-eight years, Simeon, stood in the doorway, looking at his stricken bedridden wife, his expression one of abject despair.

The sound of raised voices in such a deprived area as Laundry Lane was in no way unusual, but recognizing the voice drifting up through the open window as belonging to Doris Elkin, Michael got to his feet to look out into the street. Glancing down, he shook his head grimly.

'I'll be right back,' he said, grabbing his hat from the night-stand. He gave Maggie's grieving husband's shoulder a brief squeeze and left the room, taking the stairs two at a time and bursting onto the street just as Doris, her fist twisted in Lily's long auburn hair, was attempting to drag her back inside, while Violet implored her to see sense.

'Mrs Elkin!' Michael's voice boomed out as he strode towards them, acutely aware that the whole street had turned out to witness the altercation. Brawling was not uncommon in Laundry Lane and always provided great entertainment for any onlookers.

'Reverend!' Lily shouted. Doris yanked her hair hard. 'Ow!'

'It's family business, Reverend,' Doris warned Michael. 'Stay out of it.'

'Oh, Reverend. Thank goodness you're here.' Michael had never seen the usually unflappable Violet so agitated. 'The woman's gone completely mad! I offered Lily an apprenticeship as you suggested but Mrs Elkin is refusing to allow Lily to go with me.' She wrung her hands. The pony whinnied nervously, her ears flickering.

'Let's all stop shouting and discuss things calmly,' Michael said, rubbing his nose in consternation. 'Mrs Elkin, please, calm down.' He had understood the situation instantly. He'd always known Doris would never let Lily go without a fight. She'd had it too easy for far too long. He leaned in close, his voice low. 'Be quiet, Mrs Elkin. You're making a spectacle of yourself.'

Doris snorted. What did she care? Her standing in the community had long since sunk into the mire of public opinion. But she released her grip on Lily's hair. The frightened girl scuttled behind Michael's broad frame, rubbing her throbbing scalp.

'I decide what Lily can or can't do,' Doris spat. 'I'm her legal guardian.'

'Until she turns fourteen or finds full-time employment,' Michael reminded her, raising his voice in order to be heard above Doris's shrieking. Thank God Jim had been canny to his sister-in-law's flaws. 'Now, as I understand it, Miss Upshall is offering Lily full-time employment. Am I right, Miss Upshall?'

'Yes, indeed.' Violet nodded primly. Embarrassed as she was at being the source of entertainment for the entire street, she was resolved not to depart without Lily. Having seen first-hand how vilely Doris treated her niece, she was determined not to leave the girl in her charge for another hour. 'As soon as Lily has retrieved her belongings, we'll be on our way.'

'She's taking nothing from here.' Doris snorted. 'If she goes, she goes with the clothes she's got on her back and that's it.' The fight seemed to drain out of her, her shoulders slumping in defeat. She waved Lily away dismissively. 'Go, but don't bother coming around here with your tail between your legs when it all goes belly up. I never want to lay eyes on you again, ungrateful wench.'

Lily smiled, her heart feeling lighter than it had for years. 'Oh, don't worry, Aunt, I won't be back. You can count on that.'

'I don't know what Jez will say about all this,' Doris muttered as she turned and went indoors, slamming the door loudly behind her. Drama over, the neighbours began drifting back to their homes.

'What about your things?' Violet asked Lily, slightly bewildered by the sudden turn of events. Lily shrugged.

'I haven't much. Nothing worth worrying about.' She turned to Michael. 'Thank you, Reverend. Aunty Doris would never have given in if it hadn't been for you.'

'I didn't do much,' Michael said, clearing his throat. 'And she has no legal right to stop you. Don't let her browbeat you into believing her lies, Lily.'

'I won't,' Lily said, throwing her arms around him. 'Not anymore.'

Michael patted her head. 'This is only what you deserve. I'll call by to see you in a day or two, once you're settled.'

Lily clambered up onto the seat beside Violet. She could barely contain her excitement. As they pulled away, there were a few begrudging calls of, 'Well, done, lass,' 'God bless you,' and 'Good luck, lass, you deserve it,' from the women standing in their doorways. Lily acknowledged them with a shy smile and a wave. At the end of the street, just before they turned the corner, she twisted around in her seat to find the reverend still gazing after her. He raised his hat and waved. Lily waved back, then settled into her seat, ready for the next chapter of her life to unfold.

CHAPTER NINE

Lily woke with a start to pale sunlight streaming through floral-patterned curtains. She lay still, momentarily confused as to where she was until the events of the previous day came rushing back. She was in bed next to Gladys, in Violet's back bedroom. She stretched languidly, listening to Gladys's soft breathing and gazed around the room. Muted sunlight slanted on the rose-patterned walls. A watercolour of a ship anchored in some exotic-looking bay hung above a four-drawer chest next to a small closet. In the corner stood a wash stand, complete with a china rose-patterned jug and bowl.

Unused to lying in bed after sun-up, Lily slipped from beneath the covers, careful not to disturb Gladys. The bare boards were cool to the touch as she crossed the room to the window. She leaned her hands on the sill and gazed out at the garden below. It was a riot of colour and she breathed in deeply, inhaling the heady perfume. Insects hummed among the hollyhocks, foxgloves and delphiniums. Swallows and skylarks dipped and soared in an azure-blue sky. She wrapped her arms around her spindly frame, barely able to believe her good fortune.

Hearing footsteps on the landing, she quickly shed her borrowed nightgown and pulled on her clothes, her dismay at her shabby appearance even more acute in the face of her elegant surroundings.

She found Violet in the kitchen, still in her nightwear and brandishing the tea kettle.

'Good morning,' Violet greeted her pleasantly. 'You're up early. I was about to bring you a cup of tea. Did you sleep well?'

'Yes, Miss Upshall. Thank you. It's such a comfortable bed.' She shuffled awkwardly in the doorway, unused to being idle. 'Why don't you go back to bed and let me make the tea?'

Violet shook her head. 'You're very sweet, Lily, but I believe it's time someone did something for you for a change. You can make the tea for our elevenses later, how does that sound?'

At a loss as to what to say, Lily felt she had no choice but to nod agreement.

Gladys was just waking up when Lily followed Violet into the bedroom.

'Morning, sleepyhead.' Violet set the tray on the nightstand as Gladys stretched and grinned, rubbing sleep from her eyes.

'I hope my Geoffrey will spoil me like you do, Violet.' She giggled, plumping up her pillow, her blond hair spilling over her shoulders. 'He's got a lot to live up to.' She accepted the cup of tea Violet handed her and turned her blue-eyed gaze on Lily. 'I hope my snoring didn't keep you awake?'

'I slept like a log.' Lily grinned shyly. Seeing her hovering uncertainly near the doorway, Violet beckoned her over.

'Come on, don't be shy. On the shop floor you can be as formal as you like, but off it, we're all friends together.' She sat down on the bed and patted the counterpane. 'Come on, come and have your tea.'

Lily perched gingerly on the edge of the bed, cup of tea in her hands. Violet and Gladys were so warm and familiar with each other, more like sisters than employer and employee. Lily couldn't imagine herself ever being so easy and familiar with Miss Upshall.

'Right, Lily,' Violet said over porridge and toast in the sunny kitchen a short time later. 'A few house rules. Downstairs, I'm Miss Upshall, but off the shop floor, you call me Violet, all right?'

Lily nodded. She was still trying to get her head around the events of the last twelve or so hours. It was gone seven-thirty and the only work she had done so far was to slather butter on her toast.

'We've got a lot of work on at the moment so you'll need to work quickly and neatly. We can't afford mistakes.'

Lily nodded solemnly and Violet smiled at her.

'Don't look so frightened, Lily. We neither of us bite. You'll spend most of today cutting out patterns and tacking seams before Gladys finishes them off on the machine. We break at eleven for a cup of tea and, believe me, you'll be ready for one by then. At promptly half past twelve we close for an hour for dinner. We eat up here, so as to have a proper break. We pause for another cup of tea around four, depending on our workload. I close the shop at five o'clock sharp, but we generally keep working until eight or nine, with a break for a cold supper around half past six. Does that suit?'

'Yes, Miss Upshall,' Lily nodded. It sounded like luxury in comparison to what she had endured at her aunt's house.

'It's Violet upstairs, remember?'

'Yes, Violet,' Lily stammered shyly. She washed her breakfast down with a mug of Violet's strong tea and, by a few minutes after eight o'clock, she was hunched in a spindle-back chair tacking sleeves onto a blue and white sprigged blouse. Gladys spent the morning pinning pattern pieces together and cutting them out with a pair of long dressmaker's shears while Violet worked the sewing machine.

Several times, as Lily paused to massage her aching shoulders, she marvelled at how pleasant it was in Violet's back room. The sewing machine whirred rhythmically, the needle flying up and down with such speed it made Lily's head ache just watching it. Occasionally the bell over the shop door would jangle, jarring their concentration. Violet would bring the machine to an abrupt halt and hurry next door to deal with the customer, sometimes poking her head through the dividing door to ask either Gladys or Lily to give her a hand.

The morning flew by. Before Lily knew it, it was dinner time and she was halfway through her first day. She massaged the stiffness from her shoulders. Her head ached from concentrating so hard, but she had never felt happier.

The afternoon was equally busy. It was so pleasant to have someone to talk to while she worked, Lily mused, as she glanced at the clock. It was already ten minutes to five. The shop bell jangled, heralding the arrival of another customer.

'Lily.' The sewing machine fell silent. 'Please tell whoever it is that I shall be with them directly, and offer them a cup of tea.'

Stifling a yawn, Lily set her work aside and got to her feet. Smoothing down her skirt, she took a deep breath to steady her nerves, and hurried into the shop where an elegantly dressed woman was standing at the counter perusing the spools of thread on display. She wore a dress of dark blue with a large bustle that emphasized the colour of her eyes. Ostrich feathers sprouted from her hat, bobbing and swaying when she moved.

'Good afternoon, madam,' Lily croaked, her mouth suddenly as dry as the desert.

The woman regarded Lily with her cool gaze. 'I've not seen you here before,' she remarked haughtily, removing her black kid-skin gloves with excessive care.

'Yes, ma'am,' Lily replied, nervously, acutely aware of her too-short skirt. 'Today is my first day.'

'Please tell Violet that Lady Copperfield wishes to see her.'

'Yes, ma'am.' Lily swallowed, trying not to quail beneath the woman's supercilious glare. 'May I offer you some refreshment?'

'No, thank you. I am in a hurry so if you could ... Ah, Violet, my dear,' Lady Copperfield exclaimed, her haughty demeanour softening as Violet emerged from behind the curtain.

'Lady Copperfield,' Violet gushed. 'How lovely to see you again. What an honour. How may I be of assistance, your ladyship?'

Lady Copperfield nodded, acknowledging Violet's regard. She was similar in age to Violet, in her mid-thirties; they might have been friends had their stations in life not been so dissimilar. 'Sir Frederick and I are off to Europe next month,' Lady Copperfield explained, 'and I find myself in dire need of a new wardrobe.'

'Of course, Lady Copperfield. Lily, Lady Copperfield is one of our most esteemed clients. Your ladyship, may I introduce my new apprentice, Lily? With your permission, she'll take your measurements this afternoon.' Even before Lady Copperfield had nodded her begrudging assent, Violet's fingers were reaching for the tape measure at her waist. Lily gulped. With shaking hands, convinced her knees were about to give way, she took the tape measure from Violet.

'May, I, ma'am?'

Lady Copperfield raised her arms so Lily could wind the tape measure around her corset-slender waist.

'Is Gladys still working here?' she enquired, eyeing Lily down her long, aquiline nose.

'Gladys is leaving to be married very soon, Lady Copperfield,' Violet replied politely, scribbling the measurements in her little book. 'Lily will be taking over from her.'

'I hope you won't fall short, my girl. I expect extremely high standards. I would hate to be forced to take my business elsewhere.'

'Yes, ma'am,' Lily whispered, keeping her gaze focused on the hem of Lady Copperfield's silk gown.

'I'm grateful for your patronage, Lady Copperfield,' Violet said, giving Lily a discreet wink. 'And I'm sure you'll find Lily perfectly competent. This is only her first day dealing with customers, after all. She's bound to feel a little nervous. I'm already very impressed with the quality of her work so far.' She nodded at Lily. 'You may return to the workroom.'

'Thank you, Miss Upshall,' Lily whispered. Escaping gratefully out the back, flushed with pleasure, she found that Gladys had laid out a couple of dresses on the work bench.

'Lady Copperfield, hmm?' She gave Lily a conspiratorial wink. 'She's an old sourpuss, that one. Gives us the runaround, I can tell you. She's never happy with the finished garment until she's made us unpick it and redo it at least half a dozen times.' She grinned at Lily, who smiled back, relieved that she obviously wasn't the only one who found Lady Copperfield a trifle difficult. 'Anyway, forget about her ladyship.' Gladys pursed her lips and looked Lily up and down. 'I looked these out for you.' She pushed the dresses towards Lily. 'They might be a little on the large side but I'm sure you'll be able to make the necessary alterations. You could make a start on them this evening.'

'Thank you.' Overcome, Lily fingered the soft, finely ribbed poplin. One was a dark brown, the other a rich midnight blue. They were nothing fancy, just serviceable day dresses but a vast improvement on the limp, faded frock she had fled her aunt's house in.

The bell over the door jangled shrilly and Violet reappeared, rolling her eyes.

'A complete new wardrobe,' she sighed in response to Gladys's questioning glance. 'Everything that isn't urgent will have to be put on hold.' She turned to Lily, who was still admiring her new frocks. 'Lady Copperfield is one of our wealthiest customers,' she explained. 'We can't afford to displease her.' The worry lines across her brow eased a little as she stroked the poplins clutched in Lily's arms. 'Do you like them?' Lily nodded emphatically.

'Yes, Miss Upshall. They're the loveliest dresses I've ever seen.'

'Good, make them your own. Help yourself to any accessories you like. This' – she plucked a card of deep orange braid from one of the cluttered worktops – 'would look lovely along the collar and cuffs.' She held the braid against the brown. 'What do you think?'

'Yes, miss,' Lily agreed. In her mind's eye she was already seeing the finished article as her enthusiasm for the project took hold.

Later that evening, after a cold supper of bread, bacon and tomatoes, Lily helped Gladys bundle up the scraps of cloth and sweep the floor while Violet carefully removed a dark cloak from one of the mannequins to reveal Gladys's wedding dress. They had been working on it for weeks, Gladys told Lily as all three of them stood back to admire the gown.

It was beautiful in its simplicity. Lily could see immediately that the sleeveless white satin shift would fit Gladys's neat figure like a glove. A dress of the softest gossamer lace went over the top, trailing at the back to form a short train. The lacework on the sleeves was as delicate as a spiderweb. It was so fine, so fragile, she hardly dared exhale as she reached out to stroke it with tentative fingers.

'It's beautiful,' she breathed, withdrawing her hand and staring at it in open-mouthed awe.

'Your Geoffrey will be struck dumb when you walk down the aisle,' Violet said, unable to hide the slight wobble in her tone. Gladys blushed coyly.

'Do you really think so?'

'You'll look like an angel,' Lily said, unable to take her eyes off the beautiful creation. Perhaps one day she too would get to wear such a wonderful wedding gown.

'Apart from sewing on the buttons, there's not much more we need do to it,' Violet said briskly, wiping away a discreet tear. 'It's perfect.'

'It is perfect, Violet.' To Lily's surprise, Gladys flung her arms around Violet and hugged her tight. The sight of the two women embracing brought tears to Lily's eyes. It had been years since she had known the embrace of another woman. Not since her mother had died.

★   ★   ★

'I'm going to really miss Violet when I leave,' Gladys commented as they got ready for bed later that night. 'I was twelve when I came here, same as you. Fresh out the workhouse, I was. My mother and father both died when I was just a kid.' She laughed softly. 'I shan't say she's been like a mother to me – she'd have my guts for garters if she thought I was implying she's old enough to be my ma – but she's certainly been like a big sister, and the best friend I could have asked for.'

'Won't you be able to visit once you're settled?' Lily asked with a twinge of envy. She climbed into the bed they shared, tugging the bed clothes over her bare legs. The evening was sultry and the window was open. Laughter drifted from the Red Lion, accompanied by the tinkling of piano keys.

Gladys pulled her cap over her blond tresses and climbed in beside Lily. 'Geoffrey's uncle has offered him a position in his shipyard. We leave for Plymouth the day after the wedding.' Her lip trembled slightly. 'I don't think we'll be back this way for quite some time, if ever.'

'Surely you'll come back to visit Geoffrey's mother?'

'Oh no.' Gladys sank back against her pillow with a weary sigh. 'She's coming with us. Still, she's a dear thing really and she's already promised me she won't interfere in the way I keep house.'

Lily drew her knees under her chin. It was still quite light, the thin curtains doing little to keep out the late evening sunshine. A blackbird sang lustily outside the window and snatches of conversation wafted up from the street below.

'What about you?' Gladys asked, turning towards Lily. 'Violet says you're an orphan too.'

'Sort of,' Lily replied. 'I don't know where my real mother is or whether she's alive but my adoptive parents, Martha and Jim, passed away three years ago. That's when I was sent to live with my aunt. My parents were the kindest, nicest people. I loved them so much.' Lily's eyes filled with tears as the much-loved and much-missed faces swam into her memory. 'I really miss them. And my brother, Charlie, is an apprentice in Shaftesbury. I see him about once a month. I shall to write to him tomorrow to let him know where I am.'

'I'm sorry about your ma and pa.' Gladys groped for Lily's hand and squeezed it. Lily squeezed back, grateful for the contact.

Lily sighed. She still couldn't believe the good fortune that had brought her to Violet's. Whether by fate or divine intervention, she would never stop being grateful for the opportunity to escape her aunt's evil clutches. Doris and Jez would never be able to hurt her again.

'Do you know your real mother's name?' Gladys queried, stifling a yawn.

'Her name was Bea,' Lily replied, sleepily. 'Beatrice Cullen. Other than the fact she attended Reverend Redfern's Sunday school class, I don't know much about her.' Gladys's yawn proved contagious and Lily followed suit. She could hardly keep her eyes open.

'Come on, we'd better get to sleep,' Gladys said. 'Tomorrow's going to be another busy day.'

Lily snuggled under the covers. 'Goodnight.'

Tired as she was, Lily found sleep eluded her. She lay in the deepening twilight, her thoughts turning to the frightened young girl who had felt she had no choice but to give up her child. Lily's young heart ached with yearning for the mother she had never known.

CHAPTER TEN

Gladys left at the end of the month to marry her sweetheart. For the first couple of weeks, Lily, and Violet especially, felt her loss very keenly but as the days passed in a blur of hard work and pleasant companionship, a bond began to form between them and they settled into a comfortable routine.

Three months after Lily started working for Violet, she was summoned by the jangling of the bell that hung over the front door. Smoothing down her skirt, she went into the shop and gave a squeal of delight.

Charlie grinned. 'I bet you didn't expect to see me again so soon?'

Lily flung herself at him. 'Is something wrong? I only saw you last week.' Her joy at seeing her brother again so soon was tempered by a twinge of foreboding. Violet, having heard Lily's exclamation of delight, had followed her into the shop.

'Hello, Charlie,' Violet said pleasantly. She had met Lily's brother on two previous occasions and found him to be an agreeable, well-mannered young man. 'Come through to the parlour and join us for a cup of tea.' Her warm smile was reflected in her grey eyes. 'It's time Lily and I took a break. We've been rushed off our feet all morning.'

'That's very kind of you, Miss Upshall.' Charlie shuffled his feet awkwardly. He always felt gauche and unsophisticated in Violet's elegant presence. 'But actually, with your permission, I need to speak to Lily about something rather important.' Lily's feeling of foreboding grew. She looked at him sharply but Charlie averted his gaze, clearing his throat nervously. 'May we take a walk?'

'Certainly.' Violet smiled at Lily. 'Take as long as you need.' After quickly grabbing her hat and coat, and checking her appearance in the mirror, Lily returned to the shop. Her emerald-green coat, a cast-off from a grateful customer, brought out the deep green of her eyes, contrasting nicely with her fiery auburn hair.

'You look quite the young lady,' Charlie said, as they stepped out into the mild October sunshine. 'I feel quite at a disadvantage.'

'You look fine,' Lily reassured him, tucking her arm through his as they strolled through the bustling market. 'Oh look, there's Reverend Redfern.' Lily pointed. 'Over by the hot pie stall talking to Mrs Burridge.' She raised her hand to wave but Michael failed to notice her. 'Shall we go over?' she asked Charlie.

'I'd rather not, if you don't mind. I don't have much time, and what I need to say is very important.'

Lily's stomach contracted with anxiety.

'It must be important to bring you all this way in the middle of the week,' she said in a small voice as they ambled towards the river. 'Is it bad news?' She squinted against the low autumn sunlight, shining through the leafy canopy of a horse chestnut tree, its leaves edged with crimson and gold.

Charlie cleared his throat, his gaze fixed on the brambles along the riverbank where the last of the season's black-berries glimmered among dew-spangled spiderwebs. Water tumbled over the weir, spray dancing in the air like sparkling diamonds.

'I've been offered another job. It's better pay, and there's the chance to make a name for myself.'

'But that's good news! Oh, Charlie, I'm so proud of you.' She grinned, feeling a surge of relief. She nudged him with her elbow. 'So, why do you look like you're at your best friend's funeral?'

Charlie stood motionless, gazing out over the water, focused on a moorhen bobbing in and out of the reeds.

'Charlie?' Lily frowned, her initial sense of relief fading.

'It's not local.' Charlie looked at her, his expression bleak.

'How far is not local?' Lily queried. 'Southampton? London?'

Charlie plucked a fleck of lint from his trousers, desperate to delay the moment for as long as he could.

'Charlie?' Lily giggled nervously. 'Tell me. You're not going further than London, surely?'

'Africa.'

'Africa?' Lily stared at him in disbelief. '*Africa?*'

'The Cape Colony. A friend of mine, Danny, has a cousin out there. He's building a hotel and has invited some of us out there to work on the fixtures and fittings.' He turned to Lily, his brown eyes begging her to understand. 'It's a once in a lifetime opportunity for me, Lily. I can make good money while working alongside some of the best chippies in the business. And it won't be for long, three years maybe, five at the most, and I'll be back.'

'Five years?' she whispered in shock, fighting back tears as she digested the news. Five years was an interminable length of time.

'I'll miss you,' she whispered.

'I'll miss you too.' Charlie squeezed her arm. 'And if you'd still been at Aunty Doris's I would never have entertained the idea but you're happy at Violet's, aren't you? And safe.'

Lily nodded. 'I am, but even three years is a long time. Can't I come with you?'

Charlie shook his head. 'It's no place for a woman. I'll write as often as I can.'

Lily studied her hands. It was as if an iron vice was wrapped around her heart. Why did everyone she loved and trusted leave her?

'When?' she whispered.

'I travel down to Southampton on the twenty-third and sail two days later.'

'So soon? That's only a week away,' Lily cried, a mantle of misery settling heavily on her young shoulders. Charlie put his arm around her.

'You need to stay where you are and learn your trade. You're earning yourself a reputation as very talented seamstress. My manager said his missus speaks highly of your work.'

In spite of herself, Lily found herself flushing with pleasure. 'Mrs Kendall is one of our more amiable customers, unlike some I could mention.'

'Her ladyship still giving you grief, is she?'

Lily grinned. Lady Copperfield had recently returned from her tour of Europe, a trip that had apparently not been without its own share of problems.

'She swanned in the other day demanding that we put aside all our other commissions in order to make her some new ballgowns in time for Christmas, and she's put on an awful lot of weight while she's been away so all her other gowns will need altering. It's good money, and Violet appreciates her business, but we can't neglect our other loyal customers. We're working every hour God sends as it is.' As if to prove her point, she yawned loudly. 'Sorry.'

'She does have something of a reputation,' Charlie agreed knowingly. 'A couple of my colleagues have done some work up at Bay Willow House. Very difficult to please, I believe, was their opinion of her. Sir Frederick is a fairly decent chap by all accounts, though I believe he spends much of his time in London.'

'Probably to escape the old battleaxe,' Lily replied. They continued walking. A cool breeze ruffled the surface of the river. 'Have you seen anything of our aunt lately?'

'No, and I have no wish to.' Charlie's face grew sombre. 'I shall never forgive her for the way she treated you. I did hear Jez was up before the magistrate a while ago. The police raided one of his boxing matches. According to the newspaper report, he got away with a fine and a couple of nights in the cells.'

Lily shook her head. 'I doubt he'll ever change.'

'His father was a scoundrel before him, it's in the blood. A leopard can't change its spots, so they say.'

'Ah, well, Reverend Redfern would have us believe otherwise,' Lily said, but her laugh sounded brittle and forced.

'You'd better be getting back,' Charlie said reluctantly. Lily sighed. Much as she regretted having to cut their time together short, the work was piling up back at the shop and she couldn't leave it all for Violet.

Nevertheless, they took their time going back, reminiscing about their childhood, remembering a happier time before the untimely death of their beloved parents.

'Do you still wonder about Beatrice?' Charlie asked as they lingered on the street corner. A chill wind blew across the marketplace. A hollow-cheeked urchin snatched an apple from one of the market stalls and took off down the street, the vendor shouting after him angrily. The boy sprinted around the corner, almost knocking into Lily in his haste.

'I think about her often,' Lily replied wistfully, regaining her balance as the boy tore off down the hill. 'I just wish I knew what became of her.'

'It's a shame the reverend couldn't be more helpful.'

Lily shrugged. Right now, Charlie's imminent departure was all she could think about, hanging over her like a cloud.

'Well,' Charlie said with forced cheer as they came to a halt outside Violet's shop. 'This is goodbye, then.'

'Oh, Charlie,' Lily's voice broke. 'I wish you didn't have to go. I shall miss you so much.'

'I know.' Charlie kissed her cheek, and hugged her tight. 'Write to me, care of the White Star Line. I'll write as soon as I'm on board the ship. We're stopping off at Malta so I'll post it then. Look after yourself, Lily,' he said, his voice hoarse with emotion.

'You too,' Lily sobbed. She could hardly swallow.

Charlie gave her one final squeeze and turned abruptly away, moving swiftly down the street, his spine erect, blinking back tears. He didn't dare look back, knowing he needed all his strength to walk away from her.

Tears streamed down Lily's cheeks as she stared after him.

'Lily, whatever's the matter?' Violet appeared in the doorway behind her.

'Charlie's going away.' Lily crumpled against Violet.

'Oh, Lily, sweetheart.' Like a mother, Violet folded Lily against her. Ushering the sobbing girl indoors away from prying eyes, Violet turned the sign and shot home the bolts. 'Come on,' she said, leading Lily up the stairs to the parlour. 'I'll make us both a nice cup of tea.'

'I'm going to miss him so much,' she sobbed, as Violet bustled about the kitchen.

'I know you will.' Violet set the tea tray on the low table and came to perch on Lily's chair arm, rubbing her back. 'Of course it hurts. Charlie is your last link to Martha and Jim. You're bound to feel bereft.' She cupped Lily's chin in her hand, tilting her tear-stained face towards her. 'But remember, you'll always have a home here with me, for as long as you want it.'

CHAPTER ELEVEN

1890

'Happy birthday, Lily.' Violet entered Lily's bedroom carrying a hat box swathed in pink tissue paper and ribbons.

'Thank you.' Lily peered over the edge of the bedcovers and yawned. 'What time is it?'

'Early,' Violet replied, perching on the edge of the bed, the hat box balanced on her knees. 'But I was so excited to give you my present, I couldn't wait a moment longer. The tea's brewing and I thought we'd have crumpets for breakfast as it's a special occasion.'

Lily stretched and pushed herself up against her pillows, looking at the wrapped hat box with growing excitement.

'I can't believe you've been with me for two years,' Violet said, as Lily's nimble fingers undid the shiny satin bows.

The paper fell away to reveal a plain round hat box. Lily lifted the cardboard lid. 'Oh, Violet, it's beautiful.'

The cream bonnet was nestled in a cloud of white tissue paper. A ribbon of forest green circled the crown. On one side was a cluster of tiny flowers.

'Thank you so much.' Lily was touched. She had never owned such a beautiful hat. 'I shall look incredibly stylish when I go to church on Sunday,' she laughed, lifting the hat from the box and studying it carefully. 'Did you make it yourself?'

'I did.' Violet nodded, her grey eyes sparkling with modest pride. 'I'm no milliner but I think I've done a rather fine job, if I say so myself.'

'It's lovely.' Lily put it on, tying the long ribbon under her chin. 'There. How do I look?'

'It suits you perfectly,' Violet said admiringly. 'The green ribbon really brings out the colour of your eyes.'

Lily craned her neck to admire her reflection in the dressing table mirror, turning her head this way and that in order to admire the hat from every vantage point. 'It's really lovely,' she said again. 'Thank you.'

'It's my pleasure. These came for you too.' From her dressing gown pocket, Violet withdrew two envelopes.

'It's from Charlie!' Lily recognized his handwriting on the top envelope at once. 'Oh, it's been so long since I've heard from him, I was starting to worry.' Frowning, she studied the writing on the second. 'I wonder who this one's from. It's postmarked Buxton. I don't know anyone who lives in Buxton.'

'You read your letters,' Violet said, getting up. 'I'll make a start on the crumpets. Come down whenever you're ready.'

'I will,' Lily replied. 'And thank you again for the bonnet.'

She put her new bonnet back in its box and, taking a hair-pin from the nightstand, slit open the envelope from Charlie, unfolding the sheets of pale blue notepaper. She had received six letters from her brother in the nineteen months since he had sailed. But she'd heard nothing from him for the past three months. This letter was dated six weeks earlier.

She settled back against her pillows, a small smile on her lips. Charlie wrote that he was working hard, the hours were long but that the hotel was almost at completion and plans were full steam ahead for a grand opening later the following year. Lily felt a pang of envy and wished she could share the experience. In previous letters he had described the exotic smells, the vibrant colours, his vivid descriptions filling her head with images of awe-inspiring mountains and aquamarine seas. He had dined on strange and exotic fruits and eaten foods enriched with spices brought by ship from all corners of the globe. Lily devoured every detail, reading the letter through twice in order to imprint his words on her mind.

She tucked Charlie's letter away in the drawer of her nightstand with the others, and picked up the other letter. The neat, sloping script was entirely unfamiliar. She slit open the envelope and pulled out a birthday card. It depicted a country cottage surrounded by spring flowers on a cream-coloured background. As she opened it, a sheet of lined paper fell out. The edges were jagged, as if it had been torn from a school exercise book. The card was signed simply, Revd Michael.

She felt a rush of pleasure that the reverend had remembered her birthday. She had missed him so much. Not long after Charlie had sailed, the parish had been rocked by the news that the reverend had been taken ill with tuberculosis and had been sent to a sanatorium in the north of England to recuperate. Surely this was a sign that the reverend's health was improving? She unfolded the sheet of paper and began to read,

My dear Lily,

I'm sure you're puzzled as to why I have chosen to write to you after all this time. First of all, may I wish you the happiest of birthdays. It has been my pleasure to see you grow into a fine young woman. Your dear father and mother would have been so proud of you.

Lily paused to wipe away a stray tear.

My dear child, I'm afraid that despite my hopes for the healing waters here among the breathtaking beauty of the Peak District, my health has not improved. My doctor has advised me that I have weeks left, at the most. I'm sorry to tell you this on your birthday but, please, dear Lily, don't be sad for me. I have enjoyed a good life and my faith is such that it allows me to view death as not the end but the beginning of a wonderful eternity.

Lily blinked back more tears. The reverend was dying? She swallowed the lump in her throat.

My only regret is that I will not be around to watch you blossom to your full potential. The circumstances surrounding your arrival have always meant you are particularly special to me. My time at the sanatorium, however, has not been idle. My dear, I write with news of your mother Beatrice. I'm afraid it is not happy tidings and were it not for my unfortunate circumstances, I would have preferred to have imparted this news to you directly rather than by letter.

As you know, your mother, Beatrice, came to me when you were barely a week old, frightened and alone. Never doubt that she loved you and wanted only the best for you. Which is why she entrusted you to my care. I did what I could to secure permanent employment for her and, although I never heard from her again, I had assumed her to be happily settled. Some weeks ago, however, I sadly discovered that a young woman fitting Beatrice's description drowned in an apparent act of suicide, in the pond at Sturminster Mill, not long after she and I parted ways.

Lily gave a low moan. Beatrice had drowned herself? She sniffed loudly, wiping her eyes with the back of her hands. Though she had never known her, Lily's grief for Beatrice tightened like a vice around her tender heart. She let the tears fall, hot and swift. They ran down her cheeks and dripped on the paper, blurring the ink. All these years while she had imagined that somewhere out there her mother was loving her, missing her, she had been gone, driven to suicide by her own despair.

She wiped the tears away with a fierce swipe of her hand and took a shuddering breath. She blew her nose, forcing herself to read on.

> *Oh, my precious child, I realize how this news must come as such a bitter blow. We can only pray and trust that Beatrice is at peace.*
>
> *I do, however, have another bit of information for you. In the church that night, Bea confided to me the identity of your father. I'm sorry I have kept this from you but for a long time I have struggled to decide whether knowing his name would serve any purpose other than to cause pain. However, I do believe you have the right to know. My dear Lily, your father is none other than Sir Frederick Copperfield.*

A bubble of laughter erupted in her throat. Sir Frederick, her father? Lady Copperfield's husband? Impossible. She reread the letter in astonishment. But what reason would Beatrice have to lie if she expected no retribution? The reverend went on to explain that when Beatrice had revealed her predicament to Sir Frederick, instead of standing by her, as she had expected, he had turned his back on her. With nowhere to turn, she had confided in Mrs White, the housekeeper. Again, her trust had been misplaced and Beatrice had been dismissed immediately without references.

Lily clutched at her throat in dismay. She had caught glimpses of Sir Frederick over the years when he occasioned to pass by in his carriage on his way to the Crown Hotel. A rather distinguished-looking man, with his light brown hair and neatly trimmed goatee, she had not regarded him as callous or unfeeling, though it was common knowledge around Blandford that he had married Cynthia, Lady Copperfield, solely for her fortune. Rumour had it that the Copperfield family had lost the bulk of their brewing enterprise during the devastating fire of 1731 in which the town of Blandford had been all but destroyed. Sir Frederick's four times great-grandfather, Nicholas Copperfield, a shrewd businessman, whose wife Susannah had just come into a substantial inheritance, had plenty of time and money to plough into the rebuilding of the Copperfield empire. Within twenty years, the family's fortunes had been restored, only to be fritted away by successive generations of poor management and a weakness for gambling. According to local gossip, it was only Cynthia's substantial dowry that had enabled the Copperfield family to retain their ancestral home, Bay Willow House.

Still barely able to comprehend what the reverend had told her, Lily read to the end of the letter.

My dear, I trust you to do what you feel is right with the information I have given you. I wish you a future of happiness and joy,

I remain affectionately yours
Revd Michael

With her grief over the reverend's deteriorating health and sadness over the death of her natural mother conflicting with her astonishment over the identity of her father, and distress by the fact that his indifference may have inadvertently caused Beatrice's death, Lily joined Violet in the sun-drenched kitchen. The aroma of warm crumpets filled the air and a song thrush sang lustily on the narrow windowsill.

'Charlie is well?' Violet asked, setting the plate of crumpets on the table.

'Yes, thank you,' Lily replied in surprise. She had all but forgotten about Charlie's letter. 'He is very well. He sends his regards. The other letter was from Reverend Redfern,' she said, pulling out a chair.

Violet looked up in surprise. 'Is he better? I can't wait until he returns. I'm not sure how many more Sundays I can put up with Reverend Blanchard's dull sermons.'

'He isn't any better,' Lily replied with a sad shake of her head. 'He's dying.'

'Oh, I'm sorry to hear that.' Violet sighed. 'He's a lovely man.'

Lily nodded. 'He wrote to tell me my mother – Beatrice, I mean – drowned not long after I went to live with my ma and pa.'

'Oh, Lily, I am sorry.' Violet reached across and patted Lily's hand. 'That must have come as an awful shock for you.'

'I'll be all right.' Lily shrugged, focusing her attention on the crumpets. She couldn't bring herself to tell Violet that Beatrice's death was not accidental, nor could she say anything about Sir Frederick. His wife was Violet's best customer. One day, perhaps, she would tell her but not today. For now, it would be her secret, she decided, her thoughts miles away as her crumpet cooled in a pool of melted butter.

'Nothing from your aunt, then?' Violet said, after a few moments of silence passed between them. She licked her finger, staring at Lily intently over the steel-rimmed spectacles she had recently taken to wearing.

Lily shook her head. 'I wasn't expecting anything.' Apart from catching the odd glimpse of her aunt in the market-place, she hadn't had anything to do with the woman since she'd left. Not that she was bothered. As far as Lily was concerned, Doris and Jez Elkin belonged to another life-time. In the first few days living at Violet's, she had fretted that one or other of them would turn up and drag her back home, but as time passed and her fears proved groundless, she had begun to relax. Now she rarely thought of them at all.

'You've had quite a couple of shocks this morning, Lily,' Violet said as she got up to clear the plates. 'Would you like to take some time before you come downstairs?'

'I'd prefer to be busy,' Lily replied, getting up and rolling up her sleeves. She poured the kettle of hot water into the washing-up bowl. 'Work will help take my mind off things.'

Later that afternoon, Lily was showing a selection of ribbons to Ida Wright, the blacksmith's wife, when Lady Copperfield's horse and carriage pulled up in front of the shop. In light of the reverend's revelation, Lily found herself suddenly over-whelmed with nerves. Her palms began to sweat and her heartbeat became so erratic she could barely concentrate on what Ida was saying. Hardly daring to breathe, she fixed her gaze on the door.

She watched as the footman helped Lady Copperfield down from the carriage. Removing her gloves, she swept into the shop with a rustle of silk and a waft of heady perfume. She gave the blacksmith's wife a curt nod and fixed her haughty gaze on Lily. Over time, Lady Copperfield had begrudgingly come to admire Lily's prowess as a seamstress and often, to Lily's embarrassment, asked for her over Violet.

'I need you to attend me urgently,' she said now, imperi-ously brushing aside the needs of Lily's other customer. Flustered by coming so unexpectedly face to face with her father's wife, Lily could only stare. Lady Copperfield's brow puckered. 'Whatever's the matter, girl?' she snapped irritably. 'You're staring at me like a simpleton.'

Lily swallowed hard. 'I'm sorry, Lady Copperfield,' she whispered. 'I'll be with you in just a moment.' Shooting Ida Wright an apologetic smile, she finished wrapping her purchases and handed her the brown paper bag, hands trem-bling uncontrollably.

'Right, thank you,' Ida said, drawing herself to her full height of five foot eight. 'I'll be off then.' She paused, a smile on her thin lips. 'Good afternoon to you, your ladyship. Oh, by the way. You might tell his lordship he still owes my husband for the cost of his horse's new shoes,' she remarked sharply to Lady Copperfield as she swept past her on her way to the door. 'You wouldn't want it known around town that his lordship can't pay his bills.'

'Please ask your husband to take the matter up with Sir Frederick's groom,' Lady Copperfield retorted with a haughty toss of her head, but Lily couldn't help but notice a faint blush colour her ladyship's cheeks. 'Really, how common, discussing financial transactions in public,' she complained to Lily who, having used the short exchange between the two women to compose herself, pressed her still-trembling hands onto the glass-topped counter and plastered a bright smile on her crimson face.

'How may I be of assistance?' she asked, her serene tone belying the wild fluttering in her stomach.

Lady Copperfield laid her lace gloves on the counter. Her fingers were long and tapered at the tips, Lily noted, the nails polished to a translucent pink. She waited with studied patience while Lady Copperfield studied the array of buttons glinting in the artificial light, wondering if the older woman could hear how fast her heart was beating.

Lily wondered what Lady Copperfield would think if she knew the truth, then immediately chided herself for her foolishness. She must never find out. The scandal would destroy her and, much as Lily disliked the woman, she had no wish to cause her pain. To Lily's knowledge, only two people in the world knew the truth about her parentage, aside from herself. One was dead, the other soon to be so. And while her feelings towards Sir Frederick were conflicted, she had no wish to divulge his transgressions. For now, it was her secret to keep, one she was not yet ready to share.

'I do like those pretty red buttons,' Lady Copperfield said at length, pointing to a tray of glass buttons resembling cherries. 'I think they would look very fetching on my new ruby-red gown, Lily. Do you not agree?'

'I do, your ladyship.' Lily licked her parched lips and regarded the woman opposite her. She was very elegant, proud of her noble heritage, but her beauty had been marred by bitterness and discontent. Almost fourteen years of marriage to Freddie had brought her nothing but disappointment and financial uncertainty, and her natural aloofness had conspired to turn her into a woman who came across as cold and dismissive.

'Lily,' Lady Copperfield said, as Lily laid six buttons on the counter. 'As I've said to Violet many times, you are a fine seamstress and, thus far, I have never been disappointed with your work. Dear Violet has trained you well.'

Lily bowed her head, flushing at the compliment. 'Thank you, Lady Copperfield.'

'I have mentioned my daughter to you in the past.' Lily nodded. 'Eleanor is in dire need of a new wardrobe. I would like it very much if you would agree to come to the house and measure her for some new gowns. If Violet can spare you, I should be pleased if you could come next Thursday. Shall we say two o'clock?'

'I would be willing,' Lily said, struggling to keep her voice steady as realization dawned. She had a half-sister. A tingle of excitement crept down her spine. 'I'm sure Miss Upshall can spare me for an afternoon. But would Miss Eleanor not prefer to come here?'

'Eleanor is ...' Lady Copperfield's perfect façade faltered momentarily and Lily caught a glimpse of something bordering on vulnerability in her eyes. It was so fleeting, Lily wondered whether she had imagined it. Lady Copperfield continued briskly, her mask firmly back in place. 'Eleanor suffers a great deal with her nerves and seldom leaves the house. Sir Frederick is hoping to encourage her into society this summer. She will be thirteen in the autumn and she has no social skills at all. She spends far too much time on her own, nose ensconced in a book. But that is all about to change, hence the need for new gowns.' Lady Copperfield gave a brittle laugh. 'Make a note that the bill may be sent to our London home, care of my father, Lord Lovett.'

'Of course, Lady Copperfield,' Lily replied, as Violet came through the doorway, her arms laden with fripperies for the window.

'Ah, Violet, good afternoon. I've just been discussing my daughter's needs with your little seamstress here. Eleanor is in need of a number of gowns. Could you spare Lily to come over to Bay Willow House to measure her?'

'Of course, Lady Copperfield.' Violet smiled at Lily. 'I have every faith in Lily. You can be assured Miss Eleanor will have our best attention.'

Glowing with pride at Violet's compliments, Lily's mind was on the half-sister she had yet to meet. Going by what

Lady Copperfield had said, there was about a sixteen-month age difference between Eleanor and herself. How close might they have been had they grown up together? The thought gave her a momentary pang of regret, which she swiftly pushed aside. Sir Frederick hadn't cared what became of her or her mother. Lily would never be part of the Copperfield family, so she had better nip that silly, childish fantasy in the bud right now.

She was so lost in thought it took her a moment to realize Lady Copperfield was bidding her goodbye and getting ready to take her leave.

'I beg your pardon, Lady Copperfield,' she stammered, red-faced, painfully aware of Violet's raised eyebrows. She forced a smile.

'Don't you go wool-gathering,' Lady Copperfield told her sternly, pulling on her lace gloves. 'I shan't tolerate time wasting.'

'No, ma'am.' Lily bowed her head, chastened.

'As you know from experience, Lady Copperfield,' Violet said smoothly, one hand coming to rest on Lily's shoulder, 'our Lily is as diligent as they come. I'm sure your daughter shall be perfectly satisfied with the standard of her work.'

'I wouldn't have requested you if I didn't believe you were up to the task, Lily,' Cynthia said. 'Your work is without fault, but you are young, easily distracted, perhaps?' She pursed her lips.

'I apologize for my unprofessionalism, Lady Copperfield,' Lily said politely. 'Be assured that you and your daughter will have my full attention.'

'Very well. I shall expect nothing less. You've never let me down before, Lily. So, we're agreed. Two o'clock on Thursday.'

'Yes, Lady Copperfield. Thank you.'

'Thank you, Lady Copperfield,' Violet said as she walked her to the waiting carriage. 'I appreciate your patronage.'

Lily watched them through the window, her heart in her mouth. Despite her intention to keep her new-found knowledge a secret, she couldn't quell the rising tide of excitement welling up inside her. In just two days' time she would meet her half-sister, her own flesh and blood, and she couldn't wait.

'Lily?' Violet stood in the doorway blocking the warm sunlight. 'Are you all right?' Her skirt swished across the polished boards as she looked at Lily, concern evident in her expression. 'You've been distracted all day. I noticed you unpicking your stitches earlier. That's not like you. Are you fretting over Reverend Redfern?' Her expression softened. 'Of course you are. We're all very fond of him.' She gave Lily's shoulder a comforting pat. 'Have an early night. We're over the worst of the rush. I'll make us both a mug of hot milk later. That should help you sleep.'

Lily followed Violet into the back room. She disliked withholding the truth from her friend but how could she tell her that her best customer was the wife of Lily's biological father? Lily could hardly believe it herself. Violet wasn't a gossip by any means, but Blandford was a relatively small town and rumours, once started, spread like wildfire. The merest unguarded comment could cause a huge scandal. No, Lily determined as she climbed the stairs to her room a short while later, candlelight flickering on the walls. She would just have to keep her secret, at least for the moment. But she couldn't deny how much she was looking forward to meeting her half-sister, Eleanor. She just hoped her emotions wouldn't betray her.

CHAPTER TWELVE

Lily stood hesitantly between two weathered stone pillars and gazed up at Bay Willow House. Built of buttery Cotswold stone, it was one of the few buildings to have escaped the fire of 1731. It had been extended over the years and its many windows reflected the afternoon sunlight. Two bay willow trees stood sentinel on either side of the driveway, their leafy boughs casting dappled shade over a manicured lawn, dotted with small shrubs and beds of vibrant early-summer flowers.

It would have been an imposing sight for the young seamstress anyway, but the added knowledge that she was related to two of the people residing inside caused her heart to flutter against her ribcage like a trapped moth.

The wrought-iron gates had been left open and there were deep ruts in the gravel where carriage wheels had recently passed through. Apprehensive about what her reaction to meeting Eleanor might be, Lily took a deep breath to steady her nerves and started slowly up the drive.

The crunch of her shoes sounding abnormally loud in her ears, Lily followed the short driveway until it opened up into a wide turning circle with a rather grand stone fountain in its centre. A moss-covered water nymph poured a perpetual trickle of water from her jar into water the colour of mint sauce, a thick layer of algae floating on its surface.

Sweeping steps led up to a wide oak front door, flanked on either side by bay windows. Lily paused for a moment, wondering how it would feel to walk up those steps as one of the family. She glanced around at the tranquil grounds, the rolling, sheep-dotted hills beyond, stunned with awe that she was related to such wealth.

A rook flying overhead let out a sharp cry and she started guiltily, glancing around in the hope that no one was watching her from one of the many windows. Hastily, the handle of her workbasket tucked firmly in the crook of her elbow, she hurried along the cracked concrete path by the side of the house to the servants' entrance around the back. The door was ajar and she could hear voices.

'Hello?' she called in a small voice, rapping on the door. Getting no response, she pushed the door open and peered nervously into a large kitchen. The slate floor was scuffed with footprints. Bunches of drying herbs and copper pots and pans hung from a rack suspended from the high ceiling.

'Good afternoon. Are you the dressmaker?' A plump, dark-haired woman of late middle-age stirring a pot of something savoury smiled at Lily over her broad shoulder.

'Yes, ma'am. I'm Lily,' she replied, hovering on the threshold.

'Well, don't stand on ceremony, child. Come on in. I'm Mrs White, the housekeeper.' She regarded Lily with a quizzical frown. 'Have we met before? Your face looks very familiar.'

'I don't think so, ma'am.' Lily swallowed self-consciously. It struck her suddenly that this must be the housekeeper whose lack of compassion had sent her mother to the workhouse. Had she recognized Beatrice in Lily? Was that why the woman couldn't quite meet Lily's gaze? 'Perhaps you've seen me around town,' she offered.

'That's probably it,' Ada White agreed thoughtfully. An aging black and white mongrel padded into the kitchen and wandered over to sniff Lily's skirts. It was followed by a dark-haired man with a weather-beaten complexion wearing a homespun shirt and trousers. He stopped short at the sight of Lily standing in the middle of the kitchen stroking his dog, and shot Ada a questioning glance. So, he had noticed it too, Ada mused. She quickly said: 'Harry, this is Lady Copperfield's dressmaker, Miss Lily. Harry tends the grounds here,' she told Lily.

'Pleased to meet you, Harry,' Lily said.

'Afternoon, miss.' Harry doffed his cap.

'Lady Copperfield and Miss Eleanor are in the drawing room,' Ada said, wiping her hands on her starched-white apron. 'I'll take you to them.'

'Thank you, Mrs White.'

Harry's curious gaze followed Lily as she hastened after Ada. The housekeeper led her down a narrow, dimly lit corridor and up a flight of concrete steps, worn smooth by time and use, and along another corridor, well lit and thickly carpeted this time. Portraits of strait-laced ladies and pompous-looking gentlemen lined the papered walls.

'Her ladyship is through here,' Ada said, her voice low as she indicated a partially open door. At the end of the corridor was a wide staircase sweeping up to a galleried landing. Ada rapped softly on the door and, at the curt 'come' stepped into the room. 'Your dressmaker is here, Lady Copperfield,' she said.

'Excellently prompt,' Lily heard Lady Copperfield say. 'Show her in, Mrs White.'

Ada inclined her head and Lily, feeling as though her heart might explode with nerves, entered the drawing room.

She barely noticed the pale cream and green panelled walls and rich emerald-green curtains, nor the large bay window overlooking the front garden. She didn't register the squirrel scampering across the dappled lawn or the ornate white-marble fireplace above which hung an impressive watercolour depicting the Battle of Waterloo. Nor the vase of freshly cut flowers in the grate that gave off a heady perfume. Instead, her attention was fixed on the petite, dark-haired girl perched primly on an armchair, an open book upside down on her lap. Her complexion was peaky, as if she didn't spend much time out of doors. Despite the dark hair and walnut-coloured eyes, the similarity between the two girls' facial features was uncanny and Lily could hardly breathe. She glanced around in panic. Surely Lady Copperfield must notice?

'Lily, thank you for coming,' Lady Copperfield said placidly, seemingly oblivious to the resemblance between the two girls. 'Allow me to introduce my daughter, Miss Eleanor.'

'Pleased to meet you, Lily,' Eleanor responded shyly, her wan cheeks flooding with colour.

'Likewise, Miss Eleanor,' Lily replied breathlessly.

Although Lily had worked out that her half-sister was only a year and four months younger than herself, Eleanor spoke like a girl of a much younger age. From her manner and shyness, it was clear Eleanor's existence was quite insular and Lily found herself feeling sorry for her younger half-sister, despite her apparently comfortable surroundings.

'I'll ring for tea and then we'll go upstairs,' Lady Copperfield said, her wide skirts sweeping across the richly hued carpet. At that moment Ada reappeared in the doorway, her expression troubled.

'Oh, Mrs White, I was about to ring for you. Would you have a pot of tea sent up to Miss Eleanor's room, please?'

'Yes, ma'am.' Ada bit her lip. 'But first, ma'am, a Mr Philips is here to see you.' The colour rose in Cynthia's cheeks and she looked momentarily flustered before she stepped out of the room, pulling the door to behind her.

Left alone in the drawing room, Lily regarded Eleanor with intense scrutiny, which Eleanor returned with mild curiosity.

'I'm sorry,' Eleanor said. 'Mama may be some time. It's another creditor demanding payment, I shouldn't wonder.' She closed her book and got to her feet, going over to the window. A carriage was passing the front of the house, two large wolfhounds bounding alongside it. 'I love Papa dearly,' she said, watching and delighting in the way the sunlight was dancing on the grass. 'But he can be a bit careless about money. He drives Mama to distraction.'

Absorbing this nugget of information about her father, Lily couldn't help but wonder how Eleanor would feel should she learn of her father's treatment of Lily's mother. She exhaled slowly, sure Eleanor must be able sense her nervousness. She couldn't take her eyes off the girl. Here was her sister, in the flesh. They shared the same blood, the same father.

Eleanor turned from the window, frowning slightly, her already flushed cheeks darkening under Lily's blatant scrutiny.

'I know this will sound strange,' she said, 'but I feel as though I already know you. Have we met before?'

Lily cleared her throat, chiding herself for her unprofessionalism. 'I don't believe so, miss,' she replied with a nervous laugh. Her gaze alighted on the book Eleanor clasped against her chest. 'Do you enjoy reading?'

Eleanor nodded. 'Yes. I read a lot. Whatever I can get my hands on.' She sat down and picked up her book, absentmindedly stroking the leather cover with her index finger. 'My mother thinks I spend too much of my time closeted away with my books. She'd prefer me to be a social butterfly like her.'

'I enjoy reading too,' Lily said with a smile. 'Though I rarely get the time.'

'We have an extensive library here,' Eleanor said, her sudden smile seeming to brighten the room. 'You are welcome to borrow anything you like. I'm sure Mama and Papa wouldn't mind.'

'That is very kind. Thank you. Your father is away from home?' Lily asked in as casual a tone as she could muster.

'He has business in Dorchester,' Eleanor replied. 'We're expecting him home tomorrow.'

Lily wasn't sure whether to feel relieved or disappointed.

'Which authors do you enjoy?' Eleanor asked. Both girls were pleased to discover that they shared a liking for the novels of the Brontë sisters, *Jane Eyre* being a particular favourite, as well as the works of Jane Austen and Charles Dickens, and they were enjoying an animated conversation when Lady Copperfield returned to the drawing room, her neck flushed an ugly turkey red, her expression thunderous.

'I'm sure Lily is far too busy to waste her time reading novels,' she snapped, catching the drift of the conversation. 'Shall we go upstairs?' With an angry swish of her skirts, Lady Copperfield turned on her heel. 'You may take Miss Eleanor's measurements while we discuss her requirements,' she told Lily as she led the way up the sweeping staircase, Lily trailing behind with her workbasket. She stared in awe at the handsome tapestries and paintings that covered the gallery walls, her footsteps silent on the plush red carpet.

She followed Lady Copperfield and Eleanor into a large, airy bedroom. It was tastefully decorated in blues, creams and gold. The window overlooked rolling farmland. Through the trees, Lily caught a glimpse of the River Stour meandering through the Dorset countryside. Tufts of wispy white clouds drifted lazily across an azure sky.

'This is a beautiful room, Miss Eleanor,' Lily said admiringly, as she opened her work basket to retrieve her tape measure.

'Thank you.' Eleanor smiled shyly. 'This is my favourite place to read,' she said, indicating the wide window seat piled high with cushions. It was bathed in sunlight and Lily could understand why Eleanor would be so fond of the spot.

'We will be spending the winter months at our townhouse in London,' Lady Copperfield said, perching on the edge of Eleanor's bed. She smoothed the blue and cream floral-patterned counterpane with her long fingers, her gold rings sparkling in the sunlight streaming in through the glass. 'While we're there, we intend to spend much of our time socializing so Miss Eleanor will need a more sophisticated wardrobe.'

'I don't know why I can't just wear the dresses I already have, Mama,' Eleanor said, her arms wrapped around her body as she stood nervously in the middle of the room, wearing only her shift. She reluctantly raised her arms so Lily could measure her chest. 'I have more than enough clothes.'

'You're still so young, Eleanor,' her mother sighed. 'The dresses you wear now are suitable for a country estate, but you'll find the children of our London friends will be much more fashionably turned out.'

Eleanor rolled her eyes and Lily bit her lip in an attempt not to laugh. Secretly she agreed with Eleanor. The pale pink sprigged dress she had been wearing, and which was now flung across a chair, to Lily's mind, was exquisite. In her time as a dressmaker's apprentice, Lily had grown used to the habits of her more well-to-do clients for discarding their perfectly good dresses and gowns in order to replace them with the season's latest must-have fashions.

'Miss Upshall has sent some lovely patterns, Lady Copperfield,' Lily said, scribbling her measurements in her little notebook as Ada appeared with the tea tray. 'I'm sure you'll find them very suitable.'

Ada set the tray on the padded velvet lid of the blue and cream ottoman at the foot of Eleanor's bed.

'Thank you, Mrs White.' Lady Copperfield waved the housekeeper away with a flick of her wrist and turned back to her daughter. 'It is so important to make the right impression, Eleanor. You'll understand when you're older.

'I was the belle of the ball when I was just a few years older than you are now,' Lady Copperfield continued blithely. 'My dance card was always full.' She gave a theatrical sigh and looked at Eleanor long and hard down her nose. 'I do hope you will try to fit in, dear.' She picked up a book from the small pile on Eleanor's nightstand and looked at it disparagingly. 'We don't want our London friends thinking you dull. Bookishness is never an attractive trait in a girl.'

Eleanor remained silent but Lily could see how much her mother's words pained her.

'Do you spend winter in London every year?' she asked Eleanor once Lady Copperfield had left them to go over the household accounts with Ada.

Eleanor shook her head. 'Mama and Papa do while I remain here with my governess.' She pulled her dress over her head and turned her back to Lily whose nimble fingers made quick work of the intricate fastenings.

'You spend Christmas here alone?' Lily was appalled. Merry Christmases had been few and far between in Lily's life, but she had imagined that for a family like the Copperfields, the season would be one of lavish festivity. The thought of her half-sister alone on Christmas Day moved her to pity.

'It isn't so bad,' Eleanor said with a small, sad smile. 'Miss Clarke, my governess, comes to stay and I have Mrs White and dear Harry for company. Miss Clarke always makes sure to order a tree, which we decorate on Christmas Eve. Harry's brilliant at decorating the place with holly and mistletoe, and Mama and Papa always send presents, of course. Mrs White cooks a splendid dinner and afterwards we play charades and sing carols in the parlour. Even Harry joins in with the singing, though he is completely tone deaf.' Eleanor's smile brightened at the memory.

'It sounds a lot of fun,' Lily said, secretly thinking that a Christmas spent with the household staff sounded a better prospect than one spent with the starchy Lady Copperfield and her, presumably, equally staid London relatives. She rolled up her tape measure and slipped it back inside her basket.

'It was,' Eleanor said with a sigh, the smile slipping away. 'But now Miss Clarke is gone to another post and I am to accompany my parents to our London home for the whole five months.'

'When do you leave?' Lily asked, frantically calculating in her mind the amount of time she would need to complete Eleanor's new wardrobe.

'The end of October,' her sister replied. Lily heaved a sigh of relief. That gave her nigh on five months.

'Ah, you've finished measuring up.' Lady Copperfield appeared in the doorway, looking slightly harassed. 'Now we can discuss styles and colours. Lily, we will trust your professional eye. What would you suggest?'

Almost two hours later, Lily made her way down the lane that led back towards the town. The sun was still warm and the hedgerows were alive with birdsong. The verges were thick with frothy cow parsley and nettles. Lambs bleated in the distance. She walked slowly, enjoying the sun's warmth on her upturned face, her basket tucked in the crook of her elbow.

Already she felt a connection with Eleanor and she was elated that her sister seemed to have felt it too. Though she would never dare divulge Sir Frederick's secret, she couldn't help but wish she could confide in Eleanor. It was a dream that could never be realized, of course. The revelation would break Eleanor's heart, not to mention destroying the family's name. No, it must be her secret.

'It's only me,' Lily called out as she entered the shop. Violet appeared from between the curtains.

'How did you get on?'

'Lady Copperfield is insisting Miss Eleanor has an entire new wardrobe. Here's the list of gowns she will need.'

While Violet perused her hastily scribbled notes, Lily removed her bonnet and fluffed up her hair. 'Miss Eleanor is very shy so Lady Copperfield would appreciate it if I could do as many of the fittings as possible at the house. She would be happy to send the carriage for me.'

'That's very generous of her,' Violet approved with a smile. 'I suppose that will be all right, at least until the gowns are in the final stages of completion. When does Lady Copperfield require the gowns by?'

Lily pulled a face. 'They leave for London at the end of October.'

'Just under five months.' Violet pursed her lips, her brows puckering over the bridge of her nose. 'It's certainly doable.' She put her hands on her hips. 'What with Lady Copperfield's new gowns and the rest of our commissions, we'll certainly be burning the candle at both ends.'

'I'd better get to work then,' Lily said with a grin.

CHAPTER THIRTEEN

'Good morning, Sir Frederick.' Ada set the coffee pot on the table.

'Morning, Mrs White.' Sir Frederick lowered his copy of *The Times*. 'Just coffee this morning. I have a mid-morning meeting with my accountant, which will no doubt lead to an early lunch.' He patted his portly stomach. 'And my lovely lady wife is insisting I shed a few pounds before we leave for London. Has she risen yet?'

'Yes, sir. Lady Copperfield and Miss Eleanor are in the drawing room. The dressmaker is expected very shortly.'

'I see.' Sir Frederick shook out the newspaper. 'Very well. I shan't disturb them. Please tell Lady Copperfield I will be leaving shortly for my appointment and I'll see her on my return.'

'Yes, sir.'

He watched Ada retreat from the dining room and leaned back in his chair. Early autumn sunshine streamed in through the open French windows. The dew-soaked garden sparkled in the hazy morning light. Already the trees were turning shades of burnished bronze, crimson and gold. The cool morning breeze ruffled the pages of Sir Frederick's newspaper and lifted the edges of the lace-trimmed ivory damask tablecloth. The sky was a clear blue. It was the sort of autumn day he enjoyed, usually.

He sighed, folded his newspaper and, laying it aside, reached for his coffee cup. The rich aroma did little to lift his spirits. He was dreading having to break the news to Cynthia, again, that the Copperfield finances were in dire straits. It wasn't his fault. Granted, he wasn't very good at managing money, but the rot had started with his father and grandfather before him. Both had proved to be bad managers and prolific gamblers, a habit, thank God, in which he had never indulged. It was common knowledge that it was Cynthia's money that had saved the Copperfield family from financial embarrassment many times and now the global depression had taken its toll, Copperfield interests had plummeted. Should his father-in-law refuse to bail them out this time, they would be ruined. The thought of having to go cap in hand, once again, to his father-in-law kept him up at night. His features had turned haggard, the dark circles under his eyes a testimony to the long hours spent tossing and turning, trying to find a way to resolve the situation that wouldn't involve the pompous Lord Lovett. Sir Frederick disliked the man intensely and was all too aware the feeling was entirely mutual. The two men had barely exchanged a civil word in years.

And now, as if things weren't bad enough, his wife was frittering away a fortune on a fancy new wardrobe for Eleanor. How many gowns did one girl need? Well, Lord Lovett could damned well foot the bill.

The coffee burned his lips. His ulcer throbbed painfully in the well of his stomach as the dread of his forthcoming meeting rose like bile in his throat. He gazed desolately across the grounds. As he watched Harry pottering about in the far corner of the garden, a rake slung over one shoulder and accompanied, as ever, by his faithful dog Sky, it occurred to him that he quite envied the man. He'd much rather be out there tending the garden than having to endure another humiliating meeting with his accountant.

'Lily! Lily, wait!' Lily had finished loading the cart and was halfway down the street when she realized someone was calling after her. It was a gorgeous autumn morning and the market was already bustling. Sheep bleated in the nearby pens and a drover was coming up the road, driving a herd of young bulls, their hoofs churning up the dust into a swirling, choking cloud.

Holding her handkerchief in front of her nose, Lily turned to see Reverend Redfern's old housekeeper Mrs Fudge hurrying towards her. She was dressed in black and one look at her face, bleached of all colour, told Lily all she needed to know. She jumped down from the cart, her heart sinking like a stone as her throat closed.

'Oh, Lily,' Mrs Fudge panted. The dust was thinning now as the cattle moved further up the street, their bellowing drowning out the shouts of the market traders. 'I was just coming to see you.'

Not trusting herself to speak, Lily merely nodded. Mrs Fudge placed a black-gloved hand on Lily's arm. 'My dear, I'm so sorry. We received word at the vicarage this morning. The reverend passed away two days ago.'

Lily let out a sob. The reverend had been such a constant in her life. He had been a link to her past, to Beatrice, and now he was gone.

'I know he meant a lot to you, love,' May said, her own eyes suspiciously bright.

'Will there be a funeral?' Lily asked, endeavouring to compose herself.

'There will.' Mrs Fudge nodded. 'It's in Buxton. I'm going up on the train. I've a cousin I can stay with overnight. You're welcome to come with me if Violet can spare you?'

'Thank you, Mrs Fudge. I'd like that.'

Lily stood for a moment, staring after the housekeeper's retreating figure, trying to regain her composure. Sad as she was that Reverend Redfern was gone, she tried to find a measure of comfort in the thought that his suffering was over. Going to the funeral too would go some way to alleviating her distress.

The church clock chimed the quarter-hour and she balked. She had better not be late for Lady Copperfield. Belle, Violet's docile Welsh pony, pawed the ground as if to hurry her.

Settling herself on the rickety seat, Lily urged Belle through the crowds, down the street and around the corner. They made good progress, the noise of the market receding as they left the town behind.

As she guided Belle along the shady lane, her sadness over the vicar's passing was tempered somewhat by the prospect of seeing Eleanor again. She had been calling on Eleanor weekly for the past three and a half months and, in spite of her conflicting emotions surrounding Sir Frederick, Lily had grown very fond of her younger half-sister. She had been pleased to find that, away from her captious mother's presence, Eleanor was animated and chatty. Despite the vast difference in their circumstances, they found they had much in common. As well as their shared love of reading, they enjoyed a similar taste in music and poetry.

Eleanor had confided in Lily how lonely she was for company her own age, yet how terrified she was by the seemingly confident, assured girls of her parents' social circle. In return Lily had told her about Martha and Jim, and Charlie, and her life with her aunt and Jez. She said nothing about Beatrice, only revealing that her birth mother had died when Lily was a baby. Over time, their relationship had blossomed into a deep and lasting friendship.

Unable to procrastinate any longer, Sir Frederick drew his gaze away from the French windows and got wearily to his feet, catching sight of his reflection in the oval, gilt-edged mirror hanging on the wall. At thirty-three, he could acknowledge that he was still an attractive man. Stress over his precarious finances had flecked his dark hair prematurely grey, giving him a somewhat distinguished air, and his face still retained the remnants of a summer tan. He held himself erect, sucking in his slight paunch as he adjusted the cuffs of his pristine white shirt, and reached for his jacket.

He could hear his wife and daughter's voices emanating from the drawing room and his spirits sank even further as he contemplated the cost of the silk and satin, the ribbon and lace that would make up the new gowns his wife insisted upon. As if the pair of them hadn't enough dresses between them to clothe an entire village.

Wanting to avoid as long as possible the inevitable look of disappointment in his wife's eyes when he told her of their financial problems, he slipped past the drawing room. Grabbing his hat and coat, he quietly opened the front door and stepped outside, greeting his driver, Jenkins, with a heartiness he did not feel.

'The accountants on Whitecliff Mill Street, please, Jenkins.'

'Yes, sir.' Jenkins closed the carriage door and climbed up onto the seat. The bay mare set off at a frisky pace, but they had barely gone a few paces when Jenkins had to rein the mare in.

'What's the hold-up?' Sir Frederick snapped irritably, leaning out of the carriage window. A plump, grey pony was coming up the drive, pulling a small cart driven by a young woman in a green bonnet and cloak. Sir Frederick's first thought was that she was a gypsy come to sell her wares to the staff, but there was something about her . . .

As the cart approached, he felt his breathing quicken. *Bea?* He blinked and shook his head. No, of course it couldn't be Bea.

The cart drew alongside. 'Thank you, sir,' he heard the girl say to Jenkins. As she drew level to his window, Sir Frederick felt the blood drain from his face. The girl appraised him coolly, her green eyes seeming to reach deep into him in a way that left him totally disconcerted.

'Who are you?' he croaked. 'What do you want?'

Lily's heart raced as she looked into the hazel eyes of her father. He was good-looking, she had to admit. She could see why a young girl like her mother would fall for him.

'I'm the dressmaker, sir,' she replied, her cool tone belying the emotions raging within her. 'I've brought Miss Eleanor's gowns for a fitting.'

'Ah, yes, of course.' Sir Frederick inclined his head. He was fighting to regain his composure as all sorts of memories surfaced. Memories that were best left buried and forgotten. 'Pleased to make your acquaintance, Miss . . .?'

'Hayter. Lily Hayter, sir.'

Sir Frederick nodded. 'You must excuse me. I'm late for an appointment.' He tapped the side of the carriage. 'Drive on, Jenkins. Drive on.'

It was only once the carriage had cleared the drive and they were travelling swiftly down the lane, that his rapidly beating heart began to slow.

Lily stared after the departing carriage in consternation. She was trembling like a leaf. This was the man who had rejected her and her mother. The man who was responsible for her mother's untimely death, and yet, she couldn't help feeling strangely drawn to him. His blood flowed in her veins, after all.

'Lily, what are you doing?' Hearing her half-sister's voice, Lily turned and waved. Eleanor stood on the front steps, a blue shawl over her shoulders to ward off the morning chill. Lily couldn't speak. He had recognized her, of that much she was sure. She had seen it in his eyes, a mixture of shock and fear. For one brief moment it had seemed as though he might say something, but then the shutters had come slamming down and the connection had been lost.

'Come on, Lily,' Eleanor chided her with mock impatience. 'Mama is eager to see my gowns before her guests arrive.'

'I'm sorry, Miss Eleanor,' Lily apologized. 'Please tell Lady Copperfield I shall be there directly.'

Along with Harry and Ada, she unloaded the carefully wrapped gowns from the cart.

'No, Lily,' Eleanor admonished her as Lily made to follow Ada and Harry towards the side of the house. 'This way.'

Aware of Ada's frown of disapproval, Lily hesitated.

'Come on, Lily,' Eleanor hurried her. 'Mama is waiting.'

'You go, miss,' Harry said, earning himself a sharp glance from Ada. 'We'll carry the gowns upstairs.'

Blushing under the housekeeper's frosty glare, Lily thanked him and ran up the steps to where Eleanor was waiting for her.

Conscious as she was that it was only Eleanor's blatant disregard for propriety that enabled her to enter the house through the front door, Lily couldn't help the tingle that ran down her spine as she crossed the threshold. This was her family home, came the incredulous thought as she gazed up at the paintings adorning the walls. Was it possible these sober-looking gentlemen were her ancestors?

'Mama, Lily is here with my gowns,' Eleanor called out, interrupting Lily's musings, and leading the way into her airy bedroom as Harry and a tight-lipped Ada approached from the other direction, their arms full of gowns, which they laid gently across the bed.

'Good morning, Lily.' Lady Copperfield swept into the room. She was wearing one of Lily's creations, an elegant day dress of pale green with white lace trim at the collar and cuffs. 'Shall we start with the peach silk?' she said, smiling at Eleanor. 'I think the colour will suit your complexion perfectly.'

'Mama has friends coming for luncheon today,' Eleanor said some time later, perching on the bed as Lily repacked the gowns in their protective coverings. 'Would you like to have luncheon with me?' she asked hopefully.

'I'm sure Lily will be required back at Violet's as soon as she is done here,' Lady Copperfield interjected, with a slight raise of her brows. Initially she had been concerned that Eleanor was coming to rely on her growing friendship with Lily far too much, but recently, she had come to realize that Lily's company seemed to be doing Eleanor the world of good and, for the time being at least, Lady Copperfield was content to allow the friendship to continue – although perhaps not to the extent of inviting the girl for luncheon.

Lily took the hint. 'I'm sorry,' she said, trying not to notice Eleanor's crestfallen expression. 'Lady Copperfield is quite right. There is a lot of work to be done. Miss Upshall will be needing my help.' She also needed to be away from this house, she mused as she carefully laid Eleanor's midnight-blue silk in tissue paper.

How many times had Beatrice walked up and down these stairs? she wondered, as she and Ada carried the gowns down the back stairs to the kitchen. Eleanor followed, nursing her disappointment that instead of a jolly luncheon with her friend, she would be dining in the kitchen with Mrs White and Harry.

'Until next week, then, Miss Eleanor,' Lily said, holding Belle's bridle as they said their goodbyes.

'I look forward to your visits so much,' Eleanor said. 'I shall miss you dreadfully when we go to London.'

'As I shall miss you,' Lily responded truthfully. Though it would be a relief not to have to worry about running into their father, she mused.

Lily gently steered Belle down the driveway and into the lane, contemplating how Eleanor had certainly come out of her shell over the past three and a half months. She still suffered from chronic shyness around strangers, however, and she couldn't help wondering how her book-loving, sweet, shy half-sister would fare amidst the hustle and bustle of London's social scene.

★ ★ ★

'I don't want that girl coming to the house anymore.'

'I beg your pardon?' Cynthia said, turning her cool gaze to meet her husband's in the dressing table mirror as he stood in the doorway. She raised her brows questioningly. He had been morose throughout dinner, consuming far more red wine than usual which accounted for the high colour in his cheeks.

'The red-haired girl. She's your dressmaker, I believe.'

Cynthia's brow furrowed. She ran a brush through her hair. Freed from its pins, it hung in thick curls over her shoulders.

'Lily? Why ever not?' She fingered the lace-trimmed collar of her nightgown, her expression bemused.

Sir Frederick ran a hand over his face. He'd had a bad day. Seeing the girl had set him on edge and he'd arrived at the accountants with his mind in turmoil. The girl wasn't Bea, of course she wasn't, but there could be no doubt that she was her daughter. His daughter.

He groaned inwardly as he recalled the expression on Bea's face when she had told him she was expecting. She had looked so frightened yet she had trusted him to do the right thing. And he had let her down, badly. He rubbed his throbbing temples, as guilt washed over him like a tidal wave. It was because of his cowardice that his sweet, loving Bea had ended her life. Reverend Redfern's letter had come out of the blue, shocking in its content. Reading between the lines, Sir Frederick had been left in no doubt the reverend held him entirely responsible for Bea's tragic end. And quite rightly so. He would carry the shame and remorse for the rest of his life.

He hadn't been expecting his meeting to go well but, still reeling from the shock of coming face to face with Lily, he had barely been able to concentrate at all. Doom-mongering, that's all Messrs Smith and Lloyd were good for with their dire warnings and predictions. All of which he'd brushed aside with his usual fake bonhomie. He now faced the unpleasant task of persuading Cynthia to ask her father for the much-needed funds.

'Eleanor is becoming too dependent on this girl. She's all she talks about,' he said now. Painfully aware of his wife's scrutiny, he dropped his gaze, not wanting her to see the guilt in his eyes. For it was guilt. He was torn between wanting a relationship with his daughter, and despising her for bringing his guilt and remorse to the surface. His was a life filled with regrets, but losing Bea had been, by far, the biggest.

'I agree we need to encourage Eleanor to develop friendships among girls of her own social standing,' Lady Copperfield said. 'I have heard from our London friends. There will be parties galore. Eleanor will have her fill of society. But you have to admit, she does seem to have grown in confidence since she's become friendly with Lily.'

'Mrs White tells me the two of them are becoming as close as sisters.' Sir Frederick walked over to the bed and sat down. He didn't dare add that the housekeeper's words, said with more than a hint of a mocking, knowing smile, had sent a cold shiver of dread down his spine. He rubbed his hand over his face. He couldn't have Lily in the house. Her presence was far too unsettling. He didn't trust himself around her.

'Eleanor is very fond of Lily,' Lady Copperfield said, continuing to administer the one hundred strokes to her hair just as she had done ever since she was a little girl on her nanny's knee. 'We shall be leaving for London in just under two months,' she appeased him. 'By the time we return in the spring, Lily will be quite forgotten.'

'What if we were to leave sooner?' Sir Frederick suggested. 'We could spend more time with your parents.'

Lady Copperfield's heart dropped. 'Oh, Freddie,' she sighed, despair settling like a stone in the pit of her stomach. 'Are you in trouble again?'

'It's affecting everyone, my dear,' Sir Frederick said, going quickly to her side. 'I'm not the only businessman in this situation. If you can just persuade your father to release a little more of your inheritance, we can ride out this difficult period until things pick up again.'

'Will Violet be paid for Eleanor's new gowns?' she asked, her tone as hard as steel.

'Certainly,' Sir Frederick replied, emphatically. 'Just as soon as you persuade your father to help us out.' He got to his feet. 'We'll be leaving for London on the Monday after next. The sooner you speak to your father, the sooner we will be able to discharge our bills.'

With that he turned on his heel and left the room, leaving his wife fuming with exasperation.

CHAPTER FOURTEEN

A young boy brought the message early the following morning. Lily had just set the tea kettle on to boil when she heard the knock. Still in her nightgown, she grabbed her shawl and hurried down the stairs, the cool air nipping at her toes.

'Morning, miss.' The boy who stood on the threshold was tall and tousle-haired. He held his tweed cap in his hand, a saucy grin on his freckled face. 'Message from the big house, miss.'

'Thank you.' Lily took the sealed envelope, frowning as she closed the door and retraced her steps upstairs.

'Who was that at this hour?' Violet asked, stifling a yawn as she poured milk into the waiting teacups.

'A message from Lady Copperfield. It's addressed to you.'

Violet took the note and unfolded it.

'Well,' she said, passing it across the table. 'The family are leaving for London a week on Monday. Lady Copperfield wants the gowns by Friday at the latest.'

'So soon?' Lily read the note with dismay. She had been looking forward to spending a few more weeks in Eleanor's company.

'We're more than able to deliver the order in time,' Violet assured her, mistaking Lily's crestfallen expression for concern at the sudden urgency. 'For once, we're beforehand.' She handed Lily her tea and turned to stir the porridge bubbling away on the stove top. 'As long as we prioritize our work in order of urgency, we shall manage perfectly well.'

It seemed to Lily that she did nothing but sew and cut and stitch the entire week. They worked late into the evening, squinting at the tiny stitches in the lantern light until Lily's shoulders ached and her eyes burned. Her fingers throbbed where she had pricked them with her needle. But by mid-afternoon on Friday the gowns were ready for delivery.

The sun was low in the sky by the time Lily drove the small cart through the gate posts of Bay Willow House and up the driveway. The smell of woodsmoke and damp leaves hung heavily on the cool, crisp air. The grounds were shrouded in shadow and silent but for the baleful cawing of a solitary crow.

'Good evening, Miss Lily.' Harry rounded the side of the house as Lily clambered down from the springy seat.

'Good evening, Harry. I've brought the last of Lady Copperfield's order.' She indicated the well-wrapped bundles in the back of the wooden cart, rubbing her hands together in an attempt to warm them. Despite her gloves, her fingers were cold and stiff from clutching the reins.

'I'll help you carry these indoors, miss. It's a chilly evening. Will you come into the kitchen for a warm drink?'

'Thank you, no,' Lily declined reluctantly, gazing up at the approaching night. 'Miss Upshall will worry if I'm not home before dark.'

'Lily! Lily!' At that moment, the massive front door was flung open and Eleanor came hurrying down the broad steps, holding her rustling skirts above her ankles. She ran across the gravel, her grin lighting up her face. 'Oh, Lily, I thought I should have to go to London without seeing you again.'

'It hasn't been that long since I last saw you,' Lily teased. 'Barely a week.'

'I know, but I've missed you. Come, walk with me.' She shot Harry an apologetic glance. 'Would you mind if Lily and I walked for a while?'

'Not at all, miss,' Harry replied with a slight nod, a wry smile on his face. 'It's good to see you enjoying a bit of company.' He indicated the gate with a flick of his hand. 'You've got about twenty minutes before Sir Frederick and Lady Copperfield return home.' He nodded to Lily. 'I'll take these upstairs, miss.'

'Yes, please, Harry,' Eleanor replied. 'Mrs White is packing my trunk as we speak.'

Feeling a little guilty at leaving Harry to unpack the gowns and carry them upstairs alone, Lily allowed Eleanor to tuck her hand in the crook of her elbow and lead her across the damp lawn.

'Papa is behaving so strangely,' Eleanor complained to Lily. 'He's decided I'm spending too much time in your company, which is why he is whisking us off to London so much earlier than planned.'

Lily's stomach contracted with unease. Did Sir Frederick feel so threatened by her presence? Did he suspect that Lily was aware of who she was?

'I honestly never thought of Papa as a snob before. Mama, yes, but not Papa,' Eleanor said, letting go of Lily's arm to stoop and pick up a large brown conker that had fallen from the tree in the lane. She wiped away the dew with her hand and slipped it into her pocket. 'Mrs White likes to put conkers around the house,' she explained, stopping to gather up several more. 'She claims they keep spiders at bay.'

'Does it work?' Lily asked, making an effort to keep her tone light. She was going to miss Eleanor so much.

Eleanor laughed in response to Lily's question. 'Mrs White swears by it.' She stopped walking to look into Lily's eyes. 'Will you write to me, Lily? I shall write to you often. Spring will be here before we know it. Time will fly, you'll see.' Her eyes swam with tears and Lily felt her heart contract.

'I shall miss you, Miss Eleanor,' she said truthfully. Spring was months away and she couldn't help but worry that Eleanor might forget her amidst the excitement of London life, especially as it appeared Sir Frederick would do his best to discourage the friendship.

'And I you,' Eleanor sighed. 'I'm dreading London. Mama said I am socially inept and I need to make more of an effort.' She sighed. 'I wish I could stay here with Mrs White and Harry instead. Then you could visit every day. I feel at ease with you, Lily. As though I've known you all my life. Isn't that strange?'

Lily swallowed the lump in her throat. 'It's not strange at all, Miss Eleanor,' she said as they turned back towards the house. 'I feel the same way.'

The hills were shrouded in mist, the western sky a haze of colour. A flock of geese honked overhead, heading for the river to roost. Wheels crunched on the gravel; Harry was bringing the empty cart around.

Eleanor gripped Lily's arm. 'Please promise you'll write?'

'Of course I'll write, Miss Eleanor, though what news I shall have to tell I can't imagine. Our life here will seem pretty boring compared to London.'

'I'm sure everyone there will think me terribly dull,' Eleanor said, her brow creased in an anxious frown. 'I'm no good at talking to strangers.'

'No, they won't,' Lily assured her fervently. 'You chatter all the time. I don't think you're at all dull, and neither will anyone else.'

'I hope so,' Eleanor replied despondently, chewing her bottom lip.

'Once you get to know them, you'll be fine,' Lily assured her firmly. 'Just think of all the things you'll get to see: Buckingham Palace, Big Ben, the Christmas tree in Trafalgar

Square … Oh, Miss Eleanor, you'll have a wonderful time,' Lily said wistfully, trying but not quite succeeding in keeping the envy from her voice.

'I wish you were coming with me,' Eleanor said with a sigh. 'I could put up with anything if you were with me.' She shivered, clutching her cloak tighter around her shoulders.

'I am travelling north tomorrow, with Miss Fudge from the rectory. It is Reverend Redfern's funeral.' She noticed Eleanor's teeth were chattering. 'You're getting cold, Miss Eleanor. You must return to the house.' The shadows were lengthening and it had grown noticeably cooler in the time they had spent chatting. They walked back to the cart and, to Lily's surprise, Eleanor flung her arms around Lily's neck and hugged her tight.

Lily was in low spirits as she drove home. The fog was moving in, obscuring the sunset and settling heavily over the town, muffling the sound of Belle's hoofs on the road. The lamp-lighter had not yet made his rounds and visibility was reduced to a few yards.

A dark figure appeared, seemingly out of nowhere, star-tling Belle, who whinnied shrilly and shied to the left.

'Oh, I beg your par—' Lily's apology froze on her lips as she found herself looking into the sneering face of Jez Elkin. He was nineteen now, well built and broad shouldered. As devilishly handsome as ever, but the coldness of his gaze sent a shiver down Lily's spine.

'Well, well, well,' he drawled. 'If it isn't little Lily, all grown up.' His icy-blue gaze raked Lily up and down. 'And quite the lady too, by the looks of things.'

Lily lowered her head and urged Belle on but he grabbed the reins. Belle tossed her head, nostrils flaring fearfully.

'What's the matter, Lily? Too high and mighty to stay and chat to your cousin? Shame on you.'

Lily shrugged his hand off her arm, and glared at him. 'You're not my cousin, Jez Elkin,' she said with a firm thrust of her chin. 'And I thank God for that. You and your mother made my life a misery when I lived with you. I owe you nothing. Good day to you.'

'You watch yourself Miss High and Mighty Lilian Hayter,' Jez called after her. 'Pride comes before a fall, remember.'

Quickening her steps Lily paid him no attention. Head bent against the swirling damp, she urged Belle on, her racing heart only settling when she reached the safety of Violet's yard.

What with Lily's trip to Buxton with Mrs Fudge for the reverend's funeral and the extra work that always came in around Christmas, she was left with little time to mope over Eleanor's absence.

The two girls corresponded regularly, allaying Lily's fears that Sir Frederick might succeed in his quest to put an end to their friendship.

Eleanor's letters were full of news of parties, trips to the theatre, musical soirees and afternoon tea at the Ritz. Lily read them with avid interest, delighted that her half-sister appeared to have conquered her shyness and was, by all accounts, having a whale of a time. She was concerned, however, that once Eleanor returned home, she would find Lily very dull company indeed.

CHAPTER FIFTEEN

1893

The red velvet curtain at Salisbury's Palace Royal Theatre came down to thunderous applause. Lily rose to her feet, along with Eleanor and the rest of the audience. She had enjoyed the play. Written by the scandalous playwright Oscar Wilde, it made the perfect antidote to an unseasonably cold October night.

'I did admire Mrs Arbuthnot,' Eleanor said, as they joined the throng of theatre goers making their way down the thickly carpeted stairs to the foyer.

'I thought she gave a very sympathetic performance,' Lily agreed, smiling at her half-sister amidst the crowd as they walked through the plush foyer, heading for the revolving glass doors. Almost three years had passed since Eleanor had returned from London exuding a new-found confidence. Just turned sixteen, she radiated warmth and self-possession. Lily could only admire the confident, self-assured woman she had become.

Lily had been relieved, but pleased, by the way her friendship with Eleanor had continued to blossom after her sister's return from London. She had felt sure Sir Frederick would have somehow convinced her otherwise. Eleanor had confided to Lily in a letter that her father's attitude towards their friendship both baffled and frustrated her. 'Thankfully, Mama intervened,' she had concluded in her neat handwriting. 'As long as I make the effort to mingle in the "right circles".' Lily had imagined Eleanor raising her brow mockingly at this point. 'Mama is inclined to "indulge" my strong regard for you.'

As far as Lily knew, Sir Frederick had made no further attempts to prevent her friendship with Eleanor. Probably because, she surmised, to do so would no doubt arouse Lady Copperfield's curiosity. He had, however, insisted that Eleanor go to the dress shop for any alterations or fittings and, on the rare occasion Lily accepted an invitation to the house, he would make sure not to be home.

It was snowing as the two friends left the warm theatre arm in arm and bitterly cold. Ladies in thick furs and gentlemen in long dark coats streamed down the frosty steps, hailing the many hansom cabs lining the kerb or hurrying towards the station.

Lily turned up the fur collar of her coat. Her breath billowed in the frosty air. Snowflakes swirled in the light of the gas lamps, stinging her cheeks.

With snow settling on their hoods, the two girls hurried along Fisherton Street, following the crowds making for the railway station. They stopped at a stall to buy a bag of roasted chestnuts, listening to the tinkle of piano music drifting from a nearby public house as they waited their turn, light from the street lamp glistening on the icy pavements.

'The actor who played Gerald was very good-looking,' Eleanor said as they made their way inside the cavernous station building, brushing snow from their sleeves. 'Didn't you think so, Lily?'

'I did indeed,' agreed Lily. She cupped the brown paper bag of hot chestnuts in her gloved hands, savouring the warmth seeping into her chilled fingers as they hurried down the steps to the platform.

Salisbury's railway station was crowded and so absorbed was Lily in Eleanor's rehashing of the evening's performance that she failed to spot Jez loitering on the far end of the platform. But he had spotted her.

He'd seen her the moment she'd entered the station building. She had lowered her hood and her rich auburn hair was unmistakable, a fiery beacon in the milling crowd.

Since he'd bumped into Lily that foggy night over three years ago, she had become something of an obsession. The fact that the scrawny kid he remembered had morphed into a hauntingly beautiful young woman had shocked him to the core. Try as he might, he couldn't get her out of his head. The memory of the way she had reacted to the sight of him, first with shock then fear, had excited him. But then had come the crushing blow of her obvious disdain.

He watched her now, anger stirring in the pit of his stomach, remembering how she had looked at him, as if he were beneath her contempt. She'd certainly got herself a few airs and graces since she'd been working for that Violet Upshall, he brooded morosely. Had earned herself quite a reputation, Violet had taken delight in telling his mother one morning when they happened to bump into each other at the market. Her dressmaking skills were very much in demand and she was earning a good commission. Had she thought to send a few quid their way? Had she heck. Selfish, that's what she was. He got it in the neck almost daily from his old Ma. Hadn't they taken Lily in out of the goodness of their hearts when she had nowhere else to go? And was she grateful? Not one bit.

She needed taking down a peg or two, did Miss Lily Hayter. And he was going to be the one to wipe that superior smile off her face.

He grinned. He could feel himself growing hard just thinking about it. He groped in his coat pocket, pulled out his packet of cigarettes and lit one, savouring the moment. He'd been trying to think of ways to engineer a meeting with Lily and tonight, fate, it seemed, was on his side. He would teach the high and mighty Lilian Hayter a lesson she would never forget.

The train arrived with an ear-piercing whistle and belching clouds of steam. Lily and Eleanor found themselves seats in the second-class carriage ('My mother would be appalled,' Eleanor giggled) and settled down for the journey. Soon they were racing through the Wiltshire countryside towards Dorset.

Lily leaned back in her seat. She could see nothing in the inky blackness beyond the carriage but her own reflection in the glass. She closed her eyes, reflecting on how her life had changed over the last five years. Now seventeen and no longer an apprentice but a dressmaker in her own right, she was earning good money. She still worked for Violet in return for her board and lodging, but the money she earned from her own commissions was her own to do with as she wished. Apart from her outings with Eleanor, and material for the occasional new outfit, Lily didn't spend much. She was saving up to visit Charlie in South Africa. In every letter he issued the same invitation, tempting her with vivid descriptions of a land of wonder and excitement, the likes of which could barely be imagined in a sleepy old Dorset town like Blandford. All being well, she would be able to book her passage the first week after Christmas. She would miss Eleanor and Violet of course, as she would be away for at least six months, but the thought of seeing Charlie again after so many years was worth any sacrifice. Just thinking about it brought a warm tingle to the pit of her stomach.

The gentle rocking of the train was soporific as she listened to Eleanor's excited chatter wash over her like a bubbling stream. So often over the past three years she had longed to tell Eleanor the truth about their relationship. She was convinced that both Ada White and Harry knew she was Beatrice's daughter. How did that make Ada feel? she wondered. Did she even care to wonder what had become of

Bea after she'd left Bay Willow House? Perhaps, one day, Lily might pluck up the courage to ask ...

The train lurched violently, jolting Lily back to the present.

'Sorry, Miss Eleanor, I was miles away,' she apologized, realizing that Eleanor had been in the middle of a sentence. Eleanor laughed. She looked very pretty with her eyes shining and her cheeks pink from the warmth of the carriage.

'Father is always telling me I chatter too much. He says I remind him of the monkeys at Regent's Park Zoo.' She chuckled. 'I was just asking if you'd given any more thought to my invitation?' she asked, grabbing Lily's hand earnestly. 'I'd so love you to come with me to London this year. Mother and Father have confirmed they will be in Paris for the whole Christmas season, and I shall be so bored rattling around our London house on my own.'

'I am tempted,' Lily admitted. She had already worked out that she could spare the money from her savings to pay for her train fare and a modest amount of spending money. 'But what about your parents? I'm sure they won't approve.'

It was rare that Lily crossed paths with Sir Frederick, but on the few occasions she had, she felt as though she were invisible. If he looked at her at all, it was with such icy contempt it left her reeling. She wondered how Beatrice could ever have imagined that he loved her. Surely such a man was devoid of all feeling?

'Mama was reluctant at first,' Eleanor admitted. 'Her concern is that you may feel out of your depth in London society but I told her that was nonsense. Anyway, if you are with me, we shan't need to socialize too much.'

'But what does Sir Frederick say?'

'Surprisingly, Papa had no objections.'

Because he won't have to see me, thought Lily.

'Oh, Lily, please say you'll come. We would have such fun. We'll go shopping at Harrods and have tea at Fortnum and Mason. Oh, Lily, you'll love it. The Christmas display in Harrods will take your breath away.'

Lily laughed. 'All right, I will come, but only for a few days while Violet is away visiting her sister. I'm sure she won't mind if I come to London to see you instead of accompanying her to Bath. She is leaving on the twenty-third, so I shall do the same.'

'That's settled then.' Eleanor clapped her hands together in triumph. 'Send me a telegram once you know your timetable and I will arrange a hansom cab for you. Oh, I can't wait.' She hunched her shoulders in pleasure. 'We shall have such fun.'

Lily smiled at her sister. Christmas in the capital – she could hardly wait.

The train pulled into Blandford just after a quarter to eleven. The wide street was lined with hansom cabs and carriages. Horses pawed the frozen ground, steam rising from their warm bodies. Harry was waiting with the trap as the two girls emerged from the station. He tipped his hat.

'Miss Eleanor, Miss Lily, good evening,' he said, jumping down to help them into the trap, his voice muffled by the scarf covering much of his face.

It was bitterly cold, and their breath billowed in the frigid air. Concentrating on tucking the travel robe over her knees, Lily failed to notice Jez among the passengers swarming down the station steps. Seeing Lily getting into the trap, he hailed one of the waiting hansom cabs.

'Where to, sir?' the driver asked, opening the door.

'Market Place,' Jez replied. 'And make it snappy.'

It took a while for Harry to join the flow of traffic but finally they were on their way, the horse's hooves loud on the frozen mud. Snowflakes danced in the light of the streetlamps, settling softly on Lily's lashes and tickling her cold cheeks.

They were barely a few blocks from Market Place when they became aware of a commotion up ahead.

'What is it, Harry?' Eleanor queried, leaning forward.

'Looks like two carriages have collided, miss,' replied Harry, holding the lantern aloft to get a better view. 'Road's blocked. We'll have to make a detour.'

Lily clung on tightly as he manoeuvred the trap around, narrowly missing a collision of his own with a hansom cab, and guided the horse up Sheep Market Hill. Knowing that the detour would take them quite out of their way, Lily reached over and tapped Harry on the shoulder. He half-turned towards her.

'Drop me off on the corner of Church Lane, please, Harry. It will save you doubling back.'

Harry nodded. 'If you're sure, miss?'

'I shall come out directly next to Miss Upshall's shop.'

Harry nodded and a few minutes later he brought the trap to a halt on the corner of Church Lane.

'Are you sure you'll be all right walking from here, Lily?' Eleanor questioned, eyeing the dimly lit side street dubiously.

'It's barely a two-minute walk,' Lily assured her, slipping quickly from beneath the travel robe so as not to let the cold in. 'I shall see you soon, Miss Eleanor. Thank you for the ride, Harry.'

As Lily hurried down the street, she could hear the noises from the marketplace, voices and the whinnying of horses, but Church Lane was quiet, the grand Georgian houses dark and silent. A streetlamp hissed and spluttered and her footsteps echoed in the stillness. She hadn't gone very far when she heard footsteps coming up fast behind her.

Feeling only slightly apprehensive, she glanced over her shoulder, preparing to move aside to allow the person to pass by. She gave a cry of alarm as the shadowy figure smashed into her. Winded, she had no time to react before a gloved hand clamped over her mouth and an arm gripped her across the chest, forcing her down one of the many alleyways that crisscrossed the town. She struggled valiantly against her attacker's vice-like grip, her eyes widening in shock as his face was briefly illuminated by the streetlamp. *Jez?*

Cold tentacles of fear ran along her spine as he shoved her further down the alleyway. She could see the reassuring glow of the streetlamps at either end yet here the darkness was thick and all-consuming. With one hand still clamped over her mouth, he tugged at her coat. A button popped and rolled away into the darkness. Lily pushed against him, clawing at his face, his neck. He grunted, and shoved her against the wall. Shivering with cold and terror, she felt him hook his leg around hers and she tumbled onto the hard, cold ground. She could feel puddles seeping through her clothes.

Jez was on top of her in an instant.

She felt the rush of cold air on her thighs as her skirts were pushed aside, her stockings ripped by cruel, probing fingers.

In the cold, wet, ill-smelling alleyway she fought and scratched for all she was worth but he was too strong for her. Her muffled screams went unheard as he thrust himself into her again and again, grunting and panting like an animal. She felt as though she were being torn asunder. Pain like red-hot pokers shot through her body and the rough ground bruised her tender flesh. She squeezed her eyes shut, turned her face away and gave herself up to the nightmare she thought would never end.

Suddenly he let out a long moan and shuddered, collapsing heavily on top of her. Lily held her breath as he rolled off her. Was it over?

Jez buttoned up his flies, looking with disgust at the dishevelled figure cowering on the ground.

'Not so high and mighty now, are you, Lily?' he said with a derisive laugh. Picking up her coat, he threw it at her and, without so much as a backward glance, he sauntered off, whistling tunelessly to himself.

Alone in the alley, Lily leaned over and vomited into the gutter. She wasn't sure how long she stayed there, huddled against the wall but, by the time she managed to drag herself to her feet, the falling snow had turned to rain. Ice-cold needles bit into her head as she dragged herself home. Letting herself in the back gate, oblivious to the freezing rain, she stripped off her soiled clothing and scrubbed herself raw at the pump. Her skin was blue and she was shaking uncontrollably by the time she crept quietly though the back door and up the stairs. In her bedroom she pulled her nightdress over her head and climbed into bed. She knew she would not sleep, nor would she ever erase from her mind the expression on Jez's face as he raped her.

Violet knew immediately that something was wrong when Lily failed to appear for breakfast. Thinking she must be sickening for something, she put a pot of tea and two slices of buttered toast on a tray and knocked on Lily's door.

Huddled under the covers, Lily pressed her hands over her ears. She couldn't bear to face Violet. How could she look her dear friend in the eye without betraying her shame?

'Lily? Lily, are you all right? May I come in?'

Lily didn't reply. Instead she turned her face to the wall, tears of shame soaking into her pillow.

Now deeply concerned, Violet pushed the door open and peered into the room. 'Lily?' She set the tray on the nightstand and opened the curtains. 'Are you ill?'

'I'm fine,' Lily croaked. Her throat hurt and her eyes were scratchy. She hadn't slept a wink, and despite her several blankets, she couldn't seem to stop shivering. Violet perched on the edge of the bed, alarmed by the dark circles under Lily's eyes and her pale, waxy complexion. She laid a cool hand on Lily's forehead.

'You're burning up. You're staying in bed today. I'll send the young lad from the butchers to let your customers know you won't make your appointments today. I can manage everything else.' She stood up. 'Go back to sleep. I'll bring you up some beef tea in a while.' She drew the curtains again, shutting out the dull November sky and left Lily lying listlessly in her bed, listening to the howling wind and the rain lashing the glass.

She felt sick and dirty. The smell of the warm buttered toast made her stomach heave, though there was nothing left inside her to come up. Her whole body ached and she felt battered and bruised. A sob caught in her throat and she pulled the blankets over her head, wishing she could wake up and the nightmare would be over. But this was no nightmare; this was her reality, and Lily wasn't sure she would be able to bear it.

She stayed in bed for three days with Violet flapping around her like a mother hen but, eventually, Lily knew she had to make an effort to get back to some semblance of normality. She couldn't let Jez win. She mustn't let him win.

Pale and fragile, she sat at the breakfast table nibbling a slice of toast while Violet chattered away, bringing her up to date on the goings-on of the past three days.

'Miss Eleanor has been asking after you,' Violet said, pouring the tea. 'She blames herself for your chill. Says she should have insisted that Harry drove you all the way. She wanted to visit but I thought it best to wait until you were back on your feet. She said she'd call in later this week before she leaves for London. She said you're joining her for Christmas?'

Lily nodded dully. She didn't know how she could face Eleanor after what had happened. And the thought of going to London just seemed too much of an ordeal right now.

'I think that's a lovely idea,' Violet went on. 'You work so hard, you deserve a treat. And London is such an exciting place to be at Christmas. You'll have a wonderful time.' She smiled at Lily across the table. 'Eat up,' she said, registering Lily's barely touched breakfast. 'You'll need to build your strength up. You don't want a relapse.'

'Oh, Lily, you have been ill.' Eleanor took in Lily's pale complexion, the bags under her eyes. 'Worse than I realized.'

Lily nodded listlessly. She was sitting in an armchair close to the fire. The flames danced merrily in the grate yet she felt chilled to the bone.

'I should have come sooner,' Eleanor said, biting her lip in consternation. 'But I was afraid of exhausting you.' She removed her gloves and hat and settled herself into the chair opposite Lily, the warmth from the flames bringing a rosy hue to her cold cheeks. 'Are you eating properly? You look awfully thin and pale.'

'I haven't much of an appetite at the moment,' Lily replied. She knew she should make more of an effort but the events of the previous week still played in her mind on an endless reel. She felt sick, bile rising up her throat each time she pictured Jez's contorted face above her. The stench of his stale breath lingered in her nostrils, and the memory of his hands on her body made her skin crawl. She felt so dirty and ashamed.

Violet brought in the tea and half a Victoria sponge.

'Oh, Miss Upshall, that looks delicious,' Eleanor exclaimed, sitting forward in her seat to accept the teacup Violet handed her.

'Thank you. It's part of my ploy to tempt Lily to eat something. I know how much she loves Victoria sponge, don't you, Lily?'

Lily nodded obediently, forcing a weak smile as she accepted a thin wedge of cake. Violet set the tray on the small table and turned to Eleanor.

'When do you leave for London, Miss Eleanor?'

'Tomorrow,' she replied, licking cake crumbs from her fingertips. 'That's why I had to come today. I didn't want to leave without saying goodbye.' Her bright gaze met Lily's. 'I shall be able to bear our separation so much better knowing that you'll soon be joining me. I've got so many plans. I doubt we'll fit everything in.' She clapped her hands together in girlish delight. 'I can't wait, Lily. We shall have so much fun.'

Lily offered up a wan smile and sipped her tea. She couldn't seem to muster up any enthusiasm for the trip but at least, being in London, she'd be far away from Jez, even if only for a few days. Every time she had visited a customer since, she had been terrified that he would be lurking nearby. She hated him with every fibre of her being and she never wanted to see him again, ever.

'I will pray every day that you grow stronger,' Eleanor said as they said their goodbyes a while later. 'You'll need all your strength for when you visit me. I'm determined we shall have a wonderful time.' She stood on tiptoe to plant a kiss on Lily's pale cheek. 'Please look after yourself, Lily.'

'I shall, Miss Eleanor,' Lily replied, returning Eleanor's embrace. 'Safe travels.'

'Thank you, and don't forget to send me your time of arrival,' she said as she turned to go. The dark bay mare pawed the cold ground impatiently as the driver got down to help Eleanor into the hansom cab. She leaned out of the window, waving frantically as they set off down the street. Lily watched her go, her heart a leaden lump in her chest.

CHAPTER SIXTEEN

Lily had barely opened her eyes that cheerless December morning, a few days before Christmas, before she was driven from her warm bed by the urgent need to throw up. Hunched over the chamber pot she retched and heaved, spitting out hot, bitter bile that burned the back of her throat. When she was done, she sat back on her heels, trembling as she wiped her mouth with the back of her hand. The terrible sense of foreboding that had been steadily building since her monthlies had failed to arrive sat heavily across her chest. Her worst nightmare had just been realized. She was carrying Jez Elkin's child.

'Look after yourself, Lily,' Violet said, embracing her warmly in the shop doorway. 'You're still so very peaky, I worry about you overexerting yourself up in London.'

It was now the day before Christmas Eve and Violet was leaving for her sister's home in Bath. 'I'll be fine, I promise,' Lily assured her with false cheer.

'Of course, you will be.' Violet smiled, turning to study her reflection in the shop mirror. 'You're a very sensible and capable young woman.' She adjusted her hat and pulled on her gloves. The lanky boy she had employed to drive her to the station, and to take care of Belle while she and Lily were away, waited outside, rubbing Belle's nose and feeding her bits of apple. Violet's bags were already stowed behind the seat in the trap.

'As long as the trains are running smoothly, I should be home late Boxing Day afternoon. Goodbye, Lily, and merry Christmas.'

Climbing into the trap, Violet set off up the frosty street at a jaunty pace, the wintery sun glinting on the lacquered wood.

Lily let out a long sigh of relief. The past few days had been a nightmare as she tried to keep her condition secret from Violet. If she had heard Lily being sick in the mornings, she hadn't mentioned it. Violet was deeply concerned for her well-being and no wonder. Lily knew she looked as awful as she felt. Lack of sleep and being unable to keep much food down had contributed to her pale, wan complexion and dark circles beneath her eyes.

She lingered until she heard the distant shrill whistle of the train before pulling on her wraps and heading out into the street. The bitingly cold air went some way to clearing the fog in her head. The sky was clear above her but dark clouds were gathering over the hills, heavy with the threat of snow. A frosty wind scoured her cheeks as she made her way along Salisbury Street to the telegram office. To her immense relief, it was deserted apart from Ed Johnson, the telegram operator. He glanced up from the periodical he was reading and smiled.

'Morning, Miss Hayter.'

'Good morning, Mr Johnson,' Lily said with as much cheerfulness as she could muster. Her stomach churned with a mixture of nerves and nausea. She had already been sick twice that morning and was praying fervently she wouldn't humiliate herself by throwing up all over the wooden floor.

'I wish to send a telegram, please.'

'Of course, miss.' Ed grabbed his pen and paper, glancing over his wire-rimmed spectacles with expectation.

'It's to a Miss Eleanor Copperfield.' She gave him the address, praying he wouldn't notice how much her hands were trembling. 'Apologies. Stop. Unwell must cancel visit. Stop.'

'You don't look too clever, if I may say so, miss,' Ed said, taking in Lily's haunted expression. 'I'd get back into the warmth as quick as you can, if I were you.'

'Thank you, yes, I intend to do just that.' She handed over the fee and, nodding goodbye, let herself out of his warm office into the freezing cold.

She walked quickly, head down, not wanting to speak to anyone. The shop windows glittered and sparkled with Christmas cheer. The Salvation Army band played carols on Durden's Corner. A few passers-by had paused to sing, voices rising on the cold, crisp air. Chestnuts roasted on an open briar, their sweet scent causing Lily's stomach to churn alarmingly. She only just made it home in time.

A little later, as if in a daze, she walked from room to room and closed all the curtains. In the gloom of her bedroom, she got into her nightdress and climbed into bed, huddling under the covers, welcoming the oblivion of sleep.

For the next two days she drifted in and out of sleep, her feverish mind conjuring up frightening nightmares. She was only aware of time passing thanks to the changing light filtering through the curtains. Occasionally she heard voices in the street, the shouting of jubilant children, carollers beneath her window, the strident cacophony of church bells heralding the birth of Christ. Lily pulled the covers over her ears, seeking blissful oblivion.

She woke early on Boxing Day, weak but with a renewed sense of purpose. By the time she heard the pony and trap draw up outside, she was bathed and dressed. A good fire crackled in the hearth and a pot of vegetable soup was simmering on the stove. She filled the tea kettle and set it on the hob.

'Lily?' Violet called, coming up the stairs. 'Lily, are you home? Lily! Hmm, something smells good. I wasn't expecting you back from London so soon. I thought your train didn't get in until this evening. It's good to see you looking so much better, though.' She gave Lily a hug. 'London must have agreed with you.'

Lily took a deep breath. 'I didn't go to London.'

'Pardon?' Violet's eyebrows rose. Bobby chose that moment to appear with Violet's luggage, his freckled cheeks flushed from the exertion.

'I've settled Belle in her stall, Miss Upshall, and I've given her some fresh straw and a bucket of oats.'

'Good lad. Just leave the bags there, Bobby. Thank you,' Violet said, somewhat distractedly as she dropped some coins into his cupped hands. Violet slowly removed her gloves, as Bobby bounded down the stairs, her gaze questioning.

'Why didn't you go to London, Lily? You were so looking forward to it.'

'Violet, there's something I need to tell you.' Lily pulled out a chair and sat down, folding her hands on the table.

'My dear girl, is everything all right?' Frowning, Violet took off her hat and came to stand beside Lily, her voice laden with concern. 'Are you still unwell?' She laid a hand on Lily's arm.

'Violet.' Lily's eyes filled with tears. 'I'm in trouble.'

'Trouble? Good Heavens, what sort of trouble?' The creases on Violet's brow deepened.

Lily turned her terrified gaze on Violet. 'I'm ...' She faltered, took a deep a breath. 'I'm going to have a baby.'

Violet reeled backwards, the colour draining from her face. 'A baby?' she cried, incredulous, clutching the back of Lily's chair for support. 'No! It's impossible!' Her shoulders sagged. 'Who's the father?'

'Jez,' Lily responded miserably.

'Jez?' Violet threw up her hands in disbelief. 'Jez Elkin?' She stared at Lily with incomprehension. 'But you hate him!'

'He raped me. The night Eleanor and I went to the theatre.'

'Oh, Lily.' Violet exhaled sharply. Chair legs scraped the floor and she reached for Lily, holding her close as she sobbed against her. 'Oh, my dearest Lily,' she murmured, stroking Lily's hair. 'Why didn't you tell me?'

Lily shook her head. 'I was too ashamed.' Violet cupped Lily's chin in her hand.

'You have nothing to be ashamed of. It's Jez who should be ashamed. We'll get the law onto him straight away. He'll pay for this, Lily, you mark my words.'

'No,' Lily croaked, pulling back from Violet's embrace. 'No, I can't tell anyone.'

'Lily, you must. He deserves to be punished.'

'How can I prove it?' Lily demanded miserably. 'It will be Jez's word against mine. He'll say I was up for it. Even if most people believe me, there will always be those few who won't. They'll think I'm no better than a common trollop.'

Violet sighed. She knew Lily was probably right. Whatever the circumstances, her reputation would be sullied, especially as most people roundabout were aware of Lily's unfortunate beginnings. Like mother, like daughter, some would say.

'Have you thought what you might do, Lily?' Violet said, as the implications of Lily's predicament hit home. Once Lily's situation became public knowledge, many of her more discriminating customers would cut her dead and, by association, Violet's business would suffer too. Her thoughts were interrupted by the shrill whistle of the kettle and she got up to lift it off the stove and make the tea.

'I'm going to see Jez and make him marry me,' Lily said in a voice devoid of emotion. Violet whirled around, almost dropping the teapot in her shock.

'Lily! No! How can you even contemplate marrying that man?'

'What choice do I have?' Lily's gaze bore into Violet's, as if begging her to provide a way out of the life that stretched out before her, a life that promised nothing but abject misery. 'It's either the Foundling Hospital or the workhouse. At least if Jez agrees to marry me, my baby will have a name.'

'But at what cost?' Violet's expression radiated sympathy. 'You don't have to marry him, Lily. You could go away. You've saved enough for your fare. Go to Charlie.'

Lily shook her head vehemently. 'No. I don't want Charlie to know. I'm frightened of what he would do to Jez. No. I shall write to him, if Jez agrees to my proposal, when everything is settled.'

'However things turn out, you'll always have a home here,' Violet said stoutly, hands planted firmly on her hips as she regarded Lily, a defiant glint in her grey-blue eyes. 'You and the baby. To hell with what people say. Let them gossip.'

'You're a dear friend, Violet,' Lily said softly, shaking her head as tears squeezed beneath her lashes. 'But I can't drag you into my mess. You've worked hard to build up your business. I won't allow people's opinion of me to destroy all your hard work.'

'Oh, Lily, what nonsense—' Violet began but Lily cut her off with a shake of her head.

'You know I'm right. Will the likes of Lady Copperfield or Mrs Hodges Bennett risk being tainted by my shame? I'll be an unmarried mother, and your good name and reputation will be sullied by my shame and disgrace.' Lily's voice broke and Violet was instantly at her side.

'Oh, Lily, my dear, dear girl. I'm so, so sorry. I wish this horrible thing hadn't happened to you.'

'So do I.' Lily rummaged in the pocket of her skirt for a handkerchief and blew her nose. 'But it has,' she said stoically. 'And I shall have to make the best of it.'

She waited until the first week of January. The snow that had fallen between Christmas and New Year had all but disappeared, and Laundry Lane was a quagmire as Lily made her way to her aunt's cottage, buffeted by a raw east wind. A flock of crows flew overhead, their dark bodies silhouetted against a dishwater-grey sky.

Sick with dread, she approached Doris's front door. Memories of years of misery and bullying she had suffered at the hands of her aunt and cousin settled like a heavy yoke across her shoulders. She could feel herself reverting to the small, frightened little girl she had once been. Glancing up and down the deserted street, she noticed curtains at the cottage window opposite twitching. She held her head high, refusing to let her terrible childhood define who she had become. She wasn't that frightened little girl anymore.

Even so, it took all of her courage to knock. For a few moments there was nothing but silence from within. Then she heard the shuffling of footsteps, and held her breath as the bolts were drawn back, steeling herself in case she was confronted by Jez.

Doris peered around the door, her bloodshot eyes widening in shock. 'Well, well, well!' she sneered, blinking in the brightness. 'Look what the cat's dragged home.'

'Hello, Doris, may I come in?' Lily said in a tone that told her aunt she brooked no nonsense. Doris scowled.

'Well, aren't you the hoity toity snip? What do you want, you ungrateful cow? Haven't seen hide nor hair of you for years.'

'I have something to say,' Lily insisted firmly. 'So, unless you'd rather have your dirty laundry aired before all and sundry, I'd appreciate you inviting me in.'

Doris's brows rose almost to her hairline. 'You'd better come in then,' she said.

'I see you've slipped back into your slovenly ways now I'm not here to clean up after you,' Lily said disparagingly, taking in the thick layers of dust, the black mould sprouting in the corners of the ceiling and the damp wallpaper coming away from the walls as she followed Doris into the parlour.

She declined Doris's invitation to sit. 'I prefer to stand, thank you. What I've got to say won't take long.' She shivered, glad of her thick coat, the struggling fire doing little to dispel the winter chill. She took a deep breath, forcing herself to remain calm.

'Spit it out, then.' Doris leaned against the dresser, arms folded across her sagging chest. The shapeless dress she wore hung on her scrawny frame, her cheeks appeared shrunken and her greasy greying-blond hair was fashioned into an untidy knot. 'What do you want?'

'Is Jez about?' Lily asked, ignoring Doris's question.

'Jez?' Doris's upper lip curled in surprise. 'What do you want with my Jez? I thought the two of you couldn't stand the sight of each other.'

'That's as may be,' Lily agreed, determined not to let her aunt rile her. 'But it's him I came to see.'

'Well,' Doris smirked. 'You're out of luck. He's not here.'

'When do you expect him back?'

'Listen here, Miss High and Mighty, coming here with your posh clothes and fancy ways, you know my Jez answers to no one, not even his old ma.' Her shoulders sagged and she let out a long sigh. Lily could hear the phlegm rattling in the woman's throat and felt a momentary stab of pity for her aunt. She would be in her early forties now, yet she looked at least a decade older. 'He keeps his own hours, does Jez.' She stared at Lily, eyes narrowed in suspicion. 'Why do you want him?'

'That is between Jez and myself,' Lily said firmly. There was no way she was going to discuss her predicament with Doris, not before she'd settled things with Jez.

'Well you could be in for a long wait, missy,' retorted Doris, clearly peeved that her curiosity wasn't about to be satisfied. 'It's nigh on midnight when he comes home some days.'

191

'Then I shall call back tomorrow—' she began, breaking off as she heard the back door open. Her throat closed in fear, an emotion she saw reflected in her aunt's eyes. The door slammed shut. Lily heard the sound of a chair being scraped across the floor, followed by a grunt and what sounded like a boot being flung across the room.

Lily's heart was racing nineteen to the dozen as Jez appeared in the kitchen doorway where he stopped dead, clearly shocked to find Lily standing in the middle of the parlour. Just seeing him made Lily feel physically sick. She felt like she'd come face to face with the Devil himself.

'What the hell are you doing here?' he snarled nastily.

His blatant lack of shame or remorse over what he had done gave Lily the boldness to speak out. She swallowed hard, determined not to give him the upper hand.

'I came to see you,' she said, inwardly cringing at the tremor in her voice. Jez's lip curled.

'Oh yeah?' He leered at her, and came closer. It took all of Lily's willpower not to turn and run. She clenched her fists, forcing down the hot bile rising in her throat.

'Want a bit more of the same, do you?' He grinned lewdly.

She forced herself to remain calm. Her palms were damp and nervous sweat trickled down her spine. She bit her lip hard, willing herself to concentrate.

'I need to speak to you,' she said firmly, ignoring Jez's comment and her aunt's blatant curiosity. 'Privately.' She looked at Doris meaningfully.

Jez let out a snort of laughter. 'Marry you? Are you insane? I'm not the marrying kind, and if I were, I wouldn't choose a bitch like you.'

'Lily, I think you'd better go,' Doris murmured faintly. She'd had to sit down with the shock of it. For a brief moment she had experienced a flicker of excitement. A grandchild, a baby to spoil and love, but it was not to be. There was no way Jez would take responsibility for this child. At least Sam, feckless bastard that he turned out to be, had done that much.

'Yeah,' Jez drawled, 'You heard Ma, go on, get out. We don't want to see you or your brat around here, you hear me? Or there'll be trouble.' He half-rose from his chair, his fist clenched menacingly.

With an icy calmness that took Doris and Jez by surprise, Lily walked towards him. She thrust her face close to his, causing him to rear back in surprise.

'You forget that I've seen first-hand how you earn your living, Jez Elkin. If you refuse to marry me and give your child a name, it will be you who has to deal with the consequences.' Jez regarded her silently through narrowed eyes and a haze of cigarette smoke. She was calling his bluff, of course, but there was no way he could take the risk. He'd already had a few brushes with the law. The last thing he wanted was to risk attracting further attention to his dodgy business dealings. 'Sleep on it,' she said, her tone deceptively light as she straightened up. 'I shall expect your response by tomorrow evening. You know where to contact me. Good evening.' Her calm demeanour belying her inner terror, she walked from the house with her head held high.

A scruffy street urchin delivered the note late the following afternoon.

'I agree to the marriage. Tell me the time and place. I'll be there.'

CHAPTER SEVENTEEN

1894

They were married at ten o'clock on a bitterly cold Saturday in February. Violet and Doris were the only witnesses. Inside the Church of St Mark the Evangelist, it was cold and bleak, the richness of Christmas having given way to the austerity of Lent.

Lily's breath clouded in front of her face as she stammered her vows. She was unable to stop shivering and anxiety had tied her stomach in knots. At the last minute, Violet had thrust a posy of winter flowers into her hands. They shook violently as she listened to Jez reciting his vows in a bored monotone. He hadn't looked at her once, fixing his cold gaze firmly on the stained-glass window above the vicar's shiny bald head.

The ceremony was mercifully brief and, barely twenty minutes after she had arrived at the church, the tiny wedding party emerged into the frozen churchyard. There was to be no wedding meal, no celebration of any sort. What was the point? Her wedding band glinted in the light and panic caught at the back of her throat. She had provided her child with a father but in doing so she had the feeling she had made a pact with the Devil incarnate.

'Are you all right, Lily?' Violet's kind concern brought tears to Lily's eyes, which she blinked back furiously. She had made her bed for better or for worse. There was no point crying over it now.

She hugged Violet warmly. Right up until they had arrived at the church, Violet had done her best to persuade Lily not to go through with what she called the 'sham of a wedding', but Lily had been adamant. Her child deserved a father and Jez, for all his faults, deserved to know his child. Perhaps, she had suggested more out of desperate hope than any real conviction, once the child arrived Jez would become the father she needed him to be.

Violet's sceptical expression had left Lily in no doubt that her friend thought she was deluding herself.

'Right, I'm off,' Jez said, rudely shunning the Vicar's outstretched hand. 'I've got to see some people about business. I'm running late already.' He shot Lily a pointed look, then leered at her. 'I'll see you later, wife.'

Lily's face flamed and she looked away, unable to bear the triumphant glint in his eyes. She was dreading having to be a proper wife to him. She doubted he would show any consideration for her condition. He'd take her out of spite.

She watched her new husband saunter down the path, his shoes crunching loudly on the frozen gravel.

'We'd better get home too,' Doris said cheerfully, adjusting her hat. She alone had been looking forward to the wedding and, to give Doris her due, she had made an effort. She'd washed her hair and Lily had trimmed her old hat with fresh blue ribbon. It matched the colour of her eyes, affording Lily a glimpse of the pretty woman she must once have been.

'Oh, Lily,' Violet said, choking back tears as she gave Lily's arm a squeeze. 'It will be ever so strange not having you at home.'

'I shall be back at work on Monday,' Lily assured her, 'and every day after that, at least until the baby's born.' She hugged the woman who, along with Eleanor, was her dearest friend.

Lily and Doris spoke little on the walk back to Laundry Lane, the sombre sky perfectly reflecting Lily's mood. Her legs felt wooden and her heart was heavy. She mustn't let herself think too far ahead, she consoled herself. She would take one day at a time. That was the only way she could find the strength to survive in this new life she had chosen for herself. One day at a time.

'Just because you're expecting, I'll not let you sit around idle. I shall expect you to pull your weight,' Doris said as Lily surveyed the room she would now share with Jez. Her trunk had been delivered the day before and stood at the foot of the unmade bed. The sour smell curdled Lily's stomach. Swallowing her revulsion, she crossed to the window and threw it open, letting in a blast of ice-cold air.

'Blimey, girl,' Doris shrieked, clutching her shawl tightly around her scrawny neck. 'What are you doing? We'll catch our deaths.'

'We need fresh air, Doris,' Lily said firmly, frowning at the bedding, which lay in a jumbled heap. 'And fresh linen.' She looked at her mother-in-law. 'Do you have any? You can't expect me to sleep on this.' She picked up a frayed blanket, stiff with dirt. 'This blanket doesn't look like it's been beaten since I walked out of this house half a decade ago.'

Doris sniffed with indignation. Her daughter-in-law's criticism clearly stung.

She shrugged. 'There might be some blankets in the bedding box up in the attic. You can have a look if you're that fussy.'

Lily changed out of her best dress and spent the rest of her wedding day scrubbing and cleaning. She dragged the filthy blankets off the bed and hung them outside, barely noticing the bitter cold as she took out all of her anger and frustration on them, beating away years of grime. By the time she had finished, the muscles in her arms and shoulders screamed for relief but Lily felt strangely calm. Determined to start as she meant to go on, she went back into the dingy house and set about preparing supper. She could hear Doris snoring in the front room, and she sighed. Clearly nothing had changed in the years she had been gone.

They ate supper in relative silence and Lily washed the dishes by candlelight. Afterwards, she opened the back door to throw out the dishwater. The moon was bright and frost twinkled on the ground. She shivered on the step, her thin shawl offering little protection against the icy night air, but she was in no hurry to go back inside. There were no books or papers in her new home and the long evening seemed to stretch out ahead of her.

Finally, she could procrastinate no longer. With a quiet sigh, she returned the washing-up bowl to its peg and shut the back door, careful to remember not to bolt it, knowing Jez would play merry hell with her in the morning if he couldn't get in.

'It's like old times,' Doris slurred. She grinned, revealing a mouthful of yellow stumps. She was cradling a bottle of spirits and she held it out to Lily. 'Want some?'

'No, thank you.' Lily shook her head disdainfully and cast her eyes around the room. Despite her valiant efforts the room still reeked of stale drink and damp. She sat down on the sofa and stared into the fire. She was dreading Jez's return and every time footsteps sounded in the street, she held her breath, her stomach clenched with nerves. Only when whoever it was had passed could she exhale, her shoulders slumping in relief.

Loud snoring alerted her to the fact that Doris had dozed off. Lily glanced at the clock on the sagging mantelpiece. It was barely eight o'clock. Far too early to go to bed. Then she remembered the books she had packed in her trunk.

Quietly, so as not to wake her mother-in-law, she groped her way up the dark staircase to her bedroom. Lighting the candle on the chest of drawers, she knelt in front of her trunk, her nimble fingers working the catch and throwing up the lid. The sight of her personal possessions, so familiar to her, brought tears to her eyes. Her breath caught in her throat and she shook her head, determined not to give in to her emotions. Finding the book she was looking for, she returned to the parlour.

For the next hour, she lost herself in the world of Jane Austen, only returning to reality when the clock chimed nine. Suddenly she felt weary to her bones. It had been a long, emotional day.

Leaving Doris snoring softly, she made her way back up the stairs to her bedroom. The room was chilly and she shivered as she stripped off her clothes, folded them carefully over the wooden chair and pulled on her nightgown. The sheets were threadbare and frayed in places but at least they were clean, she consoled herself as she slipped between the covers, her teeth chattering uncontrollably. One thing she had forgotten to pack was her stone hot water bottle. Well, she would rectify that as soon as she could, she thought ruefully, rubbing her frozen feet together in an attempt to get the blood flowing.

Despite her tiredness, sleep eluded her and she lay awake for hours, listening to the mantelpiece clock chiming down the hours. Somewhere around midnight, Doris stumbled up the stairs. She missed her footing twice, cursing loudly as she crashed into the wall. The landing floorboards creaked and a door was closed, none too quietly. Presently the cottage walls began to vibrate with Doris's loud snores. And still Jez didn't come home.

Lily awoke with a start. She was enveloped in darkness but the sound of voices drifting up from the street outside told her that it must be morning. The only sound was her own breathing. Rolling onto her side, she put out a tentative hand. Jez's side of the bed was cold. She hadn't seen him since their wedding, two days earlier.

She slid from beneath the covers and dressed quickly. Doris was snoring loudly as Lily crept along the landing and made her way cautiously downstairs, terrified Jez would be waiting for her in the kitchen. She held the candle aloft, its pale, yellow light flickering on the faded and peeling wallpaper and exhaled in relief. Jez was nowhere to be seen. She lit the lamps and got on with the business of making breakfast. She had to be at Violet's by eight o'clock and didn't want to be late.

She made porridge and ate heartily, sitting at the table, her ears tuned for the sound of approaching footsteps, but none came. Though she still suffered the odd bout of nausea, she wasn't being sick anymore and had begun to regain some of the weight she had lost.

She heated water in the kettle to wash her hands and face, combed her hair and pinned it up, checking her reflection in the mirror that hung behind the kitchen door. Satisfied with her appearance, she started to wash her bowl and cup and was elbow deep in soap suds when she heard the latch being lifted on the front door. She froze. Jez was standing in the kitchen doorway. She could feel his gaze boring into her back.

Slowly, she wiped her hands on a threadbare towel and turned around. Jez was looking at her with an expression of mild surprise, as if he had forgotten Lily's very existence.

'Well, well,' he smirked, 'is my darling wife making me breakfast?' He glanced at the porridge simmering gently on the stove top.

'Hello, Jez.' Lily found her voice. 'Where have you been?'

'Where have I been?' Jez threw back his head and laughed. 'Why, did you miss me?' In two strides he had closed the gap between them. Lily flinched as he cupped her chin roughly in his hand, jerking her face towards his. Swallowing her fear, Lily stared up at him defiantly.

'I'm your wife,' she said, praying her voice wouldn't betray her fear. She was grateful for the cold porcelain sink behind her; otherwise her knees might have given way. 'I have a right to know where you've been all weekend.'

'A right?' Jez gave a hollow laugh. He jerked Lily's chin higher, his expression menacing as he lowered his face close to hers. His breath reeked of stale tobacco. 'Let's get one thing straight, Lazy Lily. In this house you have no rights, you got that? This is my house and I will come and go as I please.' His features morphed into a lecherous leer. Lily's eyes widened in fear as he squeezed her breast hard, making her wince. She bit her lip, fighting down the urge to lash out. He kept his mocking, taunting gaze fixed on her face.

'Get off me,' she hissed.

'Pardon?' Jez drew his head back, feigning surprise. 'I thought this was what you wanted?'

'I married you to give our child a name,' Lily snarled, digging to the depths of her being to find the courage to defy her husband. 'I know I will have to do my duty in due course.' The thought caused bile to rise in her throat and she swallowed it down before continuing. 'But know this, Jez Elkin. You repulse me and I will never lie with you willingly.'

Jez's face turned thunderous. He wrenched her jaw. 'Oh, you'll lie with me, wifey dear, and you'll enjoy it.' He thrust his face towards hers, his foul breath wafting across her skin. 'Don't dare cross me, Lily,' he warned menacingly. 'I promise you, you'll live to regret it.' He stepped back, his dark, brooding gaze registering that she was dressed for work.

'You can dish up my breakfast before you go to your lah-di-dah job,' he said, pulling out a chair and sitting down. 'And make a fresh pot of tea,' he added, his tone almost amiable. 'I'm parched.'

Paralysed with fear, it took Lily a few seconds before she could force her body to move. Woodenly she dished up a bowl of porridge and made a fresh pot of tea, not daring to look at him. He ate noisily, ignoring Lily completely. Without a word, she put on her coat and fled from the house.

★   ★   ★

The slam of the door woke Doris. Knotting the cord of her dressing gown, she made her way slowly downstairs.

'Is there any tea in that pot?' she mumbled, stifling a yawn.

Jez glanced up, his eyes narrowing in disgust as he took in his mother's bloodshot eyes, sleep-tangled hair and stained dressing gown. He shrugged, and pushed the pot towards her.

'My head isn't half thumping this morning,' Doris grumbled, pouring herself a mug of tea.

'That'll be the gin, then,' Jez said callously.

Doris ignored him. With an unsteady hand she lifted the mug to her cracked lips and grimaced. The tea was lukewarm and stewed. She set her mug down. Outside it was growing lighter and she got up to extinguish the lamps.

'Where's Lily?'

'Gone to work,' he replied without looking up from his newspaper.

'Are you happy with that? I didn't think you were the sort of bloke who'd allow his wife to work,' Doris said with surprise. 'Your pa never wanted me to work. A wife's place is in the home, he always said.'

'Yeah,' Jez replied drily. 'Like he was a great breadwinner. We never had two beans to rub together until I was old enough to start earning,' Jez reminded her, a dangerous edge to his tone. He folded the newspaper. 'I'm all right with Lily working, just until the baby comes. She earns good money. It's time we got some payback.' He reached over and patted

Doris's arm. 'I'll see she pays her way so don't worry, you won't go short of gin,' he added with an evil grin.

'Are you all right?' Violet asked, emerging from the back room as Lily entered the shop. 'You look very pale.'

'Yes, I'm fine, thank you,' Lily replied, avoiding Violet's concerned scrutiny as she shed her hat and coat. 'Jez stayed away all weekend,' she elaborated, following Violet into the back room where a mannequin adorned with her latest creation awaited her attention.

'Really?' Violet stood with her hands on her hips, her head cocked to one side as she gazed at Lily questioningly. 'So, you haven't seen him since the wedding?'

'Oh, I've seen him, all right.' Lily gave a hollow laugh. 'He appeared just as I was leaving this morning.'

'And?' Violet waited.

'And he laid down the law, put the fear of God into me, but other than that . . .' Lily gave Violet a tight smile. 'Everything is fine.'

'Oh, Lily,' Violet said sadly.

'Don't.' Lily held up her hand, fighting back the tears. She smiled. 'Please, Violet, don't be kind, I can't cope with it just now. Let's just get on with our work, shall we? How was Mrs Brookshaw yesterday afternoon? Is she still determined to have the yellow silk?'

Violet pursed her lips. There was so much she wanted to say but she had to respect Lily's wishes. She exhaled slowly, her shoulders relaxing as she moved towards the bench and picked up the swathe of yellow silk cloth.

'I've tried to explain to her that the yellow will not suit her, her skin is too sallow, but she is determined to ignore my advice and have it all the same.'

'Then we'd better get on with it, hadn't we?' Lily said, forcing a smile. Soon she was absorbed in her work and all thoughts of Jez and her marriage were banished from her mind as she lost herself in the pleasure of her needlework.

CHAPTER EIGHTEEN

Eleanor walked briskly down Oakley Street towards her parents' elegant Chelsea townhouse. Despite the overcast sky and a cold March wind that scoured her cheeks, the signs of spring were visible everywhere, from the gold and purple crocuses in the window boxes to the catkins and pussy willow adorning the trees in the park.

She had been bitterly disappointed to receive Lily's telegram cancelling her visit at Christmas. The endless round of balls and soirees had lost its appeal without Lily there to enjoy it with her. And over the ensuing weeks, her disappointment had turned to concern as her many letters went unanswered.

She sighed and ran up the steps to the front door, which was opened immediately by Jerome, the butler.

'Good afternoon, Miss Eleanor. Did you have a pleasant walk?' he asked, helping to divest her of her coat and muff.

'Good afternoon, Jerome. Yes, thank you. It was very pleasant, if a little chilly,' she added, catching sight of her red nose and pink-tinged cheeks in the hall mirror. 'Are my parents home?'

'Lady Copperfield is out visiting friends but Sir Frederick is in his study,' Jerome said, hanging Eleanor's fur-lined coat on the coatrack. He was a distinguished-looking man, tall and thin with slightly rounded shoulders, neatly trimmed grey hair and slate-grey eyes topped by bushy white brows.

'Thank you, Jerome. I shan't disturb Father. I'm sure he's busy.'

It had come as a shock when, in the first week of January, Eleanor's maternal grandfather had been killed in a hunting accident. Eleanor wished she had made more of an effort to be cordial when she saw him at Christmas but, sadly, both Lord and Lady Lovett viewed children as nothing more than a necessary evil and had failed to build a rapport with either their only surviving child or their granddaughter.

Lady Copperfield had shed few tears for the father she had always found to be cold and distant, yet he had made her joint beneficiary with Lady Lovett and, since then, Sir Frederick had spent his time closeted away with his accountant using his wife's inheritance to discharge his many debts and investing in his struggling businesses, the Copperfield fortunes restored.

'A letter came for you while you were out, miss,' Jerome said, indicating the silver tray on the lacquered side table. 'It came this morning.'

'It's from Lily,' Eleanor said, recognizing the writing. 'At last.'

Hugging the letter to her chest, she hurried up the stairs to the sanctuary of her bedroom and closed the door. Her window overlooked the back of the house where pink cherry blossom and clusters of crocuses and early daffodils brought a touch of spring colour to the winter-drab garden. Settling herself in the window seat, she ripped open the envelope and unfolded the single sheet of paper.

Her initial relief and excitement quickly faded, replaced by growing disbelief. She frowned in confusion. Lily and Jez were married? Jez Elkin? A man Lily had confided to Eleanor that she despised? And now Lily was expecting a baby! Surely, there must be some mistake.

Letting the letter fall to her lap, Eleanor stared unseeing into the hearth.

Why would Lily tie herself to such a man? Eleanor read the letter again, sure her eyes must have deceived her in some way, but no, there it was in black and white. Lily and Jez were married and expecting a baby. Eleanor frowned, unable to make sense of Lily's news.

Perplexed, she refolded the letter and slipped it between the pages of her book and looked down into the garden where two squirrels were chasing each other across the windswept lawn. In just under a fortnight, she would be going home and now, in light of Lily's news, she felt an urgency to see her dearest friend and discover for herself the reason Lily had chosen to marry Jez Elkin, of all people. In the meantime, she resolved to write to Lily straight away and offer her congratulations. With a deeply heartfelt sigh,

Eleanor got to her feet and went in search of writing paper and a pen.

Hunched over the bodice of a red-satin ballgown, Lily gave a sudden gasp and jerked her head up, wincing as the needle found the fleshy bit of her thumb.

'Ow!'

'Lily?' Violet set down the blouse she was basting and looked at Lily with concern. Lily was five months along now and starting to show, although her clothes managed to conceal her swelling bump well enough for now.

'The baby moved,' Lily said in breathless wonder, slightly misty-eyed as she returned Violet's gaze, sucking her bleeding thumb.

'Really?' Violet's tone was one of excitement. The baby might have a scoundrel like Jez for its father and it might have been conceived in violence but it was a baby nonetheless and Violet, now thirty-seven and having long since reconciled herself to life as an old maid, was determined to enjoy every minute of Lily's pregnancy.

'What did it feel like?'

'It was like . . .' Lily began wonderingly. She paused, unable to find the words to describe the gentle fluttering deep in the pit of her stomach. 'Oh, it's hard to describe. It feels like I'm being tickled from inside.' She laughed, then grew sober as the weight of the responsibility she was carrying dawned on her. Instinctively, she placed her hands protectively on her swollen stomach.

Her changing body fascinated her. When she undressed for bed at night, she would stare in wonder at her rounded belly. Jez had already started making lewd remarks about her swollen breasts. To Lily's immense relief, he still hadn't made good on his threat to take her as his wife in the physical sense and, as the days had turned into weeks, she had begun to relax. Dare she hope he was displaying some common decency by leaving her alone until after the baby was born? She refused to dwell on what would happen afterwards. She was focused on getting through each day as it came and saw little point in fretting about a future over which she had no control.

'Do you need to go home?' Violet asked now, her brow creased in concern.

Lily laughed. 'No, I'm fine, Violet. I'm expecting a baby. I'm not ill.'

'If you're sure,' Violet replied doubtfully. 'I worry you're doing too much.'

'I'm perfectly fine, Violet,' Lily assured her. 'And to be honest, I'd rather be here working than stuck at home with Doris.'

Now that Lily was no longer boarding over the shop, Violet had begun paying her a small wage. So, while Jez took the money Lily earned in commissions each week, he knew nothing about the savings account Violet had opened in Lily's name, nor the amount she deposited every week.

'You never know what may happen,' Violet had said when she showed Lily her new bankbook. It was the thought of her steadily growing nest egg that kept her sane, knowing that she had an escape route, should she ever need one.

For the rest of the afternoon Lily's baby remained disappointingly inactive but she was left with a glow that stayed with her until well into the evening.

The following day, Sunday, dawned bright and sunny. Church bells rang out across the town. Fluffy white clouds scudded across a pale blue sky and the sun was warm on Lily's skin as she threw open doors and windows in an effort to banish the damp mustiness left by a long, wet winter.

'Shut that blinking door,' Doris snapped, shuffling into the sunlit kitchen looking her usual unkempt self. 'It's freezing.' Jez, hunched over a mug of strong tea, scowled at her.

'You never heard of fresh air, Ma?' he asked mildly. Lily moved carefully around him to set his plate of eggs and toast on the table. Now the weather was improving the hens had begun laying again.

Nodding his thanks, Jez caught Lily's hand and pressed it to his lips. Lily forced herself not to flinch as his dark eyes mocked her.

Though he sometimes shared her bed, slipping in beside her late at night, his body cold and smelling of woodsmoke and drink, he never touched her. Where he spent the night when he failed to come home Lily neither knew, nor, as long as he was discreet, did she care. The occasional whiff of perfume on his shirt collar left her in little doubt he didn't sleep alone.

They were husband and wife in name only and that suited her, though she knew the day of reckoning would come. And she was dreading it. She pushed the thought from her mind and, ignoring the ramblings of her perpetually disgruntled mother-in-law, dished up her own breakfast. The protein from the eggs would be good for the baby and she ate heartily, pointedly ignoring Jez's comments about her ravenous appetite.

'I ate like a horse when I was carrying you, Jez,' Doris remarked in a rare show of support for her daughter-in-law. 'She's eating for two, don't forget.'

Jez raised one eyebrow in reply. 'You'd better not get too fat,' he warned, his head cocked as he leered at Lily wolfishly. 'I'm not sharing my bed with a fat pig.'

'Leave her alone, Jez,' Doris reprimanded. Blushing, Lily got up and began to clear the table. As she reached for Jez's plate, he grabbed her hand again. She stiffened, her heart pounding.

'Put on your prettiest dress,' he said, letting go of her to fold his newspaper. 'I've a mind to take my wife out.'

Lily and Doris both looked at him in surprise. Lily's eyes narrowed in suspicion. 'Where are we going?' she asked cautiously.

'It's a surprise.' Jez grinned and Lily's stomach contracted. She could tell by the mocking glint in his eyes, the surprise wouldn't be a good one.

'Can I come?' Doris asked eagerly.

'No,' replied Jez bluntly. 'You'll only show me up.' Seeing Doris's crestfallen expression, Lily almost felt sorry for her.

Trying not to let her apprehension show, Lily said, 'I'd better finish the dishes, then.' Conscious of Jez's scrutiny, she washed up, taking her time to dry and put everything away, as Doris wept noisy tears of self-pity until Jez snapped.

'Put a sock in it, Ma! You're trying my bleeding patience with your constant bleating.'

Doris only wailed louder. Shaking his head in disgust, Jez rose from the table. 'I'm leaving in fifteen minutes,' he told Lily. 'Be ready.' He left the room, slamming the adjoining door behind him, and making Doris jump.

Jez was waiting in the parlour, tapping his foot impatiently, when Lily came down the stairs twenty minutes later. He was wearing his best suit and hat, looking every inch the dapper gentleman. She held her breath while he cast a critical eye over her outfit. The dress was one of her own creations, coral-pink with puffed sleeves and a high collar, loose enough to accommodate her expanding waistline. He gave her a curt nod of approval and extended his arm. After a brief hesitation, Lily took it.

Her heart beat erratically as they walked down Laundry Lane. Being a Sunday, there were few people about. Those that were eyed Lily with mild curiosity and she knew they were wondering why, after she'd managed to escape her aunt's clutches, Lily would willingly align herself with the family by marrying Jez.

Jez walked quickly and Lily had to hurry to keep up with him.

'Where are we going?' she finally dared to ask, curiosity overcoming her fear. They were walking through the deserted marketplace and, as they passed the entrance to Church Lane, she felt the bile rise up in her throat, memories of Jez's brutal attack rushing to the forefront of her mind. Swallowing painfully, she cast a surreptitious glance sideways but he was staring stonily ahead. Did he feel any remorse at all, she wondered, or was he so evil as to dismiss the entire incident as inconsequential? Her legs wobbled and despite the sun's warmth, she shivered.

They passed Violet's shop. The upstairs windows were open. The aroma of toasting crumpets drifted on the warm spring air and Lily was overwhelmed by a longing to revert back to the carefree girl she had once been, sitting in Violet's sunny kitchen, eating crumpets and laughing with her friend.

Market Place had given way to East Street and Lily's stomach cramped nervously as she recognized the route that led towards the fire-ravaged malthouse. She faltered, her skin erupting in goosebumps as she recalled the night Jez had made her act as lookout for his illegal boxing match. As if sensing her reluctance to go any further, he tightened his grip on her arm, almost tugging her down a narrow, foul-smelling snicket. Nervously, she eyed the dirty, rough-looking men loitering in the shadows. Skin ingrained with dirt, their faces sunken and hollowed-eyed, they shrank back from Jez, allowing them free passage down the narrow, stinking alleyway.

A recent rain had turned the ground around the old ruined malthouse into a quagmire. 'Why are we here?' Lily asked in trepidation, lifting her skirts as she crossed the wooden boards that formed a footbridge through the mud. She could hear the rumble of voices from within the building.

'I thought it was time you took an interest in the family business,' Jez replied with a smirk. 'Don't look so shocked, wifey. Get rid of those inhibitions of yours and you might find you enjoy yourself.'

Lily stepped into the cavernous ruins, blinking as her eyes adjusted to the gloom. Weeds sprouted through the cracks in the brickwork and the floor was littered with animal faeces and spent matches. Dust motes swirled in the shards of hazy sunlight streaming in through the holes in the ceiling. Thick wooden beams crisscrossed overhead, shrouded in cobwebs. The rumble of conversation had ceased the moment Jez and Lily had entered the building. The men stood in small groups at the far end of the room, which had once been the main brewing room. Evidence of which could be seen in the charred remains of the wooden posts once used to support the massive vats.

They were big men, burly and wild-eyed. Some were shirtless, their naked torsos gleaming in the flickering candle-light. She was surprised to see three women among the group. They eyed Lily with undisguised contempt.

'You brought some new meat, Jez?' a petite girl with hair the colour of brass called, shooting Lily a venomous glare. Lily judged her to be about her age, and she might have been pretty but it was hard to tell beneath the heavily painted face.

'She'll need a bit of breaking in,' cackled another girl. She was taller and older, chestnut-brown hair falling in a tousled mass over her bare shoulders. 'She looks a bit green behind the ears.'

'I've broken in a few fillies in my time,' a bald, thick-muscled man shouted to the whistled approval of his companions. A tattoo of a snake coiled its way up the biceps of his right arm.

Lily licked her lips fearfully. The women's low-cut gowns and painted faces left no doubt as to their position and she was filled with dread. Surely Jez wouldn't . . .

'Jez?' she whispered frantically, her throat tight with panic. 'The baby . . .'

'Enough!' Jez snapped, a tight edge to his voice as he surveyed the men. 'This is my wife so show some respect! I thought it's time she got to see how I make my money.' He turned to grin at Lily, clearly enjoying her discomfort.

'Begging your pardon, ma'am,' the bald-headed tattooed man apologized sheepishly. 'Sorry, Jez. No offence, mate. I didn't mean anything by it.'

'None taken, Thom,' Jez replied jovially. 'Let's get started, shall we?' While the men and the girls made their way through a wide opening in the wall, Jez held Lily back, his fingers digging painfully into her flesh. 'You mind yourself, wifey,' he hissed, 'or I might change my mind and let the boys have their way with you, after all.' He nodded towards a woman Lily hadn't noticed before. She seemed to hang back from the group, her shoulders slumped. 'That's Nellie there,' Jez said with a contemptuous sneer. 'Not yet twenty-one and riddled with the pox. She'll be back on the streets before today's over. Dirty girls are bad for business.' Lily looked at the girl with pity.

Lily was about to protest but one look at Jez's face and she changed her mind. She suddenly came over queasy and would have stumbled had not Jez grabbed hold of her.

'Pull yourself together,' he hissed angrily. 'This is a very important business meeting for me. I expect you to conduct yourself in a manner befitting of my wife.' He grinned devilishly. 'You know what happens if you make me angry, don't you, Lily?'

Feeling light-headed, Lily could only nod. Jez snorted.

'Good. Now, plaster a smile on that sour mug of yours and let's go do some business.'

Stepping between the singed and crumbling walls, Lily found herself in a large, windowless chamber lit by a myriad of flickering lamps. Apart from missing large chunks of masonry, this room appeared to have survived relatively unscathed. The floor had been swept clean and hay bales had been placed at intervals around the room. She noticed several well-dressed gentlemen lounging on the bales of hay, seemingly enjoying the attentions of the provocatively clad young women plying them with drink.

'Gentlemen,' Jez exclaimed, waving his arms expansively. 'Welcome, welcome. I trust my ladies have been looking after you?' This was met by murmurs of assent form the assembled gentlemen. A few of the girls tittered and one old man – a portly gentleman with a florid complexion and thin, greying hair artfully combed in an effort to conceal his balding pate – let out a self-conscious guffaw.

'Gentlemen, allow me to introduce my wife.' Jez extended his hand to Lily, drawing her closer. Lily's ears buzzed as he rattled off a list of names. Lily swayed, and the faces before her blurred.

'My dear sir,' a younger, dark-haired man squawked in alarm. 'I believe your wife is about to faint.'

Jez's expression radiated annoyance rather than concern but he checked himself quickly. 'My dear Lily.' He clicked his fingers as he helped Lily to the nearest bale of hay. 'Lizzie,' he said, nodding at the nearest girl. 'A glass of water for my wife, please. I'm sorry, gentlemen,' he said as Lily sat down gratefully. 'My wife is with child. I forget how delicate a lady in her condition can be.'

Ignoring the hearty congratulations and backslapping going on around her, Lily closed her eyes and concentrated on her breathing. The musty smell of hay combined with the tang of pipe tobacco and sweat did little to stem the rising tide of nausea.

'Here, missus, drink this.' She opened her eyes. The young girl who had spoken to her so crudely earlier stood in front of her, holding out a glass of water.

'Thank you,' she whispered. She took a sip of the tepid water and attempted a smile. 'Lizzie, is it?'

'Yes, ma'am.' Lizzie flushed, her fingers fiddling with the buttons on her crimson bodice. 'Sorry about what I said earlier,' she mumbled. 'It was just a joke.'

Lily waved the apology away. 'It's fine, really. Think no more about it.'

Lizzie turned to watch Jez engaging the men in conversation and saw him glance over at her. Lizzie had seen it too. The expression on her face was one Lily knew only too well: fear. 'Well, if you're feeling better, ma'am,' Lizzie said, a nervous edge to her voice, 'I'd better get back to work.'

Lily laid her hand gently on Lizzie's arm. 'Can't you leave?' she asked, her voice low.

Lizzie shot a frightened glance in Jez's direction but he was facing the other way, talking to two of the young men Lily had seen when she first arrived. Their grease-smeared torsos gleamed in the lamplight.

'If I don't work, my nan and my baby boy will end up in the workhouse. Mr Jez looks after us girls. It's better than working the streets.' Her expression was one of defiance, as if daring Lily to judge her. With a toss of her brassy mane, she turned away, but not before Lily saw the tears glistening in her heavily made-up eyes.

The noise level suddenly rose several decibels as the two young men faced each other in the middle of the floor. At Jez's command they flew at each other, fists clenched. Lily watched with a mixture of abhorrence and disbelief. Bare knuckle fighting. She had heard of it, but she had never dreamed it could be this barbaric. No wonder it was outlawed. Each time a fist found purchase she winced at the sound of flesh hitting flesh. Her nausea returned.

The air was soon thick with the coppery stench of blood. The girls were passing around flagons of beer to the gentlemen. Just minutes before, they had seemed to Lily to be the epitome of high society, but now they were red-faced and perspiring as they jeered and yelled, swilling beer and cursing like navvies. The girls joined in the cheering and booing, draping themselves around the men in a suggestive manner.

Each match ended only when one of the participants went down and couldn't get back up. There was just enough time between bouts to throw a handful of sawdust over the puddles of blood before the next pair took up their positions.

It was late afternoon when the only man left standing was declared the winner and Lily was exhausted. She had eaten nothing since breakfast and felt light-headed with hunger. It was only now she noticed the metal staircase at the far end of the room, up which the six gentlemen, all now much the worse for drink, were making their way. Each had at least one girl draped on their arm.

Only the poor pox-ridden Nellie remained downstairs. Eyes downcast, she started sweeping up the blood-stained sawdust.

'Are you all right?' Lily asked. She felt dreadfully sorry for the girl. Nellie nodded, not meeting Lily's gaze.

Not wanting to think about what might be going on upstairs, she tried to engage the girl in conversation.

'Do you have any family, Nellie?' she asked. This time Nellie did look at her. She leaned on her broom, regarding Lily with a mocking expression.

'If I had family I could rely on, do you think I'd be playing the whore for your husband?' she jeered. Lily flinched and looked away, her cheeks flooding with shame. She felt sick to her stomach. Nellie's expression softened.

'Do you really want to know how that man of yours makes his money, huh?' Glancing over her shoulder to make sure Jez wasn't within hearing distance, Nellie leaned towards Lily, her voice low.

'Blackmail, that's how.' She waved her hand. 'All this, the girls, the boxing, that's just bait to tempt the punters. It's our job to get them drunk and take them upstairs. Whether they're capable of anything or not, once they get up there is beside the point. Once they've sobered up, Jez threatens to tell their wives and business associates unless they pay up. The poor chaps are so petrified they usually cough up straight away.'

'Blackmail?' Lily repeated hoarsely, hardly able to believe her ears.

'Easy money,' Nellie said, her words trailing away. Following her stricken gaze, Lily balked. Jez was standing barely three feet away.

'You've got a big mouth, Nellie,' he said mildly.

'I'm sorry, Mr Elkin,' Nellie stammered. Jez smiled lazily then, like a panther, he lunged forwards and grabbed Nellie by the throat. Lily was on her feet in a flash.

'Leave her alone!' Ignoring his wife's anguished shout, Jez squeezed Nellie's throat, his cheeks flushed with anger.

'You're out of here, Nellie Rogers, and you'd better keep your mouth shut or I'll shut it for you, permanently.'

Nellie's eyes bulged in fright, leaking tears. She made a harsh gurgling noise, her fingers scrabbling at Jez's hands in vain.

'Jez!' Lily screamed again. 'Let her go.'

With one last squeeze, Jez released his grip. Nellie sank to the floor, gasping for air and Lily flew to her side.

'Are you all right, Nellie?' She glared at Jez. 'You nearly killed her.'

'Serve her right, then,' Jez said. 'And you, keep your voice down. You'll upset our guests.'

'Guests?' Lily spat in disgust. 'You mean the stupid men you're about to blackmail? And what about those poor lads who got themselves beaten to a bloody pulp? What happens to them?' She wrapped her arms around Nellie, gently stroking her back as she sucked in deep breaths of stale air and massaged her bruised throat.

'Oh, they'll be adequately compensated,' Jez said, waving away her concern. He glared at Nellie. 'Get out, go on. Get out of here.'

'Are you sure you're all right?' Lily whispered, helping Nellie to her feet.

'Why are you still here?' Jez growled. 'Get out!' His shout made them both jump. With one last terrified glance at Lily, Nellie grabbed her hat and fled.

'I'm going home.' Lily turned her back on Jez. She could feel his gaze boring into her back, causing the hairs on the back of her neck to stand on end.

'Lily.' His tender tone took Lily by surprise as he took her elbow and gently turned her round to face him. 'We got off to a bad start, you and me, but I'm prepared to make an effort.' He shrugged his shoulders as the sound of raucous laughter drifted from the floor above. Two of the fighters, one sporting a bandage around his hand, were helping a third young man across the room. His eyes were swollen shut and his broken nose was caked with dried blood. Lily's stomach curdled.

'This is what I am, Lily. This is me in all my glory. I make a good living so, as long as you play your cards right, you and your brat will want for nothing. But you go squealing to the constable and I'll make sure you rue the day you were born. You play nice with me and I'll play nice with you.'

Stunned, Lily could only stare. His mocking smile reminded Lily of a snake, lulling its victim into a false sense of security before it dealt the deadly strike. The illegal boxing was one thing but did he really believe she could turn a blind eye to whoring and blackmail?

'You disgust me,' she said, finding her voice. 'You're nothing but a common criminal. Blackmailing those men? Pimping young girls? What sort of man are you?'

Jez's hand seemed to come out of nowhere. She fell backwards, sprawling across a bale of hay. She licked her lips, tasting blood. Jez hovered over her menacingly.

'Hit me again, Jez Elkin,' she hissed, struggling to her feet. Her cheek smarted and she blinked back tears. 'And I shall be straight down the police station. I made the biggest mistake of my life marrying you. I should have listened to Violet.' She fixed Jez with a beady eye. 'I'm leaving you. I never want to see you again.' She turned on her heel, but Jez grabbed her arm and pressed his face up against hers.

'You are not leaving me, wifey, not now, not ever. If you do, you'll never see your brat. I'm its legal guardian – you have no rights over him or her.'

'You'll never find me,' Lily said, but her voice lacked conviction. Where could she go? If she went to Violet, then Jez could make good on his threat and take her child away as soon as it was born. She could go to Charlie, the voice in her head whispered. But how could she bring her shame to his doorstep? Her shoulders slumped in defeat.

Jez let out a chuckle. 'I thought you'd see things my way. Ned! Ned!' A heavily built young man, with a crude scar running down one cheek and a deep gash above his right eye, emerged from the shadows. Lily recognized him as the man who'd emerged the victor. He ran a hand the size of a shovel over his face. His knuckles were raw.

'Boss?' He eyed Jez warily.

'Clean yourself up then see my wife gets home safely. Stay with her until I get home. I'll hold you personally responsible if she's not there waiting for me when I return,' he added with a pointed look at Lily. Her heart sank. She couldn't risk getting Ned into trouble. She was in no doubt of what Jez might be capable of, if provoked.

Ned's gaze met Lily's and he nodded. 'Yes, Mr Elkin, sir,' he said. His tone was deferential, but before he turned away, Lily was sure she saw a flash of pity in his soulful brown eyes.

CHAPTER NINETEEN

They walked in silence, Lily's few attempts at conversation met by Ned's gruff monosyllabic replies. She felt only relief, the silence allowing her to concentrate on her thoughts. Her head ached with the day's revelations. That her husband was nothing more than a pimp and an extortionist weighed heavily on her heart and her conscience. She felt for her poor unborn child. That he or she shared blood with such a man made her sick to her stomach and she made a silent vow that, no matter what, her child would not grow up to be like its father.

The church bells were ringing as they turned the corner into Laundry Lane, summoning the faithful to evensong. An elegant trap and handsome pony stood waiting outside the cottage, and Lily's spirits rose. *Eleanor.*

Her first flush of joy at the thought of seeing her sister after so long an absence was tempered by the shame. She had thought, perhaps, that Eleanor might not want to continue the friendship, once she'd received news of Lily's hasty marriage, so it was with some trepidation that Lily hastened towards the cottage, all the while praying fervently that she would find Doris sober.

'Thank you,' she told the taciturn Ned. 'I shall be all right now.'

Colouring slightly, Ned lowered his gaze. He kicked at a clod of loose earth churned up by the pony's hooves and cleared his throat.

'Ma'am, Mr Elkin said I was to remain outside the door until he returned.' He shrugged apologetically. Lily's cheeks flooded with humiliation, but before she could protest, the cottage door flew open.

'Lily!' Throwing propriety to the wind, Eleanor ran into the street and flung her arms around Lily. 'I've missed you so much.'

'I've missed you too, Miss Eleanor,' Lily said softly. Aware that curtains would be twitching and feeling the weight of Ned's curious stare, Lily ushered Eleanor indoors. She shot Ned a defiant glare and shut the door firmly in his face.

'You've got a visitor,' Doris slurred from where she was slumped on the threadbare sofa. 'One of your posh customers, is she?'

'I see you've met my mother-in-law,' Lily remarked drily, bundling Eleanor through to the kitchen. She was ashamed of the squalor, the mushrooms of damp that sprouted on the bowed ceiling, the ever-pervading smell of neglect which, no matter how hard Lily scrubbed, could never be erased. At least in the kitchen she could open the door, allowing the cool spring breeze in to alleviate the musty smell.

Eleanor sat down at the kitchen table, her purple and cream striped dress with velvet cuffs incongruous in the less than salubrious surroundings. Lily busied herself making tea as an awkward silence settled between them. Doris shouted something derogatory from the parlour, which Lily ignored.

'You'll have to excuse my mother-in-law,' she apologized, spooning tea leaves into the pot as she waited for the kettle to boil. 'She likes a drink.' She twisted her hands together, the cheap metal band on her ring finger as weighty as a millstone. 'Thank you for your letter of congratulations.'

'I felt it was the proper thing to do,' Eleanor said. Throwing a cautious glance at the adjoining doorway, she lowered her voice. 'Though I must say, it was a huge shock to hear you had married.' Eleanor chewed her lip in consternation. 'Why, after the way he and your aunt treated you?'

Lily was saved from answering straight away by the kettle coming to the boil. 'I'm afraid there isn't any milk,' she said, pouring boiling water into the teapot.

'Black's fine,' Eleanor said as she took the mug Lily handed her, cupping it in her hands. She raised her brows quizzically.

'I don't expect you to understand,' Lily said, pulling out a chair. 'But I had my reasons.' She brushed a lock of hair from her face. 'It all happened rather quickly.'

'I'll say,' Eleanor replied sceptically. 'One minute you were cancelling your visit to me because you were unwell, and the next thing I hear, you're married. He must have really swept you off your feet.' She took a sip of her tea. 'I was worried about you. You didn't reply to my letters.'

'I'm sorry. I didn't want to write until everything was settled.'

'Until what was settled? Look, Lily, I know Jez and your aunt made your life a misery when you were little. Can he really have changed that much?' Eleanor was sure all was not as it seemed. She just hoped that one day Lily would trust her enough to confide the truth.

'Things are different now,' Lily assured her. The lie left a sour taste in her mouth. 'Jez is very excited about the baby.'

'When are you due?' asked Eleanor.

'Oh, sometime towards the end of summer,' replied Lily evasively, feeling the heat creep into her cheeks. Eleanor frowned.

'Is everything all right, Lily? Only, you seem so unlike your usual self.'

'Oh.' Lily waved away Eleanor's concern. 'It's the baby. My emotions are all over the place.' She glanced out of the window, not wanting Eleanor to witness her despair.

'I trust I shall be Baby's favourite aunt,' Eleanor said cheerfully once she'd given Lily a moment to collect herself.

Lily smiled wistfully. If only she could tell Eleanor the truth. 'My baby would be honoured to call you aunt,' she said instead. For a moment she contemplated the fact that her child would be the grandchild of Sir Frederick Copperfield. What a life her child could have looked forward to, had life dealt Lily a better hand, if Sir Frederick had stood by Beatrice instead of casting her aside for the wealthy Lady Copperfield.

'Penny for them,' Eleanor queried, interrupting Lily's train of thought.

'Sorry.' Lily massaged her temples. 'Everything has happened so quickly. I'm still getting used to being a wife and mother-to-be.'

Eleanor laughed, pushing her misgivings over her friend aside. 'It's bound to take some getting used to,' she said, draining her mug of tea. 'Who was the man outside? I thought at first he was Jez but I realized by the way you shut the door in his face that he couldn't be.'

'He works for my husband,' Lily replied. 'Jez asked him to walk me home.'

'That's very . . . thoughtful of him,' Eleanor said dubiously.

Lily bit back a scathing retort and got to her feet. She was still coming to terms with Nellie's allegations of blackmail. 'I need to visit the privy,' she said. 'The baby has a habit of pressing on my bladder. I won't be long.'

New growth was evident everywhere in the garden. Lily had worked hard clearing the weeds and brambles to prepare the yard for planting. There was no sign yet of her new seedlings but, come the warmer months, they should see an abundant crop of vegetables. She wouldn't be able to work much by then so the fresh produce would make a welcome addition to the weekly meals. Birds trilled in the hedges and she could hear the sound of children out in the street.

She visited the privy and was heading back across the yard when she heard his voice. Her heart plummeted. She hadn't expected him home for hours. She heard Eleanor laugh at something he said and felt a flood of dread. Forcing herself to remain calm, she quickened her pace, pausing in the doorway as her brain tried to make sense of the tableau before her.

Eleanor was still sitting at the table, her expression animated, her hazel eyes fixed firmly on Jez, who leaned nonchalantly against the sagging Welsh dresser, rakishly handsome in his suit and cravat.

'Miss Eleanor and I have been getting acquainted,' Jez said, turning his dark mocking gaze on Lily. 'You never told me you were on such familiar terms with Sir Frederick's daughter, Lily.' He winked at Eleanor. 'You must come around more often, miss.' He smiled graciously. 'Lily's welcome to invite her friends over whenever she wishes.'

Lily swallowed the bile that rose in her throat. She had seen that hungry gleam in Jez's eyes before.

'Perhaps you'd like to stay for supper,' Jez said, his tone mocking. 'I'm afraid we're not quite as grand as Bay Willow House but I'm sure Lily could rustle up—'

'Eleanor was just about to leave,' Lily interrupted frostily. 'You don't want to be late home, Miss Eleanor.'

'Pardon?' Eleanor tore her gaze away from Jez with difficulty. Golly, he certainly was handsome, in a rakish sort of way. No wonder he had swept Lily off her feet. He brought to mind the heroes in the penny romances Eleanor kept hidden beneath her pillow away from her mother's prying eyes.

'I'm sure we can get a message to Sir Frederick,' Jez said, shooting Lily a look of annoyance. 'Though she didn't understand the subtle undercurrent in the exchange, Eleanor was astute enough to appreciate the silent plea in Lily's eyes.

'That's very kind of you, Mr Elkin,' Eleanor said, sliding her chair back. 'But I have stayed too long already.' She felt herself colouring under Jez's blatant scrutiny. A pulse throbbed at the base of her throat. 'And my parents are expecting me home for supper.'

'How disappointing,' Jez said with mock gallantry. 'It was a pleasure to meet you, Miss Eleanor.' He lifted Eleanor's hand to his lips. 'I trust it won't be too long until we see you again.'

'I hope not.' Eleanor withdrew her hand, her cheeks glowing crimson.

'I'll see you out, Miss Eleanor,' Lily said, studiously avoiding Jez's gaze. He was goading her and she refused to give him the satisfaction of knowing he had unsettled her. She led Eleanor through the front parlour where Doris was sprawled across the sofa, snoring throatily. Her mouth hung open, a line of spittle running down her chin. Turning away in disgust, and swallowing her shame that Eleanor should bear witness to such a sight, Lily ushered her half-sister out of the door and into the quiet street.

The sun was sinking in the sky and the cottages opposite cast lengthy shadows across the ground. Relieved of his duties now Jez had returned, Ned was nowhere to be seen.

The pony snickered and nudged Eleanor's elbow. She rubbed its nose affectionately.

'I can see exactly why you fell for Mr Elkin so quickly, Lily. He's as handsome as the Devil himself. I am quite jealous.

None of the young men Mama has introduced me to are half as good-looking as him.'

'You'll find yourself a lovely husband one day,' Lily assured her, inwardly praying that Eleanor's future husband would be the complete opposite of her own.

'The young men I meet seem so staid in comparison to your Jez.' Eleanor pouted petulantly. Lily gave her a tight smile and helped her into the trap.

Eleanor gathered up the reins. 'I do hope Mama and Papa aren't going to be difficult about me calling on you. They're both such awful snobs sometimes.' She gave Lily an apologetic smile. 'I told them I shall be perfectly safe, but if they make a fuss, I'll get Harry to drive me next time. They can't object then.' She raised a gloved hand, her fond gaze resting on Lily's upturned face. 'May I call again next Sunday?'

The hairs on Lily's neck stood on end and she knew Jez was watching them from the window, listening to every word. Her reply caught in her throat. Eleanor's face clouded with disappointment.

'If you're busy ...?'

Lily shook her head. 'No, I'd love to see you. Perhaps we could take a walk. The daffodils in Bryanston Park will be beautiful at this time of year.'

'That will be lovely,' Eleanor agreed with enthusiasm. 'I'll get Mrs White to make up a picnic. Until next Sunday then.' Eleanor gently shook the reins and the pony set off at a brisk pace.

Lily stood in the gathering dusk, clutching her shawl against the late afternoon chill, long after Eleanor was out of sight, shoulders drooping in despair.

That Jez had been so pleasant towards Eleanor frightened her. He would have some agenda, some plan up his sleeve, and she was determined to protect her sister from him, whatever the cost to herself.

Finally, she could delay no longer.

'You kept that quiet, didn't you?' Jez said the moment she entered the cottage.

'What?' she asked, knowing full well what he meant.

'Why didn't you tell me you were thick with Sir Frederick's daughter?'

'My friendship with Miss Eleanor is none of your concern,' Lily said defiantly. She turned to hang her shawl on the hook and Jez grabbed her arm.

'Everything you do is my concern,' he hissed. He smiled. 'This could work to our advantage.' He released his grip on Lily's arm and stood back, rubbing his chin in a thoughtful manner.

'Put the kettle on, Lily.' The sudden change in tone caught Lily off guard. 'We'll have a cup of tea and a chat.'

'What about?' Lily asked nervously.

'Make the tea first,' he said, shoving her towards the kitchen. 'I need to collect my thoughts.' He cast a glance in the direction of the snoring Doris. 'I'll drag the drunken old hag up to bed first. I don't want her waking up like a bear with a sore head and sticking her oar in.'

He hefted his mother off the sofa, slinging her over his broad shoulders like she was some old drunk he'd found in the street, and took her upstairs. Lily made a fresh pot of tea, listening to the creak of the floorboards overhead, and the squeak of the bed springs as Jez unceremoniously deposited Doris onto her bed.

'So, what is it you want to talk about?' she asked. She leaned against the Welsh dresser, trying to quell her deep sense of foreboding as she forced herself to meet her husband's beady-eyed gaze. He rocked back on the spindle-back kitchen chair, letting his gaze travel the length of Lily's body before coming back to rest on her face.

'Your friendship with Miss Eleanor could prove to be very lucrative indeed,' he said slowly.

'What do you mean?' Lily stammered, flushing guiltily. Had Jez somehow made the connection between herself and Eleanor? Did he intend to blackmail Sir Frederick with the truth?

'Don't be dense, Lily,' Jez growled. 'Her old man is minted. Word on the street is that the father-in-law popped his clogs a few months back and the missus inherited half the estate.'

'How does that affect you?' Lily asked coldly. 'I'm privileged that she calls me her friend, but I am only her dressmaker. I don't see how Lady Copperfield's inheritance is of any relevance.'

'Can't you see?' Jez demanded excitedly. 'We could take Sir Fred for a king's ransom. We just need to get him to one of my boxing matches. All you've got to do is persuade your Miss Eleanor to encourage him to come. Once he's there, the girls will do the rest.' He grinned, clearly expecting Lily to be as enamoured with the plan as he was.

She stared at him in horror. 'You're asking me to help you blackmail Sir Frederick?'

'Yes.' His eyes narrowed. 'If you don't want to do it, I could always speak to Eleanor myself. She's clearly besotted with me.' He chuckled. 'The poor girl could hardly take her eyes off me.' He leered across the room, clearly enjoying Lily's discomfort, and sniggered. 'She could probably do with having a real man for a change. I wonder how long her loyalty to you would last if I started paying her some attention?' He gave Lily a wink. 'I'd wager not very long. She was practically begging for it.'

'You're disgusting,' Lily said angrily. 'Leave Eleanor, and her father, alone,' she warned, a hard edge to her voice. She was prepared to put up with a lot for the sake of her unborn child, but she would never allow Jez to take advantage of Eleanor as he had her.

'Why? What do you care?' he sneered. 'I'm entitled to seek my comforts elsewhere until you're prepared to behave like a proper wife.' He eyed her rounded stomach. 'And there's not a man on earth who wouldn't agree with me.'

Was there no end to her husband's depravity?

Jez spread his hands in appeal. 'It's up to you. You persuade your pal to get Sir Fred along to one of my parties, and I'll leave her alone.'

'No!' Lily said forcefully. 'I will not allow you to besmirch Sir Frederick's name.'

'Why not?' Jez swallowed a mouthful of tea and wiped his mouth on his hand. 'What's he to you?'

'He's my—' Just in time Lily bit back the words. 'He's Miss Eleanor's father,' she continued weakly. 'I won't let you break her heart.'

'Very well.' Jez shot her a look of pure disdain. 'I'll do it myself.' He got to his feet, glaring at Lily as he pushed past her. 'I doubt I'll have much difficulty in convincing your little Miss Eleanor to do anything, do you?' Grinning evilly, he snatched up his hat and coat and stormed out of the house, leaving Lily reeling. Sick to her stomach, she ran to the privy and emptied the contents of her stomach, retching until there was nothing left.

CHAPTER TWENTY

Lily tossed and turned much of the night. When Jez finally stumbled into bed, reeking of whisky and cheap perfume, she feigned sleep. He fell asleep instantly while she lay awake, staring into the inky blackness, his threats whirling round and round in her head.

She would never allow Jez to bring shame on Eleanor's family. Whether Sir Frederick would be so foolish as to open himself up to blackmail was open to debate but Lily was not prepared to take the chance. As the grey dawn light crept into the room, she made her decision. What she was about to do would break her heart, and no doubt Eleanor's too, but she had no choice. She had to protect Eleanor's family, her family.

Lily slept badly, waking early the following morning. For a moment she lay in the grey dawn light, listening to Jez's loud snores, before slipping quietly from beneath the covers and hurrying downstairs in search of paper and ink.

She had agonized over what to say all night but, in the end, her message was short and to the point.

Dear Miss Eleanor,

I regret I must cancel our outing next Sunday. On reflection, I feel that now I am a wife and soon to be a mother, my family must be my priority and so I feel I must curtail our friendship. I wish you well for the future.

Yours affectionately,

Lily Elkin (Mrs)

Blinking back the tears, she waved the sheet of paper in the air to dry the ink before folding it up and tucking it into her skirt pocket. Trying not to dwell on how much her note would hurt and shock Eleanor, she went into the kitchen to stoke the fire and make a start on the breakfast preparations.

Her thoughts were still on Eleanor when she left for work some time later, almost colliding with a ragtag group of boys coming up the street.

'Oops, sorry, missus.'

'Sammy?' Recognising the son of one of her neighbours, she waved away his apology. 'Would you do me a favour? Could you drop this note into Bay Willow House on your way to school?' she asked, willing him to say yes. She had been dreading delivering the note herself and running the risk of bumping into Eleanor. 'There's a shilling in it for you.'

'A shilling? Yes, missus.' Sammy grinned. There was a gap where his two front teeth should be.

'Ask the housekeeper to please see that Miss Eleanor gets it immediately. Will you remember that?'

Sammy nodded enthusiastically. 'Tell housekeeper to give the note to Miss Eleanor.'

'You needn't wait,' Lily told him with a twinge of sadness. 'I'm not expecting a reply.'

Eleanor was eating breakfast with her parents. Her father, as usual, was engrossed in *The Times*, a hand snaking out from behind the newspaper every now and then to grope blindly for his teacup.

'It's such a perfect day, I thought we might go riding this morning, Eleanor dear,' Lady Copperfield said, spreading a thin layer of marmalade on a slice of toast.

'I'd like that, Mama,' Eleanor replied as Ada bustled in with the coffee pot.

'Pardon me, Miss Eleanor,' Ada said, reaching into her apron pocket as she set the silver coffee pot on the table. 'A message has come for you.'

'For me?' Eleanor asked, surprised.

Sir Frederick lowered his paper. 'From whom?' he queried with a frown.

'Lady Copperfield's dressmaker, sir. Lily.' Ada didn't quite meet Sir Frederick's gaze. 'The lad who delivered it was most insistent I bring it to Miss Eleanor right away.'

'Was he indeed?' Sir Frederick's frown deepened. It irked him that, despite his strong reservations, his wife continued to encourage Eleanor's friendship with Lily.

Eleanor wiped her lips with her napkin and took the note. 'Thank you, Mrs White.'

'That will be all, Mrs White,' Sir Frederick said curtly. Ada retreated with a nod, closing the door behind her.

'I was thinking,' Lady Copperfield said, setting down her knife, 'that now Lily is married, perhaps it might be best if you didn't rely on her friendship quite so much.'

'I agree with your mother,' Sir Frederick said quickly, barely able to hide his relief. 'Being overly familiar with the tradespeople is all right when one is a child, I suppose, but you're sixteen now. Old enough to start courting. You should be mixing in the right circles with a view to finding a marriage partner.'

'Oh, Papa,' Eleanor laughed, unfolding Lily's note.

'Your father's right, Eleanor,' Lady Copperfield admonished her daughter. 'You could do untold damage to your prospects if you insist on visiting places like Laundry Lane.' Just the name of the street sent a shiver of revulsion down her spine. 'We've been very patient, but it's now time to nip this friendship in the bud.'

But Eleanor wasn't listening. Frowning, she read Lily's note again, sure that there must be some mistake.

'Well,' she said at length, gazing bitterly at both her parents, 'you've got your way. Lily doesn't want to see me anymore.' She passed the note to her mother. 'Did you have anything to do with this, Papa?' she demanded.

'Eleanor!' her mother exclaimed. 'How can you even suggest such a thing?'

'Papa has never approved of our friendship,' Eleanor retorted.

'Indeed, I have not.' Sir Frederick folded his newspaper and laid it on the table, his expression stern. 'While I can assure you that Lily's decision has nothing to do with me, I am pleased that she has seen sense.' He pushed back his chair. 'I shall be in my study. I do not wish to be disturbed.'

Eleanor stared after him in misery. How could Lily cast her off so callously? And how could she think their friendship was incompatible with caring for her family? Eleanor would never try to come between Lily and her husband. She was struck by a sudden thought. There was no doubt she had been flattered by Jez's teasing. Surely Lily hadn't been ... jealous? She pushed the thought aside. Lily knew her better than that. Didn't she? She bit her lip in consternation.

'I don't mean to be unfeeling,' Lady Copperfield said dismissively, handing back Lily's note. 'Lily's a lovely young woman but she's hardly your equal, darling.'

'But Lily is my dearest friend,' Eleanor protested. 'I shall miss her.'

'Which is why,' Lady Copperfield said, daintily dabbing her lips with a napkin, 'I am advocating your father's suggestion that we move to London permanently.'

'Pardon?' Eleanor frowned. 'You mean leave Bay Willow House, for good?'

'I know you've been happy here but since Grandfather passed away, Grandmama has been very lonely. If we were in London, we could see so much more of her. She has even suggested a family who may be interested in renting this house. Do you remember the Lambert family? We met them at the Claverings' New Year's Eve party? Perhaps you don't,' she said when Eleanor looked blank. 'No matter. They seemed nice enough, though a bit new money for my taste.' She wrinkled her nose as if to emphasize the point. 'But new money or old, they've got plenty of it and they're looking to move to the country for a few years.

'So, what do you say?' she asked Eleanor hopefully. 'Would you be willing to live in London, at least for a year or two? Grandmama knows so many families; there will be summer balls, hunts, tea parties, punting on the river. Oh, Eleanor, it will be such fun, you cannot imagine.'

Still smarting from Lily's unexpected rebuttal of her friendship, Eleanor nodded.

'I suppose so.' She picked up a slice of toast and put it down again. Her appetite had deserted her.

'When do you intend to leave?'

'Well, there is much to do,' Lady Copperfield said thoughtfully, her mind racing with the scale of the task ahead of her. 'Most of the furniture will have to be put into storage, of course, but I know your father hopes to leave by the end of April, early May at the latest.'

Eleanor nodded. 'Very well,' she said, unable to inflect any enthusiasm into her voice. 'But would you mind very much if I went before then?'

'Not at all,' Lady Copperfield replied, barely able to disguise her delight. 'If that's what you'd prefer?'

'It is.' Eleanor wiped her lips. 'I need a change of scenery and I believe you are right. Moving to London will be just the thing. Please would you ask Father to telegram Jerome and tell him to expect me on Saturday?'

'Certainly,' Lady Copperfield said, pleased by the way events had unfolded. She had nothing against Lily as such, not like Freddie who seemed to have developed a dislike for the girl right from the start but, nevertheless, it was only right the friendship came to a natural end. It was time Eleanor concentrated on her future, and finding a husband of her own. She got to her feet. 'Papa can send word to Grandmama too,' she said. 'She'll be thrilled to have you nearby.'

Alone in his study, Sir Frederick leaned back in his chair, his gaze drawn to the window overlooking the grounds, his emotions in turmoil. Contrary to his daughter's accusations, it wasn't snobbery that had influenced his aversion to Eleanor and Lily's friendship, but shame. Every time he thought of Lily, or heard her name mentioned, he was filled with deep shame. Lily was the spitting image of her mother, but there was something of him in her as well, and Harry and Ada's silent reproach and unvoiced condemnation, undoubtedly aware as they were of Lily's parentage, were like burning coals to his already stricken conscience. Ada had dismissed Bea to protect Sir Frederick's reputation, and he doubted the cook had ever forgiven him for that. He didn't blame her. He had never forgiven himself. He groaned, his expression bleak. Though part of him longed to acknowledge Lily, to do so would be to destroy his family, and he was a coward. He had been a coward then and he was a coward now.

★　　★　　★

'Did you know Sir Frederick and Lady Copperfield were leaving Blandford?' Violet asked, coming into the work-room where Lily was basting the seams of a plain white calico shirt.

Lily removed the pins from between her lips and frowned up at her friend. 'No. Is Miss Eleanor going too?'

'She left this morning on the ten o'clock train. I'm surprised she didn't tell you.'

'Perhaps it was a sudden decision,' Lily replied, her gaze downcast. Her heartache at the loss of her precious half-sister was tempered with relief that Eleanor and Sir Frederick would be safely out of Jez's clutches. The notion that his evil scheme had been successfully thwarted provided her some measure of comfort.

She felt the baby move once more and experienced a twinge of regret that her baby would probably never get to meet her true blood relations. She pushed the thought aside. There was no point dwelling on what could never be. Eleanor was no longer part of her life. She had to concentrate on making a decent future for her unborn child.

'Oh,' Violet said, pausing as she unrolled a bolt of dark blue cloth. 'I forgot. You've had a letter from Charlie. I left it on the counter. I'll fetch it for you.'

Lily's mouth dried. She wiped her clammy palms on her skirt. She had put off informing Charlie of her marriage for several days, unable to find the right words. She had finally found the courage two weeks ago and was dreading his response. She exhaled in relief as she read the postmark.

'This was posted two months ago, before he would have received my letter.' She slit the envelope and unfolded the single sheet of paper. 'He's doing very well for himself and is wondering why I haven't informed him of my plans to visit.' She bit her lip in anguish as she leaned against the workbench. She cleared her throat, and continued. 'He writes that there is still much tension between the Dutch settlers and the English. Apparently, some people are predicting another war. Oh, I do wish he'd come home.'

'I'm sure that if Charlie entertained even the faintest suspicion that things would escalate that far, he would be on the first boat home, and he wouldn't be encouraging you to visit.' Violet was bent over the bench, pinning pattern pieces to the cloth. She reached for her dressmaker's shears. 'Don't worry yourself over Charlie. He can look after himself.'

Lily folded the letter and stuffed it in her pocket, unconvinced. Though he had initially only intended to be away for three to five years, five years had already passed since she had last seen him and he had made no mention of when, if ever, he may return to England. It grieved her greatly that she could barely remember what he looked like. Tears welled as she remembered how he had looked out for her when they were children. If only he had never gone away, how different things might have been. But she and Charlie were oceans apart.

She tucked the letter into her pocket and bent over her work, hiding her tears of self-pity from Violet's prying gaze. She knew that, had she even an inkling of how miserable

Lily's situation was, Violet would insist she move back in with her. But, tempting as that would be, the law would view Jez as a deserted husband and he would have all rights to Lily's baby. The thought of her child being brought up by Jez and his drink-addled mother made her blood run cold.

'Over my dead body,' she muttered.

As if she had conjured up the Devil himself, the shop door was flung open with such force it crashed into the wall. Both Lily and Violet jumped out of their skin.

'What the . . .?' Violet began. She was half out of her seat when Jez appeared in the workroom doorway, his expression thunderous.

'Jez!' Lily gasped, the colour draining from her face.

'Mr Elkin,' Violet said, her voice cold but steady. 'Please leave my workroom.'

Ignoring Violet, Jez turned his dark smouldering anger on Lily. She could tell by the way he was clenching and unclenching his fists that he was fighting for control.

'Get your things,' he said with icy calm.

'Jez, I'm in the middle of . . .' Lily's voice faltered under the weight of his simmering rage.

'Miss Upshaw,' he said, his gaze not leaving Lily's terrified face. 'My wife hereby terminates her employment with you.'

Lily and Violet exchanged nervous glances.

'Mr Elkin, might you explain why? Lily is a very accomplished dressmaker. Her skills are much sought after.'

'Good, she can carry on earning her keep from home then,' Jez said, his nostrils flaring with impatience. 'Instead of lining your pocket. You can send on any wages due. Good day.' He tipped his hat, and grabbed hold of Lily's elbow, his fingers digging painfully into her skin. Her face flaming with embarrassment and shame, Lily didn't dare look at Violet as Jez all but dragged her through the shop and onto the market-place, startling May Fudge who was chatting to the butcher's wife.

'Lily? Lily, is everything all right?' she called anxiously as Jez half-dragged Lily down the street.

'She's fine,' Jez called back over his shoulder. 'Nosy old bags.'

On the corner of Salisbury Street, Lily managed to yank her arm free. 'What are you doing?' She rounded on him, eyes blazing angrily. Jez glanced up the street. Violet had joined May and the butcher's wife outside the dress shop, watching in consternation. Lily let out a shriek as he shoved her around the corner and up against the wall.

'I needed that job,' Lily said, as he pushed his face into hers.

'You stupid, stupid bitch,' Jez hissed. He clamped her jaw in his hand, seemingly oblivious to the stares of passers-by. 'You warned your little rich friend, didn't you? She's hightailed it to London and Sir Fred is all set to follow her. You did it on purpose, you bitch. Don't ever think you can outwit me,' he snarled, spit bubbling on his bottom lip. 'If it wasn't for the fact you're carrying my brat, I'd wring your neck here and now. I'd have been set for life if old Fred Copperfield had coughed up but no, you thought you'd stick your oar in, didn't you? Didn't want to upset your fancy friends. Well, you've interfered once too often. From now on you'll stay where you belong, where I can keep an eye on you.'

'Please, Jez, I love my job.' The thought of being cooped up in the house all day with only her drunken mother-in-law for company was more than she could bear.

Jez ignored her. 'From now on you'll do as you're told. I've been far too lenient with you, given you too much leeway. Well, that stops today. And you can start by doing your God-given duty and being a proper wife to me.'

Alarmed, Lily grabbed his arm. 'No, Jez, the baby.'

'Don't take me for a mug, Lily,' Jez leered, his eyes mocking. 'My mates have told me there's no reason why I can't get my pleasure from you while you're up the duff.'

He yanked her painfully by the arm. Tears of humiliation streaming down her face, Lily could think only of her baby and how she must keep him or her safe, whatever the cost to herself. She could endure anything for her child. She had to. She had no choice.

CHAPTER TWENTY-ONE

Lily put the last of the ripe strawberries in the basket and sat back on her heels, massaging her aching back. It was barely ten o'clock, yet already her brow was beaded with perspiration. With one hand resting on her cumbersome belly, she got laboriously to her feet and surveyed her flourishing allotment. A wet, warm June had given way to a hot, dry July and August and the small tract of land was a riot of colourful sun-ripening fruit and vegetables.

Which was just as well, Lily mused, her gaze lingering on the chickens scratching at the baked-hard soil. Her home-grown produce went a long way to supplementing the house-keeping. Money had been tight since Lily had stopped working for Violet. Once her customers had realized that she was working out of a cramped cottage in Laundry Lane, orders had dried up at an alarming rate. Violet sent as many alterations her way as she could and she had her savings but they wouldn't last for ever. The money Jez made from his illegal boxing matches and extortion went mainly on himself. And, struggle as she might, Lily wanted nothing from him. She'd happily pawn everything she owned if it meant not having to accept a penny of his ill-gotten gains.

To her disgust, Jez had blackmailed one of the stewards at the Grosvenor Club, a prestigious gentlemen's club on West Street, into giving him a membership. There he mingled with some of the county's wealthiest businessmen. He thought nothing of dining with doctors, lawyers and bank managers while his wife and mother existed on whatever scraps Lily could get off the market stalls.

She arched her back and wiped the sweat from her brow, grimacing as the baby kicked against her bladder. She was almost nine months now and it seemed to Lily that she spent most of her day visiting the privy. The pain had been growing steadily worse since breakfast. And she needed to visit the privy – again.

As she followed the narrow path between the tomato vines and runner beans, her thoughts turned to Charlie. He hadn't replied to any of her letters and, in her darker moments, she fretted that he was so angry at the news of her marriage that he had cut her off. Then she would chide herself for her foolishness. Charlie loved her. He would be there for her always, no matter what, and she comforted herself with the thought that his letter had most likely gone astray.

She was quite desperate by the time she reached the privy. Sharing a toilet with four other families meant that the toilet and floor were often left in a disgusting state. Thankfully, today the floor was dry and the board across the long drop had recently been scrubbed, the smell of carbolic soap still hanging heavily in the air.

The gush of water took her by surprise. She had barely pulled up her bloomers when the first contraction rippled through her body. She sucked in her breath, more in shock than pain. Molly Ames, the neighbourhood midwife, had confidently assured Lily the baby wouldn't come for at least another week.

'Well, Molly, you got that wrong,' Lily muttered through gritted teeth as another contraction washed over her, much stronger than the first. 'This baby is coming now.'

She waited for the contraction to pass before waddling back to the house, shouting for Doris as she went.

'You all right, dearie?' her next-door neighbour, Polly Weeks, called anxiously from her kitchen door.

'The baby's coming. Will you send your Stan for Mrs Ames?'

'Of course, lovey.' Polly nodded, smiling encouragingly. 'You go and put your feet up and get that lazy good-for-nothing mother-in-law of yours to make you a cup of tea. I've pushed out four myself, and the first one always takes the longest. It'll be hours yet.'

Lily nodded, unconvinced. It felt as though the baby was about to drop between her legs any minute. Clutching her enormous belly, she stumbled into the kitchen still calling for Doris.

'What's all the racket about?' Doris appeared in the door-way. She coughed loudly, hawking up a glob of phlegm and spitting it into a grubby handkerchief. Lily grimaced. Another contraction was building and she grabbed the back of a chair, gritting her teeth as a tidal wave of pain washed over her.

'The baby's coming, Doris,' she panted. 'Mrs Weeks has sent her Stan for Molly Ames.'

'The baby's coming?' Doris's bloodshot gaze went straight to Lily's swollen stomach. 'I thought Molly said it'd be another week at least?'

'She was wrong,' Lily panted.

'Right,' Doris said, shrugging off her hangover as if it were a cloak she no longer required. 'Let's get you upstairs and into bed. I'll get you settled, then I'll put some water on to boil.'

'There are clean towels in the airing cupboard,' Lily said, grateful for Doris's supporting arm as they made their way slowly up the narrow staircase.

'Don't you worry about a thing,' Doris said. Lily found her tone surprisingly soothing as she helped her across the landing and into the bedroom. Despite the open window the room was stiflingly hot and perspiration beaded on Lily's upper lip. In a brief hiatus between contractions, she changed into her nightgown and sank onto the bed. Doris disappeared downstairs and Lily could hear her banging about in the kitchen below. She lay back against the pillows and sighed. Children's voices drifted through the open window and a dog was barking. She yawned and closed her eyes, overcome by a sudden wave of tiredness. She must have dozed, for when she opened her eyes, Molly was bustling about at the foot of the bed. Doris hovered in the doorway, pale-faced and anxious.

'Shall I send for our Jez?' she ventured.

'No,' replied Molly shortly. She was a large woman, with steel-grey hair worn in a tight bun and a reassuring no-nonsense manner. 'The birthing room is no place for a man,' she told Doris sternly. 'He'll only be in the way.' She gave Lily a wink of encouragement. 'You lie back and save your strength, Lily. Birthing babies is hard work and you've a way to go yet, so just relax and let me take care of things this end. Doris.' She turned to the older woman and clucked her tongue in dismay. 'Where's that cup of tea? The poor girl's parched. Go on, Doris, love, make yourself useful. Nothing's going to happen here for a good hour or so. You won't miss anything.'

With obvious reluctance, Doris left to do as she was bid. Molly smiled at Lily and winked again.

'She's a useless piece of work, isn't she?'

'She does her best,' Lily replied, feeling obliged to defend her mother-in-law. She would, after all, be her baby's grandmother, God help the little scrap.

'It can't be easy having Jez for a son,' Molly agreed. 'Or a husband,' she added dryly. 'You set a lot of tongues wagging the day you married him. Still, we all make mistakes.' She eyed Lily's stomach knowingly. 'I shouldn't worry, love,' she said, grinning at Lily's obvious discomfort. 'You're not the first one around here to have put the cart before the horse. There'll be a bit of talk, with baby coming barely six months after the wedding, but they'll soon get fed up and move on to someone else.'

Lily's contractions grew in frequency and severity as the day wore on. She clung to Doris's hand, her skin soaked with sweat, her lank hair fanned across the damp pillow. Doris tried not to wince as Lily's fingernails bit into her skin, remembering the awful time she'd had when her Jez had been born. For once, she felt nothing but sympathy for her daughter-in-law. She wiped Lily's face with a damp cloth, keeping her eyes averted from whatever Molly was doing down the business end of things.

The sun was low in a crimson sky and the bedroom shrouded in shadow when little Alice Elkin finally made her appearance. She slithered into Molly's waiting arms with an indignant bellow.

'Here she is, your baby girl.' Molly wrapped the still-squalling infant in a blanket and handed her to Lily. Propped against the pillows, Lily stared into her daughter's face, all the hours of pain and discomfort instantly forgotten.

'She's beautiful,' Lily whispered in awe. Alice, nestled contentedly in her mother's arms and exhausted after her lengthy ordeal, promptly fell asleep.

'She looks just like my Jez,' Doris remarked, her voice trembling with emotion. Lily studied her sleeping child's face but, to her immense relief, apart from her dark hair, she could see nothing of Jez in Alice at all.

Molly gave Alice a bath while Doris helped Lily into a clean nightgown and changed the sheets. Though she never took her eyes off Alice, she could only relax once her baby was back in her arms, suckling contentedly at the breast.

'I'll call in tomorrow to see how you're getting on,' Molly said, leaning over to stroke Alice's cheek with her forefinger.

'I'll see you out,' Doris said, moving stiffly. She coughed loudly and tugged her shawl tighter around her shoulders, cold despite the balminess of the early August evening. She hadn't been feeling herself for a while, she fretted after seeing Molly on her way. Perhaps a nip of gin would set her right, after all she'd earned a drink. It had been a pretty gruelling day for them all.

Jez threw back the covers and swung his long legs out of the bed. The pretty brunette next to him rolled onto her side and propped her head on the elbow. Her plump, kiss-bruised lips formed a pout as she watched him pull on his trousers in the grey dawn light.

'Do you really have to go?' she asked petulantly.

'I've got a busy day ahead, Patty,' Jez said dismissively, buttoning his shirt. He filled the wash bowl from the jug and splashed his face with cold water. His reflection stared back at him from the filthy mirror. Even with bloodshot eyes and day-old stubble, he knew he was a handsome man. He ran a wet hand through his thick dark hair and grinned at the girl on the bed. She was a pretty thing, experienced despite her tender years, and he was half inclined to forgo his early meeting and give in to her entreaties for him to stay a little longer, but business was business and he had a feeling his meeting with Arnold Dunwoody Esquire would prove very lucrative. The man was a buffoon with an inflated idea of his appeal to the fairer sex. It would give Jez immense pleasure to bring him down a peg or two. The man was loaded and running for local office. He would pay handsomely to prevent his good name being dragged through the mire.

The thought made Jez chuckle.

'What's so funny?' Patty whined. She was sixteen and worked as a maid at the Grosvenor Club. In the week since she had caught Jez's eye, she had begun to fantasize about how her life might be, should she bag herself a rich, handsome man like him.

'Private joke,' Jez said. He leaned down and kissed her hard on the mouth. 'I'll see you later.'

'I'll be waiting,' she said, licking her lips the way she knew excited him.

Jez winked and, snatching up his hat, headed for the stairs of the modest boarding house he used for his assignations. Patty was a sweet girl and he had big plans for her, once he'd tired of her sweet, tender body. But by the time he'd reached the foot of the stairs, he'd forgotten all about her.

He put his hat on and set off down the quiet street, whistling tunelessly as he looked up at the clear sky. The sun was just cresting the buildings, bathing the roof tiles in a soft golden glow. It was going to be another scorching hot day.

He let himself in the front door. Doris was slumped in an armchair, her slack mouth hanging open as she snored gently.

Closing the door none too quietly, Jez hung up his hat and jacket, grinning as Doris jolted awake.

'Oh, you're back.' Blinking, she pushed herself upright. 'She's had it,' she said, getting to her feet. 'The baby.' She shot Jez a warning glance. 'Now don't go waking them up,' she said sternly.

Ignoring her, he took the stairs two at a time, bursting into the bedroom to find Lily fast asleep, her auburn hair fanned across the pillow, her face bathed in pale sunlight, one arm cupped protectively around her little daughter.

Awestruck, Jez could only stare at his tiny daughter sound asleep in her mother's arm. Having viewed his impending fatherhood with disinterest, he was shocked at the strength of his emotions. He was partly responsible for the creation of this tiny, perfect human being. Alice stirred and opened her midnight-blue eyes. She seemed to look straight into her father's face and, for the first time in his life, Jeremy Elkin fell in love.

Some primeval instinct jerked Lily awake. Startled to see Jez smiling down at Alice with a benign look upon his face, she struggled up against the pillows, cradling the baby against her chest and watching Jez anxiously.

'You've done a grand job, Lily,' he said without a trace of his usual animosity. 'She's an absolute treasure.'

Lily smiled, motherly pride overcoming her usual hostility towards her husband. 'She's beautiful.' She adjusted her position and the baby squirmed, making little sucking motions with her rosebud lips.

'Can I ... May I hold her?' Jez looked almost humble. After a brief hesitation, Lily placed Alice in his waiting arms. He held her awkwardly, yet Alice didn't appear to mind. She seemed quite content in his clumsy embrace. As Doris stood in the doorway with a cup of tea for Lily, the sight brought tears to her eyes.

'She's a bonny little lass, Jez,' she said, a quiver in her voice. 'Here you are, Lily, love.' Her tone was warm, motherly even. Lily kept her scepticism at the endearment well hidden. Her mother-in-law may yet prove to be a welcome ally in the difficult times ahead.

'You should be proud of our Lily, Jez.'

Jez nodded, his gaze sweeping across Lily's face. 'Yes, you did well, old girl.'

Alice chose that moment to start crying. Jez stared at her in alarm as her tiny screwed up face turned bright crimson.

'What's wrong with her?' he demanded, clearly shocked as both Lily and Doris burst out laughing.

'She's just hungry,' Lily assured him with a smile.

'Are you sure?' Jez asked, practically shoving Alice into Lily's waiting arms. Lily lifted her to her breast and the crying stopped instantly.

'Come on, lad,' Doris said after a moment. 'Let's leave them in peace.' She all but bundled Jez onto the landing, paused in the doorway and glanced over her shoulder. 'Things will be different around here, Lily,' she said. 'You'll see. Now, get some rest. I'll see to Jez.'

'Thank you,' Lily replied softly. Doris nodded as their eyes met in mutual understanding. The door closed and Lily was left alone with her baby. She gazed down at the suckling Alice, marvelling again at the perfect curve of her cheek, the tiny button nose, the dark lashes, the tendrils of dark hair peeking from beneath her knitted bonnet.

'You are perfect,' Lily whispered, her heart almost bursting with love for her child. In that instant she knew without a doubt that she would protect Alice with her life, come what may.

CHAPTER TWENTY-TWO

Two days later, Lily had just finished giving Alice her mid-morning feed when there was a loud hammering on the door. Knowing Doris was still at the market, Lily swung her still-tender limbs from the bed and made her way gingerly to the window. She leaned out, and called to the scrawny boy hammering on the door.

'Hello?'

The boy looked up. He was a sandy-haired lad, thin and gangly, and Lily recognized him as Solomon, one of Edith Bartlett's boys. He was always out in the street playing with his brothers.

'Morning, missus,' Solomon replied with a cheeky grin. 'Is Mister Jez at home?'

'No, he isn't,' Lily replied with a frown. Before she could ask Solomon what he wanted with her husband, he turned tail and sped down the street. Lily stared after him. Shaking her head in puzzlement, she was about to get back into bed when she heard the front door open and close. She hardly dared breathe as a man's voice drifted up the stairs.

'Hello? Jez?' Her hand moved instinctively to Alice sleeping beside her, her heart racing. Who was in the house?

'Lily?' She exhaled in relief as she recognized Violet's voice. 'It's me.' Moments later Violet appeared in the doorway, beaming. 'Doris told me you'd had the baby so I just had to come.'

'Violet, I'm so happy to see you.' Tears filled Lily's eyes as she embraced her friend. 'I've missed you so much.'

'And I you.' They were interrupted by the sound of heavy footsteps on the landing. Someone coughed discreetly and Violet laughed as Lily shot her a questioning look.

'Come on in, Mr Bartlett, it's quite safe.'

The door opened and a man Lily recognized as Solomon's father, Elias, appeared in the doorway holding a large crib.

'My cradle,' Lily cried in delight. 'Oh, Violet, thank you. I didn't know when I might be able to collect it.'

'I've brought all the things you bought for baby Alice,' Violet informed her, nodding at Elias to set the cradle down. It was beautiful, made of light wood and carved with intricate patterns. Lily had spotted it in a department store catalogue and had ordered it be delivered to Violet's weeks ago.

'I'll go and help Solomon with the rest of the stuff, ma'am,' Elias said, with a shy nod in Lily's direction.

Lily thanked him before turning to Violet. 'Would you like to hold her?'

'Oh, Lily,' Violet breathed as Lily handed Alice to her. 'She is adorable.' She settled herself on the edge of the bed and studied Alice's features in wondrous rapture. 'What an absolute treasure. How is Jez with her?'

'Believe it or not,' Lily said, adjusting the bed covers, 'he's besotted with her.'

'Really?' Violet raised a quizzical eyebrow.

'I know,' Lily laughed. 'I was as astonished as you are. But whenever he's home, he just sits staring at her, as if he can't quite believe she's real. He's terrified of hurting her. He'll barely touch her, although I keep assuring him that she's not as fragile as she looks.'

Elias and Solomon returned at that moment with the rest of the items Lily had acquired in preparation for Alice's arrival, and soon the bedroom was littered with tissue paper as Lily and Violet spent a happy twenty minutes oohing and aahing over the tiny garments and toys.

Doris arrived home not long after and made them both a welcome cup of tea.

'She seems to be really trying hard,' Lily confided to Violet once they were alone again. 'It's as though Alice's birth has brought about something of a breakthrough. She promises things will be a bit better now, and so far they have been.'

'Let's hope so,' Violet said, though her tone was sceptical. In her book, a leopard didn't change its spots and, in her mind, Doris was a nasty piece of work, as was her son. Once the novelty wore off, they were bound to revert to their natural behaviour. Of course, she refrained from saying so to Lily. Her young friend was basking in the first flush of motherhood and Violet had no wish to disillusion her, whatever her own thoughts on the subject. Instead, she smiled warmly and kept her opinions to herself. She left an hour later and Lily drifted off to sleep, one hand resting on the new cradle in which Alice slept peacefully.

'You shouldn't be out of bed,' Doris scolded Lily a week later when she ventured downstairs for the first time, cradling Alice in her arms.

'I feel perfectly well,' Lily protested. 'I'm fed up of staring at the same four walls. I need a change of scenery and fresh air, and so does Alice.'

'I agree,' said Jez, surprising both his wife and mother. He finished tying his boot laces and stood up. 'There's a surprise for you in the yard,' he said, his dark gaze fastening on Lily's face. Lily hesitated. She found Jez's recent change of behaviour towards her unsettling. 'Well, come on,' he chided her. 'Aren't you going to see what it is?'

'Er ... yes,' Lily stammered, glancing towards the open door where the late-afternoon sun cast a slanting ray across the dusty slate.

'Oh, Jez, it's ... lovely.' The wicker perambulator was parked just outside the back door. Passing Alice to Doris, she ran her fingers gently over the gleaming handle and the soft leather hood. 'It's beautiful,' she said, admiring the craftsmanship.

'The hood folds up and down.' Jez showed her with all the delight of a child on Christmas Day. 'It'll keep the sun off her as well as the rain. Do you like it?'

'Of course, I do. It's lovely. Thank you.'

'I'll go up and get some sheets and that pretty blanket you embroidered, Lily,' Doris offered, handing Alice to Jez and hastening back indoors, a spring in her step. She hadn't touched the gin since the day Alice was born, and she felt a world better than she had for years.

'It really is a beautiful perambulator,' Lily said hesitantly, breaking the awkward silence that had fallen.

'I wanted to get her something,' Jez said, looking ill at ease as he jiggled Alice in his arms. 'Most of the stuff she has, you got for her. I wanted to do my bit. I'm going to be a proper dad to Alice, Lily. I promise you. She'll want for nothing.'

Lily nodded. Despite Jez's sudden change of character, she remained wary of him. She had known him too long to believe the change would be permanent.

'You're Daddy's precious doll, aren't you, my love?' he crooned, as Alice looked up at him with her unfocused gaze. 'Daddy's going to spoil you rotten, just you wait and see. You'll want for nothing.'

He looked at Lily. 'I mean it,' he reiterated, reading the scepticism in her green eyes. 'She'll have the best clothes, the best toys.'

'All paid for with money you've extorted from foolish men,' Lily retorted coldly. It still chilled her blood to think how close her own father might have come to having his reputation ruined by her husband. But Sir Frederick and Eleanor were safely in London now and another family were living in Bay Willow House.

'They've only got themselves to blame,' Jez sneered. 'I don't force them to go with my girls. Their own lustful desire is their downfall.' He grinned, his teeth appearing extraordinarily white in his tanned face. 'I just use their weakness to my advantage.'

Before Lily could protest, Doris reappeared carrying a bundle of linen. Turning her back on Jez, Lily made up a bed for Alice in the perambulator and laid her in it.

'Right, let's see how my little princess likes her gift and take her for a walk.'

Alice stared up at them, and all three adults peered down at her, smiling indulgently. She really was a bonny baby.

Feeling self-conscious, Lily wheeled the perambulator down Laundry Lane. No one in the street owned a perambulator. In this part of town, mothers carried their babies in their arms and she felt very conspicuous as she walked alongside Jez, who strutted like a peacock, calling out greetings to women he'd barely had the time of day for in the past.

'Morning, Mrs Bartlett, Mrs Webb, lovely day, isn't it?' he cried with such bonhomie that Edith and Beryl Webb had no choice but to come over and coo over baby Alice, while all the time Lily was aware of the sly looks behind the muttered congratulations. Lily knew what they whispered about her. That she was no better than she should be. Barely six months married and having delivered a healthy baby. And Lily herself a bastard child. Bad blood would out, the housewives and washerwomen of Laundry Lane would mutter to each other.

Like mother, like daughter. They might be poor, the likes of Edith and Beryl surely consoled themselves, yet they kept up standards. You wouldn't find their daughters getting themselves in the family way before they had a ring on their finger.

Lily had tried hard to ignore the malicious gossip and now, squaring her shoulders, she forced herself to look them in the eye. She had nothing to be ashamed of. She was making the best of a bad situation and she refused to be cowed by some sour-faced women who had nothing better to do all day than gossip.

'We really must be going if we want to finish our walk before Alice is ready for her next feed,' she said in her politest tone. Alice squirmed as a shaft of sunlight hit her full in the face, so Lily adjusted the perambulator's hood.

'Very fancy, I must say,' Beryl observed with a disapproving cluck and Lily flushed, knowing Alice's perambulator probably cost as much as Mr Webb earned in a week.

'Too posh for the likes of round here,' Edith agreed, with a sniff.

'My sentiments exactly,' Jez said, executing a mocking bow as Lily turned away, mortified. 'Jealous old bints,' he said none too quietly as they carried on down the road. 'It's not my fault her old man earns a pittance and her kids wear little more than rags.'

'At least their money is honestly earned,' Lily rebuked him quietly.

'Give it a rest, will you?' Jez snapped, his cheerful disposition dissipating like dew on a hot day. 'Do you really want Alice brought up like them because of your hifalutin' morals?'

'I want Alice to be able to hold her head up and not be ashamed of what her father does for a living. Everyone knows what you are, Jez.' Lily stopped walking and rounded on him in disgust. 'Please. Think of Alice. Imagine what it will be like when Alice starts school. She'll be a pariah, bullied by the others because of your reputation.'

Jez cursed loudly, causing passers-by to glare.

'I wish people would refrain from airing their dirty laundry in public,' Lily heard one matronly woman mutter loudly to her companion as they hurried by, careful to give Lily and Jez a wide birth. Jez gesticulated rudely in her direction, and Lily, mortified, felt her cheeks flame. With white knuckles, she gripped the handle of the perambulator tightly and pushed Alice down the street, her eyes swimming with tears of frustration and shame.

They continued on in stony silence, passing grand houses as they made their way up Whitecliff Mill Street. Primrose Park was an expanse of manicured lawns surrounding an ornamental lake. Jez tipped his hat to a party of well-dressed ladies as they passed through the stone gateposts.

'Perhaps it's time you had some new dresses,' he said, staring after the young ladies admiringly. 'Get your friend, Violet, to make you a new wardrobe.'

Lily was about to protest and tell Jez she was quite capable of making her own dresses, but the thought of getting to spend time with her dear friend was too appealing.

She simply said, 'Thank you,' and Jez nodded imperiously. He straightened the collar of his coat and leaned over the perambulator to smile at his daughter.

The park was busy. Little boys in sailor suits pushed toy boats on the lake, or threw crusts of bread to the ducks, watched by their doting nursemaids. Little girls in bows and ruffles walked demurely alongside their nannies and governesses. Well-dressed couples strolled arm in arm beneath the canopies of oak and chestnut trees. Primrose Park was for the affluent and Lily felt out of place. Jez, on the other hand, strutted along as if he owned the world. The admiring looks from the young ladies they passed were not lost on Lily, or Jez, who preened like a cockerel.

If only they knew the real person behind the handsome face, Lily thought, as yet another young woman smiled at him coquettishly. Jez was clearly revelling in the attention and grinned back, touching the brim of his hat.

'I'm going to see about taking one of these houses, Lily,' Jez said, indicating the fine buildings that lined the leafy, tree-lined avenue. 'I'm not having my daughter growing up with the likes of the Bartlett kids. She deserves better.'

'You want us to move here?' Lily blinked in surprise. 'Can you afford it?'

'Are you questioning me?' Jez raised his eyebrow. 'You should be grateful. You won't have to worry about Alice being picked on at school, not when we're living here. No one would dare criticize a daughter of mine, especially once I'm an elected member of the town council.'

'You? On the town council?' Lily stared at him in astonishment. 'They'd never let you on the council. You're corrupt and immoral. You don't have an ounce of integrity.'

'Shut up,' Jez hissed, noting the curious glance from a woman scrubbing the front steps of a particularly imposing townhouse. 'This is the residence of Sir Thomas Southgate. He's going to nominate my appointment to the council,' he said in a low voice. He flashed Lily a self-important grin. 'Once I'm on the council it'll be onwards and upwards for us, Lily, old girl.'

Lily sneered at him in disgust. 'You're going to blackmail Sir Thomas to get you on the council? You're despicable.'

Jez grabbed her elbow and Lily winced. Glancing around to make sure they were unobserved, he squeezed her arm hard, bringing tears to Lily's eyes.

'It's not your place to question my actions,' he told her, his eyes glittering dangerously. 'And I'm not particularly both-ered as to your opinion. You've got a choice. You can rise with me or you can stay in the muck where you belong. But hear this, Lily girl, Alice will be with me. So, if you want to be a part of our daughter's life, you'll toe the line, understand?'

'You're hurting me.' Lily tried to shake her arm free but Jez only tightened his grip. Checking that they were concealed from view by an enormous rhododendron bush, he brought his face close to hers.

'Do you understand me?' he spat. Left with little choice, Lily nodded.

'Good, as long as we understand each other.' Jez released his hold on Lily's arm and they continued on their way in silence. So much for Jez's change of character, she thought, her bruised arm throbbing painfully.

She had no doubt Jez would make good his threat. He would never let her take Alice away from him. She blinked back tears as she looked down at the innocent, trusting face of her infant daughter. They were trapped, the two of them. For Lily, marriage to Jez was little more than a prison, one from which there would be no parole, and escape was impossible. She could never leave without Alice, and if she ever dared take Alice away from Jez, she knew without a doubt that he would hunt her to the ends of the earth.

CHAPTER TWENTY-THREE

Lily stood at the window, holding Alice, and watched a flurry of golden-brown leaves scurrying down the street. It was November and Alice was coming up for four months old and just starting to roll from her stomach to her back, much to the delight of her doting father.

In keeping with his promise, Jez had spent a fortune on his daughter, and the nursery in the rented townhouse on Whitecliff Mill Street could rival the great toy store in London.

'Will you put some more coal on the fire, Lily?' Doris croaked. 'I can't seem to get warm today.' Her words ended in a hacking cough that left her gasping for breath. Lily turned from the window, her brow furrowed in concern. Her mother-in-law had been ailing for a while now. In Lily's opinion, the move from Laundry Lane had been too much for her. She had further to walk to the shops now, and though Lily was happy to do the shopping herself, Jez refused to allow her to take Alice to the market. He fretted constantly that she might pick up some dreaded childhood illness and neither Lily nor Jez were comfortable leaving Alice with her grandmother.

Twice, Lily had voiced her concerns to Jez over Doris's health but he refused to pay for a doctor.

'She's an old drunk and a hypochondriac,' he'd told Lily brusquely when she'd approached him about calling out Doctor Arnold. 'I'm not throwing good money after bad. Keep her off the gin and she'll be right as rain.'

But Lily wasn't convinced. Doris seldom drank anymore, yet her skin had taken on an alarming yellow tinge and she had little appetite. Lily was constantly trying to coax her to eat a little broth or beef tea, but for all her efforts, Doris seemed to be fading away before her eyes.

She shovelled some more coal onto the already roaring fire and helped Doris tuck the blanket over her legs. Only in her early forties, her mother-in-law resembled a woman at least two decades older and Lily felt nothing but pity for the woman who had made her life a misery for so long. Doris had certainly mellowed in the months since Alice's birth and seemed to feel genuine remorse over her past behaviour.

Lily even seemed to have reached an uneasy truce with Jez, though on the rare occasions he came to her bed, he took her without tenderness or affection, leaving her feeling bruised and humiliated. Where he spent the nights he failed to come home, she neither knew nor cared, feeling only relief that he was gone.

Alice gurgled, looking up at Lily with her large eyes that had recently changed to a rich toffee-brown. She was a beautiful, contented baby, who had started sleeping through the night at eight weeks and seldom cried. Jez was besotted with her, and whenever he was at home, he would bounce her on his knee, or spend long minutes just watching her sleep.

In his bid to become an elected councillor, Jez spent most of his evenings at the Grosvenor Club ingratiating himself with other members of the council. How he had managed to pull the wool over the eyes of so many seemingly intelligent men, Lily could only imagine. But Whitecliff Mill Street was far removed from Laundry Lane so perhaps they were unaware of her husband's reputation. His illicit business was thriving but, as Lily constantly refrained from warning him, one day he would make a mistake. He would target the wrong man, and then his carefully erected veneer of respectability would come crashing down around him. Lily could only pray that, when that happened, her precious daughter wouldn't be tarnished by the fallout.

'Would you like a cup of tea, Doris?' Lily asked now, handing Alice to her mother-in-law. Alice offered up a gummy smile, which warmed Doris's heart.

'Ah, she's a bonny one,' she said, beaming at her granddaughter. 'Thanks, Lily, that would be nice.' She jiggled Alice gently in her arms, gazing down at her with unabashed adoration. 'She's the spit of my Jez when he was this age,' she called after Lily, making her daughter-in-law grimace.

While she waited for the kettle to boil, Lily finished the washing up, her gaze drifting to the window. The lawn was carpeted in fallen leaves. Dark clouds were gathering in the distance, bringing with them the threat of rain.

What would Eleanor say if she could see me now? Lily mused wistfully, swilling the brown ceramic teapot with warm water. She was as content with her life as she could be, given the circumstances and she still saw Violet as often as she could get away with but, as dear to her as Violet was, Lily missed Eleanor with an ache that the months had failed to erase. There had been no contact between them since Eleanor had left for London and though Lily knew in her heart that it was for the best, it didn't make the sense of loss any easier to bear. Eleanor was her flesh and blood, her sister, and though she knew she had to keep their relationship a secret for the sake of Sir Frederick and his wife, Lily longed to be able to publicly declare Eleanor as her sister. It was a dream she knew could never come true. Her daughter would never know her Aunt Eleanor. She was as lost to her as Jim, Martha and Beatrice, and even Charlie, who it seemed, was gone from her life.

A black-hearted criminal for a husband and a sick, gin-ravaged mother-in-law. That was all the family Lily and Alice had left. She bit her lip. What a legacy for her child. She pushed her thought aside and poured Doris's tea, carrying it through into the front parlour.

Jez had got rid of much of the old furniture when they moved. Many of Doris's knick-knacks had been packed off to the rag-and-bone man, despite her whining and anguished pleas, and Lily found the uncluttered parlour much easier to keep clean and tidy. The high ceiling and bay windows allowed in maximum light, even on inclement days like today, brightening the already bright and airy room.

'Thank you,' Doris wheezed as Lily set the cup and saucer on the chair's broad arm. Alice squirmed with discomfort. Instantly anxious, Lily lifted her from Doris's arms. Her skin was red and warm to the touch.

'It's too hot for her this close to the fire,' she said, quickly stripping off the baby's outer layer of clothing, eyeing her mother-in-law with concern as she continued to complain about the chill, despite the roaring fire.

'I'm worried about you, Doris,' Lily said. Relieved to see Alice's colour had returned to normal, she laid the baby on the rug where she kicked her legs, gurgling happily to herself. 'I'm going to send for the doctor.'

'No, don't, Lily,' Doris wheezed, with a knowing look. 'I don't want you wasting your money on me. It's that good-for-nothing son of mine who should be forking out. He's quite happy to spend money on new toys for the baby – and I don't begrudge her anything, as you know – and he's pleased to spend a small fortune impressing his new friends on the council, but ask him to spare a few bob to sort me out, hah, I should be so lucky.' She coughed harshly, making Alice jump and burst into tears. Lily picked her up and cuddled her, calming her with soothing words.

'I'll speak to Jez again,' Lily promised. 'You need some medicine for that cough. You've had it for weeks and it's not getting any better.'

'It's good of you to try, Lily, but you'll be wasting your time. He's a cold-hearted bugger, that son of mine, I'm sorry to say. He doesn't even care about his old mum.'

You've only yourself to blame for that, Lily thought but said instead, 'I'm going to put Alice down for her nap. I'll read to you for a while when I come down, if you like.'

'That would be lovely,' Doris rasped, picking up her teacup with a trembling hand.

Lily laid Alice in her crib and walked to the window, her daughter's contented gurgles following her as she gazed out across the rooftops. The dark clouds were drawing nearer and a brisk wind had picked up, churning piles of fallen leaves into maelstroms that swept across the lawn.

She drew the curtains and crept quietly from the room, pulling the door to behind her. She had just reached the foot of the stairs when the doorbell rang. On opening the door, she was surprised to find Solomon Bartlett standing on the doorstep, cap in hand, shivering in the bitter wind, leaves swirling about his feet. He grinned up at Lily toothily as she pulled her shawl tighter around her shoulders.

Lily smiled. 'Solomon, how lovely to see you.'

'Morning, missus.' He tugged a folded envelope from his trouser pocket. 'Mum sent me. This was delivered to your old house.'

Lily thanked him, her heart quickening as she recognized the foreign postage stamp and Charlie's sloping writing. 'Let me give you something for your trouble.' She found a penny in the dish on the hall table and gave it to him. 'Please give your mother my best.'

'Yes, missus, ta, missus.' As Solomon took off down the street, Lily closed the door on the bleak autumnal day, her heart beating in trepidation. Although she was delighted to finally hear from Charlie, she couldn't help feeling anxious about what he had to say.

'Who was it?' Doris demanded as Lily entered the parlour, her anxious fingers ripping at the seal on the envelope.

'Solomon, Edith Bartlett's boy,' she replied absently as she unfolded the sheets of white paper. 'It's a letter from Charlie. I wrote giving him our new address, but they must have crossed in the post.'

Doris grunted with disinterest. She hadn't thought of her long-dead sister's son for years.

Lily curled up in an armchair close to the window. A gust of wind shook the glass frame and it started raining as Lily began to read. Charlie had obviously written the letter in a hurry. She could barely decipher his untidy scrawl.

My dear Lily,

I am sorry I have not written sooner but I have been travelling the interior of the country for many weeks and so only received your letters on my return to the Cape. To say I'm shocked to hear that you and Jez are married would be an understatement. Can he have altered that much? I'm sure you have your reasons and, while I hesitate to accuse our cousin of coercing this decision, I find I must blame myself. I should never have left you alone. If I had never left, I'm sure you would have thought twice about marrying someone like our cousin.

Lily blinked back tears. She could never tell Charlie the truth, of course. Had he known exactly what had transpired between her and Jez, he would have been on the first boat home and any confrontation between the two cousins would have been disastrous. Jez would have no qualms in hurting Charlie, would perhaps even kill him, and so she had lied about her reasons, persuading him that she had married Jez for security and a stable home.

That said, I'm over the moon to be an uncle. Finding your telegram waiting for me went some way to dispelling my doubts. God willing, I shall get to meet my little niece in the not-too-distant future. In the meantime, I trust you will shower her with hugs and kisses from her doting uncle.

Tensions remain worryingly high between the Boers and the British but I remain hopeful Milner and Kruger will see sense and some sort of agreement can be reached.

The letter went on in a similar vein and Lily was crying unashamedly by the time she had read it through to the end. Though she missed Charlie so much it hurt, she couldn't help feeling a little resentful. Perhaps he was right: if he hadn't gone away, she wouldn't be where she was now, at the mercy of a man who cared less for her than he would a stray dog off the street.

'What's he got to say for himself, then?' Doris asked, breathlessly, coughing into her handkerchief.

'Just that he's surprised to hear of my marriage, and that he misses me.' Lily folded the letter and tucked it safely in the folds of her skirt. The last thing she wanted was Jez getting hold of it.

'He's not coming home, then?'

'Not for a while, no, though I'm sure he will if tensions between the Boers and the British get much worse.' She wrapped her arms around herself, an ominous chill coursing through her body. She worried about him, so far from home. There had been some mention in the newspapers about skirmishes on the border, reports of acts of sabotage from small renegade Afrikaner farmers against the British. It had alarmed Lily to learn that several of the attacks had taken place not far from where Charlie had been living, but she had comforted herself that her brother was not a reckless man and, should the situation escalate, she was certain he would be on the first available ship home.

It was raining hard now. The wind howled down the chimney, sending a shower of sparks onto the hearthrug. Lily lit the lamp and picked up her copy of *Jane Eyre*. Pulling her chair closer to Doris, she began to read.

Doris closed her eyes. She tried to concentrate on the story, but she was so tired. Within minutes, she was fast asleep. When her snoring had reached a crescendo, Lily closed the book and sat listening to the rain dripping from the overflowing gutters.

She was eighteen years old, yet she felt middle-aged. She stared down at her chapped hands. The simple gold band on her left ring finger glinted dully in the lamplight. Her wedding band might as well be fetters and chains for all the freedom she had. Jez watched her like a hawk, seemingly terrified Lily would take Alice away. She knew he had people watching the house, too. Several times over the past few weeks, she had caught sight of Ned loitering nearby. She also suspected he was following her. Though she couldn't be sure, on a couple of occasions when she had been out with Alice, on glancing behind her, she thought she had spotted him skulking in the shadows. No doubt Jez was aware of her every move.

She was replying to Charlie's letter when Jez returned home in time for Alice's bath time. While he changed out of his wet clothes, Lily fetched the tin bath from the scullery and heated the water on the range. She watched her husband as she prepared the evening meal. He was crouched on the floor in front of the fire, shirt sleeves rolled to the elbow, one muscular arm supporting Alice's head as she splashed her little arms and legs, giggling with uninhibited joy. Lily reflected that he looked like any other doting father. He was totally focused on his little girl, oblivious to everything except his precious Alice.

Doris's hacking cough resonated through the parlour wall.

'Doris really needs to see the doctor, Jez,' Lily said, slicing carrots into a pan.

'How many times do I have to tell you? I refuse to waste good money on that old trollop,' he snarled nastily. 'Get old mother Hawkins in. The old witch is bound to have some concoction she can fob Ma off with.' He beamed at Alice. 'Is Daddy's little princess ready to get out?' He grabbed the towel warming by the range and lifted Alice out of the bath. She squealed with laughter, drawing up her little legs as he wrapped her in the towel, cocooning her in its warm softness.

'Your mother needs a proper doctor, not an old quack,' Lily protested, wiping her hands on her apron before taking Alice from Jez. She kissed her button nose, breathing in her sweet, soapy scent.

Jez felt the collar of his coat drying by the fire and shrugged it on. 'She's playing you like a fiddle, Lily,' he snorted. 'Ignore her.' He planted a kiss on Alice's forehead. 'I won't be home tonight,' he said, tickling his daughter's cheek. 'I'll see you in the morning, precious one. Sleep well.'

'Jez!' Lily followed him to the door, her brow creased in frustration. 'She's your mother. Have a heart.'

Jez pulled on his hat and yanked open the door, letting in a flurry of wind and rain. Without a backward glance, he stepped out into the night, slamming the door behind him.

'Thank you for trying, Lily,' Doris said a short time later as Lily was nursing Alice.

'I'm sorry.' Lily hung her head in shame. Doris laid a hand on her arm.

'It's not your fault. He's a nasty piece of work, my Jez. I know I'm to blame.' She sighed. 'His dad was no better. I'm sorry you're saddled with him, love, I really am.'

Lily nodded. Now wasn't the time to remind Doris that it hadn't only been Jez who'd made her life a misery.

'I'll call in at the chemist tomorrow and get you some cough medicine,' she said instead. 'If you're no better in day or two, I'm calling Dr Arnold.'

'You're a good girl, Lily,' Doris said hoarsely. 'Too good for my Jez, and that's a fact.' Lily didn't reply.

Sated with milk, Alice had drifted off to sleep. 'I'll just take Alice up and then I'll bring you a mug of beef tea,' Lily said.

She climbed the stairs, Alice sleeping soundly in her arms, and thought darkly how they were all at the mercy of Jez. A cold-hearted, cruel man, he commanded the destiny of them all.

CHAPTER TWENTY-FOUR

1897

Lily waved goodbye to Violet and wheeled the perambulator through the bustling marketplace. Rosy-cheeked from the cold, two-and-a-half-year-old Alice chatted happily, beaming up at her mother from her snug cocoon of blankets.

It was the last day of February and the first day Lily had felt able to take Alice out in weeks. Almost daily snowfalls had kept them confined to the house, huddled around the fireplace as a howling wind drove the steadily falling snow into huge drifts, some reaching as high as the upstairs windows.

Now the snow was steadily melting. Flung up by passing wagons and carriages, it soaked the hem of Lily's skirt and splashed her shoes. Water dripped from gutters and the newly budding trees. The sky was crisp and clear but the wind, whipping across the marketplace, was bitterly cold.

Humming one of her daughter's favourite tunes, Lily pushed Alice up Whitecliff Mill Street past stylish townhouses with scrubbed steps and bay windows, sunlight reflecting off the glass. The air smelled of coal fires and the residual tang of animal faeces wafting from the market.

'Gee-gee,' Alice shouted, her breath fogging the air, a red-mitten-clad hand emerging from the beneath the covers to point at a large grey horse tethered to a nearby railing.

'Horse,' Lily corrected her automatically, reaching into her pocket for the front door key. The horse snickered softly and tossed its head, making Alice laugh. 'Gee-gee, gee-gee,' she sang, bouncing in her pram while Lily unlocked the door.

'We're home, Doris,' she called cheerfully, manoeuvring the cumbersome perambulator into the narrow hallway and unbuttoning her coat. She took off her boots, hopping from one foot to the other as she massaged her frozen toes. There was no reply from the parlour but, then, Doris spent much of her day drifting in and out of sleep.

Her mother-in-law's health had been in a steady decline for the past two years. Lily had gone behind Jez's back and called in Dr Arnold and his prognosis had been grim. Cancer of the liver. Lily had spent a small fortune on medicines in an effort to alleviate her mother-in-law's suffering, but little helped. Now the cancer had spread to her kidneys and lungs and time was running out.

A few months previously, Lily had persuaded Jez to move Doris's bed into the parlour where, propped up on pillows, she could watch Alice playing with her toys. Despite her pain and the overwhelming tiredness that plagued her, Doris's favourite time of the day was about three in the afternoon. Alice would snuggle under the blanket beside her grandma and listen wide-eyed to one of Doris's stories. Though every word seemed to steal the breath from her tortured lungs, Doris wouldn't give in until Alice had fallen asleep, her head resting in the crook of her grandma's arm. Watching them, Lily would often reflect that, approaching the end of her life, Doris was finally becoming a person her sister Martha would have been proud of.

'Nana!' Alice cried now as Lily lifted her out of the perambulator. 'Go see Nana.' Her cheeks were pink from the cold.

'Nana's probably asleep, so go in quietly,' Lily cautioned her, unbuttoning Alice's coat and helping her to shrug it off. Alice nodded, her little face screwed up in concentration as she pushed open the parlour door with exaggerated slowness and peered into the dim room.

'Nana sleeping,' she said in a loud stage whisper, turning to look at Lily over her shoulder.

'Then let's leave her in peace.' Lily held out her hand. 'Come help me unpack the shopping and then when Nana wakes up we can take her a cup of tea.'

'And cake?' Alice skipped ahead of Lily to the kitchen at the back of the house. Lily smiled after her.

'Yes, we'll have a slice of Aunty Violet's lovely fruit cake.'

Listening to Alice's lively chatter, Lily unpacked the few items she'd picked up from the market and put them away. The range gave off a good heat, making the kitchen warm and cosy, and she soon shrugged off the February chill. She made tea and, placing the tea things on a tray, followed Alice down the hall.

She paused outside the parlour door. It was slightly ajar, and usually she would be able to hear Doris's laboured breathing. Her stomach lurched in fear. She almost upset the tray as she grabbed Alice's hand, preventing her from running into the room. Slowly she nudged the door wide open. The dimly lit parlour felt unnaturally quiet. Doris lay on her back, eyes closed, her mouth slack.

'Nana!' Alice shouted happily.

'No,' Lily said sharply. 'Wait here.' Setting the tray on the table, Lily slowly approached the bed. 'Doris?' she whispered hesitantly. She gave her shoulder a gentle shake. 'Doris?'

Sinking into the chair beside the bed, Lily sighed. 'Oh, Doris.' Her mother-in-law's skin was icy cold and tinged blue; she had clearly been dead for some time.

Lily blinked back tears. Despite everything, the two women had grown close over the past two years.

'Mama?' Alice wailed. She stood in the doorway, frightened and forlorn. Wiping her eyes, Lily moved swiftly. She snatched Alice up into her arms and, ignoring her angry protest, swept into the hallway, closing the door softly behind her.

'Nana, story,' Alice squealed crossly as she squirmed in Lily's embrace, her arms reaching for the door handle.

'No story today, darling,' Lily reprimanded her firmly. 'Nana's poorly.' She took Alice into the kitchen and sat her in the highchair, distracting her with a biscuit. Then she leaned against the sink and pressed her fingers to her forehead. She would have to get word to Jez. If they had still been living in Laundry Lane, she would have called one of Edith's boys to run and fetch him, but here people tended to have maids to run their errands.

Deciding there was no other option, Lily put Alice back in her perambulator and set off for the Grosvenor Club.

The temperature had dropped several degrees. Cold and fractious, and overdue for her nap, Alice grizzled all the way to West Street. Lily parked the perambulator at the foot of the sweeping steps that led up to the elegant Grosvenor Club and lifted Alice out. She hurried up the steps, buffeted by the cold wind, and made for the impressive double doors.

'May I be of assistance, ma'am?' The liveried doorman seemed to appear from nowhere. She hadn't noticed his tiny alcove to the right of the door until now. He blew on his cold hands.

'Yes, please.' Lily flashed him a grateful smile. 'My husband, Jeremy Elkin, is a member of your club. I need to see him quite urgently.' The doorman smiled at Alice and she stopped grizzling, gazing at him curiously.

'I'm afraid I can't let you in,' he said apologetically. 'No women allowed.'

'But it is important I see him,' Lily replied. 'I have sad news about his mother.'

The doorman placed a restraining hand on Lily's arm. 'I'm sorry, ma'am, but it's more than my job's worth.' He gave Lily a wry grin and shrugged his shoulders. He had a nice face,

Lily thought, open and friendly. He tickled Alice under her chin and she giggled. 'I can get a message to your husband that you're outside, ma'am? You said his name is . . .?'

'Mr Elkin. Mr Jeremy Elkin.'

Distaste flickered across the man's face. He pursed his lips. 'If you'll wait here, ma'am, I'll let Mr Elkin know immediately.' His expression was sympathetic. 'I'm sorry it's so cold. I'll be as quick as I can.'

'Thank you.' Lily nodded. The cold was leaching through the soles of her boots and, despite her gloves, her fingers were turning numb. She tugged Alice's fur-lined hood over her head. The cold had brought tears to the child's eyes and her cheeks were red and chapped. Her lip wobbled and she began to cry.

'Oh, don't cry, Alice, love.' Lily fished out her handkerchief and mopped at her daughter's cheeks, rocking her gently in her arms.

The doorman returned within minutes, looking sheepish.

'Ma'am, Mr Elkin said to tell you to take the child home at once. He'll be home as soon as his business is concluded.'

Dumbfounded, Lily could only frown at him. 'You informed him that I had bad news about his mother?'

The doorman shuffled his feet, clearly discomforted. 'Yes, ma'am.'

'And he refused to see me?'

The man looked away in embarrassment.

'I see.' Her cheeks burned with anger and humiliation. 'My mother-in-law has passed away,' she said, biting her lip in agitation. 'Mr Elkin is needed at home, there are arrangements to be made ...'

'Take the little one home, ma'am,' the doorman said kindly. 'I will inform Mr Elkin of his mother's passing.'

Thanking him, Lily hurried down the steps and strapped Alice into the perambulator.

'Papa?' Alice protested, struggling against her harness.

'Papa's busy, sweetheart,' Lily replied, trying to keep the anger from her voice. She was fuming over Jez's callous disrespect for his poor mother. How could he be so unfeeling? So cruel? Granted, Doris's mothering skills had left a lot to be desired, but she was his mother, when all was said and done, and deserved his consideration.

She smiled down at Alice. Her earlier tears had left her with hiccups, making her giggle. It was a huge relief to Lily that, so far, there was no sign Alice had inherited any of her father's perverse nature. She was a sweet, sunny-natured toddler, and she adored her father. The way she gazed up at Jez with such innocent trust frightened Lily. She just hoped and prayed that he would never do anything to destroy that trust.

Once they were home, Lily got Alice settled in her cot for a nap. She made herself a mug of tea, knowing that she was only putting off the moment she would have to deal with her mother-in-law. The doorbell rang and she went to answer it, puzzled as to who could be calling on a Thursday morning.

She opened the door to two tall, dark-suited, sombre-looking gentlemen and greeted them with a confused frown.

A black wagon drawn by a glossy black horse stood alongside the kerb, 'A. SOURBUTTS, FUNERAL DIRECTOR' emblazoned in gold across its lacquered paintwork.

'Albert Sourbutt, ma'am,' said the older of the two, removing his hat. He had a prominent Adam's apple that bobbed up and down his scrawny throat as he spoke. 'This is my assistant, Bernard Cole.'

'Good day, ma'am.' Bernard bowed his head. 'Our condolences for your loss. We're here to collect the deceased.'

'Who sent you?'

'We were instructed by Mr Elkin, ma'am. He asked us to collect the deceased and remove her to our funeral parlour.' He gave a discreet cough. 'She will be very well cared for, I assure you.'

'But I haven't prepared her . . .' Lily floundered. 'I'm not ready.'

Her sharp gaze caught the twitch of a net curtain in the house opposite and she bit back a humourless smile. The middle classes weren't averse to a bit of nosy poking, it seemed.

'Ma'am, I can assure you that Mrs Elkin Senior will be afforded our utmost care and attention,' Albert Sourbutt assured her. 'So, if you would be so kind as to take us to her, we can begin our duties.'

Feeling at something of a loss, Lily stood aside and let them in. 'In there,' she said weakly, indicating the closed parlour door.

'Thank you, ma'am.'

She took herself off to the kitchen, unable to watch them carry Doris out of the house, instead gazing out over the garden. The first signs of spring were visible in the budding trees and the clusters of tiny purple and gold crocuses along the back wall.

'Ma'am?' She turned to see Albert Sourbutt hovered in the doorway. 'We'll be on our way now. We'll wait to hear from Mr Elkin about the funeral arrangements. If Mrs Elkin had a favourite dress ... if you'd be so kind as to drop it round at your convenience?'

Lily nodded dumbly. 'Yes, of course. Thank you.'

She walked him to the door. Bernard was leaning against the wagon, smoking a cigarette. As his boss descended the steps, he flicked the smouldering butt into a puddle of melting snow and swung himself up onto the sprung seat. Albert climbed up beside him and, with a final wave of his black-gloved hand, set off down the street, leaving Lily staring bleakly after them.

It was early evening when the sound of Jez's key in the lock brought Alice running excitedly into the hallway.

'Papa, Papa,' she shrieked joyfully as Jez swung her up over his head. Lily watched grimly from the kitchen doorway, arms folded across her chest.

'Don't you think such behaviour unseemly, considering you've just lost your mother?' Her green eyes flashed angrily.

In response, Jez set Alice on the floor and followed Lily into the steam-filled kitchen. Condensation fogged the window and the air was thick with the tantalizing aroma of the beef stew simmering in the oven. The tin bath was ready in front of the range.

Alice wrapped her little arms around Jez's leg. 'Play, Papa, play.'

'In a minute, princess,' Jez said, his amiable tone belying his disdainful expression. 'Surely, you of all people can't expect me to mourn that old cow?' he asked Lily. 'She was a drunken old harridan who made both our lives a misery.'

'She was your mother, Jez,' Lily retorted crossly. 'She deserves your respect in death, no matter how you felt about her when she was alive.'

'My respect?' Jez snorted. 'That woman was a noose around my neck. Good riddance, I say.'

'Jez!' Lily glared at him, appalled. 'How can you be so callous?'

Jez shrugged. 'She was nothing to me. If you want to cry crocodile tears over the old bat, be my guest. I, for one, won't be wasting any tears on her.' He smiled benevolently at Alice. 'Come on, princess, let's get ready for your bath.'

Poor Doris's demise went largely unnoticed by the street. Lily hung a black wreath on the front door but only her next-door neighbours, as well as the lady opposite, called to offer their condolences. The secretary of the Grosvenor Club sent lilies, which Lily placed in the bay window from where their cloying perfume permeated the entire house.

The funeral was held three days later. Lily sat beside Jez in the front pew with Alice on her lap. Lily had explained to the little girl that Nana Doris was with Jesus in Heaven, but she couldn't be sure how much she really understood. Several times over the past couple of days, Alice had run about the house calling for her nana. Jez had already dismantled the bed and stacked it away in her old room upstairs, and her meagre possessions had been bagged up and were awaiting collection by a member of the Church of England Waifs and Strays Society.

Pale winter sunshine streamed through the stained-glass windows, casting rainbows over the handful of mourners who had braved the bitter cold to pay their last respects. Some of Jez's fellow town councillors were in attendance, along with their wives and one or two members of his club. Sadly, very few of Doris's old neighbours had turned out, for neither she nor Jez had been well liked. All in all, the congregation barely filled three pews, and Lily felt a stab of sorrow for her mother-in-law. How sad to be mourned by so few, she mused, as she attempted to concentrate on the vicar's lengthy and long-winded eulogy. For a man who had never met Doris, he was certainly finding a lot to say.

There was no wake, Jez having declared that he had spent enough money on Doris while she was alive. With little thought for his wife, he went off to have luncheon at the club with his cronies, leaving Lily and Alice to make their way home alone.

The early-spring sunshine was pleasant so Lily let Alice walk. The little girl was curious about everything, stopping to crouch down and study a clump of snowdrops, or craning her neck to watch a squirrel scampering along the branches of a horse chestnut tree, squealing with childish delight as it leapt from branch to branch.

When Lily unlocked the front door some time later, Alice ran to the parlour, calling for her nana, coming to a halt in the middle of the room when she realized Doris's bed was no longer there.

'Nana?' She turned her questioning gaze on Lily, her bottom lip trembling as tears welled in her big, brown eyes. 'Nana gone?'

Lily crouched down in front of her daughter, her arms outstretched. 'Yes, sweetheart, Nana is gone.'

'Want Nana,' Alice mumbled, folding herself into Lily's embrace.

'I know, darling,' Lily murmured into Alice's soft, dark curls. 'I miss her, too.' She kissed her daughter's soft, downy hair. Despite her failings as a mother, Doris had been a loving grandmother and, to Lily, something of an ally. Now that it was just her against Jez, Lily couldn't help but wonder what the future would hold, and a shiver of dread went down her spine.

Jez belched loudly as he strolled along East Street towards Sheepmarket Hill where stray piles of dirty straw and animal dung bore witness to the previous day's market. He ducked into the alleyway adjacent to the pub and rapped on the door of the first of three dilapidated cottages. It was opened by a young woman. She was wrapped in a sheet, her blond hair tousled.

'Hello, Barbie-Jean.' He grinned. 'Have you missed me?'

'I always miss you when you're not here.' Barbie-Jean pouted prettily, stepping aside to allow Jez into the sparsely furnished room. 'How was the funeral?'

'Grim, as you would expect,' replied Jez. 'I'm parched. Have you got anything to drink?' Barbie-Jean poured him a mug of ale, which he drank thirstily. Then, taking him by the hand, she led him upstairs.

Jez lay on his back, watching a shaft of moonlight inch its way across the ceiling. The sound of merrymaking drifted up from the pub next door. Beside him, Barbie-Jean stirred and rolled over. She ran her fingers lightly over his chest, smiling sleepily. Jez pushed her aside and swung himself off the bed, padding barefoot to the window. A cool breeze wafted up from the street, bringing with it the smell of stale beer and boiled vegetables.

'Come back to bed,' Barbie-Jean murmured. Ignoring her, Jez leaned on the windowsill and inhaled a lungful of air. Moonlight danced on the tiles of the rooftops opposite, a dog barked in the street below. He rubbed his finger along the bridge of his nose and turned to look at Barbie-Jean. She was a pretty little thing, if a little irritating at times, and he had no doubt that he would tire of her in due course. But in the meantime, she might just be the catalyst he needed to get rid of Lily.

He grimaced. The woman was a millstone around his neck. Why he'd ever agreed to marry her, he had no idea. Though if he hadn't, he would never have known Alice. His features softened at the thought of his daughter. She was the apple of his eye, his little princess. He hadn't wasted a moment mourning his mother, and now that she was out of the picture, he could set in motion his plan to get Alice all to himself. All he had to do was convince Barbie-Jean to go along with it. He grinned at her. She twirled a lock of hair around her finger and smiled coquettishly, leaving him in no doubt that she would willingly do whatever he asked.

CHAPTER TWENTY-FIVE

The churchyard was quiet but for the solitary call of a wood pigeon and the sigh of the wind through the pine trees. It had rained during the night and the damp grass soaked the hem of Lily's skirt as she led Alice between the rows of weathered gravestones.

They came to Doris's grave. She could scarcely believe her mother-in-law had been gone almost three weeks. She brought Alice here every week to put fresh flowers on her grave. She knew Jez would never bother and it didn't seem right, Doris lying in the cold ground, forgotten and uncared for. So Lily was determined to make the effort, if only for Alice's sake. Her daughter had adored Doris and felt her loss keenly. She swept away the brown curled-up petals and broken stems strewn across the grassy mound and nodded at Alice, who crouched down, her little brow furrowed in concentration, and gently laid the posy of freesias on her grandmother's grave.

'Good girl,' Lily said, taking her hand. 'Let's go see Grandma Martha and Grandpa Jim.' As they walked across the daisy-strewn grass towards the church, Lily felt into her pocket for Charlie's letter. She had written to inform him of his aunt's passing and had received his reply that morning. It was abundantly clear from his tone that he had suffered no grief at the news.

Martha and Jim rested beneath a yew tree close to the entrance to the church, beside their infant daughter, Annie. Letting go of Alice's hand, Lily crouched down and brushed the lichen from the headstone. It had been twelve years since she had lost her parents and, try as she might, she was finding it hard to recall their features clearly. She had seen a photograph once, not long after she had first gone to live with her aunt. It had been tucked between the pages of an old handwritten recipe book on the kitchen shelf and showed two girls sitting on a hay cart. One was clearly Doris and Lily had assumed the other to be Martha, but the lighting was such that her features were unrecognisable. Lily had looked for the photograph many times since her marriage to Jez but without success. When she asked Doris about it, her aunt had feigned ignorance, leaving Lily to conclude that she, or Jez, had thrown it away.

Lily and Alice laid flowers on the three graves. While Alice chased sunbeams and picked fistfuls of daisies, Lily took the opportunity to spend a few moments in reflective silence, listening to the birds and the wind whispering through the trees. Time had numbed her grief but she mourned the life she might have had, if Jim and Martha had lived.

Not given to self-pity, she pushed the melancholy thought aside, determined not to dwell on what she had lost.

'These are for you, Mama.' Lily smiled, and crouched down as Alice thrust a handful of crushed daisies at her.

'Thank you, sweetheart,' she said, taking the posy from Alice. The stems were warm from the heat of her hand. 'They're very pretty. Shall we call in and say hello to Aunty Violet?'

'Yes, yes!' Alice shrieked, jumping up and down and making Lily laugh. Taking Alice's hand and clutching her posy of now-wilting daisies, Lily glanced over towards the rectory where the incumbent's housekeeper was hanging washing in the garden. May Fudge had retired some years ago and passed away the previous year at the age of seventy-seven.

'Lily! Alice!' Violet exclaimed when they entered the shop. 'What a lovely surprise.' She came out from behind the counter, sweeping Alice off the ground into her embrace. 'And how is my precious god-daughter?' she asked as Alice nuzzled her face into Violet's neck. 'Have you time for a cup of tea?'

'No, thank you, Violet.' Lily shook her head with regret. 'We've just been to the churchyard, haven't we, Alice?'

'We see Nana,' Alice confirmed as Violet set her down.

'You look tired, Lily,' Violet said, her brow crinkling in concern. 'Are you sleeping all right?'

'Yes, I'm fine,' Lily assured her, wandering over to peer into the display cabinets. She missed working with Violet. She missed the pleasant companionship of sitting in the back room. She missed watching her creations coming to fruition before her eyes.

'You're not working too hard? I can stop sending you work, if so.'

'Oh, please don't!' Lily exclaimed. 'Now I haven't got Doris to care for, my days would be pretty empty if I didn't have my sewing to concentrate on. Jez is out all the hours God sends, so I've plenty of time on my hands, despite this little monkey here.' She smiled at Alice. 'She keeps me on my toes.'

'I'll bet she does.' Violet smiled too. 'Alice,' she said, taking down an old tin from the top shelf. She opened it to reveal buttons of various colours and sizes. 'Why don't you see how many different coloured buttons you can find?' She settled Alice on the floor with the tin and turned to Lily, her expression serious. 'He's going to get caught one day,' she said, her voice low so Alice wouldn't hear. 'You realize that, don't you?'

'I hope every morning that today will be the day,' Lily replied with a rueful smile.

'You need to be prepared. You know I've been putting a portion of your wage aside for you. If anything happens, Jez's assets will be seized. You'll be left with nothing. This way, you'll have a bit put by that the authorities won't be able to touch.'

'You're such a good friend, Violet,' Lily said, her eyes glistening with tears of gratitude.

'I regard you and Alice as family – it's the least I can do.'

Lily was still ruminating on Violet's generosity as she scrubbed the kitchen floor later that afternoon. Alice was playing house under the table with her dolls. Suddenly, she gave an excited shout and scrambled to her feet, toys forgotten.

'Papa! Papa's home!'

Wiping her hands on her apron, Lily stepped into the hall-way. Sunlight slanted through the fan-shaped glass at the top of the door, glancing off the dust motes swirling in the air. Racing ahead of her on sturdy little legs, Alice reached the door just as it opened, her shriek of joy dying on her lips as she realized her father wasn't alone.

'Hello, princess!' Jez cried, reaching for Alice as she shrunk back against Lily. Overcome with shyness, she peered up at the young woman standing in the doorway with Jez. She was perhaps a year or so younger than Lily, and pretty, with blond hair done up in an elaborate style, her midnight-blue jacket bringing out the colour of her eyes. She regarded Lily with disdain and Lily shot Jez a questioning look.

'This is Barbie-Jean,' he said by way of explanation. 'She's going to be living here for a while.'

'I beg your pardon?' Lily frowned, dumbfounded as the woman stepped past her into the hallway. 'Jez, what do you mean? Who is this woman?'

Ignoring her, Jez lifted Alice into his arms. 'Don't be shy, princess. Say hello to Papa's friend.' Alice buried her face in her father's neck and Jez laughed. 'Don't worry,' he told Barbie-Jean. 'She's just a bit shy. She'll come round.'

Lily rubbed her arms. She felt chilled to the bone as she watched Barbie-Jean stroke Alice's cheek.

'Hello, Alice,' she said. Her voice was high-pitched, and it grated on Lily's nerves. 'I'm your Aunty Barbie-Jean.'

'No!' Lily's vehement objection earned her a black look from Jez. Barbie-Jean raised a mocking eyebrow. 'I don't mean to be rude, miss, but I would appreciate an explanation.' She looked at her husband.

'Like I said,' Jez drawled contemptuously. 'Barbie-Jean is moving in. She's a friend of mine and you will treat her with the courtesy she deserves.'

'I see,' Lily said stiffly. 'Welcome to our home, Miss . . .' She raised her eyebrow questioningly.

'Taylor,' Barbie-Jean replied haughtily.

'Miss Taylor.' Lily inclined her head, her tone matching the other woman's in its iciness. 'She can have Doris's old room,' she told Jez, turning to lead the way up the stairs. A million questions swirled around her head, her sense of dread increasing with every step.

'Wait,' Jez commanded, halting Lily mid-step. He grinned at her, his face twisted in a vicious leer as he pushed past her on the stairs, still clutching Alice in his arms, and strode along the landing towards the master bedroom. 'Barbie-Jean will be sleeping in here, with me.' He grinned, clearly enjoying Lily's bewilderment.

'What?' she whispered, terror clutching at her throat as her mind conjured up all sorts of depraved scenarios. She felt her legs give way and had to clutch the banister in order not to go tumbling down the stairs. 'Jez, you can't.'

'Don't tell me what I can do in my own home,' Jez bellowed. Lily shrank back in fear as he advanced towards her menacingly. 'Barbie-Jean will be sharing my bed from now on. I need a woman, not a cold fish. You can move into Ma's old room and if you don't like it you can lump it.'

He flung open the door to the master bedroom and Lily heard Barbie-Jean's exclamation of pleasure.

Lily sank onto the top step, resting her head against the banister in despair. She had no idea what to do. What would their neighbours think? Hot, salty tears of humiliation stung her eyes. She heard Jez and Barbie-Jean emerging onto the landing and, hastily wiping away her tears, got unsteadily to her feet.

'Barbie-Jean,' Jez said with a benign smile. 'Would you take Alice out into the garden for a few minutes, please? I need to speak to my wife.'

'Of course, Jez,' Barbie-Jean simpered, holding out her arms. Alice hesitated for a moment, and then allowed herself to be taken. Lily watched in dismay as, throwing a look of triumph over her shoulder, Barbie-Jean carried Alice down the stairs and through the hallway.

Lily reeled back in anger and was about to go after her but Jez's hand on her arm pulled her up short.

'Don't!' he said, his voice dangerously low. Lily glared at him, her chest rising and falling rapidly, her green eyes flashing.

'What are you doing?' she hissed, trying to pull free of his grip but the more she tried to break free, the tighter his fingers bit into her flesh. 'Why would you humiliate me like this?'

'Seeing as you make it obvious you find me physically repulsive, you can't object to me taking my pleasure elsewhere.'

'I've always turned a blind eye to your indiscretions,' Lily retorted angrily. 'But this is different. This is my home.'

'Correction,' Jez snarled, his face up close to Lily's. 'This is my home. You are only here on sufferance. You can stay or go, it makes no difference to me but' – he wagged his finger under her nose – 'if you do choose to leave, you leave alone. Alice stays with me.' His words sent a cold chill down Lily's spine. He pushed past her down the stairs and Lily hurried after him.

'What will your posh friends think of your new domestic arrangement?' Lily hissed. 'And the neighbours? Don't you think there'll be a few raised eyebrows when they find out you've moved your mistress into the family home?' She could hear Alice in the garden, the sound of her carefree laughter only serving to fuel her anger.

'As far as anyone else is concerned, Barbie-Jean is employed as Alice's nursemaid.'

'And you intend to have her living here indefinitely?'

'Oh, I shall no doubt tire of her eventually.' Jez gave a wave of his hand. 'But in the meantime, yes, she'll be living here for the foreseeable future.'

'Does she know you won't be faithful to her?'

'That's none of her business or yours,' Jez sneered. He wrenched Lily's arm, propelling her out of his way. 'Barbie-Jean's trunk is being delivered this evening. And, now, we're taking Alice to the park. I shall expect you to have cleared out your things by the time we get back.'

Lily pressed her hands on the warm windowsill and watched her husband and his mistress walking down the street, swinging Alice back and forth between them. As they rounded the corner and disappeared from sight, she sank onto the chaise lounge, unable to stem the flow of tears.

When she had no tears left, she dragged herself wearily up the stairs. She stood in the doorway and surveyed what had been Doris's bedroom. Her dismantled bed leaned against the wall where Jez had left it the day she died. There was a dressing table against the window, a small chest of drawers on which stood a plain china washing bowl and jug and a narrow wardrobe, the inside of which smelled stale and musty.

She fetched an armful of clean bedding from the wooden box on the landing and, unable to face putting the bed together, simply pulled the mattress to the middle of the room and made a bed up on the floor. Her whole body ached, as if she had been savagely beaten. She stayed in her new room, watching from the window as the shadows lengthened, the sun slipping below the rooftops, and turning the sky into an artist's palette of crimson, pink and vibrant orange. The first stars began to appear in the twilight sky.

Anxiety curdled her stomach as she tried to stem the rising tide of panic. Where were they? She couldn't be still. As she prowled from room to room, her nerves on edge, it occurred to her that Jez may have taken Alice for good. By the time the hansom cab drew up in front of the house, she was over-wrought. She flew out of the house and onto the street, and all but snatched the sleepy Alice from Jez's grasp.

Shoulders sagging with relief, she breathed in her daughter's scent, relishing the solidity of her body pressed against her. 'Where have you been?' she demanded, ignoring Barbie-Jean's sly smile. 'I've been out of my mind with worry.'

'We took Alice to visit Barbie's mother in Blandford St Mary,' Jez said, his expression suggesting Lily was making a fuss over nothing. 'She insisted we stay for supper.' Lily looked from Jez to Barbie-Jean, who returned her angry glare with a sly, mocking smile.

'I'm taking Alice upstairs. It's way past her bedtime.' Before either of them could react, she turned on her heel and went inside.

She sat beside Alice's bed, listening to the gentle rhythm of her breathing. She heard the clatter of a wagon in the street below, followed a short time later by the sound of someone struggling up the stairs with something heavy.

'In here, gov?' she heard a man's wheezing voice ask.

'Room directly at the top of the stairs,' came Jez's reply. Through the crack in the door she caught a glimpse of two burly men coming up the stairs, manhandling a leather trunk between them. She heard the thud as the trunk hit the floor and felt a flash of anger at the thought of Barbie-Jean's dresses hanging in her wardrobe, but she pushed it aside. She had more pressing concerns, such as trying to figure out what game Jez was playing. Why had he taken Alice to visit

Barbie-Jean's mother? Her chest constricted painfully as it dawned on her. He wanted Alice to himself, and he was using Barbie-Jean to drive Lily away. She clenched her fists, her heart beating hard, and vowed that would never happen. If she ever left this house, it would be her decision, and Alice would be going with her.

CHAPTER TWENTY-SIX

Lily unpegged the sheet from the line, folded it into the wicker laundry basket and rubbed the small of her back. Her eyes felt sandy from exhaustion. She had barely slept in the six weeks since the usurper, as Violet called her, had moved in. On top of dealing with the rhythmic creaking of the mattress and muffled giggles emanating through the walls every night, she was also worried sick about Alice. Over the past few weeks, her once bubbly, exuberant little girl had become withdrawn and subdued. On Jez's instruction, Barbie-Jean often took Alice on outings and Lily suspected that, while Barbie-Jean was happy to play the doting stepmother in front of Jez, she wasn't quite so amiable once she and Alice were alone.

The first incident had occurred about a week after Barbie-Jean moved in. On Jez's insistence, she had taken Alice to the park. Alice had been tearful on their return several hours later and had run straight to Lily, burying her face in Lily's skirt.

'Oh, I had to scold her for misbehaving in the park,' Barbie-Jean told Lily airily when she confronted her. 'She'll get over it.'

She had tried broaching the subject with Jez, but he had merely waved her concerns aside and accused her of jealousy. The following day when Jez suggested he and Barbie-Jean take Alice into town to buy her some new shoes, she had clung on to Lily like a limpet and started to cry.

After trying to prise her away, Jez had finally lost his temper, something he rarely did with Alice. He had sat her down on a stool and told her to 'mind Barbie-Jean, or else'. He had even threatened Lily, blaming her for turning Alice against him and Barbie-Jean.

'That's not true,' Lily had responded, flabbergasted by the accusation. 'I have never said anything against you but she' – she shot Barbie-Jean a withering glance – 'upsets Alice.' Barbie-Jean smirked back, clearly assuming she had the upper hand in Jez's affections. Lily looked away in dismay.

Remorseful in the face of Alice's trembling lip and tear-filled eyes, Jez picked her up and gave her a cuddle. Alice adored Jez and, though she loved to please him, it was a very subdued little girl who left the house that day. Lily watched the three of them from the window, unable to shake the feeling that she was slowly being edged out of Alice's life.

On one occasion she had attempted to follow Barbie-Jean when she took Alice out, but the moment she stepped outside, Ned was there, strong-arming her back indoors. 'Sorry, ma'am,' he said apologetically as she protested. 'Boss's orders.' What did Jez think – that she would snatch Alice and make a run for it?

She couldn't deny the idea hadn't crossed her mind, she thought now as she rubbed her throbbing temples. The whistle of the four-fifteen train from Bath drifted on the balmy late-afternoon breeze. She lifted the laundry basket onto her hip and followed the path back to the house.

It was warm in the kitchen. Sun streamed in through the window. A bee crawled lethargically up the glass and she shooed it outside. She was about to fill the kettle when she heard voices from the parlour. It was Alice and Barbie-Jean. Lily swept down the hallway, determined to confront her husband's lover once and for all, but she was brought up short when she heard Alice call Barbie-Jean Mama. It was like a physical blow, and Lily stormed into the parlour where Alice was sitting on the footstool in front of Barbie-Jean, a skein of knitting wool wound around her hands.

'You are not her mother!' Lily shouted at Barbie-Jean, sweeping Alice into her arms and yanking the wool from her daughter's hands. Her chest heaved as she faced the other woman. Alice buried her face in Lily's neck, crying quietly. Barbie-Jean merely smiled sardonically.

'Oh, Lily,' she said with a pitying look. 'Don't you realize you're on borrowed time? It's me Jez wants.' She inclined her head and stretched her pale arms languidly, smiling like the cat who'd got the cream. 'Alice and me, we're Jez's family now.'

'Alice will never be yours,' Lily hissed vehemently. Clutching Alice to her chest, she ran out into the hall and up the stairs to her room. She untangled Alice's arms from around her neck and sat her on the bed. Quickly, she shut the door and dragged the chest of drawers in front of it. Breathing heavily, she sank onto the bed and held out her arms. Alice crawled onto her lap and pressed her face into Lily's chest. Lily stroked her soft dark curls, crooning softly.

'Mama, please don't go away,' Alice asked so softly Lily could barely hear her.

'I'm not going anywhere without you, sweetie.' She cupped Alice's chin in her hand and raised her face so she was looking into her daughter's tear-filled brown eyes. 'Did Barbie-Jean tell you Mama was going away?'

Alice nodded, her bottom lip trembling.

'She said you don't want me anymore and I have to call her Mama now.' Her eyes filled with tears. 'I don't like Barbie-Jean, Mama. She said I'm a bad girl.'

'Oh, sweetie.' Lily pulled her close and hugged her. The audacity of the woman! Anger boiled inside her. How dare she treat her child so cruelly? How dare she?

'Lily, open the door!' Jez demanded. Lily pressed her finger to her lips.

Alice sat on the bed, her brown eyes anxious, her little brow knitted in confusion. She loved her papa but it scared her when he shouted at her mama. She scuttled back across the bed until she was pressed up against the wall.

It was early evening. Shadows crept across the floor and the glass reflected the flaming sky. Jez had returned home minutes before. Lily had heard a muttered exchange in the hallway before his footsteps came pounding up the stairs. Now he was hammering on her door, demanding she bring Alice out.

Alice screamed in fright as Jez threw himself at the door. To Lily's horror, the force of the blow pushed the chest of drawers forward an inch.

'It's all right, Alice,' she whispered. She ran to the chest and, using all her strength, pushed against it. Jez put his shoulder to the door and it took every ounce of Lily's strength to stop the chest from sliding forwards.

'Alice, it's me, princess. It's Papa.'

'You're scaring her,' Lily said through clenched teeth.

'You're the one scaring her,' Jez snarled. 'With your erratic behaviour.' She caught a glimpse of his face through the crack in the door. A pulse throbbed in his temple. He shoved at the door again. Lily let out a ravaged sob. She was losing the strength in her arms. She wouldn't be able to hold out against him much longer. Suddenly the pressure lifted. She blinked in surprise, her breath coming in ragged gasps.

'Have it your way,' Jez grunted. 'You can't stay in there for ever and I'll be waiting. This time I'll teach you a lesson you'll never forget.' He smashed the doorframe with his fist, making Lily jump. Alice screamed again. Lily shut the door and heaved the chest of drawers back into place. She leaned against it, breathing heavily, as she listened to the sound of Jez's receding footsteps.

She waited until the house was silent. Moonlight cut a swathe through the darkness as she gently shook Alice awake. The little girl blinked in confusion and Lily put her finger to her lips.

'You must be very quiet,' she whispered, her ears straining for the slightest sound. 'We're going on an adventure.' Gritting her teeth, she gently eased the chest of drawers away from the door and stepped out onto the landing. She held her breath, listening. The only sound was the tick of the parlour clock and the rhythmic snores emanating from the bedroom next door.

Silently, she lifted Alice off the bed and reached for the suitcase she'd packed earlier. She had been unable to get any of Alice's things from her room. She would have to spend some of her precious savings on new clothes for Alice, but that couldn't be helped.

Her heart was beating so loudly she was almost convinced Jez would be able to hear it as she made her way along the landing. A floorboard creaked and she froze. Alice looked at her, her eyes wide in her pale face. Lily attempted a smile. Standing at the top of the stairs she looked down at the front door. Moonlight streamed in through the fanlight. She inhaled a shaky breath. Freedom was so tantalisingly close.

She started down the stairs. With every step, she expected to hear Jez coming after them. At the foot of the stairs, she set

Alice and the suitcase on the floor and grabbed their coats from the hooks.

'Mama?' Alice tugged at Lily's skirts.

'Shush!' Lily glanced nervously up the stairs, but the snoring continued without interruption. 'We must be as quiet as mice, Alice,' she whispered as she quietly opened the front door. She heard a low cough and her heart sank. In her haste to get away, she had forgotten about Ned. He was a few yards down the moonlit street, leaning against a lamp post, smoking a cigarette. He glanced in her direction and she stepped back into the hall. The door clicked shut behind her.

Heart thumping, she led Alice through the house to the back door. The back garden was silent and deserted.

'Mama, I'm frightened,' Alice whimpered.

Lily sacrificed a precious few minutes to console her daughter, then led her across the moon-dappled lawn to the back gate. She held her breath, as she slid back the bolts, and slipped into the adjacent street.

With the coats folded over her suitcase, and holding Alice by the hand, Lily took a deep breath and set off down the road.

Their footsteps sounded inordinately loud as they crossed the silent deserted marketplace. Glancing about nervously, Lily led Alice down the alleyway that ran behind Violet's shop, unlatched the gate and entered the dark backyard. A cat screeched nearby, making the hairs on the back of her neck stand on end.

'Mama, I'm scared,' Alice whispered.

'We'll be safe now,' Lily smiled reassuringly as she felt beneath the doormat for the spare key. The door squeaked as she pushed it open and stepped into the dark work room. Instantly, her senses were assailed by the familiar smell of cloth and she experienced a sudden pang of nostalgia for the times she had spent working with Violet.

She locked the door behind her. The house was silent but for the ticking of the clock. Leaving the suitcase on the floor, she hoisted Alice onto her hip and groped her way up the dark staircase to Violet's bedroom. Heart thumping loudly, she rapped on the door.

'Violet? Violet, it's me, Lily.'

She heard Violet's muffled exclamation of surprise. 'Just a moment.' Bedsprings creaked. A match flared and light spilled from beneath the door. A minute later, the door opened to reveal Violet silhouetted in the lamplight.

'What is it? What's happened?' she exclaimed as she tied the cord of her velvet dressing gown around her waist.

'We're leaving,' Lily said, her voice low. 'Is there somewhere I can put Alice? She's exhausted.'

'Oh, poor lamb,' Violet said, brushing a lock of hair out of Alice's eyes. 'Put her in my bed. I'll put the kettle on.'

'I can't stay there another minute,' Lily said a short while later as she sat at the kitchen table with Violet, her chilled fingers wrapped around a mug of hot, sweet tea. 'Barbie-Jean admitted to me tonight that Jez wants to get rid of me.'

'What? No!' Violet recoiled in shock.

'He knows I would never leave without Alice.' Lily met Violet's gaze. 'I'm frightened of what he might do.'

'In light of Jez's blatant adultery, surely you have grounds to divorce him?'

'I can't risk losing Alice,' Lily replied. 'It's Jez's word against mine, and as far as everyone else is concerned, Barbie-Jean is employed as Alice's nanny. If the court ruled in Jez's favour, he would be awarded custody and you can be sure he would make sure I never saw her again.'

'I expect you're right,' Violet conceded with a frown. 'But Jez will come after you,' she warned. 'He's a lot of things but he adores that girl. He won't let her go without a fight.'

'That's why I have to get Alice away from here.'

'I can't believe the gall of that Barbie-Jean, myself,' Violet said disparagingly. 'What sort of woman would debase herself so?'

Lily gazed at Violet over the rim of her mug and shrugged. 'She's a fool if she thinks Jez is going to marry her. I had a lot of time to think tonight and she's just a pawn in his game. He's using her to drive me away. If I leave, he can divorce me for desertion and I'll lose Alice for ever.' She massaged her temples. 'I've got to leave on the first available train. I need my savings book, please.'

'Of course.' Violet got to her feet. 'I'll get it for you.' She went into the parlour while Lily sipped her tea. Her head pounded painfully. Now that she had actually made the break, she felt overwhelmed. She had no idea where she was going, nor what she would do when she got there.

'Here we are.' Violet returned with her savings book. 'And I've got this for you.' She handed Lily a sheet of paper that had been ripped from a pad.

'Who is this?' Lily asked, frowning.

'Mary Johnson is a friend of mine. That's her address in Poole. She owns a haberdashery business in the High Street. I received a letter from her just last week and she happened to mention she was looking for someone to help out in the shop. She offers an alteration service as well. I'll give you a letter of recommendation.'

'Poole?' Lily looked doubtful. 'It isn't very far. What if Jez comes looking for us?'

'The first place Jez will come looking is here,' Violet told her with certainty. 'I'll tell him you've gone to London. That wild goose chase should keep him occupied for months.'

Lily bit her lip. 'It would be fortuitous if I could find employment with your friend,' she said, mulling it over in her mind.

'She's a very amiable woman,' Violet assured her. 'She was widowed young but she's indomitable. You'll like her, I'm sure.' Violet refilled their mugs. The church clock chimed two. 'I think the first train of the morning leaves about half past five. With luck, you'll be on your way before Jez even realizes you've gone,' Violet said, helping herself to milk. 'So, after this, I suggest you get a couple of hours' sleep. Oh, and I'd consider changing your name. Just to be on the safe side.'

★   ★   ★

Lily was as nervous as a cat on hot bricks waiting for the train. She kept glancing over her shoulder, terrified that Jez might appear at any moment. When the train finally thundered into the station, she was light-headed with relief. She hugged Violet goodbye and climbed aboard. Being the first train of the day, the third-class carriage was almost empty. She stowed her suitcase in the rack above their heads and she and Alice settled into their seats. The whistle blew and Lily and Alice waved to Violet who ran alongside them as the train made its way down the platform, gradually picking up speed until Violet was left behind, a lonely, waving figure fading into the distance.

Kneeling on the seat, Alice pressed her face to the window, exclaiming with delight at every field of grazing cows or sheep. Lily smiled. Despite the upheaval of the previous night, Alice appeared to be in good spirits and none the worse for her nocturnal adventure. Lily leaned back against the headrest and closed her eyes. Everything had happened so quickly, she'd barely had time to catch her breath.

The train stopped at many stations during the forty-minute journey but it was still too early for most commuters and they picked up only a handful of passengers. As the train swayed through the Dorset countryside, Lily found her earlier sense of peace deserting her.

What if Mary Johnson had already filled the position? Thanks to Violet's generosity, she had enough money to last them a month, six weeks if she was really frugal. If she hadn't found employment by then, she didn't know what would become of them. She pushed the thought aside. Of course she would find work. She had never shirked from hard work and she was prepared to take on even the most menial tasks as long as she could keep Alice safe from Jez's evil clutches.

After they'd changed trains at Broadstone, Lily unwrapped the bread and butter Violet had packed for their breakfast and handed a slice to Alice. Too anxious to eat, Lily leaned back in her seat, watching the row of grand villas set high upon a grassy embankment slide past the window as the train gathered speed.

Some thirty minutes later, they pulled into Poole railway station. Lily lifted down her case and the coats, and she and Alice followed the other disembarking passengers to the door. The platform was bustling with commuters waiting to embark and she clung tightly to Alice as she stepped off the train, terrified she might lose her in the crowd.

Jostled on all sides, Lily pushed her way through the crowd towards the exit. A scruffy, grubby-faced urchin appeared at her side.

'Carry your bag, missus?' he said, with an endearing, lopsided grin. He winked at Alice, making her grin.

'Thank you,' Lily said gratefully. She set the case down and was instantly pushed from behind. She stumbled. The urchin took off, darting through the crowd, followed by another, smaller boy. Lily stared after them in surprise. Instinctively, her hand went to her pocket, feeling for her purse. It wasn't there. Her savings book was missing too. Panicking, she patted her skirts, spinning around to scan the ground. If she had dropped it, it could be anywhere by now, kicked along the platform.

'My purse!' she cried out, looking around wildly as if in hope it would miraculously appear. 'Please,' she grabbed a plump woman who was passing. 'I've lost my purse.' The woman scowled and shrugged her hand away. Lily turned to the next person. 'Have you seen my purse?' She could feel herself growing hot as panic clouded her thinking.

Tugging Alice along, she struggled through the throng with her suitcase, coats trailing along the ground as she retraced her steps, constantly scanning the ground. Surely, she hadn't lost it on the train? She stood on the platform edge, staring down the track after the long-departed train and forced herself to think clearly. Alice started to cry and she picked her up, whispering soothing words of comfort into her daughter's ears as she tried to get her jumbled thoughts in some semblance of order. She hadn't taken her purse or savings book out of her pocket since the conductor had checked her ticket at Broadstone.

Her blood ran cold as realization dawned. The grubby-faced urchin and his friend. She had been robbed. There could be no other explanation. She gave a cry of alarm as a hand closed around her wrist, startling her.

'Not thinking of jumping, are you?' She found herself looking into the stationmaster's scowling face. He was a heavily built man with bristling grey sideburns that reached halfway down his ruddy cheeks. Lily shook her head dumbly. ''Cos you're wasting your time.' He checked his pocket watch. 'The next train's not due in for another hour.'

'I wasn't planning to jump.' She gave an exasperated sigh. 'I've lost my purse. I had it on the train and ...' Her words trailed away as she stared down onto the track, her slim hope that it had somehow fallen from her pocket between the train and the platform fading as she surveyed the detritus that littered the track.

'Ah.' The stationmaster nodded. 'You've fallen prey to the pickpockets, have you, love?' He had a faint Welsh lilt, Lily noticed, and kind eyes. He gave Lily a sympathetic smile. 'They're a menace around here.' He retained his grip on Lily's wrist, gently leading her away from the edge of the platform. The crowds had thinned considerably. A few passengers occupied one of the benches, awaiting the arrival of the next train. The hands on the large station clock stood at ten past seven. Pigeons perched on the iron girders holding up the roof, their cooing echoing in the cavernous building.

'Where are you headed?' the stationmaster asked kindly, as Lily bounced Alice up and down in an attempt to hush her crying, aware that they were attracting curious glances from the few people still milling about.

'The High Street,' she replied. Thankfully she had memorized Mary Johnson's address. Violet's note with the directions had been in her savings book.

'It's barely a ten-minute walk,' the stationmaster told her, his jowls wobbling as he nodded. Lily gave a sigh of relief, jiggling Alice on her hip. Her cries were beginning to subside and she snuggled her wet face into Lily's neck, tears and mucus soaking into her hair.

'Tell you what.' He scratched his chin. 'Leave your suitcase with me. You can send for it later, save you carrying it with you.'

'Thank you.' Lily's eyes welled with tears of gratitude. 'You've been very kind.'

'My pleasure, ma'am.' The stationmaster tipped his cap. He walked her to the station exit and pointed her in the right direction. Lily and Alice stood on the pavement, breathing in the warm, briny air as omnibuses, wagons, carts and carriages trundled up and down the street and gulls wheeled, screaming, overhead.

CHAPTER TWENTY-SEVEN

Despite the early hour, Poole High Street was bustling. A stall selling cockles and mussels was doing a roaring trade. The queue stretched down the street, the vinegary tang mingling with the smells of swirling dust, fish and horse manure. Uttering a silent prayer that Mary Johnson would be willing to take her on, Lily made her way slowly up the street.

A few minutes later, she was standing outside Mary Johnson's shop. Now almost three years old, Alice was heavy and it was a relief to put her down for a moment while, with a sinking heart, she surveyed the empty window, the TO LET sign hanging on the door. Violet said she had received Mary's letter only last week. For a brief moment she wondered if she had misremembered the address. But no, the painted sign above bore the distinct words; M. JOHNSON – HABERDASHERY. In desperation, she rapped loudly on the window.

'Mrs Johnson?' she called out. 'Hello? Is anyone there?' She stepped back, shielding her eyes against the sun's glare as she studied the upstairs window, anxiety forming a knot in her stomach.

'You looking for Mary?' A young blonde girl emerged from the candlemaker's next door. Lily nodded, shock and despair rendering her momentarily lost for words as she realized just how much she had been relying on Mary's help.

'I'm afraid she passed away last week,' the girl said. 'I'm sorry. Were you close?' she asked, seeing Lily's crestfallen expression. Lily shook her head.

'No, I . . .' Her throat constricted, making further conversation impossible.

'I'm Janey,' the girl said. 'I work in there.' She jerked her head towards the door of the candlemaker's. 'I didn't know Mary well, but she was always friendly when we met out in the street. It was a terrible shock when she died. She just keeled over in front of a customer. The doctor came but it was too late.' She eyed Lily sympathetically. 'What did you want with her?'

'She's a friend of a friend,' Lily said, finally finding her voice. Her thoughts went to Violet. She would have to write and inform her of her old friend's death. 'I was hoping she might offer me a job.' Her voice wobbled as the seriousness of her situation hit home. She was alone and penniless in an unfamiliar city.

'Are you all right?' Janey laid a sympathetic hand on Lily's arm. 'You've had a shock.'

'I – we – haven't anywhere to go,' she stammered, panic rising in her chest.

Janey crouched down in front of Alice, who hid her face in Lily's skirts. 'Hey, little girl, what's your name?'

Alice peeked out from behind her mother, a cheeky smile on her face.

'Will you tell me?' Janey smiled. Alice shook her head, giggling.

'Tell the lady your name, sweetheart,' Lily said automatically. She was far too concerned over their immediate future to engage in playfulness.

'Alice.' The little girl giggled, peeping at Janey through her fingers.

'That's a pretty name, Alice,' Janey said, straightening up. 'There are plenty of boarding houses around these parts,' she told Lily helpfully. 'As long as you avoid the seafront, they're pretty reasonably priced. I can recommend a few, if you like?'

'Thank you,' Lily said, forcing down her rising panic. 'It's just that I was robbed at the station. They took my purse and my savings book. I haven't any ...' Her bottom lip trembled as tears welled. She wiped them away roughly. 'We've no money and nowhere to go.'

The girl's brow creased sympathetically. 'I'm sorry,' she said, glancing at Alice. She shrugged helplessly. 'There are some places along the quay.' She eyed Alice with a grimace of despair. 'You can get a meal and a place to sleep this evening at least. And try the shops along the High Street. Someone might be looking for help.'

Lily thanked Janey, fighting down her welling nausea. She could taste the bile in her throat. Clutching Alice tightly by the hand, she followed the sign pointing towards the seafront. She could hardly think straight. Her temples throbbed. She was dimly aware of the girl, Janey, calling after her, wishing her luck.

Her first thought was to retrieve her luggage from the station. Wearily, she lifted Alice onto her hips and retraced her steps. Her back and arms ached and it was a relief to put Alice down as they entered the cool railway terminal. While Alice chased the pigeons strutting about the platform, Lily approached the baggage claim. The kindly stationmaster from earlier was nowhere to be seen. Instead, she was confronted by a pompous-looking clerk who peered at her condescendingly through his monocle.

'Do you have your claim ticket?' he asked. Checking over her shoulder to assure herself Alice wasn't getting into mischief, she handed it over. The clerk scrutinized it for an unnecessary length of time before asking Lily for the fee.

'Oh. The stationmaster didn't mention I would incur a fee,' she stammered. 'I only left it here about an hour and a half ago.'

The clerk shrugged. 'We charge per day,' he said.

'But I was robbed. I don't have any money. Please. I'll pay the money as soon as I'm earning.'

'You must think I was born yesterday,' the clerk sneered. 'Be off with you. You've got a week or your belongings will be sold off to cover the costs. Oh, and don't forget' – he grinned mockingly – 'you're being charged by the day.'

Tears of humiliation and shame burning the back of her throat, Lily called Alice to her and left the station. She had been hoping to pawn some of her gowns until she could find work.

Resisting the urge to sink onto the steps and give in to her misery, she led Alice back towards the city centre. She was no stranger to hard work, as her calloused hands bore testimony. Surely someone would hire her?

She spent the rest of the day traipsing the streets of Poole in search of work, growing more despondent as the day wore on. Hungry and tired, Alice grew fractious, whining and complaining as they made their way up one street and down the other.

Violet heard the shop bell jangle as she was putting the finishing touches onto a black mourning dress for a client who had recently been widowed.

'Just a minute,' she called, through a mouthful of pins, as she got to her feet. 'Jez!' She had known he would come, but that didn't lessen the shock at seeing him standing in her shop, his expression thunderous.

'Where is she?' he demanded, his eyes swivelling about the shop as if Lily might suddenly appear from behind the counter.

'She's not here,' Violet said, forcing herself to remain calm as she stepped forward in an attempt to prevent him from going into the back room. Her efforts were in vain. He shoved past her, almost ripping the curtain from its rail as he stormed into the workroom at the back. Finding no one there, he bounded up the stairs, Violet hurrying after him.

'You're wasting your time, Jez,' she said. 'I've told you, she isn't here.'

Ignoring her, Jez searched the flat, throwing open doors and wardrobes.

'Where is she?' Like a panther he sprung across the room and, grasping Violet by the throat, pushed her up against the wall. 'Where is my wife?' he snarled. They were nose to nose and Violet flinched. She could barely breathe. She tried to shake her head.

'She went to London,' she wheezed. Suddenly he released his grip and she sank to the ground, gasping for air.

'Whereabouts in London?'

Violet shook her head. 'I don't know, Jez, I swear.'

'She trusts you,' he said, his expression menacing. 'If you hear from her . . .'

He was interrupted by the jangle of the shop bell. He hesitated and Violet held her breath.

'I'll be back,' he said. Throwing her a venomous glare, he turned and ran down the stairs.

It was some minutes before Violet found the strength to get up and go down into the shop.

Late afternoon found Lily and Alice down by the quayside. 'Boats, Mama, boats.' Alice pointed, her fretfulness giving way to excitement as she skipped along the quayside. Ships and boats of all sizes rocked and bobbed on the green water, seagulls wheeling around their masts. Flags snapped in the breeze, timber creaked, water lapped rhythmically against the slime-coated harbour wall. The air smelled of ozone and fish. For a few minutes, Lily stood at the water's edge, peering down into the oily waters, her mind in turmoil. Alice tugged at her arm, fascinated by the burly, swarthy-skinned stevedores traipsing up and down the gangplanks, barrels slung over their broad shoulders, shouting to each other in strange tongues.

Beyond the harbour, clouds gathered on the horizon where silver sea merged with cerulean sky. Behind her were the dosshouses, squashed between the warehouses and brothels. She could smell them and her stomach tightened with such horror she was barely able to make one foot follow the other. Could she really subject Alice to a night in such a place?

'I don't like it here, Mama,' Alice whispered, her little face pinched and frightened. 'Want to go home.'

'We can't go home just yet, Alice,' Lily said, forcing herself to sound calm and cheerful. She was aware of the eyes following her as they made their way down a narrow alleyway. Shadows were lengthening, giving the already mean street a menacing air. A queue of ragged men, with unkempt hair and wild eyes stretched the length of the street. As one was admitted, the rest shuffled forward in a desultory manner, shoulders slumped, eyes downcast. Lily's stomach lurched. The rancid odour of unwashed bodies and stale liquor turned her stomach.

'Hello, my pretty,' one of the men leered, lurching drunkenly towards Lily. 'Give us a kiss.' He grinned with teeth that were blackened stumps. The man next to him gave a throaty chuckle. He pointed at Lily with a filth-encrusted finger.

'It's proper cosy in there,' he said with a meaningful leer as he tilted his head in the direction of the buildings. 'If you get my drift.' He laughed, doubling over as he was racked by a lengthy fit of coughing. He hawked a glob of phlegm and spat it out, narrowly missing Lily's foot.

Her skin crawling with distaste, she backed away, tightening her grip on Alice's hand.

'C'mon, miss,' the first man said, beckoning her closer. 'Don't be coy.'

Turning on her heel, she swept Alice up and ran back the way she had come, her heart thumping, almost tripping on the slippery cobbles in her haste.

Alice was heavy in her arms, yet she didn't stop until she had put a decent distance between herself and the row of dilapidated boarding houses. She slumped against a wall, her chest heaving as she fought to catch her breath. The sun was sinking ever lower. Soon it would be dark. She needed to find somewhere they could spend the night. Alice squirmed against her, her eyes wide with fear, a worried frown on her little face.

'Mama?' she said in a small, frightened voice, her lip quivering. 'I'm hungry. I want to go home. I want Papa.'

'We can't go home, sweetie,' Lily said wearily. 'I'm so sorry.' She swallowed. She was suddenly assailed by doubts. Perhaps she had made a mistake running away. At least with Jez, Alice had been safe and well fed. Their situation was growing more dire by the moment.

Alice buried her face in Lily's neck and began to cry. Her wails grew louder and she refused to be comforted, no matter how much Lily jiggled her up and down. She felt swamped by waves of despair. Her own hunger pains gnawed at her belly. They hadn't eaten since the bread and butter they'd had on the train hours ago.

A chill wind blew off the water and Lily shivered. A fog horn sounded out to sea. Mist was rolling in and Lily could just make out the shape of Brownsea Island in the gathering dusk.

She ached all over and a large blister had developed on the heel of her right foot. Every step was painful but she had to find somewhere for them to sleep.

After about ten minutes of aimless wandering, Alice's wails ringing in her ear, Lily found herself back on the High Street. There were few people about: a cart laden with cloth, a carriage conveying a well-to-do couple, an omnibus jammed with people heading for the outskirts of the city. No one paid Lily and her crying child the slightest heed.

Bone-weary, and unable to carry Alice any further, she slumped against the wall of a small printing company. The doorway recess was deep, providing shelter from the cool breeze, and the floor was relatively clean. She huddled down in the doorway, Alice lying heavily across her lap, and thought longingly of their warm coats, left at the station. They were as good as lost. There was no way she could afford to retrieve them. Ignoring her screaming muscles, she gently rocked Alice until she fell asleep. Lily leaned her head against the locked door. Her stomach cramping with hunger and anxiety, she slept fitfully, only to be woken some time later by a blood-curdling scream. She sat bolt-upright, instantly alert. Wherever the scream had come from, all was silent now and she was thankful Alice hadn't woken up. She remained awake for the rest of the night, too frightened to go back to sleep, watching as the sky lightened and the sun rose, promising another glorious day.

Alice woke up hungry and grizzling. She began to cry almost as soon as she opened her eyes, drawing her knees up to her chest in attempt to quell her hunger cramps.

'Oh, darling, I'm so sorry,' Lily tried to console her as she got stiffly to her feet. The chill had settled in her bones. Her mouth was dry as dust and she felt weak with hunger and lack of sleep. Balancing Alice on her hip, she brushed the dust from her skirt as the door behind them rattled and bolts were pulled back.

'What the . . .?' A short, pot-bellied man with a gleaming pate and steel-rimmed spectacles glared at her beneath thick black brows. 'Clear off,' he snorted with a wave of his little fat hand. 'We don't want beggars here. Go on, clear off!'

Alice's crying went up a notch and the man glowered at her. 'Clear off,' he said again, his expression threatening, 'or I'll call the law.'

Lily took a step backwards in alarm. She daren't risk a run-in with the police. They'd take Alice away from her. She stood on the pavement, the sun warm on her back, and surveyed the street. The shopkeepers were opening up, hauling down awnings, unlocking doors, sweeping pavements. Carts and wagons rumbled down the street; a boy went by pushing a hand cart. Alice's crying subsided as she was momentarily distracted by the bustle around her.

Lily took her down to the harbour, hoping the sights and smells might take her daughter's mind off her empty stomach. She had thought a lot about her mother, Beatrice, during the night. Faced with the prospect of not being able to provide for her hungry child, she was now able to understand the heartbreaking choice Bea had made. She shook the memory from her mind. It wouldn't come to that. She was determined to find a job today.

The harbour was a hive of activity. Fishermen were unloading their catch onto the harbour wall. Stevedores rolled large barrels down the gangplank of a large ship recently returned from a long voyage. A coal merchant's wagon rattled by. Gulls wheeled overhead, their mournful cries echoing on the salty breeze. The morning sun danced on the smooth waters of the harbour and glinted on the windows of Brownsea Castle. Lily's mouth watered hungrily as she walked past an old man frying sprats on the quayside. Her stomach rumbled noisily as she turned away in despair.

It was another fruitless day in her search for work, Alice growing more listless as the day wore on.

They spent another night huddled in a doorway. By morning, Lily was at her wits end. Her own hunger was nothing compared with the agony of watching her child suffer. She spied a man tossing a pie crust to the wind and cried out in dismay when a gull swooped down and snatched it in mid-air.

Alice was quiet and pale, her eyelids drooping with hunger and dehydration. Lily found a pump and managed to get a little water down Alice's throat. She had begun coughing too, her chest making an alarming rattling noise.

That day she went further afield in search of work, knocking on the doors of grand residences. The blisters on her heels had burst and every step was agony. Yet she was determined to keep going. She had to, for Alice's sake. She was willing to do anything to feed her daughter.

But the butlers and housekeepers took one look at Alice, flushed and feverish, and shut the door in their faces.

That evening she gravitated once more to the harbour. Weak with hunger and thirst, she could barely drag one foot in front of the other. Boats creaked and groaned in their berths. Music and ribald laughter wafted from the many taverns, lights spilling across the street. Alice was almost unconscious in Lily's arms. Her skin was hot, her eyes dull, and Lily was desperate. She needed money for medicine, for food, or Alice would die. In desperation she made a bargain with God. If Alice survived the night, she would take her to the police station tomorrow. Even the spiteful Barbie-Jean was better than life on the streets.

There were several ships docked in the harbour. Strange accents and foreign tongues echoed over the water.

Swarthy-skinned men streamed down the gangplank or strolled along the quayside, arm in arm, heading for the taverns.

Lily's legs trembled. Alice was a hot weight in her arms. Her throat closed and her knees turned to jelly as she imagined offering herself to one of the sailors. A woman emerged from the shadows into the moonlight, adjusting her ruffled skirts. A man followed, bow-legged and balding, doing up his flies. He saw Lily and gave a low whistle. Lily's insides turned to ice.

'Oi,' the woman snapped at him. 'She's way out of your league, Manuel. She'll charge you more than a pittance for a quick fumble up against the wall. Go on, on your way.' Manuel continued to leer at Lily until the woman booted him in the bottom. He yelped and flashed her an injured look. 'Hop it!' She hooked her thumb over her shoulder and with one last scowl, Manuel disappeared in the direction of the nearest tavern.

'Thank you,' Lily whispered hoarsely.

'Think nothing of it,' the woman said breezily. She had hair the colour of brass, piled up on top of her head in an untidy mess, and a heavily made-up face. Her lipstick and eyeliner were smudged. She eyed Lily curiously. 'What are you doing down here at this time of night, anyway?'

'I . . . I . . .' Lily stammered. Alice stirred in her arms, moaning softly. Her skin was clammy, a sheen of sweat on her pale cheeks. 'My daughter, she's sick. I need money . . .'

'Hmm.' The woman took a step closer. From behind a coil of thick rope came a rhythmic grunting. 'So, you thought you'd earn it by selling yourself to a sailor?'

Lily nodded. The woman shook her head in dismay. 'They'd eat you for breakfast, dearie. I'm Dolly, by the way.' She thrust out her hand. After a moment's hesitation, Lily shook it. 'Your kiddie's sick?'

'Yes. I need to get her to a doctor. I've got no money. We've nowhere to go. I've been trying to find a job but no one will hire me.' Her words dwindled in a sigh of despair. Saying the words out loud only seemed to emphasize just how hopeless a situation she and Alice were in and the tears began to fall.

'You don't want to go down this road, dearie,' Dolly told her, handing over a large and none-too-clean handkerchief. Lily dabbed her eyes and blew her nose, shifting Alice's weight on her hip. 'What's your trade?'

'Dressmaker,' Lily replied, biting back tears. 'But I'm willing to do anything.'

'You'll find it hard going finding anyone who'll give you a job with a kid in tow,' Dolly remarked, biting her plump, crimson lip. 'There's a woman over in Carter Lane who takes in kiddies, for a price.'

Lily recoiled in horror. 'A baby farmer? I couldn't. I won't.'

Dolly shrugged. 'Suit yourself.' She made to move away, then stopped, her shoulders slumping as she sighed, and turned back to Lily. 'If you go to the Wesleyan Chapel in the High Street, they'll help you. You can't miss it. They open their doors at night. If you're not averse to a bit of preaching, you'll get a warm meal and a bed for the night. You'll find a doctor there.'

'Thank you,' Lily breathed, overcome with gratitude. 'Thank you so much.' Dolly shrugged again.

'Think nothing of it,' she drawled, her attention diverted by a group of foreign sailors, slightly the worse for drink, reeling up the street. With a wink at Lily, she sauntered over to meet them.

CHAPTER TWENTY-EIGHT

Lily found the church easily enough. Its many stained-glass windows were ablaze with light. The solid oak doors were thrown wide open in welcome, lamplight pooling onto the smooth stone steps. A handwritten notice was tacked to the door frame.

NO MEN OR BOYS OVER 12

WOMEN AND CHILDREN ONLY

With Alice a deadweight in her arms, Lily dragged herself up the steps. A well-built woman of about forty wearing a white lace-edged cap met her in the stone porch.

'Welcome, my dear. I'm the reverend's wife, Mrs Beacham.'

'Lily,' Lily replied with difficulty. 'Lily ... Brown.'

'Welcome, Mrs Brown.' She led Lily into the main body of the church. The many lamps gave the church a cosy ambiance. The air smelled of beeswax polish and something deliciously savoury.

Women of varying ages occupied the pinewood pews. Some lay stretched out upon them, others were sitting up, chatting in low voices. Several were nursing tiny babies and young children. In a quiet corner, a group of five children were seated on a rug and an older woman was reading to them from a big illustrated children's Bible. A table had been set up close to the altar and three well-dressed women were ladling soup into bowls and buttering thick slices of bread.

'A few rules,' Mrs Beacham said in a low voice. 'We'll give you an evening meal and a bed for the night. We also offer breakfast but everyone has to be out of here by eight. Seven o'clock on Sundays. Strictly no alcohol is allowed on the premises and we tolerate no foul language or bad behaviour.' Alice coughed and Ada's expression softened. 'Your little girl doesn't sound at all well. I'll get Doctor Samuels to look at her when he arrives.'

'I can't pay,' Lily said, biting her lip anxiously. Mrs Beacham gave her a reassuring smile.

'Doctor Samuels doesn't charge, dear.' She glanced at her pocket watch. 'He'll be here in half an hour. In the meantime, let's get you fed.' She indicated to Lily to follow her down the wide aisle. Other women glanced up at her with tired disinterest. A baby wailed thinly.

The soup was delicious, if a little thin, and there was plenty of bread to mop it up with. To Lily, who hadn't eaten for two days, it was a banquet. She sat in a vacant pew and gently spooned soup into Alice's reluctant mouth. She was desperately worried about her hacking cough. Her skin was pale and clammy except her cheeks, which were bright crimson.

The doctor's arrival an hour later caused a stir among the women. He was a good-looking man in his late twenties with pale features and a pencil-thin moustache, but he looked tired and drawn. Mrs Beacham later told Lily that he came to the church after a gruelling twelve-hour shift at the hospital.

Such was the need for the doctor's time and attention that it was a further twenty minutes before he got to see Alice. She stared listlessly at him from beneath half-closed eyelids. Doctor Samuels frowned as he listened to Alice's chest and took her temperature. Lily held her breath, silently praying. Finally, slinging his stethoscope around his thin neck, he gave Lily's shoulder a reassuring pat.

'She's caught a chill and it has settled on her chest. Keep her warm and give her plenty of nourishment and she'll be right as rain in no time.'

Before Lily could demand how she was meant to accomplish such a task when she hadn't two ha'pennies to rub together, he had moved on to the next patient.

'It's all right,' said a girl seated close to Lily. She looked older than Lily, her face lined and haggard, her brown eyes dull, hair lank and greasy. 'If you've got a sick kiddie, they let you stay a bit longer in the mornings.' She smiled, showing a mouthful of surprisingly white, even teeth. 'I'm Claire, by the way. Claire Bunting, and these ruffians' – she indicated the three raggedly dressed boys of varying age sitting alongside her, chewing hungrily on thick wedges of bread – 'are my brothers, Bill, Tom and Nate. Ma and Da died three weeks ago and we got evicted from our cottage.' Her face clouded and she lowered her voice. 'I've done my best to keep us out of the workhouse but I'm out of options. Mrs Beacham's contacted the authorities. They'll be coming for the boys first thing in the morning.'

'What?' Lily recoiled in shock. 'They send us to the work-house?' She straightened up, her body tense and poised to flee.

Claire shook her head. 'No, they're good people. I know the city officials keep on at them to get us into the work-house. They'd rather that than have us on the streets. The posh folk don't like to see us begging on street corners, it offends their sensibilities, see? But Mrs Beacham's all right. She only got in touch with the workhouse 'cos I can't cope anymore.' Her voice trembled and she gave her brothers a sideways glance, her dark eyes filling with tears. 'I'll miss the little terrors though.'

'You're not going with them?' Lily asked, remembering how heartbroken she had been when first Charlie then Eleanor went away.

Claire shook her head. 'I need to find work. It's the only way I'll get them back.'

It was growing late. Someone dimmed the lamps while another woman doled out blankets. They were thin and musty-smelling, but Lily was so tired, she hardly noticed. Curled up on the floor, Alice tucked in the crook of her arm with phlegm rattling in her chest, Lily closed her eyes and fell asleep.

She woke to a prism of sunlight streaming in through the stained-glass windows. All around her women and children were stirring. The church volunteers were bringing in steaming pans of porridge. Lily searched for Claire in the breakfast queue but she wasn't there; neither were her brothers. She finally noticed her sitting alone in a dark corner of the church, her eyes red, being comforted by Mrs Beacham. Lily clutched Alice closer to her. She had to find work today, she had to.

The bowl of porridge revived her flagging spirits. Alice appeared marginally improved: her wheezing didn't seem quite so pronounced and she swallowed her porridge with far more enthusiasm than she had her soup the previous evening.

As Lily folded her blanket, placing it neatly on the pew as she saw the other women doing, Mrs Beacham came up to her.

'Did you sleep well, Mrs Brown?'

'Yes, ma'am,' Lily replied, surprised the woman had remembered her name.

Ada glanced at Lily's wedding ring. 'You're a widow?'

'Yes, ma'am,' Lily lied.

'And how's our little one this morning?' She smiled down at Alice, who squirmed shyly, and coughed, her chest wheezing noisily.

'She's a little better, thank you,' Lily replied, her hand going to Alice's forehead. Her skin felt noticeably cooler this morning, she noted with relief.

'Good, good. Now, you'll be welcome back tonight, of course. Because Alice is unwell, you're welcome to stay a bit longer. And you can get a midday meal at St James's Church.'

If only I'd known that yesterday, thought Lily.

Mrs Beacham leaned back, arms folded across her chest as she regarded Lily thoughtfully. 'What's your trade?'

'I'm a dressmaker, ma'am.'

Ada pursed her lips thoughtfully. 'A dressmaker? Are you any good?'

'I worked on commissions for several grand ladies,' Lily replied, a tiny spark of hope igniting deep in her belly. Mrs Beacham nodded, and patted Lily's arm.

'Wait here a moment. Mrs Goodwin,' Lily heard her say as she hurried down the church's broad aisle. 'Does your daughter-in-law still work for the drapers on Cornmarket Street?'

The women disappeared into the vestry and Lily could hear no more. She sank onto a pew, cradling Alice against her, hardly daring to allow herself to hope. She watched the other women readying themselves for another day searching for work or begging for charity with empty eyes and faces devoid of hope. One or two nodded, and murmured a few words, but for the most part the women were silent. The children, weary-faced and old before their time, clung to their mothers' skirts. Lily looked around for Claire, but she had gone. Lily hoped it wouldn't be too long before she was reunited with her brothers.

Mrs Beacham came bustling out of the vestry, her many petticoats rustling, her face wreathed in smiles. Lily sat up straighter, a flutter of excitement in her belly.

'Mrs Brown,' she said as she drew close to where Lily sat. 'I have some encouraging news.' She indicated for Lily to move along the pew and squeezed in beside her. 'Mrs Goodwin's daughter-in-law, Kitty, works for a draper on Cornmarket Street. For some time, the proprietor, a Mr Philips, has been thinking about offering a dressmaking service. As far as Mrs Goodwin knows, he hasn't taken his plan any further so, if you get on down there, you might be able to persuade him what a grand idea it is.' She paused to draw breath and beamed at Lily. 'What do you think?'

'It would be an answer to my prayers,' Lily said, hope bubbling like a spring. On her lap, Alice stirred and coughed. Lily faltered. 'But what about Alice?' she asked, wiping the stream of mucous that ran from Alice's red nose. 'I can't afford to pay anyone to mind her.' Even as she spoke, she felt her spark of hope being snuffed out like a candle.

'By all accounts, Jack Philips is a good man. Perhaps he can come up with a solution, if he's willing to take you on, mind. You haven't got the job yet.' The older woman got to her feet. 'I'd get going if I were you. It's a bit of a walk.'

Lily nodded and whispered her thanks.

'And don't forget, St James's Church. Twelve o'clock,' Mrs Beacham called after her as Lily and Alice made their way out into the cool spring morning.

The sky was overcast, dark clouds obliterating the earlier sunshine, and a chilly wind blew in from the sea. Lily shivered, eyeing the dark clouds billowing above the rooftops with concern. She could see the harbour between the buildings, ships rocking on the choppy waters. The sea in the distance was a dull grey, the horizon an indistinguishable blur between sea and sky.

The wind whipped Lily's skirts as she made her way down the High Street in search of Cornmarket Street. Twice she took a wrong turn and had to ask for directions, Alice growing ever heavier in her arms. Her breathing seemed easier, which gave Lily some consolation, but if this Mr Philips didn't offer her a job, she was at a loss as to what to do. The refuge at the church was a haven but that was not the life she wanted for Alice: living on the streets, reliant on charity. Her daughter deserved better.

She turned into Cornmarket Street just as the heavens opened. In the few minutes it took her to find Philips and Son, Drapers, Lily was soaked to the skin. Alice wailed pitifully, her cries punctuated by bouts of coughing. She was shaking like a leaf.

Weighed down by the heavy yoke of despair and desperation, Lily pushed the door open. A bell jangled loudly as she stepped into the warm, musty shop. The air smelled of the bolts of material that lined every wall.

A pretty blonde woman looked up from where she was arranging ribbons and buttons beneath a glass-topped counter.

'Good morning. Goodness, you're soaked.'

'Good morning,' Lily replied, blinking rainwater from her eyes. 'Mrs Goodwin?'

'Yes,' the woman acknowledged with a questioning smile.

'I'm Lily, Lily Brown. I'm a dressmaker and I'm in need of a job. Your mother-in-law suggested Mr Philips might have a position available? May I speak to him?'

'Of course.' Kitty emerged from behind the counter, her expression open and friendly. 'Come through to the parlour and warm yourself by the fire.'

She led Lily into a small, tastefully furnished room where an elderly woman was dozing beside a roaring fire. 'Poor Agatha suffers from rheumatism quite badly in her joints,' Kitty explained, lowering her voice. 'She shouldn't really be working but Mr Philips hasn't the heart to let her go. She's no family, you see.'

Lily gazed at the old woman with sympathy. Despite their presence, Agatha continued to snore softly, her chest rising and falling rhythmically as she dozed on, completely unaware of the intrusion.

'There, dry yourselves off by the fire while I fetch Mr Philips. May I get you a cup of tea? I can hear the shop bell from here if anyone comes in.'

Sick with nerves, Lily declined the offer of tea and moved towards the fireplace, letting the warmth of the flames absorb the dampness from her skirts. Behind her, Agatha stirred and opened her rheumy-blue eyes.

'Who're these drowned rats?' she snorted to Kitty, peering at Lily myopically.

'This is Mrs Brown, Agatha,' Kitty explained. 'She's here to see Mr Philips about joining us.'

'Good morning, Miss Agatha,' Lily said politely as Alice coughed loudly. Taking her damp handkerchief from her pocket, Lily wiped Alice's streaming nose.

'The child shouldn't be out in this filthy weather,' Agatha said sternly. Despite her lined face and liver-spotted hands, her voice was surprisingly vibrant. Her expression softened. 'You want some goose fat to rub on her chest. It'll ease the congestion. I'll fetch you some from the kitchen.' She got stiffly to her feet, leaning heavily on her silver-handled walking stick, which had been resting against the side of her chair.

Lily thanked her gratefully.

'Poor little mite,' Kitty said, her dark eyes clouding with sympathy. 'I'll see if Mr Philips can see you now. I'll be right back.'

She followed Agatha from the room and, left alone, Lily and Alice crouched in front of the fire, letting its smoky warmth soothe the damp chill from their bones.

Kitty returned a few minutes later, followed by a tall, well-dressed man of late middle age. He strode towards Lily, his hand outstretched. He was broad-shouldered with a shock of salt-and-pepper hair and a neatly trimmed beard that was almost completely white.

'Mrs Brown,' he said in a soft, lilting voice. 'Jack Philips,' he said with a slight bow. 'It's a pleasure to meet you.' He had the air of a kindly grandfather, and Lily warmed to him immediately. 'Mrs Goodwin tells me you're a dressmaker? Excellent, excellent. Come up to my study and we'll have a little chat.'

The upstairs study was cosy and warm. A narrow window looked out over the rooftops and the grey sea beyond. Two wing-back armchairs faced a cheerful fire. A framed seascape hung above the mantelpiece. A smoky-grey cat lay on the hearthrug and, seeing it, Alice scrambled to be free of Lily's arms. Once free, she squatted down in front of it, gently running her hand over its thick, grey fur.

'Go carefully,' Jack Philips warned her. 'Persephone can be a little feisty.'

He invited Lily to sit and she perched on the edge of the chair, keeping a watchful eye on Alice. Persephone purred loudly. She was clearly enjoying Alice's ministrations.

'Do you have any references?' Jack Philips asked, amiably. He seemed determined to put Lily at her ease.

'Yes, sir.' Lily handed him Violet's letter of recommendation, thanking God she had had the presence of mind to keep it in the inside pocket of her blouse. How she wished she'd done the same with her savings book. 'I have nine years' dressmaking experience. I was apprenticed to Miss Upshall for two years, and later I worked on a commission basis. I was highly recommended by my clients.'

'It seems Miss Upshall holds you in high esteem.' Jack smiled and Lily felt herself relax. 'It has been my wish to offer a dressmaking service in our shop for some time but I'm afraid I'm something of a procrastinator and so, as yet, I haven't gotten around to advertising for anyone. It would seem your visit today is providential.' He leaned back in his armchair and steepled his fingers together, regarding her with kindness. 'Tell me a little about yourself, Mrs Brown.'

Lily cleared her throat. 'I am recently widowed and only arrived in Poole two days ago. Unfortunately, I was robbed at the station.' She gave a wry smile. 'I apologize for my somewhat dishevelled appearance but my luggage is in storage and I can't afford to collect it . . .' Her voice broke. 'I'm sorry.'

Jack waved her apology away. 'How horrible for you. It sounds like you've had quite a time of it. Your little girl doesn't seem very well.'

'The doctor assures me it's just a chill.'

'Well, let me set your mind at rest. I'd like to offer you the position. You may start today if it's convenient and, if you are without lodgings, you and your daughter are welcome to share with Agatha. It's only an attic but I'm sure you'll find it suitably dry and comfortable.'

'I'm afraid I can't afford to pay anyone to care for Alice . . .' Lily's words trailed away as anxiety gnawed at her throat.

'No matter,' Jack said, brushing away her concerns. 'Alice is welcome to remain with you. I'm sure between us we can keep her amused.'

'Thank you, sir.' Lily could hardly believe her luck. 'I shan't let you down,' she added.

'I don't expect you to. Welcome to Philips and Son.' He shook Lily's hand. His skin was warm and dry to the touch.

'Thank you, sir,' Lily said again.

'Now, if you'll give me the details, I shall go along to the station and collect your baggage. You can pay me back out of your first week's wage,' he said, laughing at Lily's astonishment.

That evening, snug and warm in her attic bedroom at the top of the house, Lily sat at the small bureau and wrote to Charlie. It saddened her that she couldn't write to Violet, even if only to inform her of Mary Johnson's death, but it was too great a risk.

She slipped Charlie's letter into an envelope and sealed it. She sat back in her chair and pulled her shawl tighter around her shoulders. Thanks to the liberal amount of goose fat Agatha had applied to Alice's chest, her breathing appeared much easier. The two of them were fast asleep, sprawled in the double bed, snoring softly in unison. As the last of the light faded from the sky, Lily got up and climbed into bed beside Alice. She wrapped her arm around her daughter's lithe frame, and was asleep in minutes.

The night was dark. The ground gleamed in the moonlight as Jez let himself into the yard behind Violet's shop. The sigh of the wind beneath the eaves was the only sound as, moving as swiftly and silently as a panther, he crossed the yard and crouched by the back door, feeling under the mat for the key. He held it up in his gloved hand.

Stupid, trusting cow. He grinned. He should have finished her off when he'd had the chance. She'd reported him to the police. It had been embarrassing to say the least when the constable had turned up at the club to 'have a word'. Thankfully the constable was old-school. New to the area and with no knowledge of Jez's previous brushes with the law, once Jez had explained the circumstances – deserted by his wife, his only child taken beyond his reach – the constable had felt only sympathy for the spurned husband pushed beyond his endurance to uncharacteristic violence. He warned Jez to stay away from Miss Upshall's premises and left the club, secretly admiring the man's determination to find his errant wife.

Once inside the building, Jez lit a lamp and made his way up the stairs to the parlour, his sharp ears attuned to the slightest noise from Violet's room. For her sake, he hoped she wouldn't wake up. Holding the lamp high, its warm glow banishing the shadows, he approached the walnut-veneered writing desk in the corner of the room. Setting the lamp on the smooth, polished surface, he gently slid out the drawers, one by one. When they revealed nothing of interest, he moved the lamp aside and lifted the lid of the desk. His breath caught in his throat, his nostrils flaring at the sight of the writing pad.

He withdrew it carefully, his heart throbbing with the thrill of anticipation. He scanned the first page. He could just make out the imprint of what had been written on the previous page that had been torn neatly from the pad. A cruel smile playing on his lips, he rummaged through neat piles of old receipts and ribbon-tied letters for a pencil. Finding one, he ran the nib over the paper until the words became legible.

Poole? His eyes widened in surprise. Well, well, well! Violet had lied to him. The minx hadn't gone to London after all. He grinned. Now he knew exactly where Lily was, it would

As the weeks passed and May drifted into June, some of Lily's fears began to dissipate. For a while, she had been too fearful to leave the premises, terrified that Jez might somehow have discovered her whereabouts. But, as the days grew longer and warmer, so her worries faded. She had to trust that Violet had been true to her word and sent Jez on a wild goose chase to London.

Lily was thrilled to be working again. As soon as Jack Philips let it be known that he now offered the services of an accomplished seamstress and dressmaker, orders had come flooding in and Lily had been rushed off her feet. Agatha helped with the simpler alterations, her eyesight and stiff fingers disallowing her from anything too complex, and often, when the weather allowed, Lily and Agatha would take their sewing out into the garden. The small patch of daisy-strewn lawn was bordered by a crumbling brick wall and overlooked by their neighbours on every side, but it was pleasant to sit in the dappled shade of the apple tree watching Alice play to the accompaniment of birdsong and the ever-present screeching of gulls.

Lily knew Jack Philips was more than satisfied with her work and she was overjoyed to be earning a decent wage once again. She wrote to Charlie often, and looked forward to his replies with great expectation, though his letters did fill her with some dismay. While he wrote that he was pleased Lily had freed herself from Jez's clutches, he worried about her. Knowing his cousin of old, he was certain Jez would not let Alice go without a fight and he warned Lily to stay vigilant. She was further distressed by his news that tensions between the British and the Afrikaners were still running high and Lily finished every letter pleading with him to return to England before the rumours of war became a reality.

The third week of June dawned unseasonably cool and overcast. Leaving Alice happily baking with Agatha, Lily walked up Cornmarket Street to the High Street. Seagulls wheeled overhead in a dishwater sky, their mournful cries drifting on the salty breeze. A brisk wind whipped at her skirt and loosened the tendrils of auburn hair from its pins.

With the Queen's diamond jubilee just days away, the mood on the street was celebratory, the excitement tangible. Every shopfront was draped with the Union flag and yards of bunting had been strung between the lampposts, triangles of red, white and blue snapping in the breeze. Lily was looking forward to taking Alice to the street party for which Agatha's confectionary contributions were piling up in the pantry, and they would all be attending one of the many special church services to be held throughout the city.

Her mind on the forthcoming historical commemorations, she deftly sidestepped two young lads shovelling manure into a handcart, and darted across the busy street, veering slightly to the left to avoid a coal merchant's cart. Out of the corner of her eye, she glimpsed a dark figure standing on the street corner. Her steps faltered. Something about the man caused her heart to catch in her throat. Half obscured by shadow, the man's hat was pulled low over his face so she couldn't make out his features, yet she had the distinct impression he was staring straight at her, making the hairs on her arms stand on end. She swallowed hard and bowed her head. Pushing her way swiftly through the crowd, she hastily drew her woollen shawl over her telltale red hair.

She didn't dare glance behind her. She knew he was still there, could feel his gaze boring into her back. Choking back her fear, she resisted the urge to break into a run, forcing herself to remain calm, while chiding herself for her foolishness. There was no way Jez would think to look for her in Poole. It was her own paranoia that had her jumping at shadows. There was no reason to assume the man had been watching her. He was likely a pickpocket on the lookout for easy pickings, though his tailored coat seemed to give lie to this assumption. Lily pushed her fear aside. Fighting the urge to turn around, she slipped down a side street that led to the harbour.

Down at the quayside, the wind was blowing a gale. Fishing boats bobbed on the grey water. Masts creaked and groaned, ensigns snapping in the wind. Gulls shrieked, dive-bombing the filthy water for the entrails the fishermen tossed overboard.

Unable to shake off her sense of unease, Lily tried to make herself inconspicuous among the housewives and cooks crowding around the baskets of fresh fish from that morning's catch.

'Blimey, it's blowing a hooley today, and no mistake,' Lily heard someone say as she glanced behind her. She could see no sign of the mysterious man as she half-listened to the haggling between the bearded, weathered fishermen and the local housewives determined to get their mackerel at a fair price. Lily stared down at the dead-eyed fish laid out at her feet.

A trickle of fear ran down her spine and she turned, standing on tiptoe to scan the bustling harbour, certain someone was watching her. She watched the people milling about, half-expecting to spot Jez among the stevedores, sailors and harbour officials. Then she spotted the man again, the colour draining from her cheeks as she recognized him as Ned, the lackey Jez had tasked with making sure Lily didn't leave the house. He was standing on the steps of the customs house, and he was looking straight at her.

Lily's stomach lurched in fear as she scanned the bustling quay. If Ned was here, that meant Jez knew where she was. How had he found her? Swallowing her terror, she pushed her way free of the crowd, ignoring the indignant mutters. She didn't dare run, not wanting to draw attention to herself. Instead, she walked as quickly as she could towards the town centre, her heart racing. Once or twice she risked a quick glance over her shoulder but saw no sign of Ned. She frowned. Perhaps it hadn't been him after all?

Even so, she didn't waste any time in returning home. She was grateful to find the kitchen deserted. The smell of baking filled the air and a tray of scones cooled on the wire rack next to the open window. Taking a few moments to compose herself, she hung up her shawl and set her basket on the table.

Her heartbeat slowed and her breathing returned to normal. She was seriously beginning to doubt that the man on the quayside had actually been Ned.

She found Alice in Jack's study. She was sitting on his lap, paging through *A Children's Garden of Verses*.

'Mama!' she cried in delight, sliding off Jack Philips's lap and running to Lily's outstretched arms. Lily hugged her tightly, burying her face in her hair, inhaling her sweet smell. The pure love and trust in her daughter's expression were enough to bring tears to Lily's eyes.

'Mrs Brown, is everything all right?' asked Jack, surprised to see her back so soon.

'Thank you, yes.' Lily smiled gratefully. She scooped Alice up and made to leave.

'Are you sure?' Jack enquired with genuine concern. 'You seem a little out of sorts.'

'I walked too quickly, that is all.' She hated lying to him but how could she explain? He was a man. He would be sure to side with Jez. After all, her husband had the law on his side.

'It's certainly blowing a gale,' Jack remarked conversationally as a gust rattled the parlour windows. 'Let's hope it calms down in time for Her Majesty's celebrations next week.'

'Let's hope so,' Lily replied distractedly. She cleared her throat. 'If you don't mind, sir, I think I'll keep Alice with me today.' Jack raised a questioning eyebrow but, to Lily's relief, he didn't question her any further.

'We'll finish looking at our book later, little one.' Jack checked his pocket watch. 'I have some correspondence to attend to anyway.' He nodded to Lily. 'I'll see you later, Mrs Brown. Have a pleasant day. See you later, little one.'

Lily hastened across the landing to look out of the window. Though the street was bustling, she could see nothing suspicious. She sighed. Her sense of peace and security, so hard won, had been shattered in a matter of minutes. Would she ever feel safe again? she wondered despairingly as Alice squirmed in her arms, eager to get down. Planting a last kiss on her daughter's soft curls, Lily set her on the floor. Taking her by the hand they started down the stairs together.

Her sense of foreboding lingered into the afternoon. She was in the back room letting out the seams on a red-velvet evening gown for a customer who was expecting her first child, all the while keeping an eye on Alice who was playing in the yard just outside the back door. The shop bell jangled, tightening Lily's already taught nerves.

'Thomas Whitcher, ma'am,' she heard a voice say. 'Officer of the courts. We're here to see Mrs Elkin. Mrs Lilian Elkin. Please summon her.' Heart pounding, Lily looked around in panic, searching in vain for an escape route but finding none. Even if she did manage to scale the high wall, to do so with Alice would be an impossible feat.

'I beg your pardon, sir,' she heard Kitty's confused reply. 'You must have the wrong address. There's no Mrs Elkin here.'

'You're lying. She was seen entering this premises earlier today.' At the sound of Jez's voice, Lily's insides turned to water. Panic tightened around her chest like a vice. She grasped the edge of the work table, fear rooting her to the spot. She held her breath, listening.

'I'm sorry, sir.' Kitty's voice trembled. 'You are mistaken.'

Jez was in no mood to be trifled with. The day after his nocturnal visit to Violet's, he had engaged Thomas Whitcher to apply to the courts for custody. The moment the paper-work was in order, they had travelled down to Poole, fully expecting to find Lily and Alice at Mary Johnson's. It had been galling to find the shop deserted and no sign of either of them. The girl next door had been no help, either. It had taken weeks of his men scouring every inch of the town, Jez's ill-humour increasing with every passing day, until Ned had eventually spotted her down by the harbour. Now he was here to wreak his vengeance.

With a loud snort of irritation, Jez took a step towards the counter, his expression menacing. Kitty recoiled in shock. Thomas, a tall, gaunt-faced fellow with a pencil-thin moustache and ginger sideburns, placed a restraining hand on his arm. He gave Kitty an apologetic smile.

'I apologize for my client. He's been through a difficult time.' He cleared his throat. 'We know Mrs Elkin is here, ma'am. The premises has been under surveillance throughout the day.' He opened his jacket and withdrew a folded piece of paper. 'This is a court order requesting the immediate return of Alice Elkin to her father. Failure to do so will result in Mrs Elkin's arrest.'

Lily was dimly aware of Kitty's sharp intake of breath as she slumped against the wall. Fear clutched at her throat and she could barely draw breath. They were going to arrest her. She would never see Alice again.

'Papa!' Alice's excited shout snapped Lily out of her paralysis. In her panic, she hadn't realized her daughter had wandered indoors and was now running towards the sound of her father's voice.

'Alice?' Jez called. Lily gave a cry of alarm as the curtain was flung aside. She tried to grab Alice's arm but she was too late. Alice flung her arms around her father's legs. Ignoring Lily, Jez swung her into the air. Her uninhibited laughter filled the small space.

'Please, Jez,' Lily said. 'Just leave us alone. You don't want us. You've got Barbie-Jean now. Leave us alone.'

'You're right,' Jez said mockingly. 'I don't want you. I never did. But I do want my daughter. You had no right to take her from me.' He smiled evilly. 'I've got a court order giving me complete custody of Alice, and if you make a fuss, you'll find yourself in contempt of court and heading for the clink.' His mouth twisted in a parody of a smile. 'Don't worry about her things. I'll buy her whatever she needs.' He touched his forelock mockingly. 'Goodbye, Lily.'

'No!' Lily shouted. Every nerve ending in her body was screaming. 'No, please, Jez, don't take Alice.' She followed him onto the shop floor where Kitty cowered behind the counter, her face pale. She shot Lily a look of anguish.

'Now, now, Mrs Elkin,' Thomas Whitcher said raising a placating hand. 'I'm afraid you must abide by the court order. You left the family home of your own accord, abandoning your husband and thus depriving him of his daughter. In the eyes of the law, you are at fault here.'

'But he moved his mistress into our home,' Lily cried, her eyes wide open in panic. 'He moved her into our home while I was still there, into my bed. She was unkind to our daughter. What choice did I have but to leave?'

'Then you'll have to prove your husband's infidelity to the court.' Thomas gave her a pitying look. 'But for the time being, your daughter is to be returned to her father, immediately.'

'But I can't afford a lawyer,' Lily wailed, her heart shattering as Jez turned away, Alice riding high on his shoulders. She looked back at Lily, a frown on her face.

'She's frightened of Barbie-Jean, Jez,' Lily called after him in panic.

At the mention of the other woman's name, Alice's smile faded. She shook her head. 'Don't like Barbie-Jean,' she said, her hands wrapped around Jez's forehead.

'You don't need to worry about her,' Jez said, lifting Alice off his shoulders and looking at her earnestly. 'It's just going to be me and you from now on, princess.'

'Mama?' Alice frowned, reaching for Lily. Jez took hold of her hand, and pulled her close.

'What on earth is going on here?' Jack Philips demanded. He stood in the doorway, blocking Jez's exit.

'They're taking Alice,' Lily wailed before either Jez or Thomas could respond.

'I don't understand. Who are these men? Why do they want Alice?' Jack stared at her with incomprehension.

'Mr Jack!' Alice grinned up at him.

'Sir, I have a court order here for the immediate removal of Miss Alice Elkin from these premises,' Thomas said, somewhat pompously as he waved the court document under Jack's nose.

Jack frowned. 'But Alice's surname is Brown.' He looked at Lily for confirmation.

'Brown?' Jez sneered at Lily. 'Couldn't you have picked something a little more original?' He turned to Jack. 'Alice is my daughter. Lily is my wife.'

Jack looked at Lily in confusion. 'I see.'

'Lily deserted me, taking my precious Alice with her. Though no doubt she's spun you some fancy tale.'

'I had no choice,' Lily whimpered, turning to her employer. 'Please, Mr Philips. I had no choice. He moved his mistress into my home. She was cruel to Alice and treated me like dirt. How could I stay under such circumstances? How could I subject Alice to such depravity? Please, don't let him take her, please!' she begged tearfully.

'May I see the paperwork?' Practically snatching the document from Thomas's hand, Jack scanned the court order, his lips a thin line, his brow growing more furrowed with every word.

Wordlessly, he folded the letter and handed it back to the officer of the court, his eyes sad.

'I'm sorry, Lily,' he said, his voice heavy with dismay. 'I'm afraid you have no choice but to comply.'

Lily began to sob. 'I can't,' she whispered. 'I can't give up my little girl. Please.' She looked at Jez, imploring him with her tear-filled eyes. In response, he threw back his head and barked a harsh, bitter laugh.

'This matter will not end here,' Jack promised sternly. He laid a hand on Lily's shoulder as she sobbed loudly. 'We'll get a solicitor, Lily. We'll fight this. I promise you.'

'Good luck with that.' Jez grinned. 'Now, we'll be on our way.' He looked at his pocket watch. 'We have a train to catch.'

'At least let me say goodbye,' Lily pleaded, tears streaming down her face.

'You stole Alice from me in the dead of night,' Jez sneered. 'Why should I care about your feelings?'

'Have some compassion, man,' Jack barked. 'Let Lily spend a few minutes alone with the child. Surely it's the least you can do.'

Jez shrugged. 'All right. Five minutes.'

'Kitty, please make the gentlemen a cup of tea,' Jack said to Mrs Goodwin, struggling to hide his distaste. Jez appeared about to object but Thomas laid a restraining hand on his arm.

'I'm sure we can spare the time to have a cup of tea,' he said. With obvious reluctance, Jez handed Alice to Lily.

'I'll see you in a few minutes, princess,' he said. He shot Lily a filthy look, then followed Thomas and Kitty into the kitchen.

Lily sank to her knees. Her heart was breaking. She should never have left Jez. Now Alice would be at the mercy of her father's unconventional lifestyle and she wouldn't be there to protect her. She didn't know how she would bear the grief.

Jack motioned for Lily to follow him upstairs where they were met by an ashen-faced Agatha.

'What's happened?' she hissed. 'What's all the noise?'

'Take Alice for a moment please, Agatha,' Jack said. 'I need to speak with Lily. We haven't long.'

After a brief hesitation, Lily handed Alice over.

'What is this all about, Lily?' Jack asked sternly, ushering her into his study and closing the door. He stood before her, his hands behind his back, his expression grim. 'You led me to believe you were a widow when your husband is very much alive. Would you care to explain?'

Choking back her hot tears, Lily wiped her eyes, trying desperately to compose herself as the precious seconds ticked away.

With a quivering sigh, Lily told him as quickly as she could what had transpired to make her leave Jez, taking Alice with her, including all of the details of Jez's business dealings.

'Have you taken your allegations to the police?' he said. 'They would turn a blind eye to his dubious morals but extortion is a different matter. It's a serious crime.'

'Who would listen to me?' Lily cried. 'He's got judges and police constables in his pocket.' She shook her head sadly, her face in her hands. 'I'm sorry, sir, but I must go to Alice.'

'Wait!' Jack barked as she turned to leave. He hesitated, struggling with his conscience. He was a law-abiding man but, on this occasion, he was inclined to let his heart rule his head. 'Behind the wardrobe in the attic there is a door that leads next door. There will be a trapdoor into the ironmongers. I'll distract your husband as long as I can. Cover your head, that hair of yours is pretty distinctive. And disguise Alice as a boy. There are some breeches and shirts in the trunk that should fit her if you turn the hems up. Here.' He pulled a handful of notes from his pocket. 'Your wages, and a bit extra.'

Lily stared at him, momentarily speechless. 'Thank you,' she breathed, tucking the notes into the folds of her skirts. 'Thank you so much.' Jack waved her gratitude away.

'Don't waste time thanking me,' he said softly. 'You need to go. Your husband's patience is probably already wearing thin.'

'Thank you, Mr Philips, sir. I'll never forget your kindness.'

Lily quickly explained the plan to Agatha and hurried up the stairs with Alice. Agatha followed at a slower pace. While Lily tried to decide what to pack, Agatha rummaged through the trunk in search of something suitable for Alice to wear.

'I want Papa,' Alice grumbled as Agatha tugged a pair of patched trousers up her legs and pulled a worn shirt over her curls. Calmly, she took a pair of dressmaker's shears from her skirt pocket and, before Lily could protest, she snipped away at Alice's hair, her long, dark curls floating to the floor. Lily's hand flew to her mouth, and her eyes filled with tears at the sight of her daughter's shorn head. To her relief, Alice didn't seem at all perturbed at losing her hair. Laughing, she crouched down, tossing handfuls of fine, chestnut-brown hair into the air.

Agatha pulled a grey wool cap over Alice's cropped head and stood back to admire her handiwork. 'She looks like a proper little lad,' she said, satisfied. Her smile faded and tears filled her eyes. 'I'll miss the little tyke,' she sighed, holding out her arms for Alice to clamber onto her lap. She hugged the little girl tightly, glancing over at Lily.

Conscious that time was passing swiftly, Lily heaved the wardrobe aside, looking at the small door in trepidation.

'Go, Lily,' Agatha pleaded. She took a candle and lit it. They could hear loud voices down below. Jez was growing impatient. Lily's heart was beating wildly. Once again, she was about to head into the unknown, only this time she would be a wanted woman. Once she breached the court order, there would be a warrant for her arrest. She pushed her fears aside. If she wanted to keep Alice safe from Jez, she had little choice.

'Godspeed, Lily,' Agatha whispered. She handed Lily the candle. Taking Alice by the hand, Lily stepped through the doorway.

CHAPTER THIRTY

Lily lifted the candle and surveyed her surroundings. The flame flickered in the draughty air, its pale light falling on items of furniture, shrouded in dust. Cobwebs swung from the rafters, brushing against her hair and face. Alice whimpered.

'Mama, I'm scared. I want Papa.'

Lily hushed her softly. 'Remember our quiet game?' she whispered, trying to inject a cheerful note to her voice. 'Shall we play it now? We must be as quiet as a mouse.' Alice pouted mutinously and folded her arms across her chest. 'Good girl.' Lily smiled encouragingly. She crouched on the dusty floorboards beside the trapdoor. The hinges were stiff with lack of use and it took her several attempts to raise the heavy door. It fell back against the floor with a crash, sending clouds of choking dust in to the fetid air. Alice burst into tears.

Lily sat back on her heels, coughing and sneezing, blinded by swirling dust. Wiping perspiration from her forehead, she bundled Alice down the wooden steps.

The upper floor of the ironmongers was deserted but she could hear voices drifting up from the shop below. She pressed Alice's face to her chest in an effort to muffle her anguished cries and chewed her bottom lip as she debated which way she should go.

She heard a shout out in the street. Jez! He must have discovered she and Alice were missing. Struggling with her bag and Alice, Lily made her way down the staircase as quickly as she dared. To her relief, she spotted the door to the yard was open. Without a backward glance, she stumbled through the doorway and out into the yard, startling the delivery man unloading a cart. Pulling her shawl over her head, Lily ducked past him and out of the gate. She could hear loud shouts coming from the street. She began to run.

Thirty minutes later, Lily and Alice were sitting in a small teashop on Longfleet Road. Lily sipped her mug of milky tea, her gaze flitting from the window to the door nervously. Her arms ached from carrying Alice, and her feet hurt. She smiled across the table at Alice, leaning across to wipe a smear of strawberry jam from her cheek.

'That's a bonny lad you've got there.' The proprietor smiled as she came over to refill Lily's mug. 'What's your name, sonny?'

'Al . . .' Alice hesitated. She looked at Lily uncertainly.

'Albert,' Lily replied, holding her breath as she prayed Alice would remember and not contradict her.

'I'm Albert,' Alice blurted out triumphantly. Lily's shoulders sagged as she exhaled in relief.

'That's a fine name,' the proprietor said. 'My father was called Albert and he was a fine man.' She turned to Lily. 'Is there anything else I can get you, love?'

'Thank you, no,' Lily replied, wrapping her shaking hands around the warm mug. The bell above the door jingled, jangling Lily's already frayed nerves as a smartly dressed middle-aged couple entered.

'Give me a shout if you need anything,' the proprietor told Lily, hurrying off to attend the new arrivals.

'Mama, when can we go home? I want Papa and Mr Jack,' Alice said, her head ducked low over her pastry. 'Where's Agatha?' Blinking back the tears, Lily reached over with one hand and patted Alice's sticky hand.

'Eat your pastry, sweetheart,' she whispered, biting her lip. How could she explain to her almost-three-year-old daughter that she would likely never see any of them again?

The street beyond the windows with their pretty red-gingham curtains was quiet. Lily took a sip of her tea and set the cup back in its saucer, her gaze watchful as she scanned the occasional passer-by. A heavily laden cart rumbled past, a small boy hanging precariously off the back.

She had absolutely no idea where to go, or what she was to do. Her meagre wages wouldn't last long but she couldn't stay in Poole. No doubt Jez would have his men watching the railway stations. The police would be watching out for her as well. The thought of being arrested in front of Alice chilled her blood. But even worse than the threat of prison was the thought of Alice being brought up by a philandering blackmailer. She was determined to protect Alice from Jez if it was the last thing she did.

As soon as she was able to buy paper and ink, she would write to Charlie. If he was willing to pay hers and Alice's fare, they could join him in South Africa where Jez could never find her. But in the meantime, she desperately needed a job, preferably away from Poole. Her gaze alighted on a copy of the *Evening Echo* that had been left on a recently vacated table and she got up to retrieve it.

While Alice slurped her milk, Lily perused the Situations Vacant section of the classifieds. Halfway down the page a small advert caught her eye.

'Domestic Help required for newly refurbished hotel in Weymouth.' She scanned the details. The new owners were looking to employ around thirty members of staff to fill a range of positions. A cart would be outside the Longfleet post office at six o'clock on the morning of 19th June on a first come, first served basis. The 19th – Lily did a quick calculation in her head. Tomorrow. The idea of getting out of Poole without having to risk travelling by train was appealing. The railway station would be the first place the police would think to search for her.

'Mama, can we go home now?' Alice whined softly.

'Hush!' Lily hissed sharply, guilt flooding her as Alice's eyes filled with tears. 'I'm sorry, sweetheart,' she said, pushing her untouched teacake in Alice's direction as a placatory gesture. 'Mama didn't mean to snap.'

She remembered a poster she had once seen advertising trips to Weymouth with tempting pictures of sandy beaches and donkey rides. She had thought at the time that it looked a nice place to go.

The shadows were lengthening by the time Lily and Alice left the tea shop. A warm breeze blew down the street. Keeping her shawl pulled over her hair, Lily kept to the alley-ways and backstreets, terrified lest she bump into Jez, or the police.

She spent some of her precious money on a bottle of hair dye, and another penny on the public bath. Squeezing into the small cubicle with Alice, she stripped to her chemise and proceeded to lather the thick, treacly liquid into her auburn curls.

'What are you doing, Mama?' Alice watched wide-eyed and fearful as her mother's beautiful auburn hair was trans-formed into a mouse-like brown. Muddy water streamed down the plughole as Lily towel-dried her long hair.

'How does Mama look?' she asked Alice, combing her fingers through her thick hair.

'You look funny, Mama,' Alice said, grinning cheekily.

'I suppose I do,' Lily said with a rueful smile. There were no mirrors so she couldn't judge her appearance but hopefully the change of hair colour would be enough to keep her safe. The police would be looking for a red-haired woman with a little girl. And while their disguise wouldn't withstand close-up scrutiny, at least from a distance, Lily and Alice would pass for a brunette and a little boy.

The sky was streaked with pink and mauve, dark clouds gathering in the west. Music drifted on the salty breeze and for a moment Lily felt a pang for Jack and Kitty and Agatha but she pushed it aside. Now was not the time for sentiment.

Alice was growing tired and fractious. Using more of her sparse funds, Lily bought them each a pasty, which they ate sitting on a bench looking out over the estuary, watching as the water turned a bruised purple under the slowly darkening sky. Far out on the horizon, the lights of fishing boats twinkled like fallen stars.

Lily contemplated seeking out the Wesleyan chapel and Mrs Beacham's charity, but dismissed the idea almost immediately. That would be just the sort of place Jez would think to search for her. She needed to be first in line for the cart in the morning anyway, so as soon as they had finished eating, she brushed the crumbs from her skirt and retraced her steps. Her heat sank as they walked down the street. Already a number of hopefuls had formed a small queue outside the post office. They huddled on the pavement or in shop doorways. Lily and Alice barely attracted a passing glance as they found an empty doorway and settled down for the night. Curled up in Lily's lap, Alice fell asleep almost immediately. Lily stayed awake, listening to the hum of conversation. Soon people started to drift off to sleep. Lily closed her eyes, but she slept fitfully, waking long before dawn.

'Form an orderly queue. No shoving.' The recruitment officer and driver of the cart bellowed. He was a stern-looking man in his early forties with a head of unruly black curls and a thick beard that reached halfway down his barrel-shaped chest. The crowd of hopefuls had swelled during the night and Lily had to fight to keep her place in the queue. Clutching Alice tightly, Lily grabbed hold of the cart, ready to swing herself up.

'Oi, you.' The driver grabbed her arm. 'No kids.' Lily's throat closed.

'But I'm desperate. I need the work,' she pleaded.

'Don't we all, love?' someone muttered behind her.

'She'll be no trouble,' Lily held the man's gaze, silently begging him with her eyes. He opened his mouth to reply, but his attention was diverted by two brawny-looking men attempting to jump the queue.

'Oi,' he shouted, turning his back on Lily to wrestle the men off his cart. 'Get in line.' One of the men fell badly and cursed the driver in a loud voice. While everyone's attention was focused on the ensuing argument, Lily threw her bag over the side of the cart.

'Quickly,' she whispered, lifting Alice up so she could scramble aboard. Gripping the edge of the cart, she hauled herself up after her. She found a space for them to squat and tugged her shawl over Alice, hiding her from view. She heaved a grateful sigh of relief. She had enough money to last her a few days so, even if she didn't get the hotel job, at least she'd be away from Poole and, at the moment, putting as much distance as possible between her and Jez was her priority. She'd worry about everything else later.

The heavy cart creaked and jolted along the twisting lanes. The morning air was cool and fresh and at first it was pleasant travelling down the winding, sun-dappled lanes, the verges grown high with cow parsley, ragwort and crested cow wheat. Conversation among her fellow-travellers was brisk, jovial even, but as the sun rose ever higher, heat and discomfort began to take their toll and one by one they lapsed into bored silence. Lily tugged the shawl from Alice. A few of the women gave her funny looks but no one said anything.

The sun beat down on the weary travellers and Lily tried to keep Alice quiet, terrified that the driver would put them off the cart should he realize a child was aboard. Alice sat slumped against Lily, whimpering softly. She was hot and hungry. Lily glanced up at the searing hot sun; her throat was parched and she felt dizzy from lack of sleep and food. Her foot cramped painfully.

There was a collective sigh of relief when the driver reined the horse to a halt close to a babbling brook.

'You've got half an hour,' the driver called as passengers scrambled out of the cart, grumbling and yelping as they stretched and massaged stiff and cramped muscles. Lily waited until the driver had disappeared to relieve himself behind a tree before lifting Alice down. She rubbed her cramped muscles and, taking Alice by the hand, wandered over to the meandering stream. She splashed her face and cupped water in her hands for Alice to drink, wet her handkerchief and wiped Alice's flushed face. They took off their shoes and paddled their feet in the crystal-clear water, splashing the minnows that darted out of the shadows.

A kind, matronly-looking woman sat down heavily on the bank beside Alice.

'Is your little lad hungry?' she asked. 'I've got some bread and cheese here.'

Lily flushed with gratitude. 'Do you know how much further we've got to go?' she asked as the woman, who introduced herself as Mattie Atkins, broke the hunks of bread and cheese into manageable chunks before feeding them to Alice.

'About another three hours of travelling,' she said. She glanced behind her. 'Don't you worry about the driver,' she said. 'He's my second cousin. If he makes a fuss about your little boy, I'll give him what for.'

They were interrupted by a loud shout from the driver, signalling that the rest stop was over. Lily and Alice clambered back onto the cart to continue their arduous trip. The driver caught sight of Alice holding hands with Mattie. He glared at her, but said nothing. Tossing his apple core into the long grass, he hoisted himself up onto the rickety seat and slapped the reins. The horse moved forwards, forcing the few stragglers to make a run for it, scrambling aboard just in time.

A combination of the heat and the rocking motion of the cart quickly sent Alice to sleep. She woke up, blinking in the brightness, as the cart creaked its way along the seafront. She clapped her hands, her wide-eyed gaze delighting in the expanse of golden beach lapped by the gentle waves. The sea was a rich aquamarine blue, sunlight dancing on its surface.

Lily inhaled the fresh, salty air. The promenade thronged with people enjoying the warm weather. The tide was out and the wide stretch of sand was crowded. Alice giggled in delight at the sight of two children riding on donkeys, being led across the sand by a swarthy-looking man in a striped shirt.

'Me ride donkey, Mama,' she clamoured.

'Maybe later,' Lily hushed her. But the child's excitement was infectious and the mood of her fellow passengers lifted as they exclaimed over the sights and smells of the popular holiday town.

The seafront was lined with grand hotels. The newly renovated Seaview Hotel was at the end of the row, close to the Jubilee Clock Tower. Four storeys tall, its many windows reflected the blue sky. The walls were salmon pink and the black front door gleamed in the afternoon sunshine. Before Lily could absorb any more details, the driver steered the cart under a wide archway and into a shady courtyard complete with a working fountain and palm trees. There was a stable block to one side and a wide door, which Lily supposed led to the servant's quarters.

A thin-faced woman emerged from the open doorway. She looked harried, her gaze darting every which way. Lily eyed her warily as she climbed down from the cart. Someone passed Alice down to her and she hugged her tight, trying to quell her rising anxiety.

Once everyone had assembled in the courtyard, the woman clapped her hands, calling for quiet.

'Good afternoon,' she said, as the hubbub of conversation ceased. 'I am Mrs Frances Kitching, head housekeeper of the

Seaview Hotel.' She spoke softly and Lily had to strain her ears to hear over the shrieking of the gulls. Mrs Kitching's beady gaze swept the hopeful group, coming to rest on Alice. Lily's throat closed in despair.

'I will shortly speak with each of you individually,' Frances went on after a moment's pause, 'but firstly, I'm sure you must be hungry and thirsty after such a long journey. You will find refreshments in the kitchen. Please, follow me.'

Clutching Alice tightly by the hand, Lily joined the fourteen others who followed Frances down a short passageway that led to a large, airy kitchen where a cold supper had been laid out on a long table. Alice let out a shriek of delight at the sight of so much food.

Lily felt a restraining hand on her arm.

'May I have a quick word?' Frances said, and Lily's heart sank. This was it. She was about to get sent packing. She nodded dumbly, a cold knot of anxiety low in her stomach. 'Your son will be all right for a few minutes. Mary.' Frances motioned to the young girl scrubbing pots at the sink. 'Make sure this little chap gets something to eat, will you?'

'Yes, ma'am.' She held out her hand. 'Come on, little man.' Alice glanced up at Lily uncertainly.

Swallowing her nerves, Lily forced a smile.

'It's all right, Albert,' Lily assured her, with emphasis. 'Go with Mary. Mama won't be long.'

Persuaded by the promise of food, Alice went off quite happily.

★   ★   ★

'Please, have a seat.' Frances ushered Lily into her cosy sitting room, indicating one of two armchairs facing a small fireplace. She settled herself in the other chair and folded her hands in her lap, watching Lily with her beady-eyed gaze.

'Have you made provision for the child should you be lucky enough to secure a position here, Mrs ...?'

'Brown,' Lily replied after a brief hesitation. 'Lily Brown. I'm afraid I have not,' she admitted miserably, feeling her chance of employment slipping away. 'But I could keep him with me. He would be no trouble.'

'Mrs Brown, you will be working long days. You will be up at five and it will be rare that you'll get to bed before eleven, especially during the height of the season. There will be little time for you to take care of your ... daughter.'

Lily's eyes widened in surprise. Frances gave her a reassuring smile. 'Oh yes, I could see through her disguise.' She held up her hand as Lily opened her mouth to explain. 'I don't want to hear it, Mrs Brown. I'm not interested in your history. We all have a story of some sort. All I'm concerned about is how well you work and whether you are trustworthy.' She sighed. 'You have references?' she asked, pulling a pair of glasses from her breast pocket and slipping them on.

'I'm afraid not, ma'am,' Lily admitted miserably, staring at her hands.

'I see.' Frances slipped her glasses back in her pocket and regarded Lily thoughtfully. The clock on the mantelpiece ticked loudly in the silence. 'I too once found myself in unfortunate circumstances,' she said at length. 'If it hadn't been for a particular person who was prepared to give me a chance, who knows where I may have ended up?' She smiled. 'I'm prepared to give you a try.' Lily breathed a sigh of relief. 'Now, the child. The nuns around the corner offer a childcare service at a reasonable rate. It would mean losing your breakfast time to take her there and you'd have to forgo your evening break to collect her. You'd have to catch up on your meals when you can.' She leaned back in her chair. 'You're entitled to one full day and one half-day off a month. The rota of which days will be pinned up in the staff kitchen. So, if that is acceptable to you, Mrs Brown, I'd like to offer you a position at the Seaview Hotel.'

'Thank you,' Lily breathed, her shoulders sagging in relief. 'Thank you very much.'

The work was tiring and the days long. Lily and Alice shared a room with three other girls. They were all of a similar age to Lily and the four soon became good friends.

Rising at five every morning, Lily had already done a couple of hours' work before hurrying to wake and dress Alice in preparation for her day with the nuns. Their morning walk soon became Lily's favourite part of the day. She loved to watch the different ways the early-morning light reflected on the silver sea, and see the gulls flocking on the empty beach, pecking at the bits of flotsam and jetsam washed up by the tide. It was her one chance to relax. The rest of the day was one of endless toil, and by the time she fell into bed at night, she was bone-weary and slept the sleep of the dead, morning coming all too soon.

To Lily's joy, Alice appeared to have settled in well with the nuns. She was thriving and chatted constantly about her new friends.

The first chance she got, Lily sent a telegram to Charlie letting him know her new address, promising a letter would follow. She wrote to him that very afternoon, suggesting she and Alice join him in the Cape. She sealed the envelope and stared out over the gently undulating water, imagining getting on a ship and sailing halfway around the world. She tucked the letter into her wicker basket, turning to smile at Alice who was crouched beside her, digging in the sand with a wooden spade Lily had bought from a stall on the promenade.

She wished she could write to Violet. She was sure Violet would have written to Mary Johnson and, on receiving no reply, would surely be worried about Lily's whereabouts but now, with a warrant out for her arrest, the risk of contacting Violet was even higher.

It had been a week since Alice had last mentioned her father, to Lily's relief. Such a man deserved no place in her daughter's life, regardless of who he was.

Lily posted her letter on the way back to the hotel. Out of habit, she checked for anyone behaving suspiciously. Sadly, she mused, she would never be free of Jez's malevolent presence.

CHAPTER THIRTY-ONE

'Papa? Papa, are you awake?' Eleanor eased the door open with her shoulder and peered into the darkened room. Sir Frederick was a dark hump in the four-poster bed. He stirred and, taking his grunt as an invitation to enter, Eleanor set the silver breakfast tray on his bedside table and opened the heavy brocade curtains, flooding the room with bright sunshine.

The sky over Chelsea was a vibrant blue, with not a dark cloud in sight, a pleasant change from the recent bout of unsettled weather. The month of July had been marred by heavy rain showers and violent thunderstorms. Perhaps August would be better, Eleanor mused as she opened the window in an effort to dispel the smell of sickness.

'You would rather I die of pneumonia?' Sir Frederick grumbled from the shadows.

'Oh, Papa,' Eleanor chided him with a smile. 'The doctor said fresh air is good for you, and it is warm today.' She helped him to sit up, arranging the pillows so that he would be comfortable, then perched herself on the edge of the bed, her expression growing serious. 'How are you feeling today, Papa?'

Sir Frederick shrugged his thin shoulders. It pained Eleanor to see how her beloved father was diminishing before her eyes. Once such a robust man, he was now a mere shadow of his former self.

'Are you in pain?' she asked.

'A little discomfort, that is all,' replied Sir Frederick. Eleanor took his hand. His skin was dry and stretched over his knuckles like parchment.

'I do wish you would consider Doctor Spencer's suggestion that you convalesce on the coast. I'm sure the sea air will do you the world of good.'

'My precious child,' Sir Frederick said fondly. 'Would that I had even half your optimism.'

'Papa, you will be well again,' Eleanor insisted. 'At least think about Doctor Spencer's advice.' She sighed and leaned over to kiss her father's cool brow. 'I'm afraid I must leave you. Mother is insisting I join her for breakfast. I believe she wants to discuss my trousseau.'

'Ah.' Sir Frederick patted Eleanor's hand. 'Will we be seeing your fiancé this weekend?'

'Yes, Papa. He's coming for supper on Saturday evening, with his mother.' She rolled her eyes dramatically. Sir Frederick managed a weak smile. 'She wants to discuss the wedding plans. So, Papa, you must concentrate on getting well. You will be walking me down the aisle next spring.'

'I will do my best, my darling. Now be off with you – you know better than to keep your mother waiting.'

'Ring if you need anything, Papa.'

'I will,' Sir Frederick promised. He managed to keep his smile in place until Eleanor had left the room, pulling the door to behind her. He sank back against the pillow and grimaced. The constant gnawing pain in his abdomen was growing steadily worse. Regardless of Eleanor's hopes, he knew with certainty that he would not live to see his beloved daughter married. Doctor Spencer had been blunt. The tumour was killing him and he was unlikely to see out the year.

He glanced at the bowl of milky porridge cooling on the tray and winced. He had no appetite for it this morning.

He sighed. Shame and regret weighted heavily on his heart. He wasn't a religious man but he couldn't help but wonder if somehow, on the other side, he might be called to account for the many mistakes he'd made during his lifetime. So many people he had failed, not least his wife, Cynthia. He had married her for her money, knowing that his heart already belonged to another. Thoughts of his dearest Beatrice, dead all these long years, conjured up memories of Lily. He had been thinking about her a lot lately. He had been surprised when Eleanor and Lily's friendship had ceased so suddenly, yet he had to admit it had come as a relief. Over the three and a half years since, he had attempted to salve his conscience by convincing himself that Lily's uncanny resemblance to Bea was nothing more than a coincidence. But now he wasn't so sure.

The summer breeze stirred the curtains. He could hear voices out in the street, the rumble of a wagon. Someone was whistling on the landing. He remembered Eleanor saying something about calling in the chimney sweep. Sir Frederick closed his eyes and sighed once more. Since he had become confined to his room, he felt as though he was on the periphery of a life that was going on without him.

The biggest regret in his life was the way he had treated Bea. He had loved her. She was so sweet, so innocent. She had trusted him implicitly. He could still remember the look on her face when she had told him she was expecting. A mixture of hope and fear. And, coward that he was, he had let her down. He had gone through with his sham of an engagement, leaving Bea to face her shame and disgrace alone. He'd loitered outside his father's study the morning the house-keeper had come to tell his father that Beatrice Cullen had been dismissed. Though nothing was ever said, Sir Frederick was sure his father and Ada both knew he was the cause of Bea's disgrace, and the knowledge caused him to burn with shame. If only he could make amends. He didn't even know where she was buried. Perhaps Jessop could endeavour to find out. He would like to know Bea's final resting place, at least.

'My aunt Dorothy owns a villa in Weymouth. I'm sure she would be perfectly amenable to your father taking it for the winter.' Arthur Randall smiled across the table at Eleanor. He was an earnest young man, clean-shaven with brown hair neatly combed to the side. He was completing his Law studies in London, after his degree at Oxford, with a view to joining his father's practice.

'What do you think, Mother?'

Emmaline Randall smiled fondly at her only son. 'I'm sure she would have no objection,' she said, dabbing her lips with a napkin. 'My sister-in-law always retires to the South of France for the winter. I think she leaves about mid-August usually,' she said, turning to Lady Copperfield. 'I'm certain you'd all be more than welcome.'

'Oh, that's very kind of you,' Lady Copperfield said with a tight smile. Now forty-one, her face bore few traces of the pretty woman she had once been. The past few years had been particularly difficult. Theirs had never been a marriage made in Heaven but she and Sir Frederick had grown more estranged as the years passed and, though she would never admit it to a living soul, she had felt nothing but relief when her husband's ill health had seen him confined to his room. Happy to leave his daily care to Eleanor and the servants, Lady Copperfield visited Sir Frederick every evening for half an hour after supper. An exercise that was onerous for them both.

'I'm sure Sir Frederick would benefit from the sea air but Eleanor and I would prefer to remain in London.'

'No, Mama,' Eleanor interjected. 'I couldn't bear to think of Papa going alone. If Arthur's aunt is agreeable, perhaps we could take the villa from the middle of August. We could expect at least six weeks of fine weather.'

'We'll discuss it later, Eleanor,' Lady Copperfield said, shooting her daughter a warning glance. 'So, my dear Mrs

Randall.' Lady Copperfield smiled. 'We were thinking Claridge's for the wedding breakfast. Would you agree?'

'Thank you, Jerome.' Eleanor handed the butler her valise and climbed into the carriage beside her father. It was the last week of August and she and Sir Frederick were on their way to Weymouth. Lady Copperfield stood in the doorway, her face pinched with disapproval. She had refused point blank to join them. Though secretly relishing Sir Frederick's absence, she was annoyed that Eleanor had insisted on accompanying him. They had a wedding to plan and all the best shops were in London, after all. But Eleanor had remained adamant.

'Will you not miss your young man?' Sir Frederick now roused himself enough to ask.

'Arthur will visit at the weekends as often as he is able, Papa,' Eleanor assured him. 'Now, are you warm enough? Are you comfortable? It will be a good four hours before we stop for our midday meal.'

'Stop fussing, my dear,' Sir Frederick said. 'I am quite content.'

The horses made good time. It was harvest time and the fields were a hive of activity. The scents of late summer – freshly mown hay and sun-dried grass – drifted in through the open carriage windows. The hedgerows glistened with ripe blackberries and wild raspberries.

They spent the night at an inn in Winchester and set off again at first light, arriving in Weymouth mid-afternoon. The long journey had taken its toll on Sir Frederick and, alarmed by his grey pallor, Eleanor insisted he go straight to bed. The servant, a pleasant middle-aged woman called Clara, had prepared the front bedroom.

'It's got the best view, miss,' she told Eleanor in her Cornish accent, as she helped her get Sir Frederick upstairs. And Eleanor had to agree. The view over the English Channel was breathtaking. The late afternoon sun sparkled on the waves and the sand shimmered in the summer heat. Some children were beachcombing at the water's edge while couples strolled along the promenade. A fairground organ pumped out a rousing tune, which added to the general carnival atmosphere. She flung the window open, inhaling the warm, briny smell of the sea.

'I'll leave you to rest, Papa,' she said, crossing to the vast bed in the centre of the well-appointed room. 'I'll bring you up a light supper in about an hour or so.' She kissed his dry cheek. 'Sleep well, my dear Papa.'

Sir Frederick let out a small sigh and Eleanor gave a wistful smile. He was already asleep.

CHAPTER THIRTY-TWO

Lily wiped a dribble of ice cream from Alice's chin. It was a Sunday afternoon in early September and the promenade was bustling. A salty breeze blew off the green water. Brightly coloured bathing huts lined the shore, but only the hardiest of bathers were braving the sea. Ladies in straw hats and gentlemen in caps milled about on the sand, children darting between them, shrieking. Others paddled along the shoreline, screaming in delight as the foamy-fingered waves licked their tiny toes.

It was three months since Lily and Alice had fled to Weymouth and the tight knot of anxiety in her chest was finally starting to unravel.

'Look, Mama, look!' Alice shrieked with excitement. Holding on to her straw boater with one hand and shielding her eyes with the other, Lily craned her neck to watch the coloured kites dipping and soaring in the cloudless sky. They watched the kites for a while until Alice's attention was diverted by the organ grinder's performing monkey. She dragged Lily across the soft sand, past the Punch and Judy man setting up his puppet show and up the stone steps that led from the beach to the promenade.

The organ grinder, or rather his tiny liveried companion, had drawn quite a crowd. Lily fished into her purse for a coin for Alice to throw in the monkey's hat. She felt quite sorry for the little creature as he scampered up onto the organ grinder's shoulder where he sat staring at the crowd with sad brown eyes.

She brushed a tendril of light brown hair from her face. She was growing accustomed to her reflection now and had recoloured her hair twice in the past three months. For the first few weeks she had hardly left the hotel except to take Alice to the nuns or to run a necessary errand and she would continually scan the bustling streets, her eyes peeled for any sign of Jez or one of his many henchmen. The sight of a policeman would turn her blood to water and though they barely glanced in her direction, she would hold her breath until they had passed her by.

Now though, her fears were at last beginning to recede. She inhaled deeply, filling her lungs with the sea air, standing with her back to the coast and watching Alice running up and down, clapping her hands and chasing the gulls.

'I'm hungry,' Alice said, clambering onto the railings. Her hair was in disarray and her cheeks were flushed. Her hair had grown over the past twelve weeks and framed her face pageboy-style. She brushed a strand from her face and sneezed.

'How about some cockles?' Lily suggested. She was feeling peckish herself and it would be a nice treat. Once she had paid the nuns for Alice's care, her wages didn't stretch very far, but Charlie had enclosed a postal order to the sum of three shillings with his last letter, so she could afford this small extravagance.

Inhaling the aromas of hot grease and sugar, frying fish and vinegar, they threaded their way through the oncoming pedestrians towards the cockle seller's stall. While Lily joined the queue, Alice wandered over to the railings to watch the Punch and Judy show. The sun's warmth bounced off the street and Lily took off her hat, fanning her flushed cheeks as she gazed along the promenade, shimmering in the heat.

'Lily?' The familiar voice seemed to echo down the years and, beneath her sleeves, Lily's arms erupted into goosebumps. She turned in disbelief to find Eleanor staring at her from beneath a peach-coloured parasol, looking equally stunned.

'It is you, Lily, isn't it?' A note of uncertainty had crept into Eleanor's voice. It had been three years since she had last seen Lily, after all.

'Hello, Miss Eleanor,' Lily said nervously.

'Oh, I knew it was you. But your hair . . .?' Seeing the look of consternation on Lily's face, Eleanor immediately changed tack. 'Oh my, Lily, can you believe it?' she exclaimed instead. 'What are the chances of us both turning up in Weymouth on the same day?' Eleanor laughed, a happy, joyous sound that warmed Lily's heart. She hadn't realized how much she had missed her.

Eleanor had matured a great deal since Lily had last laid eyes on her. As always, she was stylishly dressed, in peach organza, her lustrous dark hair perfectly coiffed and held in place with a tortoise shell comb.

'Are Mr Elkin and Alice here too?' Eleanor asked, glancing around.

'My husband is not with us,' Lily replied stiffly, 'but this ...' She called Alice, who came running over. 'This is Alice.' Alice clung to Lily's skirt, staring up at Eleanor with unabashed curiosity.

'This is Alice? My, what a sweetie.' Eleanor smiled at Lily. 'She's adorable.'

'Thank you.'

'Alice,' Eleanor said, hunkering down so that she was eye level with the girl. 'I'm Mama's friend, Eleanor,' she said, making Lily wince. Could Eleanor really be so forgiving? Did she not bear any grudge for the way Lily had so abruptly ended their friendship?

'I'm three,' Alice told her importantly. 'I'm having cockles for tea.'

'My dear Eleanor, there you are.' They were interrupted by a tall, unassuming young man with dark hair. 'I thought you said you would wait by the coconut shy? I've been looking everywhere for you.'

'Oh, Arthur, my dear,' Eleanor said, standing up. 'I'm so sorry. I spotted this dear friend of mine and I just had to come and say hello. My fiancé, Arthur Randall, Mrs Lily Elkin and her darling daughter, Alice.'

'Brown.' Lily blushed. 'It's Lily Brown now. Pleased to meet you, Mr Randall,' she said politely, trying not to look at Eleanor's frown of incomprehension.

'My pleasure, Mrs Brown. Eleanor has spoken of you often. She counts you as one of her dearest friends.'

Lily's flush deepened. 'I'm honoured,' she murmured. 'When is the wedding?' she asked, to hide her discomfort.

'In the spring,' Eleanor told her. 'You must come. Are you still at the same address?'

'No, Miss Eleanor,' Lily shook her head. 'It's a long story but Alice and I live here now, in Weymouth.'

'Really?' Eleanor said with an exclamation of delight. 'What an amazing coincidence. Papa and I have just taken a house here for the winter.' Her eyes clouded somewhat. 'He hasn't been well but we are hopeful the sea air will aid his recovery.'

'I am sorry to hear Sir Frederick hasn't been well,' said Lily with genuine concern.

'Thank you.' Eleanor pursed her lips thoughtfully. 'I wonder, do you have time for tea? Arthur could take Alice to get her cockles, and take her to look at the amusements. You wouldn't mind, would you, Arthur? Only Lily and I have so much to catch up on.'

Lily experienced a brief moment of panic. Apart from the time Alice spent with the nuns, she was never away from Lily's side. Seeing her obvious distress, Eleanor laid a hand on Lily's arm.

'Alice will be quite safe with Arthur, I promise.'

'Indeed she will, Mrs Brown,' Arthur confirmed with a grin at Alice.

Lily hesitated. No one would be looking for a small girl in the company of a gentleman, she reassured herself, and what she had to tell Eleanor could hardly be said in front of Alice.

'I have to be back at the Seaview Hotel by six. But I don't like to impose on Mr Randall's kind nature.'

'Not at all, Mrs Brown,' Arthur interjected swiftly. 'I should be delighted.' He bent down and offered Alice his arm. 'What say we get ourselves some delicious cockles and then go and see the amazing Rubber Man?' he suggested. 'If the advertisement is to be believed, he's something worth seeing.'

'Excellent.' Eleanor smiled. 'Arthur's catching the ten past six train to London so shall we meet back under the Jubilee clock in an hour?'

Swallowing her misgivings, Lily watched as Alice and Arthur went off hand in hand, Alice skipping happily beside the elegant gentleman. Since that day when Jez had turned up out of the blue, Lily could never rest when Alice was out of her sight.

'Oh, Lily, don't look so worried,' Eleanor chided. She tucked her hand into the crook of Lily's arm. 'Alice will have a wonderful time with Arthur.'

They found a teashop down a flight of steps just off the promenade with pretty blue and white checked tablecloths and sat at a recently vacated table at the rear of the café.

'I'll get this cleared away for you, ladies, and then I'll be back to take your order,' the waitress said as they sat down.

She gave them a friendly smile and loaded the dirty crockery onto a tray.

'Lily, I must say I find your new hair colour somewhat disconcerting,' Eleanor said the moment the waitress was out of earshot. Lily's hand went self-consciously to her hair but before she could start to explain, the waitress reappeared to take their order.

'Does your change of name have anything to do with your choice of hair colour?' Eleanor asked, once they had placed an order for a pot of tea and hot, buttered crumpets. 'I can't bear the suspense any longer. Has something happened?'

'I've left Jez,' Lily said. She spoke so quietly, Eleanor had to lean forward in order to hear her over the hum of conversation and the noise wafting in from the promenade. 'I'm working as a maid at the Seaview Hotel.' She dropped her gaze to her lap where her fingers were twisting her napkin nervously. 'There is a warrant out for my arrest.'

Visibly shocked, Eleanor reached across the table for Lily's hand. 'Tell me everything,' she said sternly. 'From the beginning.'

Lily let out a long, weary sigh. It would be a relief to finally relieve herself of the burdens she had carried alone for so long. She hadn't been able to confide in anyone at work. As fond of the other girls as she had become, there was no one she trusted the way she did Eleanor.

Very slowly, her heart beating erratically, she began to recount the horror of the past few years, starting with the night of Jez's rape.

'Lily!' Eleanor stared at her friend in horror, her hand flying to her mouth. 'Why didn't you tell me?' she breathed, her eyes filling with tears. Lily shook her head.

'I was ashamed,' she whispered, blinking back tears. The waitress arrived with a pot of tea and golden crumpets, oozing melted butter.

'Thank you.' Eleanor smiled as Lily turned her face away, embarrassed by her tears.

Eleanor squeezed Lily's hand. 'I blame myself,' she said softly. 'I should have insisted we see you to the door.'

'Please don't blame yourself, Miss Eleanor,' said Lily. 'It's not your fault.'

'Neither is it yours,' Eleanor hissed vehemently. 'The man is an animal!' Her hands shook as she poured the tea. 'I had a feeling something wasn't right when you married him,' she said, setting the teapot on the trivet.

'I had no choice,' Lily said. She picked at a crumpet. Pools of melted butter were beginning to solidify on the edge of the pretty willow-patterned plate.

'Could Charlie not help you?' Eleanor asked.

'I couldn't tell him the truth, Miss Eleanor.' Lily said sadly. 'He would have been devastated.'

Eleanor took a bite of her crumpet. 'Can he not help you now?'

'I wrote to ask if he would send us our fare, so we could join him, but he replied that many women and children are being sent home at the moment in case war breaks out. He did send some money though.'

'He sounds a fine man,' Eleanor said. 'I hope I get to meet him one day.'

'I must confess, it's been so long, sometimes I find it difficult to picture his face,' Lily said dejectedly. 'I do wish he would come home.'

'I'm sure he will,' Eleanor assured her. 'One day. So, tell me,' she said, adding a lump of sugar to her tea. 'How did you and Alice end up in Weymouth?'

Haltingly, Lily told Eleanor about the illegal fighting, the girls, the blackmail and extortion, Barbie-Jean and, finally, the events in June that led to her and Alice having to flee Poole.

Eleanor looked shocked. 'No wonder you were so worried when I insisted Alice go off with Arthur. It was insensitive of me.'

'You weren't to know,' Lily assured her. 'You don't blame me for leaving him?'

'Goodness me, no!' Eleanor exclaimed. 'I admire your courage. Can you imagine the damage to Alice if she grew up in such an environment?' She shuddered. 'It doesn't bear thinking about. It's such a shame we didn't keep in touch,' she went on without reproach. 'I might have been able to help.'

'I'm sorry, Miss Eleanor.' Lily took a sip of tea and sighed. 'Jez wanted to use you to get to Sir Frederick. He planned to entice him into a compromising position and then blackmail him. That's why I had to end our friendship. I couldn't risk him hurting Sir Frederick, or you. I'm sorry.'

'Oh, Lily, you poor thing. When I think of how frivolous my life has been and you've been through hell these past years.'

Lily shrugged and managed a weak smile. 'Every day I get to spend with Alice is a bonus. I know I'm on borrowed time. The law's on Jez's side. It will catch up with me eventually and I will lose Alice for good.'

'No,' Eleanor said firmly. 'That is not going to happen. Papa has influence. I'm sure Mr Jessop, his solicitor, would be able to advise you.'

'Oh, please, don't trouble Sir Frederick on my behalf,' protested Lily.

'Nonsense,' Eleanor replied. 'You protected Papa, now he can return the favour.'

'How is Lady Copperfield?' Lily asked as they paid the bill and made their way up the steps and onto the promenade. The sea was as calm as a millpond, glinting in the sunlight.

'Mama is well,' Eleanor said, clearly troubled. 'She chose to remain in London.' She sighed wearily. 'I'm afraid she and Papa have been at odds for some time.' She flashed Lily a rueful smile. 'It's very exhausting being caught in the middle. I love them both, of course, though Mama can be somewhat trying. She wasn't very happy about me accompanying Papa here but what could I do? I could hardly let him convalesce alone, could I?'

'I'm sure Sir Frederick appreciates your care,' Lily said, with a pang for the father she could never acknowledge.

'This spell of pleasant weather is certainly making up for the disappointing summer,' Eleanor said conversationally, tucking her arm through Lily's as they made their way towards the clock tower. Lily scanned the beach in search of Alice, her heart lurching in relief when she spotted her eating a large ice cream and skipping happily holding Arthur's hand. Catching sight of her mother, Alice let go of Arthur's hand and ran towards Lily.

'I saw a funny bendy man,' she gabbled, brimming with excitement as Lily endeavoured not to get ice cream all over her skirt. 'And there was a dog and he could dance.' To demonstrate, Alice performed a little twirl, holding her hands out like little paws, the melting ice cream dripping onto the ground.

'Thank you so much, Mr Randall. It seems Alice has had a lovely time.'

'My pleasure, Mrs Brown.' Arthur lifted his hat. 'Alice is a credit to you.'

'Thank you.' Lily smiled. 'Well, Alice and I must be getting back. It's been wonderful seeing you again, Miss Eleanor.'

'And we shall see much more of each other now I'm here in Weymouth. When is your next day off?'

'I have a half day on Wednesday the 18th,' Lily replied.

'Excellent. Until then, my dear Lily. Goodbye, Alice, be a good girl for your mama. Uncle Arthur and I will see you again very soon.'

'Are you going now?' Alice queried, her bottom lip trembling as her eyes filled with tears of disappointment.

'I'm afraid so, sweetie,' Eleanor said.

'But we'll see you again, very soon,' Arthur added, hunkering down until he was face to face with Alice. 'And next time, if your mama gives permission, we shall visit the merry-go-round on the pier.'

Alice clapped her hands in glee, tears and quivering lip forgotten. 'May I, Mama?' She looked up at Lily hopefully.

'Of course.' She smiled at Arthur. 'You are very kind, thank you.'

'Kindness has nothing to do with it, Mrs Brown.' Arthur grinned. 'I enjoy the amusements as much as any child. It's no hardship, I assure you.'

'Well.' Lily smiled at them both. 'Thank you all the same, both of you.'

'Take care, Lily,' Eleanor said as they parted ways outside the hotel.

'You too, Miss Eleanor.'

CHAPTER THIRTY-THREE

'You won't believe who Arthur and I ran into this afternoon, Papa,' Eleanor said, drawing the curtains against the low sunlight streaming into the bedroom. She returned to the bed where Sir Frederick sat propped up against a mound of pillows. Eleanor thought he was looking so much better of late. His colour seemed less pallid, and his pain appeared to have eased a little. 'Lily,' she said. Sir Frederick frowned. 'You remember Lily, Papa. Our dressmaker? We became good friends.'

'Lily is here?' Sir Frederick asked, startled. 'In Weymouth?'

'Yes, isn't it the most amazing coincidence?' Eleanor said, drawing a chair close to the bed.

'Indeed,' her father replied, his brows knitting together as his bewildered frown deepened. His chest felt tight. Bea and Lily hadn't been far from his thoughts over the past weeks; was it possible his burning desire to make amends had conjured her here? He dismissed the notion immediately, chiding himself for his foolishness. He realized Eleanor was looking at him expectantly.

'Papa, did you hear what I said?'

'I'm sorry, my dear. My mind seems to wander a lot these days.'

'I was asking if you might be able to help Lily.' Quickly, Eleanor related the details of Lily's plight. 'I feel we should do what we can to help her, Papa,' she said earnestly, 'especially as she tried to protect our family.'

'I would never have fallen prey to his blackmail,' Sir Frederick said indignantly, though secretly he wasn't so sure. He hadn't been averse to a little illegal boxing on occasion, and he'd always enjoyed a wager. No doubt many of Jez Elkin's hapless victims were well known to him. Perhaps he did owe Lily a debt of gratitude?

'I'm expecting Jessop to call in the next week or so on a personal matter. I shall speak to him then.'

'Oh, thank you, Papa.' Eleanor threw her arms around her father's neck.

'Now, now,' Sir Frederick admonished her. 'I'm not promising anything. Unless it can be proven that this Jez character is involved in something illegal, there will be little Jessop can do to help ...' He broke off as the realization suddenly hit him that if Lily were indeed his and Bea's daughter, then it followed that Alice was his granddaughter. The thought took his breath away.

'Papa?' Eleanor cried in alarm, leaning forward in her chair. 'What is it?'

Sir Frederick waved a hand. 'Nothing, my dear,' he replied, his voice hoarse. 'Nothing at all.'

Eleanor frowned. 'I'm sorry, Papa, I shouldn't have burdened you with this.'

'No, no,' Sir Frederick patted her hand. 'I will instruct Jessop to task his investigator to do some digging. There's bound to be someone willing to come forward and press charges.'

'Thank you, Papa.' Eleanor kissed his cheek. She reached for the book lying on the nightstand. 'Now, would you like me to read to you for a while?'

'Yes, please, my dear.' Sir Frederick smiled. 'You've been a godsend to me these past weeks,' he wheezed. 'I'm sure you'd rather be at home enjoying yourself with your fiancé than wasting your days stuck indoors with a sick old man.'

'Oh, Papa, no.' Eleanor leaned forward to brush away a strand of greying hair that had fallen across her father's face. 'There is nowhere I would rather be and, besides, Arthur is so busy with his studies during the week, that I should only see him at weekends anyway.' She opened the leather-bound copy of *Great Expectations*. It had been a great delight on taking up residence to discover Arthur's aunt Dorothy was an avid reader and her drawing room shelves were crammed with books. 'Where were we?' She found her place and began to read. She had barely read a paragraph when Sir Frederick interrupted her.

'Perhaps you should invite Lily and her daughter for supper one evening,' he suggested. 'It would do you good to have some company. I feel very guilty leaving you to dine alone every evening.'

'That would be lovely. Thank you. I shall write and invite them for tomorrow evening.'

Lily was scrubbing the front steps when she was summoned to the housekeeper's sitting room. Her heart racing in dread, she wiped her shaking hands on her apron and smoothed down her hair, tucking the few escaping wisps beneath her cap. She could feel her throat constricting in terror as she hurried to Frances's sitting room and rapped on the door, fully expecting to find a couple of constables waiting to arrest her the moment she entered. Instead, she found Frances sitting behind her desk, a large ledger open in front of her. Lily swallowed hard. Her mouth was as dry as dust.

'You summoned me, Mrs Kitching?'

'Yes, Lily.' The housekeeper peered at her over her wire-rimmed spectacles. 'This note came for you a few minutes ago.' She handed over the folded piece of paper. Lily recognized Eleanor's handwriting and her heart skipped a beat.

'Thank you, Mrs Kitching.' She waited to be dismissed.

'I happened to be in the kitchen when the note was delivered,' Frances said. She set down her pen and leaned back in her chair. 'You're acquainted with the family who have taken Cranborne Lodge, I believe?'

'I was Miss Eleanor's dressmaker.'

'I see. You're an accomplished seamstress?'

'Yes, Mrs Kitching. I worked on commission for several wealthy clients.'

'That's interesting, Lily. I feel that perhaps you are wasted as a housemaid. I'm sure there are many of our guests who would make use of your services. As well as offering a laundry service, we could also offer an alteration and mending service. How would you feel about that?' She folded her hands on the desk. 'Of course, it would mean an increase in wages,' she added when Lily hesitated. 'And, if demand for your services increases sufficiently to warrant it, I am not averse to employing a girl to help you.'

'I don't know what to say,' Lily said, glancing down at her work-worn hands. It had been so long since she had done any needlework apart from the regular mending of her and Alice's clothes.

'Say yes,' Frances said, with a smile.

'Then yes, thank you.'

'I think we shall begin offering your services from tomorrow so you may as well take your afternoon off today. I expect you to be rushed off your feet for the next few weeks.'

'Thank you, Mrs Kitching.'

Dismissed, Lily quickly read Eleanor's note as she hurried back to work. It was an invitation for supper that evening. Had Mrs Kitching known? Was that why she had given Lily the afternoon off?

She inhaled nervously. Supper with Miss Eleanor. She couldn't help but feel anxious at the thought of seeing Sir Frederick again.

$\star$ $\star$ $\star$

'Will Uncle Arthur be there?' Alice asked as Lily chivvied her into a clean pinafore and dragged a brush through her unruly curls, subduing them with a pink ribbon.

'Uncle Arthur?' Lily frowned. 'Oh, you mean Mr Randall? No, I'm afraid not.'

'Aw.' Alice pouted. 'I like Uncle Arthur. He's funny.'

'He was very kind to you,' Lily agreed, ushering Alice down the back stairs to the courtyard. A gust of wind caught her skirt and she had to twirl around, holding on to her hat. A stiff breeze blew along the promenade and the sea was flecked with white horses. Gulls bobbed on the swells.

Alice trailed behind Lily, her attention drawn by two large shaggy dogs frolicking in the surf on an otherwise deserted beach. Lily tugged at her hand, hurrying her along.

'Come on, Alice, we mustn't be late.'

Cranborne Lodge was a large red-brick villa set back from the promenade surrounded by a mature garden full of hardy plants and shrubs. The low sun glinted on the bay windows. Lily pushed open the front gate with a creak of rusty hinges. Eleanor had the front door open before Lily and Alice were halfway up the front path.

'Welcome to Cranborne Lodge,' she said with a beaming smile, as Lily and Alice entered the domed porch. 'I'm so pleased you could come. I wasn't sure you'd be able to.'

'Ordinarily, I wouldn't have been able,' Lily said, removing her shawl in the wood-panelled hall and draping it over the banister. She went on to explain Mrs Kitching's unexpected offer as Eleanor ushered them into an airy dining room with French windows opening onto a stone patio bordered by lavender bushes and hollyhocks.

'That sounds perfect, Lily,' said Eleanor, indicating the table laid for three. 'Please, have a seat.'

'Is Sir Frederick not joining us?' Lily asked, nervously.

'Papa takes his meals in his room,' Eleanor explained. 'He may join us in the drawing room later, if he's feeling up to it.' Her smile broadened. 'Ah, Mrs Cowper, please may I introduce my dear friend, Mrs Brown.'

June Cowper was a slight woman with raven-black hair. The warmth of her smile was reflected in her dark blue eyes. 'Good evening, Mrs Brown. And who is this little treasure?' she asked, beaming at Alice.

'I'm Alice. I'm three.'

'I see, and what a big girl you are,' June said, ruffling Alice's hair. Despite Lily's ministrations, her curls were already escaping from the ribbons. 'I'm ready to serve, Miss Eleanor,' June said.

'Thank you, Mrs Cowper. Shall we?' Eleanor indicated the table. Lily settled Alice in a chair and took her seat beside her. Cranborne Lodge was nowhere near as grand as Bay Willow House. Nevertheless, Lily felt at a disadvantage among the antique furnishings and expensive-looking artwork and ornaments that adorned every surface.

The food was excellent and the meal passed in pleasant conversation as shadows crept across the lawn. A solitary blackbird trilled on the garden fence as the sky turned from blue to mauve. A shuffling in the hallway alerted them to a presence outside the door.

'Mrs Cowper?' Eleanor ventured, half-rising from her chair. 'Oh, Papa,' she exclaimed in delight. Lily's mouth dried instantly as, getting out of her chair, Eleanor hurried to the door to help Sir Frederick to the nearest armchair. In spite of her nerves, Lily couldn't help but be shocked by Sir Frederick's appearance. His face was sallow and shrunken, his skin stretched over his prominent cheekbones, patches of flaky pink scalp visible through his thin, greying hair.

'Thank you, my dear. I apologize for interrupting your supper.' He focused on Lily and frowned. Could this be the girl he remembered? Had his mind played tricks on him? The face was familiar and she had Bea's eyes, Bea's lips . . .

'This is . . . Lily?' His troubled gaze darted to Eleanor, who laughed. 'She looks . . .'

'Oh, sorry, Papa. Of course, you remember Lily as having auburn hair. I understand. It was a shock for me too. Lily dyed her hair, Papa.'

Lily managed a weak smile. 'Good evening, Sir Frederick. It is good to see you again.'

'I apologize,' Sir Frederick said. 'The laudanum . . . I get confused.' His smile was sad. 'We are both quite altered since we last met.' His voice was weak and hoarse and Lily felt a pang of deep sadness for the man who was her father.

'It is so good of you to join us, Papa,' said Eleanor cheerfully. 'Allow me to introduce Lily's daughter to you. Alice, this is my father, Sir Frederick.'

'Good evening, Sir Frederick,' Alice said solemnly. She was feeling slightly overawed by her grand surroundings and now this frightening-looking man was staring at her with great scrutiny. It was all quite disconcerting for the little three-year-old. She bowed her head over her dessert, peeping at Sir Frederick from beneath her long, dark lashes.

Quite unaware of the effect his scrutiny was having on his granddaughter, Sir Frederick continued to watch her. Despite her dark colouring, he could see his beloved Bea in her features and it gave him a pang to realize that Lily must have looked something like Alice as a child. The sudden realization of how badly he had failed his daughter and granddaughter weighed so heavily on his heart that he felt a physical pain in his chest.

'Papa, are you all right? You've gone very pale.'

'I think I have been too ambitious,' Sir Frederick rasped. 'I shall retire to my room.'

'Of course, Papa.' Eleanor pushed back her chair. 'Let me help you.'

'Thank you, my dear. You stay with your guests. Mrs Cowper will help me.' He nodded at Lily. 'It was a pleasure to see you again.'

'I hope you get well very soon, sir,' Lily said, filled with pity as she watched Sir Frederick leaning on the arm of his housekeeper.

'I hadn't realized Sir Frederick was quite so ill,' she said to Eleanor softly, once he was out of earshot. 'It must be distressing for you?'

'It is,' Eleanor admitted. 'But I am confident that the bracing sea air will aid his recovery.'

'I'm sure it will,' Lily affirmed, though she shared little of Eleanor's confidence. Sir Frederick looked very ill indeed, and she felt an overwhelming sadness for the father she had never been able to acknowledge and who, now, it appeared, she never would.

CHAPTER THIRTY-FOUR

'You are convinced that this is the truth, Jessop?' Sir Frederick said, his brow creased in bewilderment.

'Without a doubt, sir.' Horatio Jessop snapped his briefcase shut and stood up. For a moment his gaze drifted to the bay window. The sea was a mud-brown and choppy. Dark clouds billowed on the horizon.

'But in his letter Michael Redfern seemed quite certain.'

'I understand that, sir. A sad case of mistaken identity. The details are all documented in the papers I gave you.'

Sir Frederick thanked him absently, his mind racing. He was having one of his good days and was sitting up in a chair, facing the window. Eleanor, ever attentive, had placed a vase of dahlias on the windowsill. A few pale pink petals had drifted onto the lacquered surface. The tide was in and the narrow stretch of beach was deserted but for the gulls huddled on the sand, the cold wind ruffling their feathers. He stared unseeing into the distance.

Horatio Jessop gave a discreet cough, breaking through Sir Frederick's meanderings.

'Oh yes, sorry, Jessop. There was one other thing. There's a certain scoundrel by the name of Jeremy, or Jez, Elkin. He's into extortion, illegal boxing matches, blackmail, that sort of thing. Runs a few girls. See if your man can dig up some evidence.'

Jessop frowned, wondering at Sir Frederick's interest but, as no explanation was forthcoming, he picked up his briefcase and, shaking Sir Frederick by the hand, took his leave, leaving his client staring absently out to sea.

Lily was surprised the following Sunday to receive an invitation to tea at Cranborne Lodge.

'But I thought Miss Eleanor was in London visiting her fiancé and Lady Copperfield?' she queried. The young lad who had brought the note nodded his head in agreement.

'She is, missus. It's his lordship, Sir Frederick, what's invited you.'

'Sir Frederick?' Lily's stomach gave a lurch and her heart began to race. She returned to her room in a quandary. Alice was playing with the rag doll Lily had made her while a pigeon cooed on the windowsill. The sky was a pale blue, wisps of cloud drifting by on the breeze.

She sank onto her bed, her heart still beating wildly. Was Sir Frederick about to acknowledge her as his daughter? Or was he still against her and Eleanor's friendship? Was it his plan to warn her to stay away from his daughter? She flushed. She wiped her clammy palms on her skirt, glad that, apart from Alice, she was alone. Much as she enjoyed the other girls' company, she wasn't in the mood for their idle chatter.

The next few hours passed agonisingly slowly. She picked up some mending but she couldn't settle to any task and finally gave up. In the end, they left for tea early and tried to kill time walking along the promenade. The winds were strong and black clouds rolled across the sky. Lightning split the horizon followed by the distant rumble of thunder.

By the time they walked up the front path it was blowing a gale and the first drops of rain were beginning to fall.

The housekeeper ushered them inside and took their wraps. 'Sir Frederick is in his room, Mrs Brown,' June said, folding Alice's cape over her arm. 'Please go on up. Miss Alice, you come to the kitchen with me and I'll show you the new kittens.' Alice clapped her hands in delight and looked at Lily hopefully.

'May I, Mama?'

'Yes, of course,' Lily said hoarsely. Her legs shook as she climbed the stairs to the carpeted landing. The door to Sir Frederick's room was ajar. Lily hesitated and took a deep breath in an effort to steady her nerves.

'Come in, Lily,' Sir Frederick said as she raised her hand to knock.

Trembling, Lily pushed open the door. Sir Frederick was seated by the window. A small table had been set for tea. Several lamps cast pools of yellow light around the room. The sky beyond the window was dark and foreboding.

'Please, take a seat,' Sir Frederick said, indicating the empty chair. Lily sat down nervously. 'Would you pour?' Sir Frederick pointed to the silver teapot. With shaking hands, Lily poured the tea. There was a layered cake stand in the middle of the table with dainty, crustless sandwiches and iced fairy cakes but, as delicious as they looked, Lily had no appetite.

'I suspect you know who I am, don't you, Lily?' Sir Frederick said without preamble. Not trusting herself to speak, Lily nodded. Tendrils of steam rose between them as their eyes locked.

'How long have you known?'

'Since I was fourteen,' Lily croaked. She cleared her throat and tried again. 'Reverend Redfern wrote to me and told me.'

Sir Frederick sighed. 'I realized the moment I first laid eyes on you,' he said. 'You are the spitting image of your mother.' He allowed himself a rueful smile. 'Despite the brown hair.' He sighed. 'Even your mannerisms remind me of her.' He looked at Lily, shamefaced. 'I'm so sorry, Lily. I should have acknowledged you a long time ago.' His eyes were heavy with sorrow. 'The way I treated you was unforgivable. You must despise me.'

'No,' Lily exclaimed. 'How could you acknowledge me? It would have destroyed Lady Copperfield.'

Sir Frederick's face seemed to crumple. 'Cynthia and I should never have married. We were never right for each other. I married her for her money, to save my family from ruin.' He sighed deeply and coughed. 'I regret a lot of things in my life, Lily,' he said breathlessly. 'But I regret nothing so much as the way I've let you down, and your poor mother before you.' He reached for her hand. His fingers were icy cold. 'Do you think you could ever find it in your heart to forgive me?'

'There is nothing to forgive,' Lily said earnestly. Her shoulders sagged a little as all the hurts and disappointments seemed to slip away.

'Oh, but there is, my dear Lily.' He sighed again. 'I'm just so sorry I've left it so late, but I couldn't go to my grave without acknowledging the truth.'

'You will get well,' Lily said. 'Miss Eleanor says you are improving a little every day.'

Sir Frederick smiled sadly. 'If my dear Eleanor's faith and optimism could keep me alive then I have no doubt I should live for ever. As it is, it is unlikely I shall live to see Christmas.'

'So soon?' Lily cried in shock. 'Is there nothing the doctors can do?'

'The cancer is eating me up from the inside, I'm afraid. The laudanum helps with the pain but, soon, even that small comfort will be denied me.'

'I'm so sorry,' Lily whispered, a tear tracking its way down her cheek.

'It is I who am sorry, Lily,' Sir Frederick said wistfully. 'Sorry that I will never get to know you properly, sorry that I shall never get to see my grandchildren grow up, sorry I will never my walk my beloved Eleanor down the aisle on her wedding day.' He picked up his cup with a trembling hand. 'I am grateful to have this time with you though,' he said, his voice thick with emotion. 'I never thought I should see you again.' He smiled a sad smile that spoke of regrets and missed opportunities, memories that would forever go unmade.

'I fell in love with your mother the first time I saw her. She was only twelve, a child really. I was three years older. I thought she was the most exquisite creature I had ever beheld. She had the most vibrant fiery-red hair ...'

His gaze flickered to Lily's dark hair. She smoothed it self-consciously. 'It will grow out,' she said with a wry smile.

'I was away at school and I returned to find she was even lovelier than I remembered. She had grown up and we fell in love. She came to me to tell me she was expecting our child, and I ... I was cruel, unkind. I was terrified of my father. Officially, you see, it was known that Cynthia and I were courting. The scandal would have been huge.' He rubbed his hand over his face. 'I was weak, a coward. Bea went to Mrs White for help. Though Bea refused to name me, Ada is no fool. To protect me, Beatrice was dismissed immediately, with no references. And I let her go. To my shame, I didn't even try to help her. I went ahead and married Cynthia. My father threatened to disinherit me if I refused so that settled it. The thought of having to make my own way in the world terrified me. If I'd been made of sterner stuff, I'd have said blow it and married Beatrice and made a go of it. We would have been happy, I'm sure of it. I just hope she has forgiven me.'

'She is at peace, I'm sure,' Lily said, wiping away her tears. 'I know it is taught that suicides are refused entry into Heaven, but I don't believe that. I refuse to believe that a loving God would cast out someone who is so filled with despair that they feel their only way out is to take their own life.'

'Oh, my dear Lily,' Sir Frederick said. He sounded breathless. All the talking had taken its toll. 'Of course, the reverend would have told you the same ... Oh, Lily. Beatrice is not dead. It wasn't Beatrice who drowned that day.'

Lily stared at him in shock. 'I don't understand.'

'As I said, I have been thinking a lot about you and Beatrice of late, and I wanted to at least know where she was buried before I died. I asked my solicitor Jessop to investigate for me. Apparently, a young girl very similar in appearance to Bea did throw herself in the mill pond at Sturminster Newton but it wasn't her. Jessop's man found out that, because of the rumours going around about Bea, it was assumed that the young girl was her but it wasn't. Beatrice had been employed by a local family as a companion to their feeble-minded daughter. Jessop got this directly from a member of the family itself. The daughter, an aunt and Bea emigrated to the Cape Colony several years ago. Sadly, Jessop was unable to ascertain her current whereabouts. I was hoping to write to her myself.'

Lily had been listening in a state of shock. Now, she blurted, 'My mother is alive?'

'She is, so far as I know.'

'My brother, Charlie, he is in the Cape Colony ...'

'It is a big place,' Sir Frederick said with a smile. 'I doubt their paths have ever crossed.' He shrugged his bony shoulders and coughed. 'I'm sorry, I wish I could tell you more. Jessop will endeavour to keep searching.'

'It's a lot to take in,' Lily said. She picked up her cup, but the tea had grown cold and she set it down again. Her mind was reeling. Her mother was alive? It was too much to comprehend.

'I know you have a lot to think about,' Sir Frederick said. His breathing sounded laboured and his skin was pallid. Lily could tell the afternoon's revelations had taken their toll. 'I just hope you can forgive me for the mess I've made of everything.'

'There is nothing to forgive,' Lily assured him gently once more.

Sir Frederick smiled. 'I don't deserve your kindness,' he said wearily. His eyelids fluttered.

'Let me help you to your bed,' Lily said, rising from her seat.

She helped him across the room, and into bed.

'Please don't say anything to anyone. I should like to explain everything to Eleanor first. I will speak to her in the morning.'

'Of course,' Lily said. On impulse, she leaned over and kissed his cheek. He fell asleep almost instantly. 'Sleep well,' she whispered, adding almost inaudibly, 'Father,' as she tiptoed quietly from the room.

CHAPTER THIRTY-FIVE

Lily bent over her workbench. Since Frances Kitching had launched Lily's alteration service, Lily had been inundated with work. Now that September was drawing to a close, the hotel wasn't quite so busy, and she was just wondering if she would have to go back to servicing the rooms once the demand for her sewing skills dried up when she heard footsteps coming down the stone passageway.

'Lily?' At the sound of Eleanor's voice, she laid her sewing aside and jumped to her feet, her heart pounding in trepidation. She had lain awake much of the night trying to process everything that had happened yesterday, as well as worrying about how Eleanor would react to the news that Lily was her half-sister.

'Miss Eleanor,' Lily met her at the door of her workroom. From the laundry nearby came the hiss of steam. The air smelled of soap and damp. 'Did you have a nice time in London?'

'Well, you can drop the "miss" for a start,' Eleanor said with a smile as she flung her arms around Lily. 'Yes, thank you, I did but . . . Oh, Lily, how long have you known?'

'A long time,' Lily admitted. 'You're not angry?'

'Goodness, no! I'm overjoyed. I always wanted a sister.' She released Lily from her embrace. 'Now I look back, it's obvious,' she said, pushing aside a swathe of material and perching on Lily's workbench. 'There was such a connection between us, right from the start.'

'You are not cross with Sir Frederick?' Lily bit her lip.

Eleanor waved her hand in the air. 'Cross that he could behave so abominably to a poor young woman, yes, and annoyed that he did not acknowledge you sooner. He recognized you straight away, by all accounts, and so, he suspects, did Mrs White and Harris.'

'But Lady Copperfield . . .?' Lily asked, perplexed.

'I have known for years that Papa and Mama's marriage is not a happy one. I believe Papa is still in love with your mother.'

'That would be very sad, if that were so,' Lily said. 'Both for Sir Frederick and Lady Copperfield.' And for my mother, she added silently. So many affected lives.

She pushed her melancholy thoughts aside. The past was the past. It couldn't be altered or changed. It was the future she had to concentrate on now.

'And now the reason for my visit.' Eleanor grinned. Her eyes twinkled mischievously. 'Papa is insisting that you and Alice come and live with us at Cranborne Lodge.'

'I beg your pardon?' Lily's mouth fell open in surprise. 'Live with you?'

'You're my sister, Lily. You belong with your family.'

'But what about Lady Copperfield? Surely she wouldn't be happy with that?' Lily worried. Lady Copperfield had always treated her fairly.

Eleanor's face fell. 'The truth will be difficult for poor Mama to accept. Papa wants to speak with her face to face, of course, so he has written to invite her to Cranborne Lodge.' She gave Lily a wry smile. 'Obviously, Papa does not wish to shame Mama publicly, so he will have you legally declared his ward.'

'His ward?' Lily repeated.

'I hope you don't feel this is a slight against you?' Eleanor said quickly. 'You will enjoy all the privileges of a true daughter.'

'No,' Lily replied. 'That is not what I meant at all. I am overwhelmed by Sir Frederick's generosity.'

'Nonsense,' Eleanor assured her. 'You deserve so much more. It is only Papa's regard for Mama that is preventing him from acknowledging you publicly.'

'What about my work?' Lily asked, looking around the room at the mending and alterations waiting to be done. 'I cannot let the guests down.'

'How long will you need?' asked Eleanor. 'Papa is hoping Mama will arrive by the end of the week,' she continued with a sad shake of her head. 'I doubt she will stay long.' She felt desperately sorry for her mother. No matter how estranged her parents had become over the years, her father's revelations were going to come as a huge shock to her mother.

'Once Mama has returned to London, you may move in any time you please.'

'I will speak with Mrs Kitching and make arrangements to work my notice,' Lily said. 'Depending on Lady Copperfield's departure, Alice and I could be ready to move in by the end of next week?'

'That would be perfect,' Eleanor agreed. 'And now,' she said with twinge of apprehension, 'I shall write to dear Arthur and tell him I have acquired a sister.'

The second Saturday of October dawned grey and overcast and a fine drizzle was falling as Sir Frederick's hired man loaded Lily and Alice's meagre belongings into his hand cart. The hotel had been buzzing all week as news of their good fortune had spread among the staff. Frances stood under the archway to see them off, wishing them well.

'Thank you for everything you've done for us, Mrs Kitching,' Lily said, tugging her shawl over her hair and taking hold of Alice's hand. 'And don't forget that I am available should you need me.'

They walked slowly along the windswept promenade, Alice skipping along happily and humming to herself. A grey mist loomed over the water, muting the sound of the waves on the beach. The smell of frying fish hung on the air. Out to sea, a fishing trawler was heading for the harbour, a flock of screeching gulls wheeling around its mast.

Lily had written to Charlie giving him an account of the astonishing turn her life had taken recently. Under Sir

Frederick's wardship and feeling safer than she had for months, she had finally felt able to write to Violet, and she smiled now, imagining her dear friend's amazement and relief on receiving her letter after so long a silence.

She was still thinking about Violet when, up ahead, she spotted a figure leaning against a lamppost, cap pulled low over his eyes and her heart dropped.

'What is it, Mama?' Alice asked, as Lily stopped walking. She stared through the drizzle at the figure, grateful for Sir Frederick's hired man's solid presence.

'Everything, all right, ma'am?' he asked now, following Lily's gaze with a puzzled frown. Lily was about to speak then the figure suddenly pushed away from the lamppost and waved. A horse-drawn cart was coming down the street. The driver raised his whip and the figure, a young man, Lily could see now, little more than a boy really, scrambled aboard.

Alice tugged Lily's hand. 'Come on, Mama. I want to see Aunty Leanor.'

The cart rumbled past them, the driver and the boy deep in conversation. Neither even glanced in Lily's direction. She exhaled in relief.

'Yes, sorry. Everything is fine. Shall we continue?' Her heartbeat slowly returned to normal, yet she knew that all her life she would live with the fear of Jez, or the police, catching up with her.

Eleanor was watching from the upstairs window, reflecting on her mother's recent visit. Lady Copperfield had been understandably hurt and angry to discover her husband's secret and it had been a difficult three days. Eleanor's sympathy for her mother had conflicted greatly with her regard for Lily and it had been something of a relief when Lady Copperfield had returned to London.

'Lily and Alice are here, Papa,' she called now, flying down the stairs like an exuberant child on Christmas morning. Pausing only to grab her shawl, she flung open the door and was waiting on the front step when Lily and Alice came up the path.

'Aunty Leanor,' Alice shrieked with glee, holding out her arms. Eleanor gave a whoop of joy and swept Alice into the air, making her chortle with unbridled laughter.

'Welcome home, Lily,' Eleanor said, giving Lily a warm hug. 'Papa is resting just now. He had a bad night but he will see you this evening after supper. I'll show you to your room.' She turned and led the way indoors. The hired man followed with the luggage.

Sir Frederick's bedroom door was ajar and Lily caught the distinct odour of sickness wafting onto the landing. She met Eleanor's gaze, seeing her grief and the dark shadows beneath her eyes, and smiled sadly.

'Today is a special day,' Eleanor said stoutly. 'We shall not be sad. Here.' She pushed open a door further down the carpeted landing. 'This is your room. What do you think?'

'Oh, Miss Eleanor, it's beautiful.' Lily gazed around the room in awe as she took in the wallpaper with its delicate duck-egg blue scrolls, the lacy blue curtains, the matching lace-edged quilt that covered the generously sized double bed.

'I told you to drop the "miss",' Eleanor said. 'I'm your sister, for goodness' sake.' She walked over to the large wardrobe, flinging open the doors. 'There's plenty of storage space for your clothes.' They both looked at Lily's small collection of luggage, which the hired man now set in the middle of the blue and white patterned carpet, and burst out laughing. Her and Alice's clothes together would barely fill one shelf.

'It's too much, M ... Eleanor,' Lily said. 'You and Sir Frederick have been generous to a fault.'

'Nonsense.' Eleanor grinned at Alice who was bouncing on the bed. Lily grabbed her arm and made her stop.

'Hush, you'll disturb Sir Frederick.'

'It will do Papa good to hear a child's laughter,' Eleanor said. She grabbed hold of Alice and tickled her until the little girl was screaming with laughter. 'I don't want you standing on ceremony, Lily. You must think of this as your home from now on,' she said, rolling onto her stomach and pulling faces at Alice.

Lily wandered over to the window. The rain was coming down hard now. It lashed at the windowpane and formed huge puddles on the deserted promenade. The sea was barely visible through the swirling mist and she hoped that the little fishing trawler had made it into the harbour safely.

Could she really think of this as her home? As Sir Frederick's ward, she would be entitled to his protection but what would happen when they returned to London? Lady Copperfield would certainly not want to give house room to her husband's illegitimate child. What would become of her and Alice then?

CHAPTER THIRTY-SIX

It wasn't until after supper that Eleanor took Lily and Alice up to Sir Frederick's room.

He greeted them cheerfully, though he looked tired. 'My dears, good evening. Forgive me for not getting up, but my legs are refusing to cooperate.'

'There's nothing to forgive,' Lily said, hastening to her father's side. 'It is good to see you sitting up.'

'Are you all settled in? Is your accommodation satisfactory?'

'Very much so, Sir Frederick,' Lily said. 'It is a lovely room. We are very grateful.'

Sir Frederick nodded. 'It is only what I should have done years ago, my dear Lily. And Alice, my little treasure.' He beckoned Alice to him. She looked at her mother doubtfully. Lily nodded.

Reluctantly, Alice moved a few steps closer, frowning at the old man in the bed. She wrinkled her nose. He smelled a bit too. Sir Frederick reached out his hand and stroked Alice's cheek.

'Do you know who I am, Alice?' he asked in his rasping voice. Alice nodded. 'Who am I?'

'You're Sir Frederick,' she said. 'Aunty Leanor's papa.'

'That's right, but do you know I'm also your mama's papa?'

Alice looked at Lily, who nodded. 'It's true, sweetie.'

'So, do you know what that makes me?' Sir Frederick asked Alice. She shook her head. She stood with her hands clasped behind her back, as she had been taught by the nuns, her dark curls tumbling down over her shoulders.

'It makes me your grandpapa. What do you think of that? Would you like to have me as your grandpapa?' Alice seemed to consider this for a moment. She shrugged.

'I had a nana, she went to live with Jesus,' she told him loudly. 'But I don't have a grandpapa.'

'So, what about me? Will I do, do you think?'

Again, Alice seemed to take an inordinately long time considering Sir Frederick's remark. Lily nudged her shoulder. 'What do you say, Alice?'

'I think I'd like you to be my grandpapa,' she said at length.

'Excellent!' Sir Frederick clapped his hands together. 'Eleanor, my dear, perhaps you would like to take Alice down to the parlour. I'd like to talk to Lily alone.'

'Of course, Papa. Come on, Alice. I'll teach you how to play the piano. Would you like that?' The two of them went off happily, leaving Lily and Sir Frederick alone.

'The nights are drawing in,' he said conversationally, as Lily drew the curtains. The rain had stopped but a chill wind rattled the window frames and she added a shovel of coal to the fire before drawing up a chair and taking Sir Frederick's hand in hers.

'Now, my dear, as my ward, I expect no more of this "Sir Frederick" nonsense. I know I don't deserve it. My behaviour towards you has been abominable, but I would be honoured if you would call me Papa, or Father, if you prefer.'

Lily hesitated.

'If it's too soon . . .?'

'No, no.' Lily laughed self-consciously. 'I would be very happy to call you Papa.'

'Excellent,' Sir Frederick said again. He sagged against his pillows. 'I'm just so sorry that our time together will be so short. But' – he patted Lily's hand – 'let's not dwell on melancholy thoughts. I am determined to make the best of what little time I have by getting to know you and Alice as well as I can.' He coughed, the harsh, hacking sound racking his thin frame and leaving him exhausted and gasping for breath.

'Here, let me pour you a glass of water.' Lily filled a glass from the jug on the nightstand and handed it to him. Sir Frederick managed a few sips before sinking back against the pillows.

'I have tired you,' Lily apologized. 'I shall leave you to rest.'

'No,' Sir Frederick rasped, his fingers clutching at Lily's hand. His grip was weak and Lily could feel the tremor running through his hand to hers. 'Wait. I must speak . . .'

'It can wait,' Lily said, her eyes filling with tears at the sight of her father's distress. He shook his head.

'I have had word from Jessop,' he whispered. 'He has contacted his office in Cape Town ... with instruction to try and find your mother.'

Lily choked back a sob. 'Oh, Sir Fred ... Papa, I don't know what to say.'

'There is ... nothing that needs to be said,' he wheezed. 'I only wish I could see her one last time.' He smiled sadly. 'I have also instructed Jessop to settle some money on you. You will have enough to buy yourself a little house, maybe set yourself up in business if you wish.'

'Papa.' Tears were streaming down Lily's cheeks now. If she had money, she would be able to go anywhere she wanted, somewhere far away, the Cape perhaps, somewhere Jez would never find her. She could open her own dressmaker's shop like she had always dreamed. 'Thank you,' she whispered. 'Thank you.'

'Sir Frederick ... Papa,' Lily amended with a wry smile the following morning, 'seems to have had a better night.' She and Eleanor were walking along the promenade with Alice. The autumn day had dawned unseasonably warm and bright. The sea was as calm as a millpond, shimmering silvery-blue under a pale blue sky.

'He did.' Eleanor smiled, letting go of Alice's hand to allow the little girl to run off and join the small crowd watching a mime artist performing under the clock tower.

'It is days like this that allow me to hope for his recovery,' she continued. Lily took her arm. The sun was warm on her face as they leaned against the railing, listening to the ripples of laughter drifting from the mime artist's audience.

'What does the doctor say?' Lily asked.

'He is annoyingly vague,' Eleanor replied with a sigh of exasperation. Lily bit her lip. It broke her heart to see her sister's steadfast hope, knowing that it was unlikely to be rewarded. 'But I'm so happy that he has rectified your situation, Lily. Will you take a house near us in London, do you think?'

'I was thinking about going to the Cape. There is bound to be a need for seamstresses and dressmakers in a new country. Charlie says there are new towns springing up all over the colony.'

'So far?' Eleanor's face fell.

'I need to get away from Jez, Eleanor. In the eyes of the law I am still his wife, and the court order still stands. No amount of money in the world will change that and I can't take the chance of losing Alice to him. He's evil, Eleanor, and, much as I don't doubt that he loves Alice, eventually he will destroy her.'

'I would miss you terribly,' Eleanor said wistfully.

'I have no definite plans yet,' Lily reassured her. 'Charlie may yet advise against it. He's worried that there will still be a war.'

'You would be safe in London,' Eleanor insisted. 'I doubt Jez would find you, but if he did, Papa would hire the best lawyers. But we do not need to worry about this just yet. Our rent on Cranborne Lodge is paid until the end of March.'

The mime artist finished his performance and the small crowd began to disperse. Alice came running over.

'Can I play in the sand?' she begged, hopping from one foot to the other impatiently. Lily laughed.

'It's such a warm day, it would be a pity to waste it,' she said. Alice ran ahead, one hand clutching her straw boater, its ribbons trailing behind her, while Lily and Eleanor followed at a more sedate pace.

'Don't you envy her exuberance?' Eleanor laughed. 'How I would love to be able to run on the sand like a child.'

'She's having the time of her life,' Lily agreed, watching her daughter running across the damp sand, pausing every now and then to inspect a tangled clump of seaweed or to gather pretty shells. Soon the pockets of her pinafore were bulging with treasure.

'You haven't said how Mr Randall reacted to the news that I am your sister,' Lily remarked as they strolled along the sand.

'Oh, Arthur is as easy-going as they come,' laughed Eleanor, 'and took my revelation in his stride.'

They walked the length of the beach and were nearing the steps up to the promenade when Eleanor grabbed Lily's arm. 'Look, Lily, it's Papa.' Shielding her eyes against the light, Lily looked to where Eleanor was pointing. Sure enough, Mrs Cowper was pushing Sir Frederick along the promenade in a bath chair. He was well wrapped up against the sea air.

'Papa,' Eleanor called, waving as she quickened her pace. Calling Alice to her, Lily followed Eleanor up the steps.

'I thought I might join you for an outing,' Sir Frederick said as they hurried towards him. To Lily's relief, his voice sounded stronger than it had last night and the fresh sea air had added a splash of colour to his cheeks.

'It's so lovely to see you out and about, Papa,' Eleanor said joyfully.

'It is good to be out,' Sir Frederick agreed.

'Thank you, Mrs Cowper. I shall take over from here.'

'Very good, miss,' June Cowper nodded. 'I shall see you back at the house.' She frowned and laid a hand on Eleanor's shoulder. 'I shouldn't keep him out too long,' she said, her voice low. Eleanor nodded.

'Grandpapa, watch me run.' Eleanor parked Sir Frederick's chair near the railing so he had a clear view of the beach and the gently undulating sea, and could watch his granddaughter turning cartwheels on the sand and chasing seagulls.

The time passed all too quickly, but soon it was clear that Sir Frederick had had enough. The colour had gone from his cheeks and he was finding it difficult to keep his eyes open.

'It is time to return home,' Lily said firmly, when Sir Frederick tried to protest. She called Alice up from the beach and the little girl ran over to her grandfather. Without preamble, she clambered on his lap, and wrapped her arms around his neck.

'I love you, Grandpapa,' she said with simple childlike sincerity. 'Would you like to see my treasure?'

Together, Lily and Eleanor pushed the heavy chair back towards the house, listening to Alice's continual chatter, as she snuggled against Sir Frederick.

'Here we are,' Eleanor sang out as they manoeuvred the bath chair through the narrow gateway. 'Home sweet home.'

Yes, Lily mused, gazing down at Sir Frederick's thinning crown with fondness. Her broken heart had healed and any animosity she had harboured towards her father had dissipated. She was filled with love and compassion for him and for Eleanor. The secret family she had carried in her heart for so long was a secret no more.

The front door opened and June Cowper stood on the threshold, wiping her floury hands on her apron. Alice slithered off Sir Frederick's lap and ran to fling her arms around the housekeeper's waist.

Watching her daughter going off happily with June, Lily let out a deep sigh of contentment. Alice was happy and, for the time being, they were safe, surrounded by her family who loved her. Lily's true family. They had finally come home.

CHAPTER THIRTY-SEVEN

November brought days of wet and stormy weather. The rough sea battered the shore, sending clouds of spray into the air. In the harbour, boats rocked and swayed, masts creaking, flags snapping in the stiff wind. Rain lashed the promenade and anything that wasn't nailed down was whipped along the by the strong gusts.

Huddled against the driving rain and howling wind, Lily left the post office, tugging her hood over her head. The brown dye was growing out now, her vibrant red colour returning. She was eager to get home and spend some precious time with Sir Frederick. Contrary to expectations, her father had had several good days since his morning out the previous month, even rallying enough to join them for the occasional meal. He and Alice had grown close. She loved nothing better than to crawl onto his lap and be regaled with his stories of a wild and misspent youth.

The gate rattled on its hinges as Lily pushed it open and hurried up the garden path. Leaves blew across the sodden lawn, the shrubs bent and bowed by the force of the gale. The air smelled of damp leaves and coal fires.

'It's me. I'm home,' she called as she blew in the front door and shed her wet coat and hat. Hurried footsteps sounded overhead and Alice came charging down the stairs to fling herself at Lily.

'You must be soaked, Miss Lily,' June said, emerging from the steam-filled kitchen, her cheeks flushed. 'Get out of those wet things before you catch your death. I'll bring you up some hot water.'

'Thank you, Mrs Cowper.' She kissed Alice's cheek and buried her face in her curly hair. 'Have you had a good day, sweetie?'

'Yes, Mama. Aunty Leanor and I baked biscuits for Grandpapa's visitor.'

'Grandpapa has had a visitor?' She wondered if it had been Lady Copperfield. As far as she was aware, Sir Frederick's wife had not been in contact with him since her return to London. Even her letters to Eleanor lacked their usual warmth. She knew it grieved her sister that Lady Copperfield saw Eleanor's continued regard for Lily as a betrayal.

'Yes. Mr Jessop,' Alice said.

'Ah, Lily, you're home.' Lily looked up at Eleanor leaning over the banister. Her eyes twinkled with mischief and Lily was instantly suspicious.

'What is it?' she demanded with a grin.

'Papa would like to see you in the drawing room,' Eleanor said. 'He has some news.'

'Not until you've changed out of them wet things,' June said firmly, coming to stand in the kitchen doorway. Lily and Eleanor exchanged a smile.

Burning with curiosity, Lily hastened upstairs to shed her damp clothes and wash her face and hands. She dressed quickly, choosing a rose-pink dress with long sleeves, a high neck and lace trim. Having brushed her hair, she wound it up on top of her head, securing it with a number of pins.

'You look pretty, Mama,' Alice said. She was sitting at the dressing table, watching Lily in the mirror.

'Thank you, sweetie.' Lily kissed the top of her head. Her heart was pounding as she made her way downstairs, wondering what Sir Frederick wanted to see her about. Had Jessop brought more news of her mother? Her chest constricted in anticipation.

Eleanor took Alice into the parlour, leaving Lily standing outside the drawing room door. She hesitated, then raised her hand and knocked.

'My dear, Lily, come in,' Sir Frederick said as she pushed the door open. 'This is Mr Horatio Jessop, my solicitor. Jessop, my daughter, Lillian Brown.'

'Mrs Brown.' Jessop bowed. He was a small, neat man with a pencil-thin moustache and a bald head, which shone in the lamplight.

'Mr Jessop, good afternoon.'

'Sit down, Lily. Jessop has some news.'

Lily swallowed hard. Her throat was dry. She sat down and folded her clammy palms in her lap.

'Mrs Brown.' Jessop coughed. He stood erect, his hands clasped behind his back, his moustache twitching comically. 'I am here to inform you that your husband, Jeremy Elkin, has been arrested on charges of extortion.'

Lily's hand flew to her mouth. 'Arrested?' she repeated weakly.

'He is in prison in Dorchester awaiting trial. He has also been charged with two lesser offences. Holding an illegal boxing match and living off immoral earnings.'

'Do you see what this means, Lily?' Sir Frederick rasped with a smile. 'You are free of him. He will go to prison for a very long time. Jessop has applied for the court order regarding Alice to be rescinded. We expect confirmation of that within the week.'

Lily stared at the two men, stunned. 'I can't believe it,' she whispered.

'Believe it, my dear. And it's all thanks to Jessop here. His investigator managed to find one of Jez's victims who was willing to press charges. Once the newspaper ran with the story of Jez's arrest, several more victims came forward. It's a cut and dried case, Lily. The evidence against him is overwhelming. There's no chance he'll get off.'

'Thank you so much, Mr Jessop,' Lily said. She could hardly believe that she was free at last. 'I feel as though a huge weight has been lifted from my shoulders.' She sighed.

'I'm happy for you, my dear,' Sir Frederick said.

'What of Barbie-Jean?' she asked as she got up to leave.

'She was seen boarding the train to London not long after Jez was arrested,' Jessop informed her. 'No one has heard from her since.'

Lily nodded. She wasn't surprised. It had been Jez's money and status Barbie-Jean wanted. With his assets seized and Jez facing a long prison sentence, there would be little incentive for her to stay loyal to him.

'You can drop the Brown as well,' Sir Frederick said. 'In fact, I would be honoured if you were to take my name.'

Lily paused. With one hand resting on the door handle, she looked her father in the eye. 'That's very generous of you, Papa,' she said, earnestly. 'But, if you don't mind, I'd like to revert to my maiden name, Hayter. Jim and Martha were the best parents I could have wished for and I hope that one day, if I ever get to meet Beatrice, I can tell her that she did the right thing, giving me to them. The first nine years of my life were the happiest I ever had . . . until now.'

Sir Frederick gazed at her fondly. 'I understand, my dear, and I shall be forever in their debt.'

As November drifted towards December and the mild wet weather gave way to cold blue skies and frosty ground, Sir Frederick's health declined rapidly. Lily and Eleanor spent as much time as they could by his bedside. They took it in turns to read to him, the pages blurred by tears as his pain became so intense that he cried out in agony, his body drenched with sweat. It broke Lily's heart to watch him suffer but though the doctor called every day there was little he could do alleviate Sir Frederick's torment.

Three weeks before Christmas, Lily was reading aloud to Sir Frederick. It had been one of his better days. Despite a

heavy dose of laudanum, he had been lucid enough in the afternoon to allow Alice to spend a few precious minutes with her beloved grandpapa. Now he appeared to be sleeping peacefully. His skin was parchment thin, his lips dry and cracked, his complexion the colour of dishwater. The sound of his laboured breathing filled the room. The temperature was tropical, the fire roaring fiercely in the grate. Perspiration pricked Lily's armpits and trickled down her spine. She paused, her brow furrowed in concern as she glanced at her father, watching his chest rise and fall with every struggling breath.

Suddenly, as if aware of Lily's scrutiny, he opened his eyes. His lips moved silently. Lily put the book aside and leaned over him.

'Are you thirsty, Papa?' Sir Frederick moved his head ever so slightly. Lily took one of his skeletal hands in hers. His skin was cold and dry to the touch. She wet a cloth and gently dabbed it to his parched lips, letting a few droplets seep into his mouth. His lips moved again, as if he were trying to speak. She leaned closer, her ear to his lips. His sour breath brushed her cheek.

'Beatrice?' It was barely audible, her mother's name, whispered on a dying breath. Had her father, in his dying moment, mistaken her for Beatrice? The one true love of his life. The woman he had loved and never forgotten for over twenty years.

At that moment the bedroom door opened and Eleanor came into the room.

'How is he?' she asked, her expression turning to one of alarm as she registered Lily's ashen face.

'I think ...' Lily choked on a sob. 'I think he's ... gone.'

Eleanor flew to the bed, falling to her knees at her father's bedside. 'Papa? Papa?'

Lily shivered. Despite the roaring fire, the room seemed suddenly icy cold.

'Papa, can you hear me? It's Eleanor.' There was no response and she burst into tears. With tears sliding down her own cheeks, Lily slipped quietly from the room to inform June Cowper and ask her to call the doctor.

'Is Grandpapa an angel now, Mama?' Alice asked. It was the following week and Lily and Alice were waiting in the grand entranceway of Sir Frederick's Chelsea townhouse, waiting for a hansom cab to take them to the station.

The funeral had been a sombre affair. Lady Copperfield's reception of Lily and Alice had been frosty. For propriety's sake, Lily and Alice had sat at the back of the church, well away from the family pew and unobtrusive among the many mourners. At the graveside, Lady Copperfield had glared at Lily across the casket. Seemingly contemptuous of Lily's grief, she had stood alone, regal and aloof in her black widow's weeds, studiously ignoring Eleanor, who sobbed unashamedly in the arms of her fiancé.

Lily had declined Eleanor's invitation to stay for the lavish wake, electing instead to make the arduous journey back to Weymouth immediately.

'I'm sure Grandpapa is an angel, sweetie,' she replied now, kissing the top of Alice's head. She looked stiff and formal in her black dress, her thick hair held back from her face by a black velvet ribbon.

'Is he watching us now?' Alice asked, gazing up at the domed ceiling.

'I'm certain he is,' she assured her daughter, turning as she heard footsteps behind her.

'Miss Hayter, condolences on your loss.' It was Jessop.

'Thank you, Mr Jessop.'

'Miss Eleanor tells me you are heading back to Weymouth today?'

'We are waiting for our transport to the station now,' Lily replied.

'Might I beg a moment of your time before you go?'

Puzzled, Lily agreed.

'As you are aware, Sir Frederick settled a large sum of money on you and Alice.' Lily nodded, her frown deepening. 'Very good.' Jessop coughed into his fist. 'As I am sure you are also aware, Sir Frederick tasked me with liaising with our sister company in Cape Town. Three days ago, I received a telegram from a Mr Armstrong, one of their partners. It would appear that they have managed to track Miss Cullen down. May I have your permission to arrange contact on your behalf?'

'Yes,' Lily blurted, stunned. 'Yes, of course. Please do.'

'Very well.' Jessop smiled. 'I believe you have a relative in the Cape?'

'My brother, Charlie, yes.'

'May I suggest we use Charlie as point of contact? Would he be agreeable?'

'Yes.' Lily shook her head in bewilderment. 'I'm sure he would. Goodness.' She leaned against the wall, afraid her legs were about to give way. Jessop's smile broadened.

'With luck we shall hear back from Miss Cullen very soon. In the meantime, I wish you a safe journey home, ma'am.'

Lily stared after him, barely able to comprehend his words. Beatrice had been found? Was it possible she might finally get to meet the woman she had dreamt about so many times as a child? She could scarcely take in how much her life had changed over the past year. She was now a woman of means. She could afford to buy a little house somewhere and open her shop. Now she need no longer fear Jez, she could go wherever she wished. Would she stay in England, or venture further afield? The possibilities were still whirling around her head when Jerome, the butler, appeared to inform her that the hansom cab had arrived to take her to the railway station.

EPILOGUE

Southampton Docks, May 1898

A warm breeze swept the docks as Lily and Alice made their way through the crowds thronging the quayside. Blinking in the bright sunlight, Lily took a moment to adjust her hat and calm her rapidly beating heart. She clung to Alice's hand, terrified of losing her in the crowd. The ship RMS *Pembroke Castle* loomed above them. It sat low in the water, a coiling rope of grey smoke billowing from its red and black funnel. Tall masts creaked in the breeze and flags fluttered. The gangplanks were a hive of activity. Men in short-sleeved shirts and striped bandanas scurried back and forth unloading trunks and crates amidst a cacophony of shouting and clanging.

Shielding her eyes against the sun, Lily craned her neck, staring up at the crowded railings on the upper decks. The smell of fish, tar and damp hung heavily on the warm air. Oily water slapped rhythmically against the harbour wall.

The deep rumble of the ships' engines reverberated in her stomach.

'Can you see Uncle Charlie, Mama?' Alice asked, clamouring to be picked up. She was a big girl of nearly four now, and heavy. Nevertheless, Lily hoisted Alice onto her hip and together they scanned the throngs of passengers waiting to disembark. It had been nearly ten years since she had last seen her brother. What if she didn't recognize him?

Her stomach fluttered nervously. She had barely slept the night before in their little boarding house close to the bustling port. Eleanor and her new husband had offered to come with Lily for moral support but, while she had appreciated their concern, this was something Lily needed to do alone, just her and Alice.

The last few months had flown by. Early in the new year, Lily had written to Jack Philips to thank him for his help and assure him that she and Alice were safe and well. To her delight, he had written back immediately. He, Agatha and Kitty were well, he wrote, and sent their love. He ended with the news that Kitty was expecting a baby in the summer.

Late January had brought the exciting news that Mr Armstrong had made contact with Beatrice, and in February, Lily had received word from Charlie that he had met her mother and they were making plans to return to England as soon as they could secure their passage.

In March, Lily had purchased the lease on a small shop tucked down a little side street just off the esplanade. It boasted a small back garden and a spacious flat above. Violet had come to stay for a few days at the end of March and, while she was there, two police constables had turned up at Lily's door to inform her, in the gravest of tones, that her husband, Jeremy Elkin, had been killed in a prison brawl. Lily could only stare at them in disbelief, hardly daring to believe what they said was true. Jez was dead? She had managed to keep her emotions at bay until they were gone, before collapsing to the floor and sobbing with relief that she would never have to fear him again.

'You realise this means you are free to marry again,' Violet had pointed out over a cup of tea once Lily had regained her composure.

'I'm quite content as I am for the moment,' replied Lily with a smile. But perhaps, one day in the future . . .

In April, Lily and Alice had travelled to London for Eleanor and Arthur's wedding. To Lily's dismay, Lady Copperfield had been as frosty as ever but, as Eleanor kept telling her, Lily could hardly be blamed for events that had taken place before she was born.

Soon after Lily and Alice returned home, and Eleanor and Arthur had left for their honeymoon in the Scottish Highlands, Lily received a telegram from Charlie informing her that he and Bea would be arriving at Southampton on 17th May.

And now here she was, shuffling nervously from foot to foot as the passengers began to disembark.

'Lily! Lily!' Charlie's voice was unmistakable above the racket. Lily glanced up and gasped as she spotted his dark head among the crowd. He waved and Lily waved back, crying unashamedly as the full force of how much she had missed him over the past decade hit her like a ton of bricks. She lost sight of him as the crowd surged towards the exits, and then, there he was, pushing his way through the crowds towards her. He seemed taller, broader. He had filled out and his skin was tanned a deep mahogany.

'Lily.' He wrapped her and Alice in his arms. 'It's so good to see you.'

'It's been so long,' Lily sobbed. 'You still look the same, though,' she said, smiling through her tears. Charlie laughed. His voice was deeper, gruffer.

'You wouldn't have thought that if you'd seen me a few weeks back,' he said, grinning. 'I had a full beard down to my chest and hair so long I had to tie it back. I hadn't seen a barber for months until I got back to Cape Town.' He tickled Alice under the chin. 'So, this is my little niece. Hello, Alice, I'm your Uncle Charlie.'

Alice cocked her head. 'Hello,' she said, boldly.

'And now, there's someone I believe you're eager to meet,' Charlie said, with a smile. He stood aside and Lily's heart stopped. It was as if the noise and the hustle and bustle of the docks disappeared as she watched the woman making her way slowly towards them. She looked to be in her late thirties, with the weathered complexion of some-one who had spent many years under the hot sun. Her dress was simple, homespun, her fiery red hair scraped back from her face in an untidy bun. Her green eyes flashed with recognition and, beneath the suntan, she looked pale.

The woman bit her lip apprehensively, and held out her arms.

'Hello, Lily,' she said softly. 'I'm Beatrice. I'm your mother.'

ACKNOWLEDGEMENTS

Once again, grateful thanks must go to my agent, Judith Murdoch, for her continued encouragement and support. Your instinct and insight into what will make a good story are invaluable. Thank you.

To my editor, Alice Rodgers of Simon & Schuster UK Ltd, thank you for encouragement, guidance and support. To Paul Simpson, thank you for your meticulous copyediting and for, once again, correcting my historical errors. And to all the staff at Simon & Schuster UK Ltd, a huge thank you.

Thank you, also, to all of you who bought and read my previous book, *The Shopgirl's Soldier*. To those of you who stopped me in the street to tell me how much you enjoyed it, to the manager and staff of my local WHSmith for tirelessly promoting it, and to all of you who sent messages via Facebook or email, I am truly thankful.

To my husband, John, thank you again for your unwavering support and encouragement. And to Mum, Dad, Amanda,

Andrew, Warren, Melanie, Mark, Leigh-Anne, Gareth and Michelle, Venessa Hastings and Jane Churcher, a huge thank you to you all.

And last but not least, to my friend Ros. Thank you.

Discover more from Karen Dickson ...

The Shop Girl's Soldier

'An exciting, fresh and talented new voice
– a five-star read!' **Carol Rivers**

Southampton, 1905. Ellie-May and Jack have been
inseparable since birth. But when Jack and his mother
fall on hard times they are thrown into the workhouse,
and he and Ellie-May are forced to say goodbye.

Four years later, now aged sixteen, Jack returns to
Southampton and is reunited with Ellie-May. Quickly
they both realize that their feelings for each other
go beyond friendship. But when WWII approaches,
Jack's duty to his country is hard to ignore, and when
he enlists to fight, they are once again torn apart.

**Will Ellie-May and Jack find their way
back to each other before it's too late?**

AVAILABLE NOW IN PAPERBACK AND EBOOK

**SIMON &
SCHUSTER**